Amid the back-room dealing and power plays of a presidential convention, Jokers and Aces alike rise up to assert their rightful place in society. But terror stalks the halls of Atlanta's Omni convention center. For a fanatical religious leader has vowed to crush the rights of all Wild Cards, and a hidden Ace wields a terrifying power to determine the outcome of the convention.

Against this backdrop of passion and intrigue a handful of Aces and Jokers struggle for control of a nation:

PUPPETMAN—The ruthless manipulator who can bend others to his own unholy will.

MACKIE MESSER—The vicious young punk with flesh of smoke and hands of steel.

DEMISE—The twice-killed Joker who can deal death with a touch.

DR. TACHYON—The flamboyant extraterrestrial who brought the Wild Card plague to Earth and now carries the virus in his own veins.

GOLDEN BOY—The ageless mighty hero of the forties who risks his life to atone for past sins.

ACE
IN
THE HOLE

A Wild Cards Mosaic Novel

edited by
George R.R. Martin

assisted by
Melinda M. Snodgrass

and written by
Walton Simons
Victor Milán
Melinda M. Snodgrass
Stephen Leigh
Walter Jon Williams

BANTAM BOOKS
NEW YORK · TORONTO · LONDON · SYDNEY · AUCKLAND

ACE IN THE HOLE
A Bantam Spectra Book / February 1990

ISBN 0-553-28253-0

Published simultaneously in the United States and Canada

Bantam Books are published by Bantam Books, a division of Bantam
Doubleday Dell Publishing Group, Inc. Its trademark, consisting of
the words "Bantam Books" and the portrayal of a rooster, is
Registered in U.S. Patent and Trademark Office and in other
countries. Marca Registrada. Bantam Books, 666 Fifth Avenue, New
York, New York 10103.

PRINTED IN THE UNITED STATES OF AMERICA

OPM   0 9 8 7 6 5 4 3 2 1

to Barb,
with fond memories of a dozen years of friendship,
and fond hopes of at least two dozen more

ACE
IN
THE HOLE

CHAPTER ONE

Monday
July 18, 1988

6:00 A.M.

Spector pulled down on the padlock with a gloved hand. The lock snapped open. He unlatched the corrugated tin door and put his weight against it, pushing it up and sideways, trying to make as little noise as possible. He slid his thin body through and shut the door behind him. So far it was going just like they said.

The place smelled of dust and fresh paint. The light was dim, coming from a single overhead lamp in the center of the warehouse. He paused to let his eyes adjust. There were boxes of masks all around. Clowns, politicians, animals, some just normal human faces. He picked up a bear mask and put it on; might as well be safe if someone flipped on the lights. The plastic pinched his nose and the eyeholes were smaller than he would have liked. His peripheral vision was shot. Spector moved slowly toward the light, turning his head back and forth to make sure no one was closing in on him.

He was a few minutes early. He figured it was the smart thing to do. Someone had gone to a lot of trouble tracking him down and arranging this meeting. They were either desperate, or they were setting him up. It could mean trouble either way. Dust irritated his eyes, but he couldn't do anything about it with the mask on. He stopped a dozen or so feet from the light and waited. The only sound was the moths pinging against the metal light fixture.

"Are you there?" The voice was muffled, but definitely male, and came from the other side of the lighted area.

Spector cleared his throat. "Yeah, it's me. Why don't you move into the light so I can see you?"

"I don't know who you are, and you don't know who I am. Let's keep it that way." There was a pause. Paper crinkled in the darkness.

"So. Let's hear it." Spector took a long, easy breath. This didn't feel like a setup, and he had the upper hand.

An arm reached forward into the light. The person was short enough to be a kid, but the arm was thick with heavy muscle. The fingers on the hand were short. The edge of a plastic glove peeked out from under the leather one. This guy was obviously being very careful. The hand held a manilla envelope. "Everything you need to know is in here."

"Toss it over." The arm threw it toward him. The envelope landed heavily and skidded to the edge of the lighted area, stirring up dust and paint flecks. "Like the sound of that." Spector walked over to the envelope. Hell, let the guy see him in the bear mask. It wouldn't matter. He picked the envelope up and popped it open with a thumb. There were several carefully batched stacks of hundred dollar bills, a round-trip ticket to Atlanta in the name of George Kerby, and a piece of paper that had been folded over twice. Spector figured there was over fifty thousand.

"Half now. The rest when the job's finished." The voice had moved, and was now between Spector and the door.

Spector opened the slip of paper and held it up to the light to read. He took a sharp breath. "Shit. Never ask for anything small. And Atlanta, too. What a mess that'll be. Why not wait until he's back in town and get a refund on George Kerby's plane ticket?"

"I want it taken care of in the next week. Tomorrow wouldn't be too soon. We got a deal?"

"Yeah, okay," Spector said, bending the envelope over and tucking it into his shirt. "You must hate this guy something fierce."

The door opened. Spector got a glimpse of the man before he pulled it closed again. Four feet tall and built like a linebacker—a dwarf. Not many of those around. And only one who had it in for the guy he'd been hired to nail.

"I heard you were dead, Gimli." No answer. But he couldn't expect any from someone who was supposedly stuffed and mounted in the Famous Bowery Wild Card Dime Museum. Still, Spector knew better than anyone that just because a person was supposed to be a stiff didn't necessarily make it so.

It was Rat's Alley, where the dead men lost their bones. Where Jokers Wild was, was Rat's Alley.

It was probably a good alley for rats.

The last of the customers stumbled out through the door, set like a scream into a blank brick imbecile face of wall. The doorway was normal height, but most of them kept heads ducked low into collars wilted with the sweat of fear, anticipation, and sweet release, kept them that way as they picked their way through mother-of-pearl puddles, the faded glory of plastic food wrappers, stale city smell of tired proteins and complex hydrocarbons aging without grace.

An insignificant figure loitered next to the doorway, James Dean with a hunchback, his black Ked propped against the wall behind him, his white one down in the muck, nodding and humming low in his throat to make sure the night's clientele kept heading in the right direction. It was no sweat. The ones still inside were leaving to put the rubbery, giggling menace of Moon Goon behind them, and once outside the right direction was away from *him*.

On the other side of the door a bulky figure, bagged in black cloak and pantaloons, nodded and murmured floor-walker endearments through a seamless clown's mask: "Thank-you. Please come again. Thank you. Always a pleasure." At most they nodded back.

Last out were a handful of Beautiful Youths, late teens who still managed to look fresh and scrubbed beneath their flattops and floppy *nouveaux* dos, the Jokers Wild wait staff. James Dean *manqué* watched them walk. His pupils dilated when his eyes fixed the boys, jocks as clean limbed and muscled as fledgling Howard heroes. He wasn't aware. They were probably queers anyway. There were queers everywhere; you never could tell. Mackie's scrotum and fingertips itched at the thought; there were things he liked to do to queers. Not that he got much chance. The Gatekeeper and the Man were always on him to be careful where he used his powers. And whom on.

When the last were gone from Rat's Alley, the man with the clown face shut the door. Its outside was enameled a chipped green. He took hold of the frame with white-gloved fingers, pulled it away from the wall. What lay behind was brick. He folded door and frame into a bundle, like a collapsed artist's easel, and tucked it into the billow of one armpit.

"Be good, Mackie," he said, reaching up to pet the thin cheek, just showing a scum of downy whiskers. Mackie didn't pull away. Gatekeeper wasn't queer, he knew that. He liked it when the masked man touched him. He liked approval. A skinny teenage expatriate hunchback didn't get much of that. Especially when Interpol wanted to talk to him.

"I will, Gatekeeper," he said, grinning lopsidedly and bobbing his head. "You know I'm always good." His words had a broad loopy north German lilt to them.

Gatekeeper regarded him a moment longer. His eyes were only visible sometimes. Right now they were just hooded blacknesses in his mask.

His gloved fingertips slid down Mackie's face, rasping softly. He turned and walked away, down the alley with a slight waddle, carrying his bundle beneath his arm.

Mackie went the other direction, picking his way carefully around the puddles. He hated to get his feet wet. Tonight, Rat's Alley would be somewhere else. He'd find it, no worry. He'd feel the call, the siren's song of Jokers Wild, like the rest of those who belonged, the victims and the audience, whose thrills sprang in part from the knowledge that their roles were interchangeable.

Not Mackie, though. In Jokers Wild, Mackie was untouchable. Nobody fucked with him in the nightclub of the damned.

He emerged on Ninth into a breeze full of Hudson River and diesel fumes. Motile features contorted in a brief twitch of nostalgia and loathing: it was just like the Hamburg docks where he'd grown up.

He stuck his hands in his pockets and turned his higher—right—shoulder to the wind. He had to check a message drop in a Bowery flop. The Man was doing something big down in

Atlanta. He might need Mackie at any time. Mackie Messer couldn't bear to miss a moment of being needed.

He started to hum his song, his ballad. Ignoring a tortured rabbit squeal of bus air brakes, he walked.

7:00 A.M.

The crazies were out early. Once he walked past the police perimeter at the Atlanta Marriott Marquis, Jack Braun saw hundreds of convention delegates, dressed mostly in casual clothes, silly hats, and vests covered with campaign buttons; several stretch limos carrying Party Elders; a 1971 primer-gray Chevrolet Impala with a swastika flag fluttering from the aerial and three uniformed Nazi storm troopers sitting stonefaced in the front seat—for some reason no one was in back—and two gangs of jokers hanging their disfigured heads out of battered VW microbuses, waving at the crowd, and laughing at the reactions of the pedestrians. The microbuses were covered with Hartmann stickers and other political slogans. FREE SNOTMAN, said one. BLACK DOG RULES, said the other.

Gregg Hartmann, Jack Braun thought, would not approve. Associating the next president in the public mind with a joker terrorist was *not* approved political strategy.

Jack could feel sweat beading on his scalp. Even at seven-thirty in the morning, Atlanta was humid and sweltering.

Reconciliation breakfast. In an hour he and Hiram Worchester were supposed to become good friends. He wondered why he'd let Gregg Hartmann talk him into it.

The hell with the stroll, he thought savagely. He'd clear his head some other way. He turned around and headed back to the Marriott.

Jack had spent the previous night in his suite at the Marriott, getting sloshed with four uncommitted superdelegates from the parched Midwest. Gregg Hartmann's campaign manager, Charles Devaughn, had called with the suggestion that a little Hollywood charm might swing the uncommitted over to Gregg's camp. Jack, resigned by now, knew perfectly well what that meant. He made a few calls to some agents he knew. By the time the superdelegates arrived, the room had been stocked with bourbon, scotch, and genuine Georgia starlets, veterans of locally produced films with names like *Chain Gang Women* and *Stock Car Carnage*. When the party finally broke up about three in the morning and the last congressman from Missouri stumbled out with his arm around Miss Peachtree 1984, Jack figured he had put at least a couple more votes in Hartmann's pocket.

Sometimes it was easy. For some reason politicians often crumbled around celebrities—even, Jack thought, famous traitor aces and washed-up TV Tarzans like himself. Faded Hollywood charisma, combined with cheap sex, could sap the will of even the most hardened politico.

That, of course, combined with the unvoiced threat of blackmail. Devaughn, Jack knew, would be delighted.

A kettledrum boomed in Jack's hollow skull. He massaged his temples as he waited at a red light. The wild card's gift of enormous strength and eternal youth hadn't saved him from a hangover.

At least it hadn't been a Hollywood party. He would have had to provide a party bowl of cocaine.

He reached into his Marks & Spencer bush jacket and got the first Camel Unfiltered of the day. As he bent over to shield the match in his big hands, he saw the Impala heading down the street toward him again, swastika flag fluttering. The flat caps of the storm troopers were silhouetted in the front window. The car increased speed as the light went yellow.

WHITE POWER. Bumper-sticker slogans. AUSLANDER RAUS!

Jack remembered, years ago, picking up a Mercedes staff car full of Peronistas and flipping it onto its top.

He remembered screaming in anger as German machine guns turned the Rapido River to white froth, the way his arms ached as he drove the sinking rubber raft across to the north bank where the brush was already full of the black helmets and cammo ponchos of SS Division Das Reich, the shells called by the spotters at Monte Cassino splashing down everywhere, half his squad dead or wounded, bodies sprawled on the bottom of his boat in a mixture of river spray and their own blood. . . .

The hell, Jack thought, with politics.

All he had to do was step out in front of the Impala. He could make sure the impact pushed him under the car, and while he was underneath he could rip out the engine supports and leave the Brownshirts stranded in downtown Atlanta, surrounded by militant jokers, a large urban black population, and all the crazed and potentially violent lunatics attracted by the madness and confusion of the 1988 Democratic Convention.

Jack tossed away his match and swung one foot off the curb. The Impala sped closer, trying to beat the yellow light.

Jack stepped back and watched as the Nazis raced by in their car. The black swastika burned itself into his eyeballs.

The Four Aces had been dead for almost forty years. Jack just didn't do that sort of thing anymore.

Too bad.

8:00 A.M.

U2 blared from the radio, and the teenager beat out the rhythm line with a fork as he sucked down a glass of orange juice. His blood-red hair had been cut into a brush over the round skull, with a long skinny braid hanging down the black leather jacket. High-top black tennis shoes, fatigue pants completed his ensemble. The image was aggressively punk, but the face beneath the shock of red hair was too soft, too young for real bad-ass punk.

The contrast to his grandsire, who stood in front of the television, was startling. Dr. Tachyon, eyes slitted with interest as he listened to Jane Pauley of *Today* interview a panel of political pundits, had his violin tucked beneath his sharp chin and was busily sawing through a Paganini violin sonata. He was hearing perhaps one word in three, but it didn't matter. He had heard it all. So many many times before. As the months of campaigning ground down to this place—Atlanta. This time—July 1988. One man—Gregg Hartmann. One prize—the presidency of the United States of America.

Tachyon turned to Blaise, gestured toward the television with his bow. "It is going to be a desperate battle."

And as if in preparation for that upcoming battle, the alien had dressed in boots and breeches, with a black stock wrapped about the high lace collar of his shirt. An officer in Napoleon's Army could not have been more of a peacock than the slim, diminutive figure in his shimmering green outfit. On his breast in lieu of a Garter order hung a plastic ID card indicating that the bearer was one of the press contingent from the *Jokertown Cry*.

Blaise pulled a face and took a big bite out of a croissant. "Boring."

"Blaise, you are thirteen. Old enough to leave behind childish matters and take an interest in the larger world. On Takis you would be leaving the women's quarters. Preparing for your intensive education. Taking responsibility within the family."

"Yeah, but we're not on Takis, and I'm not a joker, so I don't care a fuck."

"*What* did you say?" asked his grandsire in freezing accents.

"Fuck, you know, fuck. Anglo-Saxon word—"

"Crudity is never the mark of a gentlemen."

"You say it."

"Rarely. And please do as I say, not as I do." But Tachyon had the grace to grin sheepishly. "But child, jokers or not, we *must* care. We too are unique individuals, and if Barnett and his philosophy of oppression were to reach the White House it would devour us as well as the most miserable inhabitant of Jokertown. He wishes to place us in sanatoriums." Tachyon gave a snort of derision. "Why doesn't he just say the ugly word—concentration camps.

"We are aliens, Blaise. You may have been born on Earth, but my blood runs in your veins. You bear my power, and it will set you forever apart from the groundlings. For a time that natural tendency of all species to cling to the *us* and shun the *them* has lain quiet in the human spirit, but that could change—"

Blaise was yawning. Tachyon closed his teeth on the endless flow of words. He *was* becoming a bore. Blaise was young. The young were always callous and optimistic. But Tach had little room for optimism in his life. Ever since that desperate night in June 1987, Tachyon had carried in his DNA the twisting, mutating pattern of the wild card virus. For the moment it lay dormant, but Tachyon knew that an instant of stress, extreme pain, terror, even joy could trigger the virus, and if he were not fortunate enough to draw the black queen and die, he too might become a joker. It was too much to hope that he would fall into that lucky minority who became aces.

There was a tap on the door of the suite. Brows arching in

surprise, the alien sent Blaise to answer while he recased the violin.

"*George!*"

Tachyon stood tensely in the door to the sitting room, gripping the jamb so he didn't release the furious anger and fear that held him. "What are you doing here?" he asked in a low, controlled tone.

George Steele, a.k.a. Victor Demyenov, a.k.a. Georgy Vladimirovich Polyakov, met the alien's thinly veiled hostility with a bland raise of the eyebrows. "Where else would I be?" The boy released his tight embrace on the portly older man, and George kissed him loudly on each cheek. "I work for the *Brighton Beach Observer.* I have a story to cover."

"Oh, Ideal, you're a goddamn Russian spy in a hotel that's crawling with Secret Service agents. And you're in *my* suite!" Tachyon suddenly pressed a hand to his heart, quieted his breathing, became aware of Blaise listening interestedly. "Go downstairs, and . . . and . . ." He dug out his wallet. "And buy a magazine."

"I don't want to."

"For once in your life don't argue with me!"

"Why can't I stay?" The whine was in place.

"You're only a boy. You shouldn't be involved in this."

"A minute ago I was old enough to take an adult interest in adult matters."

"Ancestors!" Tachyon dropped onto the sofa, held his head in his hands.

Polyakov allowed himself a small smile. "Perhaps your grandpapa is right . . . and this will be boring, Blaise, my child." He dropped a companionable arm over the boy's shoulders and urged him to the door. "Go and amuse yourself while your grandpapa and I discuss darker matters."

"And stay out of trouble." Tach yelled as the door closed on Blaise's heels.

The alien smeared jam on a croissant. Stared at it. Dropped it back onto the plate. "Why can you handle him better than I can?"

"You try to love him. I don't think Blaise responds well to love."

"I don't want to believe that. But what are these dark matters we must discuss?"

Polyakov dropped into a chair, worried his lower lip

between thumb and forefinger. "This convention is critical—"

"No joke? No pun intended."

"Shut up and listen!" And suddenly the voice held all the old steel and command it had possessed those long years ago when Victor Demyenov had picked a drunken and shattered Takisian out of the gutters of Hamburg and trained him in the delicate tradecraft of the modern spy. "I need you to do a job for me."

Tachyon backed away, palms out. "No. No more jobs. I've already given you more than I should. Let you back into my life, close to my grandson. What more do you want?"

"Plenty, and I deserve it. You owe me, Dancer. Your *omission* in London cost me my life, my country. You made me an exile—"

"Just another something we have in common," said Tachyon bitterly.

"Yes. And that boy." Polyakov gestured toward the door. "And a past that cannot be erased."

There was again that nervous worrying of lips between fingers. Tachyon cocked his head curiously, and firmly suppressed a desire to slip beneath the layers of that secretive mind. Takisian protocol dictated that one did *not* invade the privacy of a friend's mind. And there was enough friendship left from those years in East and West Berlin to dictate that courtesy. But Tach had never in all the years seen Polyakov so rattled, so jumpy. The alien found himself remembering incidents from the past year: late nights of drinking after Blaise had gone to bed; Polyakov providing an exuberant and uncritical audience as Tach and Blaise had charged through a Brahms Hungarian dance for piano and violin; the times that the Russian had kept Blaise from exercising his terrible power on the helpless humans who surrounded him.

Tachyon crossed the room, squatted before the old man, rested his arm on Polyakov's knee for balance. "For once in your life don't play the enigmatic Russian. Tell me plainly what you want. What you fear."

Polyakov suddenly gripped Tachyon's right hand. *PAIN!* The bite of fire from within, rushing up his arm, through his body, boiling the blood. Sweat burst from his pores, tears from his eyes. Tach sprawled on his elbows on the floor.

"BURNING SKY!"

"An appropriate exclamation," said Polyakov with a humorless smile. "You Takisians, always so apt."

Tachyon scrubbed a handkerchief across his streaming face, but the tears continued to flow. He gulped down a sob.

The Russian frowned down at him. "What the devil is wrong with you?"

"You couldn't just tell me you are an ace?" cried Tach bitterly.

Polyakov shrugged. Rose and pulled a handkerchief from his breast pocket. Tachyon's fingers were closed frenziedly about the sodden mass of his own.

"What the hell is the matter? I gave you only the merest lick of my fire."

"And I am carrying the wild card so your little *lick* could have triggered the virus."

Tachyon found himself crushed into a burly embrace. He fought free, gave his nose a hard blow. "So today is a day for secrets, is it not?"

"How long?"

"A year."

"If I had known—"

"I know. I know, you would never have scared me out of a thousand years of life with that little demonstration." His clothes smelled rankly of sweat and fear. Tachyon began to strip. "So now I know why you are so interested in this convention."

"It goes beyond the fact that I am a wild card," grunted Polyakov. "I am a Russian."

"Yes," Tach threw over his shoulder as he walked into the bathroom. "I know." The thunder of the water drowned out Polyakov's words. "WHAT?"

Grumbling, Polyakov followed him into the bathroom, lowered the toilet cover, and sat. From behind the shrouding curtain Tach heard the clink of metal on glass.

"What are you drinking?"

"What do you think?"

"I'll take one, too."

"It's eight in the morning."

"So we'll go to hell drunk and together." Tach accepted the glass, allowed the water to beat on his shoulders while he sipped at the vodka. "You drink too much."

"We *both* drink too much."

"True."

"There's an ace at this convention."

"There are a shitload of aces at this convention."

"A secret ace."

"Yes, he's sitting on my toilet." Tachyon stuck his head around the curtain. "How long is this going to take? Can't you be a little less cautious and trust me just a little?"

Polyakov sighed heavily, stared down at his hands as if counting the hairs on the back of fingers. "Hartmann is an ace."

Tach stuck his head back through the shower curtain. "Nonsense."

"I tell you it is true."

"Proof?"

"Suspicions."

"Not good enough." Tach shut off the water, and thrust a hand through the curtain. "Towel." Polyakov dropped one over his arm.

Stepping from the shower, the alien studied his image in the mirror as he towel dried his shoulder-length red hair. Noted the scars on his left arm and hand where the doctors had repaired the bones crushed in an eleventh-hour rescue of Angelface. The puckered scar on his thigh—legacy of a terrorist's bullet in Paris. The long scar on the right bicep—memory of a duel with his cousin. "Living takes a hell of a toll, doesn't it?"

"Just how old are you?" the Russian asked curiously.

"Adjusting for Earth's rotational period; eighty-nine, ninety. Somewhere in there."

"I was young when I met you."

"Yes."

"Now I am old and fat and in the grip of a terrible fear. You can so easily establish if my fears are real or mere delusions. Probe Hartmann, read him, then act."

"Gregg Hartmann is my friend. I don't probe my friends. I don't even probe *you*."

"I give you permission to do so. If it will help to convince you."

"Ideal, you must be in terror."

"I am. Hartmann is . . . evil."

"Odd word from an old material dialectician like yourself."

"Nevertheless, it applies."

Tachyon shook his head, walked into the bedroom, rummaged in a drawer for fresh underwear. He could sense George behind him, a portly irritating presence. "I don't believe you."

"No, you don't *want* to believe me. A fundamental difference. How much do you know of Hartmann's early life? His passage through this world has left a trail of mysterious deaths and shattered lives. His high school football coach, his college roommate—"

"So he's had the misfortune to be on the periphery of violent events. That does not make him an ace. Or would you have him damned by association?"

"And what of a politician who is kidnapped *twice*, and escapes both times under mysterious circumstances?"

"What's so mysterious? In Syria, Kahina turned upon her brother and stabbed him. In the resulting chaos we escaped. In Germany—"

"I was working with Kahina."

"*What!*"

"When I first came to America. Gimli too, that poor fool. Now Gimli is dead, and Kahina has vanished, and I fear she too is dead. She came to America to expose Gregg Hartmann."

"So you say."

"Tachyon, I don't lie to you."

"No, you merely tell me only as much as suits you."

"Gimli suspected, and now he's dead."

"Oh, so now Gregg is responsible for Typhoid Croyd? Gimli died from that virus, not from Gregg Hartmann."

"And Kahina?"

"Show me a body. Show me the proof."

"What about Germany?"

"What about it?"

"One of the GRU's top operatives was in charge of that operation, and he ran like a raw recruit. He was *manipulated*, I tell you!"

"You *tell* me! You *tell* me? You tell me nothing! Just slurs and innuendos. Nothing to back up this fantastic allegation."

"What does it cost you to probe him? Read him and prove me wrong."

Tachyon's mouth tightened mulishly.

"You're afraid. You're afraid that what I'm telling you is

true. This is not Takisian honor and reticence. This is coward-ice."

"There are very few men who would be permitted to say that to me, and live." Tachyon shrugged on his shirt, and resumed in a dry, almost lecturing, tone, "Being an ace you must have considered the political climate. Supposing for the moment that you are correct and Gregg Hartmann is a secret ace—so what? There is nothing very suspicious in a man with political aspirations hiding his wild card. This is not France, where it is the height of *chic* to be an ace. You damn him for keeping a secret that you have kept all your life?"

"He's a killer, Tachyon, I know it. That's why he is hiding."

"The hounds are gathering, George. They're snapping at our heels. Soon they will want to taste blood. Gregg Hartmann is our only hope to keep the hate at bay. If we smear Hartmann, we open the way for Barnett and the crazies. You'll be all right. You can hide behind that bland, ordinary face. But what of the others? What of my bastard stepchildren waiting in the park, their deformities obvious for all the world to see? What do I tell them? That the man who has protected and defended them for twenty years is evil and must be destroyed because he *might* be an ace, and because he kept it secret?"

Tachyon's eyes widened as he considered a new possibility. "My god, this might be why you were sent here. To bring down the candidate that the Kremlin fears. A Hartmann presidency—"

"What is this nonsense? Have you taken to reading sensational spy fiction? I fled for my life. Even the Kremlin thinks I'm dead."

"How can I believe you? Why should I trust you?"

"Only you can answer those questions. Nothing I say or do will convince you. I'll say only one thing—I would hope that this past year would have at least demonstrated that I am not your enemy."

Polyakov walked to the door.

"That's it?"

"It seems pointless to continue a circular argument."

"You waltz in here, and calmly announce that Gregg Hartmann is a killer ace, and then waltz back out again?"

"I've given you all that I have. Now it's up to you,

Dancer." He seemed to struggle with himself for a moment, then added, "But if you don't act, be warned—I shall."

After Jack crossed the street, he realized he didn't have to deal with the July heat any longer: he could get back to the Marriott by way of Peachtree Mall. The conditioned air was a relief. He rode the escalator to the top level and came face to face with a group of Charismatic Catholics for Barnett, all walking circles, counting their rosaries, and chanting the Hail Mary while wearing posterboards with their candidate's picture. STOP WILD CARD VIOLENCE, some signs said. This week's cover slogan for *Put wild cards in concentration camps*.

Weird, Jack thought. Barnett professed the Roman Church a tool of Satan, and here they were praying for him.

He passed by. Sweat cooled on his forehead. Two black kids loaded with Jesse Jackson buttons were throwing large foam-plastic gliders back and forth. Delegates in silly hats mobbed the restaurants, looking for breakfast.

One of the gliders fluttered toward Jack, heading for the pavement. Jack grinned and snatched it from the air before it hit the floor. He cocked his arm to throw it back to its owner, and then stopped and stared at the glider in surprise.

The foam glider had been created in the image of Peregrine, her wings outspread to almost two feet. The famous bosom, which Jack had gazed at on many memorable occasions aboard the *Stacked Deck*, was rendered in loving detail. Only the tail structure, presumably required for proper aerodynamics, was nonanatomical. Small letters were printed on the tail: *Flying Ace Gliders (R)*, they said, *collect them all*.

Jack wondered if Peregrine was getting any royalties.

The two kids stood about fifteen yards away, waiting for their glider. Jack cocked his hand back and threw, the same motion he'd used playing football years ago, and added just a touch of his power. A mild golden aura flickered from his body. The glider fired in a fast, straight line, the length of the mall, buzzing like an insect in flight.

The kids stared, first at the glider, then at Jack, then at the glider again. Then they took off, running after their Peregrine.

People were staring. Jack felt a delirious rise of optimism. Maybe returning to public life wasn't going to be so bad. He laughed and loped up the mall again.

On the way he met the glider-seller, his samples assembled on a folding table in front of him. Jack recognized J.J. Flash and Jetboy's JB-1. There was one Frisbee-like object obviously intended as the Turtle.

Jack showed his ID and room key to the police cordoning off the Marriott and walked into the cavernous venturi shape of the atrium. The Marriott was Hartmann headquarters, and almost all the people in sight were wearing Hartmann regalia. Flying Ace gliders, thrown from the balconies above, swooped in daring loops above their heads. Off out of sight, someone was playing *charge* on a portable organ.

Jack stepped to the desk to see if anyone had left any messages. Charles Devaughn wanted him to call; so did one of the Georgia starlets. Which one, Jack tried to recall, was Bobbie? The stacked redhead? Or was it the blonde chain gang woman who spent half the party talking about her expensive dental implants and demonstrating her anticellulite exercises?

There wasn't likely to be any time at this convention for a personal life anyway.

Jack put the messages in his pocket and turned away from the desk. A Flying Ace glider spun into the ground before his feet. He automatically reached down to pick it up, saw the molded white scarf, flyer's helmet, leather jacket.

Jack stared for a long moment, the glider hanging from his hand. *Hello, Earl*, he thought.

For a while he'd thought it would really be okay. He'd reached a truce with Tachyon; maybe Gregg Hartmann could talk old diehards like Hiram Worchester around. Maybe everyone else had forgotten the Four Aces, and HUAC, and Jack's betrayal; maybe he could step out in public and do something worthwhile without messing up, without being haunted by reminders of the past.

Better straighten up, farm boy. Funny how after all these years he still knew exactly what Earl Sanderson would say.

Jack rose to his full height and looked over the heads of the crowd, wondering if someone out there had meant the glider to fall where it did, wanted to remind him that everything hadn't been forgotten. Jack must have looked ridiculous enough, heaven knows, hunched over the glider with his guilty conscience welling out of his face, and the effigy of his friend and victim dangling from his paw.

Bye, Earl, he thought. *Take care, now.*

He cocked his arm back and fired. The glider whirred as it rose into the atrium, rising forever until it was lost to sight.

Gregg could feel the hunger.

It had nothing to do with politics or the expectation that by the end of this week he could well be the Democratic nominee.

Coming down in the Marriott elevator for his breakfast meeting with Jack Braun and Hiram Worchester, the hunger burned in his gut like glowing phosphorus—a pulsing violence that a few croissants and coffee would never touch.

The hunger was Puppetman's, and it demanded pain.

His face must have reflected some of the inner struggle. His aide, Amy Sorenson, leaned toward him and touched his shoulder hesitantly. "Sir . . . ?"

Billy Ray, assigned to Hartmann's personal security for the convention, glanced over the shoulder of his spotless white Carnifex uniform from the front of the elevator. Gregg forced a yawn and a professional smile. "Just tired, Amy. That's all. It's been a long campaign and, by god, it'll be a longer week. Give me a few cups of coffee and I'll be fine. Ready to face the hordes." Amy grinned; Billy Ray returned his solemn attention to the door, ignoring the view of the Marriott Marquis's immense and surreal lobby.

"Ellen wasn't having trouble, was she?"

"No, no." Gregg watched the lobby floor rise toward them. A large foam glider spiraled lazily past them toward the crowded restaurant below. As the elevator passed it in mid-flight, Gregg could see that the body was that of a woman with bird-shaped wings. The features looked suspiciously like Peregrine's. Now that he'd noticed the first one, Gregg saw that there were several more of the gliders performing acrobatics above the lobby. "She hasn't had morning sickness since the first trimester. We're both fine. Just tired."

"You've never told me—do you want a boy or a girl?"

"It doesn't matter. As long as it's healthy."

The floor indicators flickered down. Gregg's ears popped with the pressure change. Inside, Puppetman snarled. *You're not fine. Give me a few cups of coffee . . .* The presence radiated disgust. *Do you know how long I've been waiting? Do you know how long it's been?*

Be quiet. We can't do anything about it now.

Then it had better be soon. Soon, do you hear me, Greggie?

Gregg forced the power back into its mental cage. The effort cost him. Puppetman struggled, its anger a rasping, continual presence. Shaking the bars.

Lately, it was always shaking the bars.

The problem had only begun in the last few months. At first it was rare, something he thought of as some strange fluke, a quirk attributed to the weariness of a long campaign. But it had happened more and more often.

A mental wall would slam up between Puppetman and his victims. Just as he was about to feed on those dark and violent emotions, he would be cut off, pushed back by some outside force. Puppetman would howl as the link to the puppet was severed.

He'd prayed that problem would disappear; instead, it worsened. For the past two weeks the block had reared up every time Puppetman had tried to feed. Lately, he'd begun to sense a mocking laughter riding with the interference, a faint, whispering voice just on the edge of recognition.

The power inside Gregg was becoming desperate and uncontrollable. And Gregg was afraid the internal struggle was beginning to show.

Make me wait much longer and I'll show you the real puppet. I'll give you a goddamn graphic demonstration of which one of us is in control.

The power slipped loose of Gregg's hold for a moment, defiant. Gregg willed it to be silent, but still it screamed at him as he set the mental bars around it once more. Puppetman gibbered and spat. *You're the fucking puppet, do you hear! I'll make you crawl! Understand? You need it as much as I do. If I die, you die. You have nothing without me.*

Gregg was sweating with the effort, but he won. He closed his eyes and leaned back as the elevator lurched to a halt at the ground floor. Puppetman lapsed into brooding silence inside; Amy watched him with concern.

The doors opened, and the coolness and noise of the lobby hit them. Some of the crowd in the lobby, most of them sporting Hartmann buttons and hats, had spotted him—there were screams and a rush toward him. Waiting Secret Service men stepped smoothly between them, cutting off the support-

ers; Gregg waved and smiled. They began to chant: "Hartmann! Hartmann!" The lobby echoed with it.

Amy shook her head. "What a circus, huh?"

Ray ushered Gregg toward the private room where he
was to meet Hiram and Braun, and then took his station just
outside. Gregg went in. The air-conditioning here was more
oppressive than the lobby's. He shivered and rubbed his arms.

Only Jack—Golden Boy—was present, a handsome, tall
man who looked as if he hadn't aged a day in the four decades
since the heyday of the Four Aces, still the image of the movie
star he'd once been. He rose to greet Gregg. Braun seemed
subdued, which didn't surprise Gregg. He hadn't figured Jack
would much care for the attempt at reconciliation. Frankly, he
didn't give a shit whether Jack was happy with it or not—
Gregg was going to make the two of them bury this particular
hatchet; publicly, at least.

"Senator, Amy," Braun said. His eyes lingered a bit too
long on Amy. Which also hardly surprised Gregg; he knew
they were having an affair. Puppetman knew lots of hidden
things. "Good morning. How's Ellen?"

"Getting bigger each day," Gregg replied. "And tired a
lot. Like all of us."

"I know what you mean. Ready to begin the good fight?"

"I thought we'd already begun, Jack," Gregg commented.
His voice sounded glum and irritable against Braun's hearti-
ness. He made himself smile.

Braun glanced at Gregg strangely, but he laughed. "I
suppose so. You know Californians: it's bad enough everyone
was a little jet-lagged. I was up most of the night with your
uncommitted superdelegates. I think we have things worked
out. Listen, I thought you said Worchester was going to be
here."

"You haven't seen him this morning?" Gregg frowned,
irritated.

"Not yet. And it isn't exactly like him to pass up a
meal—though he'll probably bring his own in since I hear even
the Bello Mondo isn't up to his standards." A grimace and
shrug. "Hey, I know the reason you wanted this breakfast
meeting was to get the two of us to patch up our differences,
and I appreciate the sentiment—I'd like it, too. But maybe
Hiram isn't quite as forgiving as you think."

"I don't believe that, Jack."

Jack gave Gregg a lopsided, bitter smile. "He's never served you a plate of thirty silver dimes, either."

"Amy . . ." Gregg began.

"Already gone, sir," his aide said. "I'll find him or starve trying. Save me a roll, okay?"

As she left the room, Gregg turned to Braun. "Okay, we'll go ahead and eat. If Hiram shows, he shows." The words snapped out more sharply than Gregg intended. He was in no mood for games, not with Puppetman slamming against his restraints. Braun was looking at him strangely again, but before the ace could say anything, Gregg shook his head and waved the anger away. "God, that sounded horrible, Jack. I'm sorry. I'm just not myself this morning. Point me in the direction of the coffeepot, would you?"

Strange, Jack thought. He'd never felt uncomfortable in the presence of Gregg Hartmann before. Yet here he was, face to face with the man he hoped would be the next president, the man who had talked him into coming out of his public isolation and joining his crusade for office, and something was missing.

I'm tired, thought Jack. So is Gregg. No one can be charismatic every minute.

He poured himself coffee. The cup rattled in the saucer—hangover, maybe, or nerves. If it hadn't been Gregg asking for this meeting, he wouldn't have come. "I saw a car full of Nazis outside," he said. "Nazis in uniforms."

"The Klan are here, too." Hartmann shook his head. "There's potential for a serious confrontation. The crackpot right likes that kind of thing—it gives them publicity."

"Lucky thing the Turtle is here."

"Yes." Hartmann gave him a look. "You've never met the Turtle, have you?"

Jack held up a hand. "Please." He smiled to cover his nervousness. "Let's keep it down to one reconciliation a day, okay?"

Hartmann knit his brows. "Is there a problem between you?"

Jack shrugged. "Not that I know of. I just . . . sort of assume there would be."

Hartmann stepped toward Jack, put a hand on his shoulder. There was concern in his eyes.

"You assume too much, Jack. You think everyone's got a chip on his shoulder about your past, and it's just not true. You've got to let down the defenses, let people get to know you."

Jack stared at the coffee swirling in his cup and thought about Earl Sanderson spiraling to a crash landing at his feet. "Okay, Gregg," he said, "I'll try."

"You're important to this campaign, Jack. You're head of the California delegation. I wouldn't have chosen you if you weren't suited for the job."

"You could get some heat on account of me. I've told you that."

"You're important, Jack. You're a symbol of something bad that happened a long time ago, something we're trying to prevent from happening again. The other Four Aces were victims, but so were you. They paid with prison or exile or their lives, but you . . ." Hartmann gave his boyish, half-apologetic smile. "Maybe you paid with your self-respect. Who's to say that isn't worth more in the long run? Their agony ended, but yours hasn't. I think it all balanced long ago, that everyone's paid too much." He squeezed Jack's shoulder. "We need you. You're important to us. I'm glad you're aboard."

Jack stared at Hartmann, cynicism ringing in his mind like funeral bells. Was Gregg serious—lives and sanity and prison terms balanced against his own worthless loss of dignity? Hartmann *had* to be laughing behind that sincere expression, making fun of him.

Jack shook his head. From the time he'd met him aboard the *Stacked Deck*, Hartmann had been a man who could make Jack feel good about himself. What he was saying now wasn't substantially different from what he'd said to Jack before. But now the message seemed the reflex posturing of a politician, not the message of a concerned friend.

"Is something wrong, Gregg?" Jack blurted.

Hartmann dropped his hand, turned partly away. "Sorry," he said. "Things have been a little strained."

"You need some rest."

"Guess we all do." Hartmann cleared his throat. "Charles said you did some good work for us last night."

"I got some congressmen drunk and laid, is all."

Hartmann gave a laugh. "Charles has given me their

names and room numbers. I'll be phoning them as soon as
we've finished breakfast. Perhaps—"

The door opened. Jack jumped, spilling coffee. He turned
and saw, not Hiram Worchester, but Amy. Embarrassed at his
nervousness, Jack reached for a napkin.

"Sorry to interrupt, gentlemen. I just got a phone call
from Furs in Jokertown. It's a potential problem. Chrysalis
has just been found dead in New York. Ace abilities were
involved."

Surprise stumbled into Jack's mind. He'd spent months
with Chrysalis aboard the *Stacked Deck*, and although he'd
never been comfortable around her—the organs and muscle
visible through the transparent flesh reminded Jack of too
many things he'd seen in World War II and Korea—he'd
developed an abstract admiration for the way Chrysalis han-
dled her deformity, the cultured accent, cigarette holder,
antique playing cards, and dry style.

Hartmann's face went rigid. When the candidate spoke,
his voice was strained. "Any more details?"

"Beaten to death, looks like." Amy pursed her lips.
"Barnett can make some propaganda out of this—it's more
'wild card violence' that will have to be restrained."

"I knew her well," Hartmann said tightly. The mask-like
face seemed unusual in a man who was so open around his
friends. Jack wondered if there were aspects to this death he
hadn't known about.

"Tony Calderone checked in late last night," Amy said.
"Maybe you should get him preparing a statement in case
Barnett tries to use this."

Hartmann gave a sigh. "Yes. I'll have to do that." He
turned to Jack. "Jack, I'm afraid I'm going to have to abandon
you."

"Should I leave?"

Concern entered Hartmann's eyes again as he looked at
Jack. "I would appreciate it very much if you'd stay. You and
Hiram Worchester are two of my most visible supporters—if
you could settle your differences, it would mean a lot to me."

Jack thought for a moment, wondering if Judas and St.
Paul ever settled *their* differences.

He sighed. It had to happen sooner or later. "I don't *have*
a problem with Worchester, Gregg. He's just got one with
me."

Hartmann smiled. "Good," he said. He raised a hand and squeezed Jack's shoulder again.

The room seemed very empty after Hartmann and Amy left. Jack watched breakfast turn cold on the buffet.

Earl's glider crashed again and again in his mind.

9:00 A.M.

"Sara," Ricky Barnes said, "you've got to get off this Hartmann thing. It's making you crazy. You're acting obsessive/compulsive."

They sat at a round table covered in green-checked oilcloth near Le Peep's front window. Outside, a clot of farm-state delegates in loud ties floated down the tiled rectilinear intestine of Peachtree Center, headed for the Hyatt lobby. More delegates vied with ferns for elbow room around them, trying to fortify themselves on lightweight New Egg Cuisine. It was that, fast food, or hotel restaurants, which had waiting lists past the turn of the century.

"*Rolling Stone* says that's the disease of the Eighties," Sara Morgenstern said, dissecting her omelet with her fork. Her winter-pale hair was swept from the left side of her head to the right today. She wore a simple pink dress that came to the tops of her crossed knees. Her stockings were sheer black, her shoes wedge-soled and white.

Barnes took a bite of his own tofu and spinach omelet. The coat of his severe black two-piece was draped over his hooped chairback. With his suspenders and white shirt he might have passed for an *Inherit the Wind* epoch Southern Methodist minister, except for his gold-wire yuppie granny glasses.

"It's getting a lot of competition from AIDS," he said. "But seriously, you're a long way off your usual Jokertown beat; your Washington desk is handling everything that comes out of Atlanta this week, and they won't be as indulgent of your little foibles as the New York bureau is. Senator Gregg's the *Post's* special pet. It's as if Katie Graham invented him. They're not going to be happy with you throwing rocks at him."

"We're journalists, Ricky," she said, leaning forward, reaching as if to touch the hand resting beside his plate. The white fingers stopped millimeters short of the milk-chocolate ones. Ricky didn't react. He was an old friend, who'd taken a journalism seminar from her at Columbia a few years back, and knew her reticence had nothing to do with his race. "We have to report the truth."

Ricky shook his long and neatly groomed head. "Sara, Sara. You're not that naive. We report what the owners want or what our peers want. If the truth happens to fall inconveniently in between, it doesn't have much constituency. Besides, what is truth, as the man who washed his hands asked?"

"The truth is that Gregg Hartmann is a murderer and a monster. And I'm going to expose him."

When Hiram Worchester shambled into the room, Jack gave a start and reflexively began to rise from his chair before deciding not to. He settled back into the chair with his coffee and cigarette. He and Hiram had been on the *Stacked Deck* together; even if they hadn't been friends, there was no need for formality.

Hiram looked as if he hadn't slept. He headed wordlessly for the buffet, took a plate, began to fill it.

Jack felt perspiration speckling his scalp. His heart seemed to change rhythms every few seconds. Why the hell, he demanded of himself, was he so nervous? He took a long drag on his Camel.

Hiram kept filling his plate. Jack began to wonder if his wild card had suddenly run to invisibility.

Hiram turned, chewing a cruller as if he wasn't really tasting it, and took a seat opposite Jack. On the *Stacked Deck* he had used his control of gravity to remove a lot of his weight, something that made him oddly agile. He didn't seem to be doing that now. He looked at Jack out of dull, marble eyes. "Braun," he said. "This meeting wasn't my idea."

"Mine either."

"You were a hero of mine, you know. When I was young."

We all have to grow up sometime, Jack thought, but decided against saying it. Let the man have his moment.

"I've never made any claims to heroism myself," Hiram spoke on. Jack had the feeling it was a speech he'd been working on for some time. "I'm a fat man who runs a restaurant. I've never been on the cover of *Life* or starred in a feature film. But whatever else, I'm loyal to my friends."

Good for you, chum. This time Jack almost said it. But he thought of Earl Sanderson fluttering to the floor of the Marriott and instead said nothing.

He blinked sweat out of his eyes. Why am I doing this to myself? he thought.

Hiram spoke on, robot-like. "Gregg tells me you did good work in California. He says we might have lost without all the celebrity support and money that you organized. I'm grateful for that, but gratitude is one thing and trust is another."

"I wouldn't trust anybody in politics, Worchester," Jack said. And then wondered if that piece of fashionable cynicism was true, because he *did* trust Gregg Hartmann, knew him for a genuinely *good* man, and he wanted the man to win more than he had wanted anything in thirty years.

"It's important that Gregg Hartmann win this election, Braun. Leo Barnett is the Nur-al-Allah in American dress. Remember Syria? Remember jokers stoned to death in the streets?" There was a weird gleam in Hiram's eyes. He raised a fist and clenched it, forgetting it contained half a cruller. "That's what's at stake here, Braun. They'll do *anything* to stop us. They'll bribe, smear, seduce us, resort to violence. And *where will you be, Braun?*" Loudly. *"Where will you be when they really start turning the screws?"*

Suddenly Jack's nervousness was gone. A cold anger hummed through him. He'd had quite enough.

"You . . . weren't . . . there," Jack said.

Hiram paused, then became aware of pastry dough ballooning out between the fingers of his upraised hand.

"You . . . weren't . . . fucking . . . there." The words grated slowly from a place inside Jack that seemed like a twilight graveyard, a place without warmth, an endless plain of autumn grass marked with gray stones that noted the passing of Earl, of Blythe, of Archibald Holmes, of all the young men he knew in the 5th Division, all those who died at the Rapido crossing, little stick figures scattered like so many handfuls of dust beneath the pounding guns of Cassino . . .

Jack stood up and threw the cigarette away. "For someone who doesn't claim to be a hero, Worchester, you sure make a great speech. Maybe you should consider a career in politics."

With quick, vicious movements of the napkin, Hiram swabbed dough from his hand. "I told Gregg you can't be trusted. He told me you've changed."

"Could be he's right," Jack said. "Could be he's wrong. The question is, what can *you* do about it?"

Hiram threw the napkin away and rose massively to his

feet, a pale mountain lumbering to battle. "I can do what I have to do!" he said sharply. "It's that important!"

Jack's lips skinned back from his teeth in a wolverine smile. "You don't know that. You haven't been tested. You haven't been there." He gave a stage laugh, Basil Rathbone standing on the parapet and mocking the peasants. "Everyone knows about me, Worchester, but nobody's put the screws to *you* yet. Nobody's *asked* you to betray *your* friends. You haven't been there, and you don't know what you're going to do till it happens." He smiled again. "Take my word for it."

Hiram seemed to wilt before Jack's smile. Then his color drained away, and to Jack's surprise the big man seemed to stagger back and fall. Springs burst in the chair as Hiram collapsed into it. He tugged at his collar as if he were choking, revealing a painful sore on his neck.

Jack stared in amazement. The granite mountain had melted into a marshmallow.

And suddenly Jack was very weary. A faint hangover residue throbbed in his temples. He didn't want to watch Hiram any more.

He headed for the exit.

He paused by the door. "I'm here for Gregg's sake," he said. "I guess it's the same for you. So let's tell Gregg we're the best of friends and do what we have to do. Okay?"

Hiram, still dragging at his collar, nodded.

Jack stepped into the corridor and closed the door of the suite behind him. He felt like the school bully picking on the class fat kid.

From down the corridor came the raucous cry of conventioneers on their first day in town. Jack headed toward it.

10:00 A.M.

Gregg was tired of talking to the delegates Jack had gotten laid the night before. He was tired of sounding enthusiastic.

Alex James had been a puppet since the beginning of the campaign. Most of the extra secret service people assigned to Gregg had been uninteresting to Puppetman, too dutiful and without the hidden flaws on which he fed. But Alex . . . he had slipped through the battery of psychological examinations and background checks. Like that of Billy Ray, Alex's soul was marbled with a delicious streak of sadism, tinted with the jade-green urge to flaunt and abuse his power. Left alone, he might have been only a little overzealous in his duties, a touch harsh when he moved people away, preferring to confront a situation rather than defusing it. No one would have noticed.

But Puppetman knew. Puppetman saw all the cracks in the veneer of a soul and he knew best how to make them gape wide open.

Gregg sat in the living room of his suite. The Zenith bolted to the wall cabinet was on, set to CBS and Dan Rather's coverage of the convention's opening. Cautiously, Gregg let down the bars that held Puppetman. The power surged out, searching for Alex's presence. Gregg had just seen the man in the hall outside, knew that Ray had just sent him to check the stairwells. There were often people on the stairs: lobbyists looking for a way to the candidate's floors, reporters, groupies, or just the curious. The chances were good that Alex would find someone. Puppetman reached out and curled into the familiar recesses of the guard's mind. *This time*, the power sighed. *This time*.

Be careful, Gregg warned him. *Remember what's been happening lately. Go slowly.*

Puppetman snarled in reply. *Shut up! It's all right now. Everything's turning our way again. Chrysalis is finally taken care of. Oddity is going to find the jacket and we've sent Mackie after Downs. The convention's started well. I need this one. Can't you feel the hunger? Remember, if I go, you go down with me. I'll make damn sure of it.*

With the threat, the power turned away, suddenly rapacious. Through Puppetman, Gregg could feel a surge of anticipation in Alex. He knew what that must mean—the guard had found someone. Gregg could imagine the scene: some nat kid, probably, dressed in stone-wash jeans, a T-shirt studded with oversized "Hartmann in '88" buttons, and a cheap J-town mask over his all-too-normal face. Alex would be staring, his hands a shade too close to the bulge under his sports jacket, barking orders.

Puppetman lanced into Alex's emotional matrix, thrusting aside the heavy blue layers of duty and the leather-brown binding of morality until he uncovered that orange-red core of psychotic brutality. Puppetman nurtured it, fanned it into flame. It flared easily into heat. *Now* . . .

(Alex would be shouting by this time, his neck corded,

and his cheeks red with blood. He'd reach out, grab a fistful of the T-shirt, as campaign buttons rattled like tin pie plates, and shake the kid like a disobedient puppy. The mask would fall to the floor and crumple under Alex's Florsheims.)

. . . *yes.* Puppetman could taste it, and Gregg tasted with him. There was raw fury there, a waiting feast. Puppetman leaned toward it hungrily, tweaking the emotions again, turning the settings just a little higher . . .

(Alex's hand would come back, and the open palm would slash across the kid's cheek, snapping the head to one side. Blood would be drooling from a cut on the lip and the kid would be crying in fear and pain, suddenly terrified.)

. . . and it happened again. In Gregg's mind, the interference seemed like a cold, obsidian wall, cutting between himself and Alex and sending Puppetman reeling backward. The power inside Gregg wailed in frustration and rage, hurling itself at the wall again and again and always being slammed back down. Gregg could hear the laughter behind the wall, and that faint voice.

Only this time, *this* time, he could hear the words.

You're a fucking son of a bitch, Hartmann, but I finally got the way to take you down, don't I? I found your goddamn weakness, Greggie old friend. I found the fucking playmate inside you, the ace you used on me and Misha and Morgenstern and everyone else. Only now I can play with your ace the way you played with us. I can keep him away from the puppets; I can make him fucking starve, and then what happens to you, Senator? What happens to you when the power turns against you? The words faded, leaving behind a mocking chuckle.

And Gregg, with a rising horror, knew that he recognized that voice. He knew who was behind the wall, and the realization left him cold and shaking.

Gimli. It was Gimli.

You're dead, he shouted after the voice. *You're dead—your stuffed skin is sitting in the Dime Museum; I saw it. Typhoid Croyd killed you.*

Dead? The laughter came again. *Do I sound dead to you, Hartmann? Ask the friend you keep locked up inside you if I'm real or not. No, not dead. Just changed. It took me a long time to get back . . .*

The voice faded and was gone. The wall vanished.

Puppetman screamed wordlessly at the place where it had been.

Let me out again, the power demanded. *It's not too late, Alex . . .*

No! Gregg looked at his hands; they were trembling on his lap. He could feel sweat running down the back of his shirt. Adrenaline pounded in his chest. He wanted to run, to scream himself. The ordinariness of the hotel room and the droning voice of Rather seemed to mock him.

He was very, very scared.

You have to let me out. There's no choice.

No!

No choice, do you understand? The power leaped at him, spearing deep into Gregg's own will. Gregg gasped in surprise, and felt his own presence falling away. His hands clenched; he started to push himself off the couch. Like an automaton, Puppetman walked him stiff legged across the room. The muscles of Gregg's face were locked in a painful grimace, spasms rippled down his legs as he struggled to regain control. He watched, helpless, as his hand reached for the doorknob to the bedroom, twisted, and pushed.

God, no . . .

"Gregg?" Ellen was reading on the bed, the book propped up against her swelling stomach. "Put your hand here; the baby's been giving me flutterings all morning." She turned to look at him, and her aristocratic, fine New England features went quizzical. "Gregg? Are you all right?"

He could feel his whole body quivering, balanced between Puppetman's will and his own. Each tugged on the strings of the body, trying to yank them from the grasp of the other. Even as Gregg made that visualization, Puppetman scoffed. *We're both the same person, you know. I'm just your ace, your power. I'm doing what we need to do to survive. Ellen's here. Use her.*

No! Not that way.

She's just another damn puppet. More pliable than most, in fact. Her pain is as good as anyone else's.

It's too risky. Not here, not now.

If not here and now, you stand to lose everything anyway. Do it!

Gregg felt his body take another stumbling step forward. His fist clenched and raised. There was definite fear in Ellen's eyes now. She closed the book, tried to struggle up from the bed. "Gregg, please, you're frightening me . . ."

Gregg let go all his holds on the body, as if he were exhausted by the battle. Puppetman shouted in victory. Then, as his arm lifted for the first blow and Puppetman relaxed in anticipation, Gregg grappled with the power again. Surprised by the renewed onslaught, Puppetman was stripped of control. Ignoring its struggling and cursing, Gregg wrestled it deep, deeper than it had been in years, slamming and locking the mental cage, and then burying it far back in his mind. When he could no longer hear it, he stopped and came back to himself.

He was gasping alongside the bed. The hand was still upraised; Ellen cowering beneath. Gregg unclenched the fist, and brought it slowly down to her face as he sat next to her. He felt her draw back, then slowly relax as he began to stroke her hair.

"You don't have anything to be afraid of, darling," he said. He tried to laugh and heard pain instead. "Hey, I wouldn't hurt you, you know that. Not the mother of my child. I'd never hurt you."

"You looked so angry, so violent. For a second—"

"I'm not feeling well. It's nothing; stomach cramps. Nerves—I've been thinking about the convention. I took some Maalox. It'll pass."

"You scared me."

"I'm sorry, Ellen," he said, soothingly. "Please . . ."

With Puppetman, it would have been easy; he could have made her believe him without effort. But that power wasn't safe, not now. Ellen stared at him, and he thought she was going to say more, then she slowly nodded. "Okay," she said. "Okay, Gregg."

She snuggled against him. Gregg leaned back against the headboard. Through the faint tendrils of his ace ability, he could feel her relaxing, forgetting. Since she'd become pregnant, she'd become more inward focused; things outside were not as important. It was less threatening to accept his excuse, so she did. The realization eased his mind very little.

My god, what am I going to do?

He could hear Gimli's laughter. It pounded in his head.

The phone by the bed rang. Gregg picked it up, thinking it might drive the dwarf away. "Hartmann."

"Senator?" The voice on the other end was breathless, agitated. "Amy. Bad news. The word is that we're in for a big fight tonight over the California delegation's credentials . . ."

He barely heard her over Gimli's roaring amusement.

Jack's hangover finally muted itself after two shots of vodka. He had spent the last hour in his suite, talking on his bank of telephones with Emil Rodriguez, his second-in-command, and trying to round up all his delegates and have them briefed for the platform fight that would come tomorrow.

There was a knock. Jack told Rodriguez he'd call him back and opened the door. Amy Sorenson stood outside, carrying a pile of briefing papers in an envelope. Her chestnut hair was pinned up atop her head.

"Hi, Amy." Jack kissed her warmly, then drew her inside and tried to kiss her again. She turned her head away.

"Not this time, Jack. This isn't like Buenos Aires. My husband's here."

Jack sighed. "You're on business, then."

Amy stepped out of his arms and straightened her fetching blue suit. "Brace yourself," she said. "I've got bad news."

"I'm braced. I've been braced for months."

Amy's nose wrinkled at the appalling stench of tobacco, liquor, and the residue of perfume. She perched on the edge of a chair, then carefully pushed a cigar-filled ashtray as far away as she could. Jack pulled up a chair and sat on it backward, gazing at Amy over the chairback.

"What's up?"

"You're not going to like this at all. There's going to be a big credentials fight tonight over the California delegation."

Jack stared at her.

"The Jackson people are gonna spring it on us. They're claiming that a winner-take-all primary is inherently discriminatory against minorities."

"Crap." Jack's reply was immediate. "The California primary's been a winner-take-all for as long as I can remember."

"The challenge gives everyone a chance to dismember our largest bloc of delegates, and do it in a righteous cause."

"We followed all the rules. We won the primary fair and square."

Amy looked exasperated. "The rules, Jack, are what the convention *says* they are. If they strip our delegates, they open the convention to a series of parliamentary and procedural battles that could unhinge everything. That's what Jackson, Gore, and Barnett *want*—if things get chaotic, it improves their chances of getting the nomination. If they can fuck us over and hand us a procedural defeat before the first ballot, they can hope to acquire defectors from our camp during the second ballot."

"Great. Just great." Funny how he just couldn't get used to women who used words like *fuck*. Hell, Jack couldn't get used to the way *men* used the word these days.

Some days more than others he felt like a relic.

"The showdown's all going to be about the rule books and who can manipulate them best. Who's the parliamentarian for your delegation?"

Jack shifted uncomfortably in his chair. "I guess I am."

"Do you *know* anything about parliamentary procedure?"

Jack thought about it. "I've sat on a lot of corporate boards. You'd be surprised at some of the tricks they pull."

Amy sighed. "Do you know Danny Logan? He's our campaign parliamentarian. I want you to take your instructions from him."

"When I last saw Logan, he was lying under a bar stool at LAX."

Amy's eyes flashed. She tossed her chestnut hair out of her eyes. "He'll be sober *tonight*, I promise you."

Jack thought for a moment. "Do we have the votes?"

"Can't tell. Dukakis is hedging, like always. The people who can save us are the superdelegates. Most of them are congressmen and senators who would do anything to prevent a bloodbath. They may vote for us just to keep things sane. And of course they know Gregg a lot better than they know the Duke and Jackson, let alone Barnett."

"This is all crazy."

"The Democrats haven't had a convention that's gone past the first ballot since 1932. Everybody's making it up as we go along."

Jack rested his chin on his big hands. "I remember that convention. My family listened to it on our radio. We were Roosevelt all the way. I remember my dad breaking out the bootleg hootch when Texas Jack Garner defected from Smith and gave Roosevelt the nomination."

Amy smiled at him. "I keep thinking of you as my

younger . . . indiscretion. I just can't picture you as old enough to live through those times."

"Till Gregg came along, the only presidential candidate I voted for was Roosevelt in '44, when I was overseas. Before that I was too young to vote. In '48 I couldn't make up my mind between Truman and Wallace, so I never cast a ballot at all."

"You almost voted for George Wallace?" Amy seemed a little shocked. "That seems unlike you."

Jack felt terribly old. "*Henry* Wallace, Amy. Henry Wallace."

"Oh. Sorry."

"Just to make it absolutely clear, the Roosevelt I mentioned was Franklin, not Teddy."

"*That* I knew." Grinning. "How'd your meeting with Hiram go? Or should I ask?"

Jack shook his head. "It was weird. I really don't know what to make of it." He looked at her. "Is Worchester okay? I wondered if he was ill. He didn't look healthy."

"Mmm."

"He's got this big sore on his neck. I read somewhere that sores like that could be a symptom of AIDS."

Amy blinked in astonishment. "*Hiram?*"

Jack shrugged. "I don't know the man, Amy. The only impression I had was that he really wasn't interested in me."

"Well." She ventured a brief smile. "I guess that means you got along all right."

"He didn't hand me any more dimes, anyway."

"That's encouraging." She cocked her head and looked at him. "I met a celebrity this morning. Josh Davidson. You ever met him?"

"The actor? What's he doing here?"

"His daughter's one of our delegates. He's here as an observer. I thought you might know each other, being actors and all."

"There are a few actors I haven't met. Honest."

"He's charming as anything. Real smooth."

Jack grinned at her. "Sounds like you're considering an older, uh, indiscretion."

Amy laughed. "Well. Maybe if he'd shave off the beard."

"I doubt it. That beard's one of his trademarks."

One of Jack's phones rang. He looked at the row of

telephones on his desk and tried to decide which one wanted him. Amy stood.

"Gotta go, Jack. That's probably Danny Logan anyway."

"Yeah." Parliamentary tactics, Jack thought. Oh, great.

Another phone began to ring. Jack crossed the suite and picked up a receiver. He heard only a dial tone.

It was setting out to be that kind of day.

11:00 A.M.

With a nasal squeal of fury Mackie ripped the calendar off the petechiate wallpaper. It displayed an open-lipped pussy presented for his approval—which wasn't coming—framed in dark hair and olive-thigh flesh, the tentative smile of a Puerto Rican girl hovering off above it in the middle distance.

Mackie put a buzz on his fingers and ran them across the photo. Bits of woman went everywhere, a flurry of colored-paper snow. That made him feel better.

It was almost as good as the real thing.

But while it could be assuaged, nothing was changing the thing that was pissing him off in the first place: the man he had come to kill wasn't here. Mackie didn't take disappointment well.

Maybe if he hung out a while Digger Downs would return home. He kicked over a low table of blond, wood-like veneer, purchased from some rental store, and went to the kitchen, while tabloids, racing forms, and issues of *Photo District News* fluttered around the floor like wounded birds. The SounDe-sign stereo on the cinderblock-and-board bookcase spritzed robopop at the fading seams on the back of his leather jacket.

The icebox was like a fifties Detroit car, big and bulging, and banded with chrome from which even phony luster was long since gone. All it lacked was fins. He yanked the door open. Inside were a bunch of white cardboard fast-food containers; half a deli sandwich, entombed in Saran Wrap, the meat gone the color of a morning-after bruise; a carton of eggs with the top ripped off, and two eggshells punctured, as if by a drunken thumb while some of their comrades were on their way to a morning-after omelet; two six packs of Little King and one of no-name creme soda; and plastic margarine tubs filled with this and that, mostly mold. There were a few little gray plastic cylinders that obviously held film. These Mackie opened and unspooled, gleefully bathing them in the dubious radiance of the one bare bulb protruding like a hemorrhoid from the ceiling.

He closed the door, buzzed a hand, and slashed across. The thick-gauge metal parted with a shower of sparks and a satisfactory vibration up his arm and down his dick. Only skin was more fun to cut than good metal. He grabbed the refrigerator, pulled, got it rocking with a strength that was surprising in his skinny, twisted little body, and pulled the thing over with a satisfying bang on the cracked linoleum. Then he turned his attention to the cupboards that crowded around a sink filled with caked and crusty dishes, which gave off a fruity fecal wino smell, something you could dip a spoon into.

The cupboards were layered, like a televangelist's wife, with enamel. Though they hadn't been refinished in living memory they gave off an odor of paint, overlaid with eons of cigarette smoke that had permeated the cabinets to their presumed bedrock of wood, that actually competed with the organic decay in the sink. Inside he found sixteen bags of Doritos, two cans of beans, one of them opened, replaced, and forgotten during binge munchies, and a box of Frosted Flakes. Tony the Tiger looked ill. The beans smelled like a dead cat.

"This is Randy St. Clair, and I'll be coming back at you with more sounds of your city from WBLS-FM, 107.5 at the end of your dial," the radio was saying when he came back in the living room. "But first, on Newsbreak, Sandy will tell us how the delegates are preparing for a long, hot summer week in Atlanta, and update us on continuing reports of genocide in Guatemala, and she'll have the latest on a grisly celebrity murder in Jokertown. Sandy?"

He frowned. It was too bad about Chrysalis. The Man had promised he could do her himself one day. Now he'd never find out what it would be like to put his hand in that glass-clear meat.

That was a brand new bitch, and it made him mad all over again. He went from room to room of the cramped apartment breaking what he found, alternating between exhilarated and clinical: Will this make me feel better? It was vandalism as designer drugs.

The bed was propped up with textbooks under one corner: French, darkroom technique, a police text on interrogation. There was no spread. The sheet was tie-dyed with bodily fluids of the kind you were supposed to encase yourself in Latex rather than come in contact with. He shredded things.

When he emerged he was starting to feel cranked at Downs again. *Der Mann* wasn't going to like this, not for one little minute.

Well, Downs just wasn't here. The Man could hardly blame him for that; it wasn't *his* fault. Fuck it. He phased through the outer wall, into the corridor.

As he did, a door across and down one opened.

"I tell you it's those Chinese people," a woman was saying in that nosy whine that made these New York people sound to Mackie like big, fleshy insects. "They're all drug dealers, you know. I saw all about them on the *60 Minutes*. This Mr. Downs, he's, like, a crusading investigative reporter. I figure he got too close to them, the tong sent somebody over to mess his place up. There must be a dozen of them, the noise they were making. With sledgehammers and chain saws."

She pushed out into the hallway like an East River tug in housecoat and fluorescent-pink, fuzzy slippers, with a hankie tied over curlers, and a super in tow. The super was a black man not much taller than Mackie, with a mustache and gray-stippled hair bushing out in back from beneath a Montreal Expos baseball cap. He had on paint-smeared, gray coveralls. He nodded distractedly at the woman while grumbling to himself, and tossing his big steel ring of keys for the master to Digger's apartment. He didn't notice Mackie.

The woman did notice Mackie. She screamed.

He smiled. It was the nicest thing anyone had said to him all day.

The super looked up at him, his mouth a shout of pink in his dark face. Mackie felt his hands begin to vibrate as of their own accord. This wasn't going to be a total loss after all.

Jack saw the weird red pyramids, looking like some strange form of acoustic tile, that crowned the Omni Center, and headed in their direction. He'd got lost in Peachtree Center looking for cigarettes, and taken the wrong route to the convention.

Ted Turner's Omni Center was built of a new type of steel that was *designed* to rust. The theory was that the rust would

protect the steel underneath, and from what Jack had seen—
and Jack had built a lot of buildings over the last thirty
years—the theory was perfectly correct.

Still, the damn thing was so *ugly*.

He was approaching one of the convention's back en-
trances. A uniformed guard stood outside the closed door. Jack
nodded into the man's shades, then tried to step past him to
the door.

"Wait a minute." The guard's voice was sharp. "Where do
you think you're going?"

"Into the convention."

"Like hell you are."

Jack looked at him. *Connally*, the man's name badge said.
He had a broken nose and a little silver Christian cross pinned
to his collar.

Great, Jack thought. Probably a Barnett supporter. He
unclipped his ID and floor pass from his pocket and waved
them in the guard's face.

"I'm a delegate. It's okay."

"No one gets through this door. Ever. Those are my
instructions."

"I'm a *delegate*."

Connally appeared to reconsider. "Okay. Let's see that
ID."

Jack handed it over. Connally squinted as he looked at it.
When he looked up, there was an evil grin on his face. "You
don't look sixty-four to me," he said.

"I'm well-preserved."

The guard reached for his walkie-talkie. "This is Connally.
Situation Three."

Jack waved his arms. "What the hell is that?"

"You're under arrest, asshole. Impersonating a delegate."

"I *am* a delegate."

"The Secret Service are on their way. You can talk to
them."

Jack stared at the guard in rising despair.

This, he realized, was only Monday.

12:00 NOON

"Devils and ancestors. What are you doing here?"

Jack Braun eyed Tachyon sourly. "I'm headed for that

bar." His long arm speared the underside of the raised piano bar. "For a drink . . . or two . . . or three, and if anybody tries to get in my way—"

"You should be on the convention floor."

"I was trying to *get* to the goddamn convention floor when this lard-assed security guard accused me of impersonating a delegate, and had me *arrested*. It took Charles Devaughn to cut me loose. So I've had a rather trying morning, Tachyon, and I'm going to get a drink."

"The Barnett forces are desperately politicking for delegates. You need to be there to keep California solid."

"Tachyon, in case you've forgotten; I'm the *head* of the California delegation. I think I can handle it." Braun roared, and several ever vigilant reporters craned to see the fight. "Jesus, you've been an American citizen what, five, six months, and already you're an authority on American politics?"

"Anything I do, I do well," replied Tachyon primly, but he was working to subdue a smile. Braun spotted it and suddenly grinned.

"Relax, Tachyon. Gregg's not going to lose California."

"Jesse Jackson wants to talk to me," said Tach with one of his bewilderingly abrupt changes of topic.

"Are you going to?"

"I don't know. I might learn something."

"I doubt it. Jesse's one smart operator. And besides, you're not working for the Hartmann campaign. Objectivity of the press and all that."

Tachyon frowned. "What do you think he could want?"

"At a guess I'd say your support."

"I have no delegates, no influence."

"Balony. Tachyon, these conventions are like a big shambling dinosaur. A prod in the ass can sometimes start the whole beast off in a new direction. If you were to switch your support, many of the jokers would follow. People might decide that you knew something. It could tilt things toward Jackson, and *that's* what he's after."

"Then I won't see him. This convention is too close already."

"Drink?"

"No, thank you. I think I'll head over to the convention center."

Jack started up the stairs. Tachyon stared at that broad back and powerful shoulders and wondered if he could shift some of his burdens onto those shoulders.

"Jack."

Something of his confusion and fear must have penetrated, for Braun paused part way up the stairs, and walked slowly back down. Laying his hands on Tachyon's shoulders, he frowned down at the smaller man. "What? What's wrong?"

"Do you think . . . do you think it's possible for one of the candidates to be an ace?"

"What, here?"

"Yes, of course here! No, the candidate for dog catcher in Shawnee, Oklahoma. Don't be an imbecile!"

"I'm not, you just took me off guard, that's all. Why? You got something?"

"No," he said airily, and suspicion flared in the big ace's blue eyes.

"It's hooey . . . bunk. Nobody could keep a thing like that hidden from the press. Remember Hart."

"He was careless."

"Look, if you're worried check it out. You could do it easily enough."

"Yes, but information received telepathically is not admissible evidence. Also, given the current climate in this country, what would they do if they discovered I had been using alien mind powers on potential presidential candidates?"

"Hang your skinny alien ass out to dry."

"Precisely." Tach shrugged. "Well, never mind. I just thought I'd mention it . . . get your opinion . . ." His voice trailed away into silence.

"Forget it, Tachy." Jack gave him a shake. "Okay?"

"Okay."

"Now I'm going to get that drink."

"Don't be too long," Tach yelled after him.

"Oh, go to hell."

"American whiskey. Straight up. A double. *Two* doubles."

"Hard day, sir?"

"Hard liquor for a hard day," Jack said. He lowered his briefcase to the ground and noticed for the first time—what was wrong with him anyway?—that the petite blonde waitress here in the atrium lounge was really quite attractive. He gave her the Hollywood smile that he'd practiced in countless mirrors throughout the late forties. "They've probably got you working overtime, too," he said. "Call me Jack, by the way."

"Overtime sucks, Jack," she said, and waggled away with a swing to her hips that hadn't been in evidence for any of her other customers. Jack began to feel slightly better.

After the Secret Service had testified to his bona fides and let him go, Jack spent most of the morning telling his delegates they were about to have their votes taken away if they didn't look out. Then Tachyon had harassed him for not doing his job, handed him the jive about a secret ace; and the campaign parliamentarian Logan, who was supposed to meet him here in the Marriott lounge, was already late.

The cheerful waggle of a waitress's butt, he thought, is enough to give a man heart for the struggle. Flying Ace gliders swooped overhead in dancing accompaniment to his thoughts.

The waitress brought his drinks. He chatted with her— her name was Jolynn—and tossed down the first drink. Logan still hadn't showed. Jolynn had to leave to see to another customer, and Jack tipped her ten dollars, reflecting that all in all he enjoyed being rich, even at the cost of having to pretend intelligent conversation with a chimpanzee on TV for four years. He watched as a young man in a white dinner jacket crossed the atrium lounge to the white piano, then sat down and banged out the opening chords to "Piano Man." Jack felt his head try to retreat, like that of a turtle, between his shoulders.

Moss Hart, Jack thought desperately. Kurt Weill. George and Ira Gershwin. Richard Rodgers—Jack could still remember the opening night of *South Pacific*.

Maybe he could just tip the guy a hundred bucks and tell him not to play *anything*.

"Honky Tonk Women" was next, followed by "New York, New York." Where, Jack thought, was Morrie Ryskind when you needed him?

Logan still hadn't showed up. Jack sipped his second drink and stared fixedly at Jolynn's heart-shaped ass as it perambulated about the other end of the lounge.

Then another female form drew his attention. Sluts on the *right*, he thought, an expression he'd acquired decades ago in Camp Shenango.

The woman was walking right for him.

Then he saw she was wearing a Barnett button. A slut for the Lord, he concluded.

Then he recognized her. She was Leo Barnett's campaign manager—that was bad enough—but there was an old score between them that made everything far worse.

Oh, god.

The piano struck up the opening bars of "Don't Cry for Me, Argentina." Another whole set of memories invaded him, including being spat on the year before in Buenos Aires by a female *Peronista*.

Jack rose, his heart sinking like a lead plummet, and prepared his face for more spittle.

"Jack Braun? You have no idea how long I've looked forward to meeting you again."

I'll just bet, Jack thought.

The voice, he realized, was different. Blythe had had a New York patroon accent of the kind that didn't exist anymore, that had died with Franklin and Eleanor. And Blythe would have worn red lipstick like all the women did in the forties, a bright crimson contrast to her pale face and dark hair.

"Fleur van Rensselaer, I presume," Jack said. "I'm surprised you remember me."

Which was the civil thing to say, but perfectly ridiculous. According to some, Jack had murdered her mother, and Fleur must have found that impossible to forget even if she wanted to.

The heart-shaped face tilted far back to look him in the face. "I was—how little? Three or four?"

"Something like that."

"I remember you playing with me on the floor of my father's house."

Jack gazed at her with a face of stone. She was dragging this out incredibly. Why didn't she spit on him or claw his face or otherwise get it over with?

"I've always wanted to say how much I admire you," Fleur said. "You've always been one of my heroes."

Shock ran like cold fire through Jack's veins. It wasn't that he *believed* in the sincerity of the words . . . the shock came from the fact that Blythe's daughter would prove this adept at sadism.

"I hardly deserve it." Truthfully.

She smiled. It was a very warm smile. He realized she was

standing very close, and his groin tingled at the thought she might try to bring her knee up between his legs. His wild card would keep him from harm, but old reflexes died hard.

"Aside from the Reverend Barnett," Fleur said, "you're the bravest man I know. You risked everything to bring down the aces and . . . that alien. I think you've been treated shamefully ever since. After all, your whole career was wrecked by those Hollywood liberals."

Jack's thoughts dragged with glacial slowness. She was, he realized dumbly, absolutely sincere. Something cold crept like a stalking insect up his back.

"I'm . . . surprised," he said.

"Because of my mother?" She was still smiling, still standing close. Jack wanted to run as fast as his legs would carry him.

"My mother was willful and obstinate. She deserted my father to whore with . . . that alien creature. The one who brought us the plague." She couldn't say Tachyon's name, he realized. "I was well-rid of her," she went on, "and so were you."

Jack remembered he was holding his drink in his hand. He took a long swallow, needing the bite of the whiskey to return his staggered senses to reality.

"Surprised at my language?" Fleur said. "The Bible is explicit about whoredom and its consequences. *The adulterer and the adultress shall surely be put to death.* Leviticus 20."

"The Bible was also clear about who got to throw the first stone." Jack's tongue was thick. He was surprised he could talk at all.

Fleur nodded. "I'm glad you can quote scripture."

"I learned a lot of Bible verses when I was a kid. Most of them in German." He took another drink. "Don't Cry for Me, Argentina" rang in his skull.

"What surprises me," Fleur said, "is who you're keeping company with these days." She took a step closer and touched his wrist. Jack managed barely to keep from jumping out of his skin. "Senator Hartmann is surely the moral heir of the Roosevelt-Holmes clique that almost destroyed our country in the forties. You saved us from those people then, and now you've fallen for the liberal humanist line again."

"That's me." He managed to grin. "Fallen."

"I thought I might raise you again." Her fingers ran up and down his strong wrist.

Slut for the Lord indeed, thought Jack.

"I wanted to talk to you in person. That's why I'm here in the—" She gave a bell-like laugh. "These unhallowed halls."

"Everyone needs to go slumming now and again." He stared at her, sickness rising in his belly. Fleur van Renssaeler, he realized, was the most twisted bitch he'd ever met in his life. His third wife included.

"I thought perhaps we could get together. Talk about . . . politics. Talk about Senator Hartmann, Reverend Barnett."

"Barnett wants to put me in a concentration camp."

"Not *you*. You're a proven patriot. The Lord has turned your curse into a blessing."

Jack could taste bile. "Glad to know I'm immune to the Lord's roundup. How about every other poor sucker who's got a wild card?"

"If I could just explain it to you. Talk you back onto the right path. The path of Reverend Barnett and my father."

Finally Jack's anger rumbled to the surface. He saw Logan's head above the crowd of delegates, and knew it was time to go.

"Barnett's path I can't say anything about," Jack said as he picked up his briefcase. "But your father's I knew fairly well. He ate like a hog at the public trough, and for fun he fucked black boys in Harlem."

The first time he'd ever used the F word to a woman, he thought as he headed for Logan.

Though he had to give Fleur credit. She was a real professional. The smile hadn't gone, though it had, he thought, stiffened a bit.

He felt slightly cheered. Cheap and lukewarm triumph was better than none.

2:00 P.M.

"Listen, Sara," Charles Devaughn said. "Whatever happened between you and Gregg on that world tour is history. It's over. Accept that." Hartmann's campaign manager had the sort of brusque preppie good looks people felt the senator had; nobody envisioned Hartmann as the round-shouldered ordinary he was.

Sara felt her cheeks begin to glow like a spoon in a microwave. "Damnit, Charles, that's not the point. I need to talk to you about the way the senator's been acting—"

He turned a shoulder to her, immaculately tailored and midnight blue. "I have no further comments for you, Ms. Morgenstern. I would like to ask that you refrain from harassing the senator's campaign staffers any further. The press has certain responsibilities you'd be wise not to overlook."

He walked. "Charles, wait! This is important—" Her words bounced off his wedge of back and chased each other like arboreal animals up the Marriott's soaring organiform atrium, which she'd overheard a reporter from some fringe journal describe as Antoni Gaudí's trachea. Delegates bumping elbows in the lobby outside the function rooms turned to stare, their faces pale blank moons hanging over gardens of gaudy ribbons and campaign buttons, and in the middle of each a little square shine of plaque, like an exhibit at a botanical garden, identifying which subspecies of small-time political hustler or wanna-be this specimen belonged to.

She struck herself twice on the thighs with the heels of her hands in frustration. *You're losing it, Sara.*

On cue, the projector inside her mind brought up an image of Andrea, her elder sister, fine and beautiful as an ice sculpture. A laughing, taunting crystal voice, eyes like snow-melt: perfection tiny, mousy Sara could never hope to attain. Andrea, who had been dead for thirty years.

Andrea, murdered by the man who would be president. Who had the power to twist others to his will. As he had twisted *her.*

There was no proof, of course. Lord knew it had taken her years to acknowledge first the suspicion and then the awful certainty that there had been more to her sister's brutal death than the random urges of a retarded adolescent. It had taken her long enough to realize that that was why she went into journalism in the first place, why she was drawn to Jokertown: deep down, she knew there was more. And over the years, as she was establishing a rep as *the* reporter on joker affairs, she had come to be aware of a presence in the joker slum, covert, manipulative . . . evil.

She'd tried to track it down. Even a star investigative reporter—even an obsessed investigator—didn't find it easy to trace the invisible strings of a demented puppet master. She persevered.

She was convinced it was Hartmann even before she boarded the *Stacked Deck*. She was certain she would discover the final evidence to convict him on the W.H.O. tour.

She had. She felt cool sweat start at the roots of her hair as she remembered how her suspicions had begun to erode, then whirl away beyond her reach, like driftwood from a drowning woman's fingers. She had actually come to think she *loved* him—and all the time a minute internal voice cried, *no, no, what's happening to me?*

She recalled sweaty skin friction, and him thrusting inside her, and she wanted to douche and never stop.

He had controlled her, as he had controlled poor Roger Pellman that Cincinnati afternoon when her sister died. Had used her because he perceived her as she perceived herself: as a poor imitation of her beautiful lost sister. At least they shared that obsession with what was lost.

She had her proof, all right; she could still feel the points in her psyche where the puppeteer's strings had been attached. And sometimes when they coupled she heard the word *Andrea* grunted among the endearments, and something within her chilled even as her body and mind responded with eager need.

But it was no proof at all to anyone who could not read her thoughts.

. . . She found herself drifting, realized she was being drawn by some journalist tropism toward Cluster 3, the function rooms clumped beyond the circular escalator well. In her growing frenzy to nail down some evidence that might convince an outsider, make him look beyond the sober statesman's mask, the air of compassion for all those touched by the wild card, that hid the puppet master from view, she had paid little attention to the phenomenon of the convention itself. The guilt stung her: *You're supposed to be dealing with wild card affairs.*

Self-anger flared: *What could be more important to jokers—to anybody—than that a psychopathic ace may become the next president of the United States?* She thought of the puppet master's finger poised above the famed red button and wanted to vomit.

Delegates and reporters were streaming from the big

corner Sidney Room, flushed and noisy as schoolkids. "What's going on?" she asked one, mainly because he was little taller than she was.

"It's Barnett's crazies," he told her. "They came up with something juicy on Hartmann." He was vibrating with gratified malice. He wore glasses and a big Dukakis button.

Could this be it? she wondered, starting to feel cheated that it wasn't her hand that had driven the stake through the monster's heart.

"They got to someone who was on the W.H.O. tour last year. Turns out Hartmann spent the whole time having himself a fling with some bimbo reporter from *The Washington Post*."

The parade of delegates and politicians through Gregg's suite seemed endless—Gregg had to admit that Amy had done a tremendous job contacting people on extremely short notice. But then most delegates were anxious to meet with the front-runner among the candidates, and none of the elected officials wanted to offend the man who might possibly be the next president.

As for Gregg, the afternoon was interminable and taking its toll. He thought he'd locked Puppetman away tightly. He'd even begun to hope that maybe, just maybe, the voice inside his head would stay silent for the rest of the week. But the bars holding Puppetman were beginning to weaken again. He could hear the power, alternately pleading and threatening.

Let me out! You have to let me out!

He ignored it as well as he could, but his temper was shorter than usual, and his smile was sometimes more a grimace. It was worst with the politicians, most of whom he could have gotten to agree, with a touch of Puppetman's influence, and who now could say no with impunity. That was when Puppetman howled the most.

Ohio Senators Glenn and Metzenbaum showed up on schedule. Ellen greeted them at the door; Gregg was changing his shirt in the bedroom. Gregg could hear Metzenbaum being his usual ingratiating self. "So it *is* true. Expectant mothers *do* glow."

Ellen laughed as Gregg walked in. "John, Howard," he said, nodding to them. "Please grab something from the bar if you want, and thanks for coming on such short notice. I'm trying to meet as many influential people as I can on this—you were both at the top of that list."

Get out. That's what he really wanted to say. *I'm tired and ragged and my mind's splitting in half. Leave me alone.*

Metzenbaum smiled politely; Glenn, with the old astronaut's exaggerated calm, simply nodded, if anything more stonefaced than usual. The two were looking at Ellen pointedly. Gregg didn't need to say anything; Ellen was well-experienced at picking up such cues.

"Well, I'll leave you folks to your politics," she said. "I've a meeting of my own with the NOW delegates. You *are* backing the ERA, aren't you?" She smiled again and took her leave. Gregg walked her to the door. On impulse, he gathered her into his arms and kissed her deeply. "Listen, Ellen, I just want you to know how much I appreciate all your help today, without you . . . well, that incident this morning. Please don't think any more of it. I'm just tired, that's all. The stress . . ."

He couldn't seem to stop talking. The words just kept tumbling out and he felt closer to her than he had in months. "I wouldn't do anything to hurt you . . ."

Glenn and Metzenbaum were staring. Ellen stopped his words with a quick kiss. "You have guests, dear," she said, looking at him strangely.

Gregg smiled apologetically; it felt more like a death's-head grin. "Yes, I supppose . . . I'll see you in a bit for dinner: Bello Mondo, right?"

"Six-thirty. Amy said she'd call to remind you." Ellen hugged Gregg wordlessly. "I love you." She gave him another long look, and stepped out.

Down below, Puppetman howled for attention. Gregg felt sweat beading on his brow. He wiped it away with the back of his hand and turned back into the room.

"Ohio's been very good to me, gentlemen," he said. "You two are largely responsible. I suppose you're both aware that we're looking for support on 9(c) and the California—" They weren't listening. Gregg stopped in mid-sentence. "What?" he asked.

"We have a bigger problem, Gregg," Glenn said. "Bad news, I'm afraid. There's a nasty story going around about you and Morgenstern on the aces junket . . ."

Gregg was no longer listening. *Sara Morgenstern.* His

career seemed to be inexorably linked to hers. Puppetman's first victim had been thirteen-year-old Andrea Whitman, Sara's sister. Gregg had only been eleven at the time. It was only bizarre coincidence that had caused Sara to suspect, many years later, that Gregg had been involved in Andrea's death. To nullify Sara, and to satisfy Puppetman's own needs, he had taken Sara as a puppet the year before. On the wild cards junket, as discreetly as possible, they'd become lovers.

Gregg could see it all unraveling—the nomination, the presidency, his career. What had happened to Gary Hart could, after all, just as easily happen to him.

Inside, hardly muffled at all, Puppetman screamed.

For a while she simply wandered.

When she got back to her room in the Hilton the message light on the phone was glowing like a telltale on the console of a reactor on overload. When she called the desk, there were about twelve-thousand messages from Braden Dulles in D.C. waiting for her. Another call came in as she was getting the word, and the harried-sounding hotel operator patched it through.

"Is this true?" he asked.

She felt her breath congeal in her throat. It had been like this the one time she tried cocaine, back when she was still married to upwardly mobile lawyer David Morgenstern: the muscles of her chest just refused to work.

"Yes."

At the door, the first knock came.

5:00 P.M.

Amy Sorenson met Gregg and Ellen behind the podium screen. On the other side of heavy velvet curtains, Gregg could hear the loud conversations of the reporters; the glare of video lights washed under the red folds. "They're all primed," Amy said. "I have your guests next door; I'll get them after you go in." She touched the wireless receiver in her ear and listened for a second. "Okay, Billy Ray says everything's fine. Are you ready?"

Gregg nodded. It had been a long, hard afternoon— trying to get news from New York, working with Jack and a mostly soused Danny Logan (Logan was definitely one puppet

he'd driven too far) on the strategy for the California fight later
tonight, putting out brushfire rumors about his affair, arranging things with the Justice Department, setting up this press
conference. He'd worried that the stress would bring Puppetman back to conciousness, but the power was still silent and
buried. He could sense only the barest rustle of its struggling.

But Gimli—if it *was* Gimli . . . That presence was still
very much with him. Gregg could hear the dwarf's evil
chuckling, and he wondered, as he'd wondered much of the
afternoon, if he weren't approaching some kind of breakdown.
With the thought, the Gimli-voice surged forward.

You are, Greggie, he said. *I'm going to fucking make sure
of it.*

Gregg took a deep breath and pretended he'd not heard
the voice. He took Ellen's hand, squeezed it, then patted the
swell of her belly. "We're ready. Let's get on with the circus,
Amy."

Gregg fixed a smile on his face as Amy held the curtains
aside. He took the three steps up to the stage at a bound, Ellen
following slowly. Cameras clicked like a plague of mechanical
insects; electronic flashes stuttered their brief lightning. At the
podium, Gregg waited until the reporters had quieted in their
seats, looking down at the outline of Tony Calderone's speech
in his hand. Then he raised his head.

"As usual, I don't have much in the way of a formal
statement," he said, waving the single page of handwriting.
That received the small laugh he'd expected—Gregg had a
reputation as an off-the-cuff speaker who regularly strayed
from Tony's prepared text, and most of the reporters in the
audience had been with him on the campaign trail for months.
"There's a good reason for that, too. I really don't have much
to say at this press conference. I feel that the less one responds
to vicious and unfounded rumors, the better. And I know what
you'll all say to that: 'Don't blame us. The press has its
responsibility.' I hope you all feel better for having that out of
the way."

There was more chuckling at that, mostly from those he
knew were in his camp. The rest waited, solemn.

He paused, glancing again at the notes Tony, Braun,
Tachyon, and he had made. At the same time, like a person
constantly probing at a broken tooth, he felt for Puppetman
and sensed nothing. He relaxed slightly. "We all know why

you're here. I'm going to say my piece, answer a few questions
if you want, and go on to other things. I've already seen a
fellow candidate ruined by what was essentially innuendo and
circumstance. Whether Gary Hart actually did anything is
immaterial. He was injured by rumors and might have lost
credibility even if he'd actually done nothing at all.

"Well, I'm not Gary Hart; he's better looking. Even Ellen
says so."

They grinned at that, almost universally, and Gregg let
himself smile with them. He placed his notes carefully and
visibly to one side, and leaned on his elbows toward them. "I
think I can point out a few other differences. The *Stacked Deck*
wasn't the *Monkey Business*. We went to Berlin, not Bimini.
And Ellen was along on the entire trip."

Gregg glanced over to Ellen and nodded. On cue, she
returned his smile.

"Senator?" Gregg squinted into the glare of lights and saw
Bill Johnson of *The Los Angeles Times* waving his notebook.
Gregg gestured for him to go ahead. "Then you're denying that
you and Sara Morgenstern have had an affair?" Johnson asked.

"I certainly *know* Ms. Morgenstern, as does Ellen, and
she's been a family friend. She has her own problems, and I
have no knowledge of precisely what she's said or hasn't said
recently. But I don't go sneaking around behind my wife's
back."

Ellen leaned in close to Gregg with a mischievous look.
"Bill, I *did* catch Gregg eyeing Peregrine from time to time,
but he was hardly the only one doing that."

Laughter. The cameras began flashing again, and the
tension in the room visibly dissolved. Gregg grinned, but the
expression went cold and dead on his face. Gimli's voice
seemed to whisper just behind his ear.

*You screwed her, Hartmann. You spread her legs on five
different continents, and your little ace made her smile and
think she enjoyed it. But she didn't, did she? Not really. She
doesn't think much of you now, not at all. Not without
Puppetman.*

Ellen sensed Gregg's distress. He knew his hand was
clammy in hers. She was still smiling, but behind the eyes was
worry. He shook his head slightly, pressing her fingers.

*Such a fucking professional wife you have, too. She knows
exactly what to do, doesn't she? Smiles at just the right time,*

*says just the right thing, even lets you knock her up so she'll be
nice and matronly for the convention. You're so proud, such a
good daddy. You're a bastard, Hartmann. I am too, and this
little bastard's going to wreck your life. I'm going to make your
pet ace rip you open so everyone can see.*

Listening to the voice, he'd waited a beat too long. He
could hear the laughter dying, the moment passing. He
hurried to catch them again, refusing to listen to Gimli's
continuing stream of invective.

"Okay, as Ellen has pointed out, I'm guilty of some of
Jimmy Carter's lust of the heart. I doubt there's very many of
us who aren't—Peregrine would be disappointed if it were any
other way. Beyond that, I'm afraid that you've been duped.
There's a rumor, and nothing else. From today on, I'm going
to consider this whole question answered, and we'll try to
concentrate on real issues. If you want more of a story about
this, look at your sources. Ask yourself what ulterior motives
were responsible for spreading this kind of trash."

"Are you accusing Leo Barnett or his staff?" A voice from
the back: Connie Chung of NBC.

"I'm not naming names, Ms. Chung; I don't have them.
I'd like to believe that a God-fearing man such as Reverend
Barnett would refuse to use such tactics, and I'm certainly not
going to cast the first stone." Another wave of laughter. "But
the lie started somewhere—track it down. I notice Ms.
Morgenstern hasn't been quoted directly by any of you. I
haven't seen any tangible proof at all. That should tell you
something immediately, I'd think."

He had them. He'd turned it around. He could see it, feel
it. Yet there was very little sense of triumph in Gregg. Beneath
everything, he could sense a familiar stirring. Puppetman was
rising, still deep down, but heading for the surface. *Just
another day*, he thought. *Give me that much time.*

*You can't keep it down even that long, Hartmann. You're
addicted. That's all Puppetman is: your goddamn drug. And
you both need a fix, don't you?* Gimli chuckled. *To get it,
you've got to get around me. Ain't it a fucking pity.*

Both Ellen and Amy were staring at him. He was standing
stock still, frozen. Gregg gave them an apologetic shrug and
continued.

"A few minutes ago, Bill Johnson called me 'Senator.'
Now, it's been over a year since I gave up my seat to run for

this candidacy, but I understand the mistake. Bill's been calling me Senator—when he hasn't been calling me other things—for years now."

A slow amusement moved through the ranks in front of him. "That's habit," Gregg told them, sliding easily back into Tony's speech. "It's easy to let habits rule us. It's easy for us to cling to ancient prejudices, clouded outlooks, and outright fables. But we can't do that, not now. We hear too many rumors and believe them without foundation. We've had the habits and listened to the lies for years: that jokers are somehow accursed; that it's right to hate people—jokers or otherwise—because they look or act differently; that people can't change, and the way it is is the way it must be. If you believe opinions and feelings are set in concrete, you're right—you can't change, you can't grow. But when we can do something that defies such beliefs, well, to me that's worth more coverage than sensational rumors about infidelity."

Gregg glanced over to Ellen; she nodded back. Gimli was still there and Gregg's head ached with the sound of his voice, but he blinked and went on. He wanted to get off the podium, to be alone in his room. He was rushing, speaking too fast; he forced himself to slow down.

"I'm pleased to say that some things we think eternal pass. I've based my entire campaign on the idea that *now* is the time to heal the wounds. Opinions change. We can embrace those we once hated. *That's* important. *That's* newsworthy. And it's also not my story. I can understand a person who takes his or her fervor too far. I can understand passionate convictions even when I don't agree with them. We all have things we believe in strongly and that's good. It becomes a problem when such passion crosses the line beyond fervor to violence. There have been joker organizations that have sometimes stepped over that line."

Gregg gestured to the back of the stage. "Amy, please bring them out."

The curtains at the back of the stage parted, and two jokers stepped into the light. One had skin marked with fine serrated ridges; the other was shadowy and the ghost of the curtains could be seen through him. The press began to murmur.

"I'm sure I don't need to introduce File and Shroud to you. Their faces were prominent in your papers and on your broadcasts last year when the JJS was finally broken up." Gimli laughed inside at that; Gregg swallowed hard. "Some of the JJS, those who seemed peripheral members or harmless, were simply fined and released. Others, the ones deemed truly dangerous, were incarcerated. File and Shroud have been in a federal prison since that time. Perhaps deservedly so—both have admitted to extremely violent acts. Yet . . . I was the direct victim of some of that violence, and I've spoken to File and Shroud extensively in the last year. I feel that they've both learned a hard and painful lesson and are genuinely remorseful.

"I will stand by my own words and convictions. I believe in reconciliation. We need to forgive, we need to strive to understand those less fortunate than ourselves. Today, in agreement with Governor Cuomo of New York, the Justice Department, and the New York Senate, I've arranged to grant parole to File and Shroud."

Gregg placed his arms around the jokers: the rough skin of File, the misty shoulders of Shroud. "This is far more important than rumors. This is genuine, and it's also not my story—it's theirs. I'll let them convince you as they convinced me. Talk to them. Ask them your questions. Amy, if you'd moderate—"

As the first questions were shouted from the crowd and File stepped to the microphone, Gregg took a deep breath and retreated.

Don't you understand? Gimli taunted as Gregg left the room and headed for the elevators. *You haven't gotten rid of me. You can't run away from my particular obsession. I'm here. And I'm staying. I don't forgive. Not at all.*

With fingers without feeling Sara replaced the receiver in its cradle.

She'd fled her room in tears, trusting in her small size and a certain knack of invisibility that had served her well at various points in her career to hide her in the mob. At first it worked. When they paged her in the lobby, it set a fresh pack of reporters baying after her, hungry to worry bones from which Hartmann's bland denial hadn't filleted the last scraps of meat.

Is Hartmann telling the truth? Why did Barnett's announcement specify you? What's your connection to the Bar-

nett campaign? The questions split half and half between trying to get her to admit she'd hit the rack with Hartmann and trying to get her to admit she'd conspired with the fundamentalists to wreck the senator's good name.

Part of her ached to use the proffered forum, to announce, *Yes, I slept with Gregg Hartmann, and I learned that he's a monster, a covert ace who makes people into puppets*. Cowardice intervened. Or was it sanity? Her revelations—allegations,was the only way they would be viewed—were extravagant enough without turning them into *Midnight Sun* headline fodder.

She turned her face away and said, "No comment."

And swallowed whole the steaming chunks of abuse: "Where do you get off trying to pull that shit? The public has a right to know. You're a *journalist*, for Christ's sake."

Finally a cocktailer in leotards and one of those short black skirts took her by the arm and steered her here, into the office of the manager of the Marriott's lounge.

The receiver clicked home with the finality of a breech closing on a cartridge. *Somebody* took what she had to say seriously.

The caller was Owen Rayford of the *Post's* New York bureau. Chrysalis was dead. Murdered. Ace powers were involved.

Was it a puppet? She doubted that. Hartmann's strings quickly attenuated and broke with distance; she knew that from experience. There were bent aces—Bludgeon, Carnifex, maybe the Sleeper if he were far gone in amphetamine psychosis—who were capable of such a deed. That was an irony about Hartmann; in his position you hardly needed ace powers to get into serious evil doing. Money, power, and influence weren't exactly any weaker forces in human affairs than they'd been up until the fifteenth of September, 1946.

The fear lived within her; it coiled like a serpent, burned like a star. It brought with it terrible knowledge: the only hope of safety lay in risking all.

The manager and the waitress who'd rescued her stood by, watching with polite curiosity. She arranged her face in a smile and stood.

"Is there a back way out of here?" she asked.

6:00 P.M.

She had to take a Valium before she could get the damned acoustic coupler to work right. Her laptop had an inboard modem, but hotels were leery of modular jacks, preferring to keep their phones tethered firmly to the wall by old-fashioned cords. So she had to fiddle with the antique external modem, which was unforgiving if you didn't get the phone's handset into its twin-cup cradle *just so*.

Eventually she got it going. Then she sat in gloom, lit only by afternoon light straggling through the room's heavy curtains, smoking and squinting at the screen as the records-transferred count spun on and her story spun down the wires that connected her NEC laptop to the *Post*'s computers.

It had all come out of her in one orgasmic gush: Andi's death, her suspicion, the sinister hidden presence in Joker-town who had flashed tantalizing clues as to his existence—and identity—during the riots attending another Democratic convention twelve years ago; her own personal quest, leading to her entrapment in the very web she'd been struggling to delineate. And finally murder.

There were two people, she'd written, who had their fingers on the Jokertown pulse. Actually there were three; Tachyon was the third, literally as well as figuratively. But he was blinded by personal regard for Hartmann, and the political plums the senator had thrown his way, the grants that kept him living in a style fit for a prince, which he was. Sara would not invoke his name.

The others were herself and Chrysalis. The Crystal Palace had never been more than a front for Chrysalis's real avocation, which was brokering information on everything that went down in J-town. Close observers of the scene took it for granted that sooner or later she'd reel in a thread and find it had a cobra tied to it.

The cobra was named Hartmann. And Chrysalis pulled his string just at the moment when he was swollen with venom and quickest to strike.

Why didn't I confide in her? she asked herself as liquid crystal numbers flickered in the dim. There had been plenty of time, when they gained a guarded sort of friendship aboard the *Stacked Deck*, during the year that intervened. But Chrysalis had remained in some sense a rival. And Sara was not a woman who found sharing confidences an easy thing.

UPLOAD COMPLETED, her screen said, with a beep for emphasis. She quickly broke the connection and began to disconnect the modem. Calm had come upon her, strange and a little frightening. The calm of an accident victim.

I'm a target, she thought without emotion. *If Chrysalis learned his secret, he has to assume that I know*. She regretted pushing so hard at Hartmann's staffers earlier in the day. He had to have heard about that, and the inference would be unavoidable.

You're such an innocent, she chided herself. *Naive, just as Ricky said you were*.

But she wasn't a total fool. She was wading in the shark tank now. She'd learned a lot of moves during a long and successful journalistic career. None of them would suffice to get her to dry land intact. That was maybe the most important thing she knew right now.

She turned off the NEC's power and clicked its cover closed. She tucked the miniature computer into her shoulder bag. Stood.

It has to be Tachyon, she knew. He had to have his suspicions about what had been happening in Jokertown over the years—about what had happened in Syria and Berlin. He could read her mind, if he doubted her words.

Besides, he thinks I'm . . . attractive. Even if he refused to believe her, there was a way to attach herself to him. She had been prepared to offer herself to him before, when she was convinced the Doughboy case would lead to Hartmann. He had a certain magnetism. It might not even be so bad.

Don't kid yourself. She had not been with a man since—since the tour. She hadn't felt the lack. Even before the famous affair, sex hadn't been her biggest priority.

But survival was. At least until Andrea was avenged.

At least Tachyon seemed the type to take his pleasure in a hurry and be done with it—no protracted grunting and groaning and Was It Good for You Too? She stabbed her cigarette to death on the Hilton logo embossed in the plastic ashtray. Pausing to dab some perfume on the insides of her wrists, where blue veins met white skin, she walked out the door.

7:00 P.M.

The convention had broken up for dinner and would reconvene at nine. Jack shared the glass elevator with a man who carried a tall stack of Domino's pizzas, and stood with his face turned firmly to the door—he *hated* heights, a phobia that developed after Tachyon pointed out, forty years before, that a long fall was one of the few things that could kill him. The elevator doors opened, and Jack thankfully followed the pizzas down the hall to Hartmann's headquarters. Floating up from the atrium lobby were the chords of "Don't Cry for Me, Argentina." Bar pianists, he thought, seemed a bit overspecialized.

Billy Ray, chest puffed out as he stood guard in the hallway in his white Carnifex suit, passed the deliveryman, but with a martial artist's quickness, stepped in front of Jack as he tried to follow.

"Did the senator send for you, Braun?"

Jack looked at him. "Don't push. It's been a hard day."

Ray's face, which had quite literally been rearranged in a fight, gave Jack a leer. "Your plight touches my heart. Let's see what's in the case."

Jack bit back his annoyance and opened his briefcase, revealing the cellular phone and computer-operated dialing system that kept him in touch with his delegates and Hartmann HQ.

"Let's see your ID."

Jack dug the laminated card out of his pocket. "You're really a prat, Ray."

"Prat? What the fuck kinda word is that?" Ray's twisted face leered at Jack's ID. "That's not the word the strongest ace in the world would use. That's the kinda word some insignificant shivering weenie might use." He licked his lips as if savoring the idea. "Golden Weenie. Yeah. That's you."

Jack looked at Ray and folded his arms. Billy Ray had been riding him for over a year, ever since they'd met on the *Stacked Deck.* "Get out of my way, Billy."

Ray stuck out his jaw. "What are you gonna do if I don't, weenie?" He smiled. "Give me your best shot. Just try it."

Jack comforted himself for a moment with the mental picture of squashing Ray's head like a pumpkin. Ray's wild card gave him strength and speed, and his kung fu or whatever gave him skill, but Jack figured he could still demolish him with one punch. On second thought Jack decided it wasn't what he was here for.

"Right now, my job's getting the senator elected, and fighting with his bodyguard isn't going to do that. But after Gregg's in the White House, I promise I'll kick a field goal with you, okay?"

"I'm holding you to that, weenie."

"Any time after November eighth."

"See you at one minute after midnight on the ninth, weenie."

Ray stepped aside and Jack entered the headquarters suite. Open pizza boxes were surrounded by gorging campaign workers. TV monitors babbled network analyses to media-deaf ears. Jack found out which room Danny Logan was using, took a pizza box, and set off.

The campaign parliamentarian was a white-haired, paunchy former congressman from Queens who had lost his seat when his Irish constituency was replaced by Puerto Ricans. Now he advised Democratic candidates on how to collect Irish-American votes.

Jack saw him spread-eagled alone on his bed, surrounded by empty bottles and crumpled yellow legal-sized sheets, covered with numbers. "Better eat something," Jack said, and dropped the pizza box onto Logan's wide stomach.

"It's not going to make a bit of difference," Logan said. His voice was thick. "We don't have the numbers. We're going to lose 9(c)—the test case."

Jack rubbed his eyes. "Refresh my memory."

"9(c) is a formula for apportioning delegates formerly committed to candidates who have dropped out of the race. According to 9(c), the ex-candidates' delegates are divided among the remaining candidates in proportion to the number of votes the survivors won in those states. In other words, after Gephardt dropped out, his delegates from Illinois, say, were divided between Jackson, Dukakis, and us according to the percentage of the vote."

"Right."

"Barnett and a few of the party elders are challenging 9(c). They want to free the delegates to vote for whoever they want. Barnett figures he can pick up a few votes; the party elders want to start a movement for Cuomo or Bradley among the uncommitted." Logan ran a hand through his thinning white hair. "We announced our support for the rule—thought we'd see who lined up for and against, to give us a hint how the California challenge will go."

"And we're losing on 9(c)?" Jack reached for a bottle and drank from the neck.

"Gregg's making some phone calls. But since Dukakis came out against 9(c), we're fighting a losing fight." He slammed his fist into the bed. "Everyone keeps asking about those stories about the senator and that reporter lady. That we're going to have another Hart fiasco. That's where the resistance lies. Everybody's smelling Gregg's blood."

"What can you do?" Jack said.

"Just try to delay." Logan belched massively. "Lots of ways to delay in this game."

"And then?"

"And then Gregg starts working on his concession speech."

Anger crackled in Jack like a burst of lightning. He waved a big fist. "We won the big primaries! We've got more votes than *anybody*."

"That's why we're a target. Aw, shit." Tears were rolling from the corners of Logan's eyes. He swiped at them with the back of one red paw. "Gregg stuck by me when I lost my seat. There isn't a more decent man alive. He deserves to be president." His face crumpled. "*But we don't have the numbers!*"

Jack watched as Logan began to weep, the pizza box jogging up and down on his broad stomach. Jack left his drink on the bedside table and wandered out of the room. Hopelessness sang in him like a keening wind.

All that work, he thought. All the renewed hope that had got him into public life again. All for nothing.

In the main HQ, campaigners were still clustered around pizza boxes. Jack asked where Hartmann was and was told the senator was cloistered with deVaughn and Amy Sorenson, plotting strategy. Then they'd try a last-minute phone blitz to win over some of the uncommitted superdelegates. Without anything else to do, Jack took a piece of pizza and settled down in front of the television monitors.

"It'll be a close vote." Ted Koppel's voice rang in Jack's

ear, speaking from the nearly empty floor of the convention to a cynical-looking David Brinkley in the sky booth. "The Hartmann forces are counting on this test to show their strength prior to the showdown over the California challenge."

"Isn't. That. A risky. Strategy?" Brinkley's curt manner seemed to inflate each word into its own sentence.

"Hartmann's strategy has always been risky, David. His articulation of liberal political principal in a race dominated by glib media personalities has always been thought risky by his own strategists. Even if he loses California tonight, Hartmann's campaign manager told me that he'll still stand by the Jokers' Rights plank in the platform fight tomorrow."

Brinkley affected curmudgeonly surprise. "Are you telling me, Ted. That in this day and age. A man can get. To be front-runner. By a consistent public articulation. Of principle?"

Koppel grinned. "Did I say that, David? I didn't mean to suggest that Hartmann's campaign wasn't media-wise—just that it's been consistent in the image it's presented to the voter, just as the campaigns of Leo Barnett and Jesse Jackson, the other two candidates nearest the prize, have been equally consistent. But, like I said, any strategy has its risks. The campaign of Walter Mondale in '84 stands as an example to any politician who dares to be *too* consistent and articulate."

"But let us suppose. That Hartmann loses the fight. How can he possibly. Regain momentum?"

"He may not, David." Koppel was obviously excited. "If Gregg Hartmann can't win by at least a small margin in the fight over Rule 9(c), he may lose everything. The big challenge over California may just prove an anticlimax—he could lose the whole shooting match right here in the fight over 9(c)."

Drama, Jack thought. Everything had to be dramatized. Each vote had to be *the* vote, the significant vote, the critical vote, or else the voracious media gods were unhappy and had nothing to fill the air with but their own meanderings.

Jack tossed his half-eaten pizza slice back into the box. He crossed the room and met Amy Sorenson coming out of her meeting. There was despair in her dark eyes. Hartmann was on the phone, she said, trying to round up last-minute votes.

Hopeless, Jack thought. He picked up his briefcase, left HQ, and headed down the hall to Logan's room. The parliamentarian was passed out on the bed, clutching a whiskey bottle as if it were a woman.

Alone in the corner, the television rattled on. Cronkite and Rather were analyzing Hartmann's strategy and concluding that he may have overreached this time. They reminded Jack of a pair of television movie critics chewing up a new film.

What if there wasn't any drama? Jack thought. What if the vote came and nothing happened, it was just some little procedural thing? Wouldn't everyone be surprised if someone came along and took the drama away? What if someone, some media god or something, went and canceled Leo Barnett's showdown?

Jack realized he was staring at his briefcase.

He opened the case, picked up the phone, told the little computer memory to get him Hiram Worchester.

"Worchester?" he said. "This is Jack Braun. I'm speaking for Danny Logan."

"Has Logan come up with any numbers yet? From what I can see, we're in real trouble."

Jack reached to the bedside table and swallowed the remains of his drink. "I know," he said. "That's why, when the fight over 9(c) comes up, I want you to give half your votes to Barnett."

"You better not be selling us out, Braun."

"I'm not."

"That would be your classic Judas ace style, wouldn't it? A quick stab in the back, then a new job in the media courtesy of Leo Barnett."

Jack closed his fist. The glass in his hand exploded in a flash of gold light.

"Are you going to do this or not?" Jack demanded. He watched as crushed glass drained like sand from his fist.

"I want to discuss this with Gregg."

"Call him if you like, but he's busy. Just get ready to cut your delegate count in half."

"Would you mind explaining to me what's going on?"

"We're canceling the showdown. If Barnett wins by too large a margin, it's not going to prove anything. All it'll mean is that we didn't fight. In the pictures, you can't have a gunfight with just one man in the street. The audience'll walk out."

There was a long silence on the other end of the line. Then: "Let me talk to Logan."

"He's on another line."

"Why do you expect me to trust you?" The fat man's furious anger beat at Jack's ear.

"I don't have time to argue this. Do it or not, I don't care. Just be ready to answer for your decision later."

"If you cost Gregg the election . . ."

Jack gave a laugh. "Have you seen ABC? They've already got our man conceding."

Jack cut the connection, then phoned his own assistant Emil Rodriguez. He told Rodriguez that he wouldn't be on the floor tonight, that the delegation was his to command; but cut his vote in half on 9(c), and then stand like a rock against the California challenge.

He began to call every other delegation head, in order of number of votes. By the time he made his last call, to the man who controlled Hartmann's two votes from the Virgin Islands, the convention had reconvened.

Danny Logan, unconscious on the bed, began to snore.

Jack turned on the television and sat in the corner with Logan's whiskey bottle. The atmosphere on the convention floor was intense. Delegates were scurrying into place around their floor leaders. The orchestra was playing—good lord—"Don't Cry for Me, Argentina."

A knot of fear began to tighten in Jack's stomach.

Jim Wright, speaker of the House and the chairman the convention had elected that afternoon, gaveled the convention to order. A senator from Wyoming stood up to move the repeal of 9(c). All the troops were already in line and there was no debate.

Jack took a long, long drink, and the roll call began.

For the next ten minutes, Peter Jennings, seconded by his people on the floor, spoke in serious tones about Gregg Hartmann's stunning defeat. Jack could hear people outside the room marching up and down. Twice someone knocked, and twice he ignored them.

Then David Brinkley, his sardonic grin firmly in place, began to wonder aloud if he smelled a rat. He and Koppel and Jennings tossed this notion around while the lopsided numbers added up, then unanimously concluded that the whole showdown had been a sucker play, and that Barnett, Gore, et al had fallen for it.

There was more pounding on the hotel door. "Logan?" Devaughn's voice. "Are you in there?"

Jack said nothing.

After the reporters' analysis leaked back to the convention, bedlam broke out on the floor. Mobs of delegates lurched back and forth like wood chips caught in a flood. Jack reached for his phone and called Emil Rodriguez. "Move the California question. Now."

Hartmann's opponents were in total disarray. Their entire strategy had come unhinged.

Hartmann won the California challenge in a walk. A roar of celebration began to come through the hotel room door.

Jack opened Logan's door, put a Do Not Disturb sign on the outside, and stepped out into the hallway.

"Jack!" Amy Sorenson, her chestnut hair flying, ran toward him through a crowd dizzy with celebration. "Were you in there? Did you and Logan come up with this?"

Jack kissed her, not caring in the least if her husband was present. "Got any pizza left?" he asked. "I'm getting hungry."

8:00 P.M.

A knot of people at the main entrance to the Marriott reared back in alarm as the Turtle settled onto the sidewalk. Blaise drummed on the side of the shell with his heels as he slid off. Tachyon gave the shell a fond pat before he climbed down. "Thank you, Turtle, for a lovely afternoon. It's an elegant city when seen from above."

"Any time, Tachy." The shell floated away.

"Dr. Tachyon."

The alien turned at that smooth, well-modulated voice with its strong Southern accent. "Reverend Barnett."

They had never met, yet recognition was instantaneous. They stood on the steps of the Marriott, devouring one another's faces, searching for the key to the character of the other man. Leo Barnett was a young man of medium height, blond hair, blue eyes, a dimpled chin. It was a nice face, and for an instant the Takisian struggled to reconcile the hated image of his dreams with this soft-spoken man. Then he recalled the exquisite faces of his kith and kin—all of them murdering thugs—and the moment of dislocation passed.

"Doctor, didn't anyone ever tell you that there are some

things we don't do in the streets because it alarms the children and frightens the horses?"

Humor laced the words and Tachyon, who had tensed for an attack, relaxed. "Reverend, I've been on Earth longer than you've been alive, and I don't believe I've ever heard that expression."

A woman stepped out of the crowd surrounding Barnett. "It generally refers to sex, and you know all about that."

Shoulder-length sable hair, cascading onto her breast, long sooty lashes fluttering on alabaster cheeks, lashes lifting to reveal eyes of a profound midnight blue . . .

No, *brown!*

Reality shifted like a cable car being wrenched off its track. Tach's breath seemed to be clogged somewhere between diaphragm and throat. He tottered, groping for Blaise's shoulder, and Leo Barnett leaped forward to support him on the other side.

"Doctor, are you all right?"

"I've seen a ghost," Tach murmured thickly. The faintness was passing, and he lifted his eyes to hers.

"My campaign manager, Fleur van Renssaeler," said Barnett with a nervous glance to the woman.

"I know," said Tachyon.

"You're very quick, Doctor." Her opening words had been aggressive, now bitter sarcasm laced each syllable.

"You bear your mother's face . . . ." He quailed slightly under blazing anger in those brown eyes. "But her eyes were blue."

"What an extraordinary memory you have."

"There is not a detail of your mother's face that I have forgotten."

"Am I supposed to be pleased by that?"

"I hope so. I am inordinately pleased to see you. Every week for almost two years we played." He laughed gently. "I recall you were dreadfully fond of that horrid sticky candy corn. My pockets would be gummy for days afterward."

"You *never* came to our house. My father wouldn't permit it."

Tach felt his jaw sag. "But I mind-controlled the servants. Your mother wanted to see you so desperately—"

"My mother was a damn slut. She abandoned my father and her children for you."

"No, that's not true. Your father threw her out of the house."

"Because she was whoring with you!" Fleur's hand lashed out, snapping his head around with the force of the blow.

Tentatively he touched his burning cheek, started to advance on her. "No—"

Barnett laid a hand on Tachyon's shoulder. "Doctor, this conversation is obviously upsetting both you and Miss van Renssaeler. I think we should move along."

The minister held out his hand to Fleur. Her lips seemed slack, and somehow heavier. An aura of sex surrounded her. Barnett handed her into the taxi as if he were eager to release her.

"Perhaps sometime we can talk again, Doctor. I confess I'm very curious about the religious beliefs of your world." Leo paused with a hand on the taxi door. "Are you a Christian, Doctor?"

"No."

"We should talk."

The entourage was whisked away, Tach staring blankly after the taxi containing Fleur.

"What, by the Ideal, was that all about?" The Takisian phrase spoken in Blaise's heavily accented English added to Tachyon's sense of disorientation.

Tach pressed steepled fingers to his lips. "Oh, ancestors." He wrapped his arm tightly about Blaise's shoulders. "1947."

"No kidding? What the fuck are you talking about?"

"Watch your language."

They started into the hotel and Blaise asked, *"K'ijdad,* who is the old *femme?"*

"She's not old . . . a little older than her mother when I lost her. And you've got to stop using French and Takisian in the same sentence. It drives me mad."

"Tell me this story," the boy demanded.

Tachyon's eyes flickered from the elevators to the bar. "I need a drink."

The pianist was on duty tinkling out a jazzed-up version of "Smoke Gets in Your Eyes."

"Brandy," the alien snapped to a waitress as he passed.

"Beer." Blaise drooped under a gimlet stare from his grandsire. "Coke," he amended in a subdued tone.

They sat in silence until the drinks were delivered, and Tachyon had a long swallow. "It was only a few months after the release of the virus. Blythe had contracted the wild card, and was brought to the hospital where I was working. She was the most beautiful woman I'd ever seen, and I think I loved her from the first moment I saw her." Blaise rolled his eyes. "Well, I did," said Tachyon defensively.

"So what happened?"

"Blythe's power enabled her to absorb minds. Archibald Holmes recruited her for an antifascist organization called the Four Aces. Jack was a member, and Earl Sanderson, and David Harstein. Blythe became the repository for the minds of Einstein, Oppenheimer, and many many others, mine included. Meanwhile, Jack and Earl and David were flitting around the word overthrowing dictatorships, capturing Nazis and the like.

"Then in '48 they tried to resolve the China problem. David was the key to the negotiations because he possessed a powerful pheromone power. When you were with him he could get you to agree to anything. He had Mao and the Kuomintang kissing and swearing eternal friendship. Then he and the others left China, and naturally the whole thing collapsed."

Tach raised a finger for another brandy. "There was growing suspicion toward the wild cards during this period. A lot like today. China gave them the excuse they needed. They went after the Four Aces, accusing them of being communists. But it was just an excuse. Their real sin was that they were different—more than human. We were all called before the House Un-American Activities Committee. They wanted the names of all the aces I had treated. I refused, but then—" Tachyon took a long swallow of brandy. Somehow this story never got any easier.

"Go on," pushed Blaise, his dark eyes bright with excitement.

In a voice drained of all emotion, Tachyon resumed. "Jack had become a so-called 'friendly witness.' He told the committee that Blythe had absorbed my mind, my memories. They put her on the stand and began to grill her. Because of the stress of juggling so many minds Blythe was . . . fragile. She was about to reveal the other aces. I could not allow that to happen. I controlled her, and so broke her mind. She became hopelessly insane, and her husband had her committed. She died in a sanatorium in 1954."

"Who was the husband?"

"A congressman from New York. There were also three children. Henry Jr., Brandon and Fleur. I lost track of them during the years I was roaming Europe."

"Which is when you met George."

"Yes."

"This is so confusing."

"You should have tried living it."

"So this is the ancient history you won't discuss whenever I ask you why you and Jack fight so much."

"Yes. For years I blamed Jack for Blythe's destruction. Then I realized that *I* was the one who destroyed her. Jack was just one of a long line of contributing factors: my family for developing the virus in the first place, Archibald Holmes for recruiting her, her husband for rejecting her, Jack for being weak, and humans for being venal."

Blaise sucked noisily through his straw, dragging up the last of the Coke. "Boy, this is really heavy, you know?"

"She's beautiful, isn't she?"

"Fleur?" A shrug. "Yeah, I guess."

"I have to see her, Blaise. Explain, set the past straight. Have her forgive me."

"Why should you care?"

"Burning Sky, look at the time! I was supposed to meet the Texas delegation five minutes ago. Go buy some dinner, put it on the room, and stay out of trouble! I've got to change."

The phone was ringing as he entered the room. Snatching it up, Tachyon heard the hiss of long distance. An operator's cool, bored tone asked, "Will you accept a collect call from Mr. Thomas Downs?"

For an instant, disbelief at the journalist's brass held him silent, and Tach could hear faint and far away Digger babbling frantically. "Tachy, you gotta listen—"

"Sir, this call has not yet been accepted." Admonishment from the frigid operator.

"Tachy, listen! Something terr—"

"Sir!"

". . . help me . . ."

"Sir, will you accept the charges?"

". . . in big trouble!" Digger's voice soared into the soprano range.

"*No!*" Tachyon slammed down the phone so hard that it gave a ring of protest. He was halfway out of his shirt when it rang again.

"Collect call—"

"NO!"

It rang seven more times. After the third time Tach stopped answering. The shrill ringing was a drill biting into his head. He dressed quickly in his usual elaborate finery. Pale rose and lavender with silver lace. The phone was still ringing as he stepped into the hall. For a moment he hesitated. *Help me.* Help him how? Tach gave his head an emphatic shake, and pulled the door shut. Too often Digger had embroiled him in the sleazy journalist's sleazy little problems. Not this time.

I have enough problems of my own.

Spector hadn't been to the store for a year and a half, not since the Wild Card Day when the Astronomer went out in a blaze of glory. With a little help from him, of course. The suit he'd bought then didn't last out the day, but then a lot of things hadn't made it through *that* day. The old guy who ran the place had seemed okay to him. What the hell, might as well throw him some more business. He couldn't stay at a swank hotel and not have some decent clothes. He'd stand out like a joker at a fashion show.

He knew it was a mistake as soon as he stepped in. Before, the store had been old, dim, and dusty—like the old man who ran it. Now the place had been repainted and new, brighter lighting had been put in. The room even smelled new.

As Spector turned to leave, a voice called out to him, "Hey, come on in, sir. If you're looking for fine clothing at great prices, you've come to the right place. Just tell me—I'm Bob—name's on the sign outside—what you want and I'll fix you up in no time."

Spector looked Bob over. He was dressed well enough, although the clothes didn't disguise the fact that he was creeping into middle age, but he had a hustler's eyes and smile. Spector just wanted to buy some clothes and get out. "I'll need two suits, one dark gray and one light gray. Thirty-eight long. Not too expensive."

Bob stroked his chin and made a face. "I don't think gray

is really your color. Something in a tan maybe. Come on over here." He grabbed Spector by the elbow and guided him over to one of the mirrors. "Wait just a second."

Spector looked around the store. He didn't see anyone else. It was just Bob and him.

Bob trotted back over, holding a tan coat. He turned Spector toward the mirror and held the coat up in front of him. "What do you think? Great, huh. And a steal at four-hundred-and-fifty dollars. Plus alterations, of course."

"I want two suits. Just like I said. One light gray. One dark gray."

Bob sighed. "Look around outside. You know how many people are wearing gray suits? If you want to stand out, make an impression, you have to dress for it. Trust me."

Spector wasn't listening. He was breathing evenly and concentrating. Remembering the pain. The agony of his own death.

"You okay, mister?"

Spector turned to face Bob and stared into the man's eyes. They linked. Bob couldn't look away, and Spector didn't want to. The memory of his death blotted out everything else. And he gave it to the man in front of him. His insides twisted and burned. Skin ruptured and sloughed off. Muscles tore and bones snapped. Spector's death lived again in his mind. And Bob felt it, too. Spector shuddered as he recalled his heart bursting. Bob gasped. His legs went rubbery and he fell over. Dead. Just as Spector had been before Tachyon brought him back to life.

Spector glanced around. They were still alone. He grabbed Bob under the armpits and dragged him into one of the dressing booths, then walked back to the rack and picked out two gray suits. One dark and one light.

He wrapped them in plastic and headed for the street. "The customer's always right, Bob. First rule of business."

9:00 P.M.

"The problem with Jackson on the ticket is that it could cost us the election. Not to sound bigoted or nothin'—"

"But you do," interrupted Tachyon. A frown of jovian proportions creased Bruce Jenkins's forehead. Since the only hair remaining to the man was a tiny ruff over each big red ear it looked as if his entire head was buckling like earthquake-torn Earth. "Not to suggest that you *are*," Tachyon hastened to add, realizing that Takisian tactlessness might not be in place at a political convention. "But why are we discussing third-place runners, no matter how interesting or charismatic? The real issue is Senator Hartmann and Leo Barnett."

"Reverend."

"Eh?"

"Reverend Barnett. You give Hartmann his title. Leo's deserving of his, too."

"Are we finally getting down to business, Mr. Jenkins?"

"Yeah. Texas went solidly for the Reverend."

"And you intend to keep it that way?"

"If I can. Now this ain't to say that Gregg Hartmann isn't a good man. He is, that's why I think a Barnett/Hartmann ticket might have some real strengths."

"Impossible!"

"Now, don't be so hasty. Politics is a lot like horse trading, Doctor. You can't be too rigid."

"Mr. Jenkins, if the issue is the triumph of the Democratic ticket in November, then a ticket headed by Leo Barnett would be a disaster. There are still enough people who would oppose a religious figure running this country. Besides, Barnett is a one-note candidate."

"No, sir, there you're wrong. *You* see him as a one-note candidate because you're obsessed with wild cards, but Leo speaks for a lot of simple Americans who are worried about the moral decay of this country."

They stepped out of the Bello Mondo restaurant. To their left came the clatter of cutlery on china as the journalists, hangers-on, and less wealthy delegates dined in the Marriott's coffee shop. Tachyon frowned up at the banners stretched across the dizzying expanse of the lobby atrium.

Heard the sharp tick of high heels. Jumped and whirled as he felt cold fingers nuzzle up beneath his hair, touching the nape of his neck. Sara winced at the pressure of his hand around her fingers. Bright color flamed in each cheek, but it looked angry against the unnatural white of her skin.

"I came for a statement, and to see if I could help."

Tachyon shook his head. "What?"

She reared back slightly, nostrils flaring. "Chrysalis."

"What about her?"

"She's dead." The flat tone snapped him around as surely as Fleur's slap. He took two quick steps, groping for support. His hand closed on the sharp point of Sara's shoulder.

"*Dead!*"

"You mean you didn't know?"

"No . . . I . . . I've been busy. All day."

"Yeah." Her tone was bitter; then abruptly she dropped a gentle sympathetic mask over her pale features. "I'm sorry to be the one to tell you."

Jenkins tiptoed over. "Doctor, it seems you've had bad news. We'll talk another time."

Sara gripped Tachyon's arm with both hands and tugged him toward the elevators. "This has been a shock. You're very pale. Maybe you should lie down."

"I need a drink."

Sara hung on grimly to his arm. "Don't you have something in your room?"

He frowned at her. "Yes."

"Let's . . . let's go there." Pale tongue running briefly across those too thin lips. "I . . . I need to talk to you."

Physical vertigo added to his emotional vertigo as the elevator shot upward. "Chrysalis." He shook his head. "Tell me."

She did, in quick terse sentences, her pale eyes locked on his lilac ones. She seemed to be pressing for a mind contact, and he tightened his control. He didn't really want to know what went on behind that intense face.

He led them into the suite. Stood staring into the mirror over the wet bar, a hand closed limply about a brandy bottle.

Mirrors. Chrysalis had loved mirrors, and had filled her boudoir with them.

He pictured the skull head with its trademark swirl of glitter on one transparent cheek. Pictured it battered to a bloody pulp. The tink of glass on glass was loud in the room. He turned, and held out the glass, but Sara was gone. Hearing the squeak of a mattress, he walked into the bedroom, and stared in bewilderment at her pose. Elbows resting on the coverlet. One leg cocked over the other. Skirt hiked to mid-thigh. She accepted the drink, and coyly patted the bed next to her. Feeling like a man sharing a bench with a spider, he sank warily down.

"Secrets." He sighed and drank. "I suppose Chrysalis at last found the secret that killed her."

"Yes." Sara stared rigidly at the far wall. Gave a shake, and placed her hand on his arm. It lay there heavy and lifeless. "I know how much this must hurt you. You two were very close."

He removed her hand, squeezed it, and sat it aside. "I don't know if I would go that far."

The hand crept back, fingers tightening suddenly on the big muscle in his thigh. She began to rub him. Tach rolled a nervous eye in her direction. Sweat had broken along her hairline, and her lips were compressed into a thin line. She sensed his scrutiny, and smiled at him, eyelids half lowered, pouted her lips. Tachyon drained his glass. His leg muscle was beginning to cramp under her furious assault.

"Another?" He waved the glass.

Throaty, husky. "Oh, yes. Please."

They sat drinking in silence. Tachyon felt his guts cramping. "I wonder—JESUS!"

He hit the edge of the bed, slid off onto the floor, brandy sloshing across his crotch. Thrust his little finger into his ear, and wiped out the moisture left by the sudden thrust of Sara's tongue. It had felt like someone driving a Q-tip dipped in icy Vaseline into his ear.

She hung over the bed staring down at him with fever-bright eyes. Gasped out, "I want you! I want you!"

It was like getting hit with a rake. Bony knees, elbows, pelvis digging into his chest, groin, thighs as she flung herself upon him. They thrashed for a few moments, Sara dropping inexpert kisses onto whatever part of his anatomy she could hit. Tachyon threw her off, and tottered to the far side of the bed.

"*What in the hell are you doing?*" Tears of shame and rage filled his eyes.

"I want to make love with you."

"If this is some kind of joke, it is in pretty goddamn bad taste! Or actually, it's in perfect taste if you go in for cruel Takisian humor."

"What are you driveling about?" she screamed, raking back her hair.

"I'm impotent! Impotent! *IMPOTENT!*"

"Still?" Honest amazement filled the word.

It shredded his last vestige of control. "Yes, fuck you! Now get out! Just get the hell out of here!"

Blotchy red patches flamed in her cheeks. Sara flung herself on his chest, hands clasped frenziedly behind his neck. "No, please, I can't leave you. I'm next, don't you see? Only you can keep me safe!"

"Are you out of your mind? Keep you safe from what?"

"Hartmann! *HARTMANN*! He killed Andi, he killed Chrysalis, and now he's going to kill *me*!"

"I'm not going to listen to any more of this."

"He's a monster. Inhuman. Evil."

"A year ago you were fucking your brains out with him." Her breath came in harsh pants. "He made me."

"Now I've heard everything. You are crazy." Tach threw himself through the sitting room, dragging Sara like a recalcitrant foal. Flung open the door. "Out, out, out, out."

She ran from him, and threw herself onto the bed. Curled up with a pillow clutched to her chest. "No, no, you can't make me. I won't leave. You've got to *help me*," she wailed as he bundled her into his arms, and staggered back to the door. "Read me! Go into my mind!" she hissed, clinging to his lapels.

"I wouldn't *touch* that cesspool that you call a mind."

Fire flared as her nails raked across his face. "WHEN I'M DEAD YOU'LL BE SORRY."

"I'm already sorry."

Tach slammed the door, brushed distastefully at his coat, and crossed to the bar. Seized the cognac and drank directly from the bottle. Spewed as the heat became too much for his throat. He drew a hand across his face, and yelped as the liquor entered the cuts left by her nails.

Help me.

You don't want to believe.

When I'm dead you'll be sorry!

The bottle exploded against the far wall.

"I'M TIRED OF FEELING SORRY!"

11:00 P.M.

Spector combed his hair up and went at the ends with the scissors. Lank brown strands fell into the dirty sink. The job was near barber standards. He'd cut hair on the side when working his way through school, and had gotten pretty good at it. He picked up the cracked hand mirror and checked the neckline in the back.

"Not bad, my man," he said to himself. He scooped up a fingerful of skin lotion, and rubbed it onto his reddened upper lip. Without the mustache and long hair he looked years younger, not much different from his old college self. Only the pained eyes were forever changed. With his hair washed and blown dry he'd be unrecognizable to anyone who'd met him since he became Demise. Except Tachyon. He'd know regardless.

The thought of the little alien knocked him from his normal sullen mood into a gnawing rage. Making the hit, that would hurt Tachyon. He nodded to the mirror and walked into the living room. The decor was nicer than his apartment in Jokertown. The walls were gray-green; the furnishings were mahogany or other dark woods. He even picked up occasionally. He'd made the move back to Teaneck after the Sleeper had roughed him up. Considering the hell that had broken loose not long after, it had been a good idea.

He flopped into the black futon and reached for the TV remote control. His flight wasn't until ten the next day. There would be plenty of time to pack in the morning. He punched up WABC. The set crackled to life and Ted Koppel came into view.

". . . little was known about this woman with transparent skin who chose to create her own kingdom in the center of New York City's Jokertown." Koppel's brows were knit together even more tightly than usual. "While police are saying little about the apparent murder, it was seemingly a very brutal affair. There is the possibility that an ace with abnormal strength was involved. Before giving you what limited background we have on this woman named Chrysalis, here's what Angela Ellis, captain of the Jokertown precinct, had to say earlier today."

The video cut to a drab press area. A short woman with dark hair and green eyes stood in front of a nest of microphones. She coughed, then paused, and placed her hands palms down on the podium. "The woman popularly known as Chrysalis was found dead at her place of business this morning. Should the medical examiner determine that a homicide has occurred, this office will of course conduct a thorough investigation. We have no further information to give at this time." Voices of questioning reporters immediately rose into a roar. Ellis raised one hand. "That's it. We'll keep you informed as facts become available."

Spector reached for the bottle of whiskey he always kept by the futon. He twisted off the cap and took several swallows.

"Shit." He'd never cared one way or the other for the bitch, but something about her being dead made him uneasy. There was blood and death in the air already, and while that ordinarily made him feel right at home he had a gut feeling that he was really going to be putting it on the line to make this hit. That was too bad, though. The money from the Shadow Fists was almost gone, and he needed another big score. This had dropped into his lap and he wasn't going to blow it.

Several more slugs of whiskey and Koppel's familiar monotone relaxed him. He drifted off to sleep wondering what the weather was like in Atlanta.

Tachyon hunched at the bar, ankles wrapped about the rungs of the high chrome stool. The light reflecting off the hanging wine glasses hurt his aching head, but he couldn't find the energy to look away.

Mirrors. The mirrors of the Funhouse shattering as the kidnappers had come for Angelface. A skull face reflected in a hundred different angles as he entered Chrysalis's boudoir on the upper floor of the Crystal Palace. The invisible lips painted a pale pink, the swirl of glitter across one transparent cheek, the blue eyes floating eerily in their bony sockets.

He had drunk in both those bars for more years than he cared to remember. Now the Funhouse was closed following Des's death a year ago.

What would become of the Palace?

Drunken self-pity brought tears to Tachyon's eyes, and he considered his bereft state.

"Hey, buddy?" asked the cheerful young bartender. "Another one?"

"Sure, why not." The bartender set up another brandy, and Tach raised it high. "To the lost and mournful dead."

Tach drained the glass, scrawled his room number across the bottom of the bar bill, slipped off the stool. There was still a lot of activity in the lobby even at this hour, but he spotted no one he knew. Tachyon considered calling Jack, but he wanted to drink and talk about Chrysalis, and the big ace hadn't known her.

His aimless wanderings led him to the floor housing Barnett's party. Behind the doors he could hear the low murmur of voices. He stared hard at one door, willing Fleur to emerge. It didn't work. His silent scrutiny of the suite drew the attention of a Secret Service guard. Tach saw him coming, and stumbled back to the elevators.

Back in his own room he stared down at Blaise's tousled head. Sobs shook him as he knelt by the bed, and enfolded the sleeping boy in his arms.

Everyone always leaves me. Everyone I love leaves me. I love you so very much. Don't ever leave me.

CHAPTER TWO

Tuesday
July 19, 1988

8:00 A.M.

He'd been so drunk and upset last night that he hadn't noticed the message light on the telephone. Having now arrived at a state where his eyes focused and his head felt less like an enemy growth mounted on his shoulders, Tachyon sipped Alka-Seltzer and listened to the distant ringing.

"Blythe van Renssaeler Memorial Clinic."

"This is Tachyon, get me Finn."

"Hi, doc, you must have heard by now."

"Yes."

"Things are in an uproar here. There was a firebombing at Barnett's mission last night, and what I can only describe as free-form demonstrations in Chatham Square. I tried to reach you all afternoon."

"I didn't get back to the room until very late."

"I assisted on the autopsy. You want details?"

Tachyon sighed. "I suppose I must."

Finn ran down the findings. In the background, Tach could hear a sharp four beat tapping as the pony-sized centaur danced on nervous dainty hooves. The joker physician concluded with a wry, "It'll sure as hell be a closed-casket service."

"Damn, the funeral. When is it?"

"Tomorrow morning at eleven."

"I will of course be there."

"How are things down in your neck of the woods?"

"Confusing. I don't even know the current delegate count." He checked his watch. "Look, I've got to go. I'll see you tomorrow."

Snatching up a hat, Tachyon paused at the bathroom door, and yelled over the thunder of running water. "I'm off to breakfast with Jack. Meet me at ten-thirty, and we'll go over to the Omni. And *be there*."

There was no answer. Blaise was either plotting or sulking. Neither was an encouraging prospect.

"Ms. Morgenstern." Braden Dulles was younger than she was, but he had this State Voice he put on, an authoritative Ben Bradlee rumble like driving over a gravel road on a New England winter day, complete with frost crackling and the occasional squeak. "You have put this newspaper in a very difficult position."

She shifted in her bed, pulled a wad of pillow closer to her breasts. She had on a heavy blue-flannel nightgown. It was how she always did hotels: in winter leave the heat down, in summer crank up the air-conditioning and bundle up. She liked the insulation a lot of bedding gave her.

She worked her eyelids ponderously up and down. She was normally a morning person. But last night after Tachyon had brushed her off—*the bastard!*—she'd been completely out of resources, had no idea what to do but take her chances returning to her room, where she slept the sleep of the clinically depressed. She turned an eye toward the clock radio on the nightstand. 8:00 A.M. If Dulles's call hadn't roused her she might have gone on until afternoon.

When she didn't respond, Braden went on, "It has been of concern to us here that you have of late been conducting what appears to be a personal vendetta against a major candidate for the presidential nomination."

Bitterness popped like a blister. "Your fair-haired boy, you mean."

"The *Post* has a tradition of awareness of its responsibili ties as the newspaper of record in the nation's capital. Senator Hartmann is obviously the best qualified candidate at this point in time."

"You think this point in time's a good one to put a psychopathic ace in the White House? Christ, all Ronnie

Reagan's done is invade some new country where we didn't belong every two years. This man—this *creature*—feeds on human misery, Braden."

Anguished silence. She could just see the expression on his Young Patrician face, the constriction around the nostrils, the deepening of the network of grooves beyond his age that surrounded his mouth and radiated from the corners of his eyes, which he cultivated because they lent him *gravitas*. As if he'd just detected an aroma of dog turd within the sterile hallowed sanctum of the *Post*.

"We feel your . . . obsession . . . does credit neither to you as a journalist nor to us as a paper. Your latest report, if I may call it that, was simply incredible. Even were we inclined to accept such a farrago of wild accusation and innuendo, our legal department would never let us print it.

"And this attempt by Leo Barnett to smear Senator Hartmann—really, Sara, how could you have lent your name to such a, well, frankly sleazy undertaking?"

"Barnett's people didn't *ask* me, Braden. I didn't know anything about it, I swear to God." She clung to the receiver as if it was the only thing holding her up. It was cool talisman hardness on her cheek.

"You told me the allegations were true. Yet within hours Senator Hartmann had issued a denial, which we feel to have been quite convincing."

Because you wanted it to be. She tried to envision the *Post* accepting such an offhand denial of dubious dealing from a politician they didn't shine their golden light upon. A Nixon, a Robertson, even a Bush; they'd hunt him to the end of the earth.

But she could not speak. She had a good reporter's patter when she needed to draw people out. Somehow, though, the spoken word always managed to betray her when she tried to express something that really mattered to her.

"Finally, Ms. Morgenstern, we are very concerned that you have evinced no intention of returning to New York. You are the acknowledged journalistic authority on Jokertown. We find it most unsettling that you refuse to take an interest in the murder—which involved the use of ace powers, I might add—of one of that community's most prominent citizens. One I was given to understand was a personal friend of yours. It would seem your story lay there."

"The story's *here*, Braden. This is bigger than a killing in Jokertown. This concerns everybody—you, me, aces, jokers, people in Uganda, the whole world. The president has so much power, so many—" She stopped herself before she stumbled and fell headlong. That was a reason she'd always preferred the written word; the ones you spoke tended to get away from you. She drew a breath.

"Besides, Braden, he's here. Chrysalis's murderer is here. Didn't you read my article?"

"Are you suggesting Senator Hartmann personally beat Ms. Jory to death?"

"*No*. Damn you, Braden, don't be so obtuse. He had it done—he used his ace, he used his position, what the hell difference does it make? He's still guilty, just like a mafia don who orders a hit."

Dulles sighed. "I truly regret that it has come to this. Your personality disintegration has seriously degraded your professionalism. We therefore feel it is in neither your best interests nor ours for your association with this newspaper to continue."

"You're firing me?" Her voice rose toward the ceiling. "Say it, Braden. Just have the balls to say it."

"I've said everything that needs to be said, Ms. Morgenstern. I will add my personal hope that you will soon seek therapy. You have too much ability to throw it away over addiction."

"*Addiction?*" She could barely produce the word.

"Addiction to fear. Addiction to excitement, to the thrill of being a central figure in a vast and shadowy and menacing mystery. Addiction is the disease of the eighties, Sara. Good-bye."

She heard a click and the white-noise line. In her mind she could see Braden Dulles's hands, already scrubbed to a pink-white luster, washing each other in air.

She threw the phone across the room and rose from the bed to dress. She felt like a cracked porcelain doll. As if any movement, any random breath of air, might splinter her all over the carpet.

9:00 A.M.

Tach noticed with a flare of almost guilty pleasure that even among the greats of the nation he was still newsworthy.

The discrete hints that he and Jack had dropped yesterday had borne fruit. Reporters milled and jostled, ran microphone tests, camera checks. Jack had done a nice job of stage-managing the entire affair, selecting a table flush against the low divider separating the atrium coffee shop from the walkway. A tech snapped on a floor light, bleaching the big blond ace. Jack squinted, and shaded his eyes.

"Bad night?" inquired Tach, sliding into a seat opposite Jack. He kept his voice very low to avoid the foam phalluses that were already thrusting in their direction.

"Late night. We had that challenge to Rule 9(c) governing the apportioning of delegates formerly committed—"

"Jack, spare me the tedious details. Did we win or not?"

"Yes, thanks to me, which set us up to win the California challenge." Jack took a sip of coffee, and lit a cigarette. "Do you have any idea how we're going to play this scene?"

"No."

"Great," came the sour reply.

The edges of Tachyon's mouth quirked. "I suppose I could just come around the table, and give you a great big kiss."

"I'd kill you."

Tach shaded his eyes with a hand, and scanned the crowd, noting the presence of Brokaw and Donaldson. Peregrine, who always knew how to time an entrance, came flying down from the tenth floor. The beating of her great wings fluttered menus and ruined blow-dried hairdos. Cameras swiveled up to document her landing.

Tachyon reached out to her with his telepathy. *Good morning, sweet one, ready to shill for us?*

All ready, Tachy, dearest.

"Mr. Braun, Doctor, aren't you rather unusual breakfast companions?" sang out Peri.

"In what way?" asked Tach blandly.

Sam Donaldson picked up the ball, rapping out his question in his sharp staccato manner. "Your antipathy for one another is well-documented. In a 1972 interview with *Time* magazine, Doctor, you said that Jack Braun was the greatest betrayer in American history."

Jack stiffened, and ground out his Camel. Tachyon felt a momentary regret at what he was going to be put through.

"Mr. Donaldson, you might note that that interview is sixteen years old. People change. They learn to forgive."

"So you've forgiven Mr. Braun for 1950?"

"Yes."

"And you, Mr. Braun?" sung out Buckley of *The New York Times*.

"I have nothing to forgive. What I have are regrets. What happened in the 1950s was a travesty. I see it happening again, and I'm here to sound the warning. Dr. Tachyon and I share more than just a past. We were drawn together because of our admiration for Gregg Hartmann."

"Then the senator arranged for your reconciliation?"

"Only by example," said Tach. "He was one of the driving forces behind last year's World Health Organization tour to investigate the treatment of wild cards worldwide. The senator spoke movingly of reconciliation and the healing of old wounds." Tach glanced at Jack. "I think perhaps both of us took that lesson to heart."

"We also have another bond," said Jack. "I'm a wild card. One of the first. Tachyon's spent forty-two years working among the victims of that virus."

It was a pleasant overstatement, but Tach didn't correct him. It would have brought up the fact that for thirteen years, from 1950 until 1963, Tachyon had been a useless alcoholic derelict, roaming the streets and gutters of Europe and Jokertown. And the reason for his disintegration and deportation had been those fateful hearings before HUAC, and Jack's betrayal.

". . . and we don't like what's been happening in this country. The hate is back, and we fear it."

Tachyon fought free of the memories.

"Then you accuse the Reverend Barnett of fanning the flames of hatred and intolerance?" asked a serious-faced young man from CBS.

"I believe Leo Barnett is acting from principle—as he sees it. But so was the Nur al-Allah in Syria, and in that sad country I saw innocent jokers stoned to death in the streets. Is that anguish something that we wish to see translated to our country?" Tach shook his head. "I think not. Gregg Hartmann—"

"Is a secret ace, and a killer," came a thin, tight voice from the crowd.

People drew back, repelled by the madness in Sara's narrow face. Tachyon came half out of his chair.

"*Shit!*" muttered Jack.

"What are you going to do, Dr. Tachyon? He's one of yours. One of the devil's stepchildren, and only you can stop him." Tears blurred Sara's words.

"*Do* something. Mind-control her. Something," whispered Jack.

And make a bad situation worse? he shot back in a bitter telepathic message to the ace.

The crowd of reporters had turned on the woman like a pack scenting blood. She blanched and shrank back.

"Miss Morgenstern! On what . . . Do you . . . evidence . . . does the *Post* . . ."

The clamoring voices rose in intensity. To Tachyon's overstretched nerves the sound seemed to take on a physical manifestation, a wave about to break over that fragile form. Sara whirled and vanished into the crowd of interested onlookers. Tachyon stared at the eager hungry faces of the press, and bowed his head. They had to be fed.

Mothers of my mother, forgive me, he prayed, and threw Sara to the wolves.

"That unfortunate girl does not deal well with stress," he called in a clear, penetrating voice. "Yesterday's revelations concerning her and Senator Hartmann—"

"Then there *was* an affair?" snapped Donaldson.

"No. The child was in love with the senator, and could not accept his continued refusal. I think she is torn between love for him, and a desire for revenge. Remember, hell hath no fury . . ." His voice trailed away.

"Yeah," put in Jack. "I tried to interest the young lady in my charms during the tour, but she was obsessed with the senator."

"Sad," concluded Tachyon. *But not as sad as what I've just done to her.*

"Who the hell are *you*?" Sara demanded shrilly. The man who had hold of her arm ignored her. Or maybe the tumult of questions and rage breaking over them like a tsunami drowned out her words.

Something in his manner said he was ignoring her.

The discrete security goons had come out of it first, of course, advancing in their dark three-pieces, muttering into throat mikes as they converged on her. She was standing there erect and alone, challenging in her tea-green skirt and long-

sleeved white blouse, chin elevated above a ruff considerably
more modest than Tachyon's. She let the noise roll off her. She
had spilled the truth out on the carpet like a turd shining and
stinking in the hot TV lights, where it could not be overlooked
or covered up. Now she would accept the consequences.

A hand caught her wrist. She turned, ready to aim a kick
for a gaberdine crotch. Instead of a husky young jock, it was a
small, gray, balding man with a round belly hanging in a
Mickey Mouse T-shirt. The watchdogs weren't even close.

Now the gray man was towing her out a side door with the
modest but irresistible authority of an East River tug. The
security toughs got caught up in the back eddies of delegates
and reporters shouting questions at each other. Her last view
of the function room was Jack Braun staring after her with his
face rumpled up into a look of Sonny Tufts's bemusement,
Tachyon beside him gazing about with neurasthenic dismay,
like an underfed Regency buck whose man's man just farted in
the wardrobe.

Her rescuer—or whatever the hell he was—dragged her
down a corridor past incurious idlers, into a side service
passageway. He used the momentum he'd imported to spin
her around, back to a wall. A pack of reporters charged by,
down the corridor, baying on the wrong trail.

"Is not the way to go about it," he said. He had the kind
of gruff avuncular face only TV character actors have. His
accent was . . . *Russian?*

Sara lost it. This was simply too strange. She yanked her
hand away, panicked more by the fact of contact than any
ramification.

He pressed in on her. "No! You must listen. You are in
very great danger—"

You're telling me, buster. She squirmed past him and
raced away, throwing a high heel in the process, toppling into
the wall, scraping along, supporting herself with her hands
while she kicked frantically to free herself of the other.

"Little fool!" the man yelled after her. "The truth you have
can kill!"

The shoe finally came away, cartwheeling into the far
wall. She ran.

10:00 A.M.

Gregg didn't remember sleeping at all during the night.

At six, Amy called to give him the early morning schedule and remind him of a seven o'clock breakfast meeting with Andrew Young at Pompano's. By seven-forty-five he was in conference with Tachyon, Braun, and other key lobbyists and delegates about the Joker's Rights plank and the party platform. At eight-ten, it was minor difficulties with the Ohio delegation, which seemed to consider Gregg a favorite-son candidate since he'd been born in their state, and felt they deserved privileged access to him; eight-thirty was a discussion with Ted Kennedy and Jimmy Carter concerning tomorrow's nomination speeches. Amy and John Werthen huddled with him to confirm the rest of the morning's schedule, then Gregg spoke briefly with Tony Calderone about the progress of his acceptance speech.

Around nine-thirty, Tachyon came storming up complaining that Sara Morgenstern had finally gone too far. He informed Gregg of her outburst downstairs. "She's entirely insane," the alien raged. "Paranoid, delusions of persecution. We have to do something about her."

Gregg agreed with that more than Tachyon could know. She'd become unpredictable and dangerous, and he didn't dare use Puppetman to neutralize her. There was too much danger of Gimli's interference. With the problems he'd had with Puppetman in the last few weeks, he couldn't afford the chance. A public scene would ruin everything.

A little after ten, he was finally able to retreat to his room for a few minutes. Ellen was away handshaking with delegates and campaigning outside; their rooms were blessedly deserted. A headache was pounding against his temples, and it had Gimli's voice.

Why worry about Morgenstern? Sure, she's a fucking loose cannon, but she's not the problem I am, is she? You could handle her if you dared let Puppetman out. Can you feel him yet, Greggie? Can you hear him howling for his fix? I can. You will too, any time now.

"Shut up, damn you!" He didn't realize he'd spoken aloud until he heard the faint echo of his voice.

Gimli laughed. *Sure. I'll be quiet for a little while. After all, I've already got you talking to yourself. Just remember that I'm still here, still waiting. But then, I doubt you'll forget that, will you? You can't.*

The voice went away, leaving Gregg moaning and holding his head. *One problem at a time,* he told himself. *Sara first.*

He composed himself, reaching for the phone and dialing. There was the slight hiss of a long-distance connection, and then the phone at the other end rang. "Hartmann in '88," a voice said with a strong Harlem accent. "New York office, Matt Wilhelm speaking."

"Furs, how are things up north?"

There was a laugh from the other end of the line. Wilhelm—also known in Jokertown as Furs—preferred his joker name, as Gregg knew. "Senator, it's good to hear from you. I should have known it was you coming in on this line. Everything's going smoothly, if a little slow. We're waiting for the official announcement that you're our nominee, then we'll move into overdrive. How's Atlanta?"

"Hot and steamy, and awfully warm down on the floor, from what I understand."

"Lots of resistance to the plank," Furs said. Gregg could imagine the joker's leonine features set in a scowl. "I expected as much."

"I'm afraid so. But we're going to keep hammering away at it."

"You do that, Senator. In the meantime, what can Furs do for you?"

"I'd like you to make a few phone calls. I could do it myself but I've a meeting in a few minutes and Amy and John are tied up with this platform business. You or someone on our staff got the time to give me a hand?"

"Absolutely. Go ahead."

"Good. First, check with Cuomo's office—be sure to relay thanks for his help yesterday with File and Shroud and find out exactly when he's expected to arrive in Atlanta tomorrow. I want to know what arrangements have been made, and be sure one of our people picks him up at the airport. Then call our headquarters in Albany and have someone there confirm my reservation for the first week in August; Amy says she's never heard back from them. I also need you to call and make certain the New York apartment's ready for Ellen on Monday time into Tomlin, by the way, but John will be calling you with those details."

"Got it, Senator. Anything else?"

Gregg closed his eyes, sinking back into the padded embrace of the couch. "One more thing. There's another call." He recited the number he'd memorized before leaving New York. "You won't get anything but an answering machine there," he told Furs. "Don't worry about it. All you need to do is leave a short message on the machine. Just say to book a flight to Atlanta soonest. They'll know what that means."

"Book a flight ASAP. No problem. That all?"

"That's all. Thanks, Furs. I'll be seeing you soon."

"Just get us jokers a platform we can stand on."

"We'll do our damndest. Take care. Give my regards to your staff. We couldn't do anything without their help."

Gregg placed the receiver carefully in its cradle.

It was done. Mackie would be coming. Gregg hadn't wanted the volatile ace in Atlanta, but he had to do something. Mackie should have disposed of Downs already; now he could take care of Sara.

Very faintly, a sardonic voice answered him from beneath. *But what about me? What about me?*

"A KGB man hanging out at the Democratic Convention?" Ricky Barnes shook his long trim head. "Everybody already thinks you're in cahoots with Barnett, but maybe you should think about going to work for Robertson. Sounds like something his people would come up with, along with raising the dead and knowing where the hostages from Flight 737 were being kept in Calcutta."

"That isn't funny, Ricky." She sat on the edge of his tautly made bed, methodically tearing a Kleenex into shreds. She spoke without heat. Ricky was maybe the first person she'd met in her life who could tease her without causing real pain.

"Well, I mean, first you pitch your little scene in the midst of the Tach'n'Jack love feast. Then you say you're hauled out of the pot you set boiling by some old dude in a Mickey Mouse shirt. Who ever heard of a KGB man in a Mickey Mouse shirt?"

"What do KGB men wear, Ricky?"

"Rumpled suits and phony Rolexes. I've *met* KGB men, Sara. So have you."

She tossed the ruined Kleenex on the floor. "Well, who was he, then?"

"Somebody with a hell of a lot more sense than you were showing, sweetheart."

She pulled her legs up on the bed, crossed them, put her head in her hands. Ricky watched her from the table, where he had his antique Epson Geneva laptop set up. He was wearing a dark-brown pinstripe vest and trousers with a pale-pink shirt and brown bow tie. With his elongated face and big horsey white teeth he reminded her of poor Ronnie, Gregg's aide, who always disapproved of his boss's liaison with Sara. The Red Army Fraction had executed him when they kidnapped Hartmann in Berlin. She blamed Hartmann for his death.

But it was only in appearance that he resembled Hartmann's hapless aide. Ricky approved of her. He always did. Sometimes, she suspected, a bit too much.

"Do you think I'm crazy?" she asked.

"Hell, yes. Think about what if you're *right*, Rosie." *Rosie* was his pet name for her; he claimed she looked like an albino Rosanna Arquette. "Standing right up there in front of God and everybody and announcing that Senator Gregg's a killer ace—can you think of a quicker way to bring him down on your case if he *is*?"

"I mean it about Hartmann. Everybody treats me as if I'm a leper because I don't think Gregg's the reincarnation of Abraham Lincoln or something."

Ricky bit his lip and rubbed his chin with his fingertips. He was a pretty fair pianist in his spare time, and he had the hands for it, long and thin and fine.

"I have to say it strikes me as kind of improbable. All this ace mind control and stuff; how could he have kept it a secret all these years?" She started to cloud up; he held one hand protectively between them, fingers outspread. "But wait, wait now. You're a damn fine reporter, a damn fine *person*—I think your stories have maybe done more to promote understanding of jokers and their problems than Senator Gregg's posturing and his well-publicized handouts; Brother Malcolm knew all about what it means when the Man extends a helping hand. I know you're not just making this up.

"But still . . . still. I know you still feel the loss of your sister very deeply. Is there any possibility that might be affecting your judgment?"

She let her face drop between her hands, seeming to hold her head up by her almost-white hair.

"When I was a child," she said, "whenever I did something cute or clever, I could tell my parents were thinking *if only it were Andi*. Do you know what I mean? When I was bad or clumsy, it was, *Andi wouldn't do that*. I mean, they'd never say anything that horrible, not out loud. But I *knew*. It was as if I had a wild card of my own, a poison psychic gift that let me know what they really thought."

She was crying, then, the tears rushing out as if someone had punched a big awl through her eyes and hit a giant reservoir of grief. Ricky was beside her on the bed, cradling her against his racquetball-trim chest, stroking her hair with those splendid fingers, while the mascara eroded from her face and stained his Brooks Brothers shirt in big ugly blotches.

"Sara—Rosie—it's all right now, baby, it's all right, we'll get it straightened out. Everything will be okay. You're fine, sweetheart, everything's going to be fine . . ."

She clung to him like a baby opossum, welcoming human contact for one rare moment, letting him murmur his soothing words, letting him hold her.

I just hope he doesn't press too far, she thought.

The passengers walking the LaGuardia concourse gave plenty of sea room to the thin young man in the faded black jacket. It wasn't just the stale smell of sweat emanating from his seldom-washed clothes and body. Mackie was so full of excitement at getting The Call that he wasn't able to keep it all in; parts of him kept going off into buzz. The subliminals were unnerving people.

He looked up at the TV monitors next to the Eastern gate. The gray alphanumerics confirmed once again that his flight was departing on time. He could actually see it there through the polarized glass, fat and white and glistening like snot in the July morning sun. The paper jacket that held his ticket and boarding pass was beginning to wilt in his hand; he didn't want to let go of it, even to slip it into a pocket.

Chrysalis was dead, Digger vanished, but he got to kill one who was even better. The woman. The Man had told Mackie about her. She had *done it* with the Man on the tour. They broke up and she got crazy and might try to do something to the Man—his Man. He'd wanted to go out and find her as soon as he heard that, put a good buzz on and cut her, and watch the blood well up, but the Man said, no. Wait for my word.

It had come a half hour ago in the form of a coded call to the Bowery message drop.

He was glad there was no smoking on airplanes. He hated smokers: *smokers jokers*. He'd been on an airplane once, when he'd come across from Germany to be close to the Man.

He held his pass up to his face, opened it, shuffled through it. He could barely read the red type, and not just because it was blurred. He hadn't gotten what you called a good education in Germany. He never learned to read real well, even though he did learn to speak English. From his mother. The whore.

The ticket had been waiting for him when he asked at the Eastern counter. The clerk there was afraid of him. He could tell. She was a fat nigger bitch. She thought he was a joker. You could see it in those calf-stupid eyes. People always thought he was a joker. Especially women.

That was probably why the Man sounded funny. That woman after him. Women did that. Women were shit. He thought of his mother. The fat, cognac-swilling whore. The bottleneck stuck in her mouth in his mind turned to a fat nigger cock. He watched it slide in and out for a while, moistened his lips.

His mother had fucked niggers. She'd fucked anybody with the ready, in Hamburg's Sankt Pauli district. *Reeperbahnstraβe*. Where he'd grown up. One of them had knocked her up. When she got drunk and beat Mackie up, she told him his father was a deserter, a GI Stockholm-bound from 'Nam. But his father was a general. *He knew.*

Mackie Messer was maximum bad. His father couldn't have been just anybody, could he?

His mother had abandoned him; *natürlich*. Women did that. Made you love them so they could hurt you. They wanted you to put that man-thing in them so they could take it away: *bite it off*. He tried to imagine his mother biting off the huge black dick, but it dissolved into tears that streamed down his face and dripped off his chin onto the collar of his Talking Heads T-shirt.

His mother had died. He cried for her again.

"Eastern Airlines Flight 377, for Raleigh-Durham and

Atlanta, will now begin boarding passengers holding passes for rows one through fifteen," the ceiling said to him. He wiped away tears and blew his nose on his fingers and joined the big flow. He was going where he was wanted, and was content.

Spector stood in the jet's cramped restroom and splashed some water from the sink over his face. His stomach was churning and his skin was cold. He'd gone into the bathroom hoping to throw up, but no luck. He was so nervous he couldn't even manage to take a leak.

There was an impatient knock at the door.

"I'll be out in a minute," Spector said, drying the water from his face with his coat sleeve.

Another knock. Harder this time.

Spector sighed and opened the door.

A hunchbacked joker in a Talking Heads T-shirt was standing outside. He pushed past Spector and closed the door. The little creep's eyes were like something dead, even worse than Spector's.

"Fuck you, too, shrimp." Spector clutched his way back to his seat without waiting for a reply.

It was the first time he'd ever flown. The plane was much smaller than he'd expected and was getting bounced around by what the captain called "some minor turbulence." He'd already put away two little bottles of whiskey and asked the stewardess to bring a couple more. She hadn't gotten back to him, though. He was sitting between a guy who had been a helicopter pilot in Vietnam and some reporter. The reporter was playing around with a lap-top computer, but the ex-pilot hadn't stopped chattering since they boarded.

"You see that redhead over there?" Spector followed the line of his finger to a woman a few rows away who was looking over at them. Her lipstick and tight knit dress were bright crimson. Her eyes were green and heavily made up. She was licking her lips in an exaggerated manner. "She wants me. I can tell. Wants me bad. Ever make it in a plane before?"

"Nope." Spector was clacking the two empty bottles together in his sweaty palm.

The ex-pilot leaned back, brushed a piece of lint from his lapel, and sucked in his gut. "Gonna play it cool, though." He looked out the window and nudged Spector. "You see those black dots out on the wing. That's where the rivets have been

working back and forth. God, I hate flying in these death traps.
I saw one miss the runway at National in Washington once.
Nobody walked away from that one. If the impact doesn't get
you, the fire and poison gas will. I was safer back in 'Nam."

Spector slipped the bottles into his suit pocket and turned
to look for his stewardess. She was nowhere in sight. Probably
in first class sucking off some rich shithead. He'd been an idiot
to fly coach, but was a prisoner of his middle-class upbringing.

"Time to make the big move," the ex-pilot said. He made
eye-contact with the redhead and walked slowly to the rear of
the plane. She smiled back at him and nodded, then started
giggling when he disappeared into the restroom.

"Don't let him fool you," said the reporter, without
looking up. He was in his early thirties, about Spector's size,
and already balding. "These babies are safe as they can be."

"Really," Spector said, trying to sound as nonchalant as
possible.

"Yeah. He could tell you're a white-knuckler. Just having
some fun with you, I expect." The reporter folded up his
computer and looked over at the redhead. "Hope he has fun
jerking himself off."

The stewardess, a blonde with cropped hair, who seemed
slightly too large for her uniform, handed Spector a plastic cup
of ice and two more miniature Jack Blacks. "Thanks," he said,
fishing in his wallet for a small bill. He had one bottle opened
and poured before she could make change.

"You going to Atlanta for the convention?" The reporter
asked.

"Uh, no." Spector took a long, cool swallow. "Not really
into politics myself. Got other business."

"Not into politics?" The reporter shook his head. "This
could be the most exciting convention since New York in '76.
It'll be a real dogfight. Me, I'm betting on Hartmann." The
reporter sounded like someone who'd gotten a tip at the
racetrack.

"Funny things can happen. Especially in politics." Spector drained the glass and opened the other bottle. A warm,
empty feeling spread comfortably through his insides. "If I
were you, I wouldn't bet the farm."

The ex-pilot stalked slowly up the aisle, his hands thrust
deep into his pockets. He glared at the redhead. The plane
lurched and he bumped into the hunchbacked man. The

joker's hands seemed to blur for a moment, and Spector thought he saw bits of dust spray up from the armrest. He hoped it was just the Jack Black kicking in.

"No such thing as a sure thing," Spector said.

11:00 A.M.

Five television sets were blaring in the living room of the suite the Hartmann contingent had taken as staff headquarters, all tuned to different stations. On the screen nearest Gregg, Dan Rather was holding forth with a patriarchal Walter Cronkite, back on the air for special convention coverage. Cronkite, as always, sounded the way you'd expect God would sound.

". . . perception is that despite the majority recommendation, Hartmann simply isn't strong enough to guarantee passage of the Joker's Rights plank. Does this indicate that Hartmann isn't strong enough to win once the delegates are released from their first-vote obligations; that Barnett, Dukakis, Jackson, or a dark horse like Cuomo may eventually emerge as the nominee?"

"Walter, no one has a lock on this convention. The closeness of the primary results showed that. Hartmann is seen as a Northern liberal who can't win in the South, and frankly, his long involvement with joker causes is a liability outside the coasts and metropolitan areas. Barnett has Southern appeal and could woo voters from Bush, especially among the fundamentalist factions. Still, he's too conservative and strongly religious for the Democratic constituency. Dukakis is Mr. Bland, with nothing particularly against him, but nothing particularly for him. Jackson has charisma, but the question remains whether he can win outside cities with large black populations. Gore, Simon, Cuomo or any dark horse's only hope is a deadlock convention that turns to a compromise candidate. All this is reflected in the bitter platform fight. Of course—"

Gregg twisted the knob, turning off the sound in mid-sentence. The other sets babbled on. "Rather has his head up his ass," John Werthen commented. "The right vice-presidential candidate and—*boom*—there goes any regional weakness."

"C'mon, they all know that," Tony Calderone threw in

from across the room. "They're just going for drama. Blame their writers."

Gregg nodded tiredly to no one in particular. Puppetman was quiet, Gimli seemed to be gone for the moment, and Mackie would be on his way soon, if not already in flight. He felt drained, lethargic.

The staff meeting had been going for an hour. Plastic cups of cold coffee sprawled everywhere, floating old cigarette butts; stacks of paper spilled from table to floor, Danishes were petrifying in cardboard boxes stacked on the floor. Gregg's staff bustled through the blue-tinged air, a half dozen conversations competing with the TV sets.

Amy came through the hall door in a rush. "Barnett's made it official," she announced as everyone turned to her. "The minority report's not only against *any* Joker's Rights plank, Barnett's personally calling for a return to the Exotic Laws."

The room was loud with disbelief. With the surging emotions, Gregg felt Puppetman for the first time that day. "That's crazy," Tony said. "He can't be serious."

"Too damn stupid. It doesn't have a chance of being adopted," John agreed.

Amy shrugged. "It's done. You should see the convention floor—goddamn chaos. Devaughn's going nuts trying to keep things calm with our delegates."

"Barnett's not worried about the floor. It's the outside convention he wants to influence," Gregg told them.

"Sir?"

"The jokers outside the Omni, in Piedmont Park. When they hear the news, they're going to explode. More fodder for his anti-joker rhetoric." Puppetman stirred below at the thought, rising. Gregg pushed him back.

"He'll lose the delegates on the fence. They'll think he's too militant." John again.

Gregg waved a hand. "He's a one-issue candidate: the jokers. He's obsessed."

"The man's not rational."

"*That* only gets said *here*."

A quick laugh skittered around the room. Gregg swung to his feet and tugged his tie into place, running fingers through gray-flecked hair. "Okay. You folks know where to start," he said. "If Barnett's going to start pushing, we have to push right back. Get on the phones. Start using all the influence we have. What we need to do is get all the neutrals out of their corners. We're all agreed that Barnett's course will lead to greater violence out on the streets, to say nothing of the lack of compassion it shows. Tell 'em, pressure 'em, convince 'em. Get all our people doing the same. Amy, you might see if you can set up a meeting with Barnett for me; maybe what he's really after is a compromise. In the meantime, I need to touch base with Ellen and see how she's doing.

"Then I'm going to see if I can do any good outside."

The last words held a strange sense of anticipation, a feeling he hadn't expected. Gregg began to wonder if Puppetman was buried as deeply as he thought.

12:00 NOON

Spector followed the reporter into the men's room. The concourses were crammed with people, and he was sure that the man hadn't noticed he was being tailed. Spector didn't know the reporter's name. He preferred it that way when he was going to kill someone.

The reporter went to the far end of the busy bathroom and took the last stall. Spector walked calmly over to the one that adjoined it and closed the door. He felt sort of bad about this. But the guy had shot off his mouth about how tight security was going to be at the hotel, and how he'd greased a lot of palms to get his room there. These were things Spector hadn't taken into account. He hadn't had time to make any plans. He usually played things by car anyway.

Spector heard the pages of a magazine being turned in the next stall, but no sounds of progress. He leaned down to make sure no one was close enough to see what he was up to. All the pairs of feet were facing toward the mirrors or moving toward the exit. He took a deep breath and slid off the toilet onto his back. He could feel the cold, damp tiles through his suit. Spector grabbed the metal wall between the stalls and hauled himself under.

The reporter folded up his magazine and looked down. He managed to blink a few times before Spector locked in. His death experience rushed unchallenged into the reporter's mind. The man dropped the magazine and keeled over to one side, saliva dribbling from the corner of his mouth. The man's

pants were crumpled around his ankles. Spector fished into
the pockets and pulled out his wallet, then slid back into his
own stall, and up onto the toilet seat. He waited several
moments for some sound indicating he'd been seen. There was
only the incessant noise of shoes on tile and running water,
punctuated by an occasional flush.

Spector flipped open the wallet. Everything he figured
he'd need was there—driver's license, a non-photo press card,
Social Security card. The lack of ID would make it hard for the
cops to identify the corpse. They'd probably figure that some
opportunist lifted the wallet before calling them in. Things
were going better than usual. He stood and flushed the toilet,
then opened the door and walked to the mirror. He lifted his
chin and turned his head side to side. Sharp and cool, he
thought. He winked at the mirror and smiled crookedly. If
everything worked out, he'd be on a plane back to Jersey
tomorrow. And the Democrats would have one less hat in the
ring.

It was as if New York's Jokertown had been turned upside
down and dumped on the Atlanta streets.

Every large city has its small version of a jokertown, but
Atlanta had never witnessed this kind of display. A blinding
sun burned from cloudless blue onto a sea of signs, masks, and
strangely distorted bodies. The crowd—estimated by the
authorities at 15,000—had marched from Piedmont Park and
besieged the Coliseum. Ranks of police and National Guards-
men watched, waiting.

Mid-morning, when it was apparent that the majority
report was not going to be quickly adopted, a bonfire had been
started just down from the Omni. Before the encouraging
cameras, shouting and chanting jokers burned their masks in
the flames. A Flying Ace Glider sailed from the crowd a little
too close to the flames. The styrofoam melted, the wings
turned brown, shrunken and deformed. A joker picked up the
smouldering mess. "Hey, a Fucking Flying Joker!" he shouted.
The rest of the jokers picked up the bitter humor. Gliders all
over the area sailed into the bonfire or were altered by holding
them over Bic lighters.

The Atlanta police unwisely chose that moment to clear
the area. A double line of helmeted officers hit the ranks of
demonstrators. The jokers predictably shoved back: rocks

were thrown, someone's minor ace sent a few police sprawling, and suddenly it was a full-fledged melee. Jokers, reporters, and bystanders were clubbed indiscriminately.

The Turtle appeared late in the fray and bellowed for order. His telekinetic power forcibly pushed apart the remaining jokers and police. Some sixty people were arrested, and though the injuries were largely minor, the shots of bloodied heads were spectacular.

The mood of the demonstrators, already fragile, turned ugly.

A few blocks from the convention site, the jokers re-formed. Fire hydrants were opened by the jokers to abate the day's heat; each time, the police moved in to shut them off again but avoided direct confrontations. Taunts were exchanged across the lines.

A counter demonstration by the KKK arrived downtown in the late morning, producing scattered skirmishes between clansmen and jokers in the streets. If anything, the Klan was more brutal than the police: shots were reported, and jokers were treated for gunshot wounds at the local hospitals. Wildfire rumors spread through the crowd that two jokers had died, that the police were not arresting KKK members and had in fact let them through the barricades.

At noon, word arrived that Leo Barnett was calling for a return to the Exotic Laws. Barnett was crucified in effigy in front of the Omni. The Turtle's shell hovered overhead as if herding the demonstrators, keeping a clear space between jokers and police.

"I don't like it, Senator," Billy Ray told Gregg as they stepped from the limo near the barricades; other secret service men in three-piece suits flanked them. The joker crowd bristled with shouts and curses. "I don't think this is a good idea."

Gregg grimaced, irritated. He gestured harshly at the ace. "And I'm getting tired of people telling me what I should do." Ray's mouth tightened into a hard line with the rebuke. Before Ray could answer, a shadow fell over them and a voice boomed from loudspeakers. "Senator! Hey, you come out to help?"

The noise brought the cameras around. Gregg waved up at the Turtle's shell—the Turtle had a squadron of Turtle-shaped Flying Ace Glider frisbees hovering around him like electrons around a nucleus; a few melted Fucking Flying Jokers were mixed in with the group. "I was hoping we might keep things calm, at least. I know you're doing what you can."

"Yeah. Frisbee tricks. Latest in crowd control." The frisbees began whirling faster, looping in intricate patterns.

"Think you can get me into the crowd?"

"No problem." Frisbees rained on the pavement. The shell dipped gracefully, banking behind the barricades and swiveling so that it faced into the crowd. The loudspeakers hissed as the volume was nudged higher. **"OKAY, MOVE THE BARRICADES ASIDE. MAKE A PATH FOR THE SENATOR OR I'LL HAVE TO MAKE IT FOR HIM. C'MON, PEOPLE!"**

Hovering at head height, the Turtle eased through the barricades and into the jokers like a plow. Gregg stepped forward in his wake. Carnifex, the secret service people, and several of the police followed. Reporters and cameramen jostled for position.

Gregg was recognized immediately. The chant began to rise on either side of the Turtle and his entourage. *"Hart*mann! *Hart*mann!" Gregg smiled, reaching out to brush the hands that stretched toward him from the front ranks. *"Hart*mann! *Hart*mann!" He was beaming, his jacket off and his tie loosened, a patch of sweat darkening his spine: The Candidate At Work. He knew the scene would be featured in all the evening reports.

Inside, he was not so complacent.

The crowd was charged with emotional energy. The current was nearly visible to him, pulsing and surging, and it drew Puppetman like a lure. He could feel the power strengthening, rising, growing. *Let me out*, it told him. *Let me taste.*

There's Gimli, he reminded Puppetman. *Remember '76.*

As if Gregg had spoken an invocation, Gimli's faint voice echoed. *I remember '76, Hartmann. I remember it very well. And I also remember what happened yesterday with Ellen. Tell me, how did you like being the fucking puppet? Go on, let your friend out. I might not stop you this time. Of course, if I did, he might get mad. Maybe Puppetman would walk you around again. The news services would all love that.*

Puppetman snarled at Gimli, but Gregg shivered behind his smile. Puppetman shook the bars of his cage as the jokers' energy shimmered around them. Gregg held the doors shut with an effort.

"*Hart*mann! *Hart*mann!"

He smiled. He nodded. He touched. The temptation to let Puppetman out and ride with him was maddening. In that, Gimli was right—Gregg wanted it too. He wanted it as much as he wanted anything.

The Turtle came to a halt in the middle of International Boulevard near the effigy of Barnett. "Get on, Senator," he said. The shell swayed lower until it was only a foot above the pavement. Gregg stepped up; Billy Ray and the others circled the Turtle.

An enormous shout went up as he climbed the shell. Sensitive despite his burying of Puppetman, he was nearly staggered by the emotional impact of their massed adulation. Gregg slipped and nearly fell; he felt the Turtle lift him with an almost tender push. "Jeez, Senator, I'm sorry. I guess I wasn't thinking—"

Gregg stood on top of the shell. Joker faces peered at him, pressing against the Turtle's telekinetic barrier. The sound of their cheering echoed from the Omni and the WCC, deafening. He shook his head, smiling in the modest, half-shy way that had become the Hartmann trademark during the long campaign. Gregg let the chant go on, feeling the insistent beat hammer at him.

Puppetman rode with it. Though Gregg held him in, he could not keep the power from rising to the surface of his mind. He looked out at the jokers and saw familiar faces among them: Peanut, Flicker, Fartface, Marigold, and the one called Gravemold, who had finally brought down Typhoid Croyd. Puppetman saw them too, and the power slammed hard against the mindbars, growling and tearing.

Gregg trembled with the effort of controlling the ravenous personality, and knew he could not stay out here long. His hold was crumbling under the assault of their emotions.

(Brilliant, undiluted primary colors, swirling all about him. Puppetman could almost touch them and see them sway like tinted smoke . . .)

Gregg raised his hands for silence. "Please!" he shouted, and heard his amplified voice rebound from the buildings around them. "Listen to me. I understand your frustrations. I know four decades of ill treatment and misunderstanding are aching to be released. But this isn't the way. This isn't the time."

It wasn't what they wanted to hear. He felt their distaste and hurried. "Inside that building, we're fighting for jokers' rights." (. . . shouts of encouragement: aching green and knife-edged yellow . . .) "What I'm asking is that you help me in that fight. You have a right to demonstrate. But I tell you that violence in the streets will be used as a tool against you. My opponents will point and they will say: 'You see, jokers are dangerous. We can't trust them. We can't let them live anywhere near us.' Now's the time for all jokers to finally cast off their masks, but you *must* show the world that the face underneath is the face of a friend."

(. . . the shaded currents turning muddy brown with confusion and uncertainty. The brightness dimmed . . .)

With me, you could do it. Easily. Puppetman mocked him. *Look out there. Together, we could turn this around. We could end the demonstration. You'd walk away a hero. Just let me out.*

Gregg was losing them. Even without Puppetman's direct link, he knew that. Gregg Hartmann was suddenly saying the same words they'd heard all along from everyone else. There was no magic anymore. No Puppetman.

(. . . shifting to a dark, somber violet: a dangerous hue, a feeding color. Puppetman screamed . . .)

Gregg had to leave. The emotions, like a storm-tossed tide battering the shore, eroded the tenuous hold on his power. Puppetman would leap out.

He had to end it. Had to get away from the feast spread before his power.

"I'm asking—begging—you to help those who are down there on the floor. Please. Don't let anger ruin it all."

It was a horrible, abrupt ending; Gregg knew it. The crowd stared at him, silent. A few tried to begin the chant again, but it died quickly. "Get me down," Gregg whispered. The Turtle lifted him slightly and lowered him to the concrete. "Let's get out of here," Gregg said. "I've done all I can do."

Puppetman clawed at Gregg in desperation, lashing out in his mind like a mad animal. The Turtle backed slowly through the crowd toward the waiting limo. Gregg followed, frowning.

He saw and heard nothing of what was in front of him. It took all of his concentration simply to hold Puppetman in.

1:00 P.M.

He'd been in the cab for more than an hour. Traffic was snarled almost as soon as they left the airport. Cars were jammed bumper to bumper, horns blaring, all the way into downtown. Pedestrians, mostly jokers, were massed in the streets. Some wore masks. Some carried signs. All were in a dangerously surly mood. More than once they had rocked the cab as it cruised slowly through them. Spector had given the driver an extra c-note to get him within a block of the hotel. Judging by the grumbling from the front seat, the cabbie was having second thoughts in spite of the money.

The driver's license had been easy. He'd doctored them before. After removing the lamination, he'd carefully razored out the reporter's photo and replaced it with one of his own. Then he'd used a laminating machine at the airport to finish the job. The reporter, his name had been Herbert Baird, was close to the same height, weight, and age as Spector. Right now, though, getting caught with fake ID was the least of his worries. Spector just wanted to get to the Marriott in one piece.

A joker with huge folds of wrinkled, pink skin jumped onto the hood and waved a sign that said "NATS ARE RATS" on one side and "WHAT ABOUT US?" on the other. There was chanting up ahead. Spector couldn't make out what they were saying.

"Far as we go, mister," said the cabbie. "I ain't playing joker-bait for a hundred dollars or a hundred thousand."

"How far to the hotel?" Spector had his luggage in the back seat with him. He'd figured it would be a mess downtown, and he didn't want to spend any more time than absolutely necessary picking through a crowd of pissed-off jokers.

"About two blocks straight ahead." The driver looked around nervously as one of the taillights was kicked in. "I'd move it if I were you."

"Right." Spector opened the car door carefully and stepped out onto the crowded sidewalk. Some of the jokers made faces at him or raised their fists, but most didn't give him any trouble. He moved forward slowly, unhappily aware that his new suit and luggage would make him conspicuous, and a likely target.

After about ten minutes of pushing and shoving, the hotel was just across the street. Spector was covered in sweat and starting to smell like the freaks around him. A joker with needle-like fingernails stepped in front of him and took a swipe at his suitcase, shredding one side. Spector caught his eye and fed him just enough death-pain to make the joker collapse. He didn't want to risk stirring up this mob with a killing. Hot as it was, these bimbos wouldn't think twice about someone passing out.

The crowd was beginning to break up, doubtless to re-form somewhere else, as he stepped into the hotel lobby. It was open all the way to the roof. The building's curves reminded him of the inside of something dead. Spector took a breath of cool air and walked over to the security area. *Herbert Baird, you're Herbert Baird, Herbert Baird*, he thought.

There were several uniformed cops and suited men with earpieces waiting for him. "Identification, please," said one of the cops.

Spector pulled out his wallet, trying consciously to relax, and handed over the driver's license. The cop took it and passed it over to a man sitting at a computer terminal. The man typed for an instant, his fingers blurring on the keys, then paused, and finally nodded.

"Can I have your luggage, Mr. Baird?" The officer looked at the claw marks on the side. "A bit rough out there, eh?"

"Plenty more than what I'm used to." Spector smiled. They were bored and not paying much attention to him. He was going to get in.

The officer set the suitcase onto the x-ray machine and pointed to a metal detector. "If you'll please walk through, sir."

As he stepped under, the metal detector's alarm beeped. Spector stopped dead and reached slowly into his pocket. He could feel at least twenty people staring at him. He pulled out a fistful of change and handed it to the cop. He'd needed it for the laminating machine. "Mind if I try again?"

The cop motioned him forward with a slow sweep of his hand. Spector stepped through noiselessly and sighed. The officer reached around and handed him his change. Spector pocketed it and smiled again.

"Your bag's right there." The cop pointed and then turned back to the hotel entrance.

Spector picked up his suitcase; it was heavy and almost

slipped out of his sweaty palm. He walked slowly across the lobby to the registration desk. There weren't many suits that didn't have bulges under them. Getting his room took longer than it should have. The clerk was a fat officious prick who gave him the fish-eye when he said he'd be paying in cash. The little creep was trying to impress the Secret Service boys or something equally stupid. It was probably his once-in-a-lifetime chance to be a big cheese. Spector would come back some day and drop the guy. He snatched the key when the clerk finally offered it, and headed quickly for the elevators.

He was almost there when he heard someone call out. "James. James Spector. Hey, Specs." The voice sounded familiar, but that wasn't necessarily good. He turned around slowly. The man walked up to him smiling and held out a hand. He wore an ash-gray suit and had carefully styled hair. He was a couple of inches shorter than Spector, but much more muscular.

"Tony C." He let out a breath and relaxed his shoulders. "No way this is happening." He and Calderone had grown up together in Teaneck, but Spector had lost track of him years ago.

Tony reached down, grabbed Spector's hand, and gave it a firm shake. "My main man. The pick-and-roll prince. What are you doing here?"

"Uh, lobbying." Spector coughed. "What about you?"

"I work for Hartmann," Tony replied. Spector opened his mouth; shut it quickly. "Hard to believe, I know. But I'm his top speech consultant." He rubbed his palms together. "I always did have a good line."

"Especially for the girls." Spector shuffled uncomfortably. Apparently, none of the cops who'd checked his ID card had heard Tony, but he still felt exposed. "Look, it's great to see you, but I'd like to get settled in. It's a real zoo outside, I tell you."

"If you think it's a zoo out there, you should see what's going on inside." Tony slapped Spector on the shoulder. There was real warmth in the gesture, the kind Spector hadn't been exposed to in years. "What's your room number?"

Spector held up his key card. "1031."

"1031. Got it. I want to have dinner while you're down here. We've got plenty to go over." Tony shrugged. "I don't even know what you've been doing since high school."

"Fine. I've got plenty of time to kill while I'm down here," Spector said. The elevator pinged behind them. Tony backed away and waved. "See you later." Spector tried to sound like he didn't dread the idea. This was turning out to be weirder than Freakers on New Year's Eve.

Hiram was hosting a reception in his suite at the Marriott. Gregg was supposed to put in an appearance, so the rooms were packed with New York delegates and their families. Most of the suites Tachyon had entered stank of cigarettes and old pizza. This one stank of cigarettes, but the trays dotted strategically through the rooms held tiny quiches and piroshki. Tach snagged one, and the flaky pastry exploded in his mouth, followed quickly by the rich flavor of its mushroom filling.

Brushing crumbs from his fingertips and the lapels of his coat, Tach reached up and patted Hiram on the shoulder. The big ace was dressed with his usual flair, but circles hung like bloated bruises beneath his eyes, and his skin had the unhealthy look of moist dough.

"Don't tell me you had time to slip down to the kitchens and cook all this," teased Tachyon.

"No, but my recipes . . ."

"I suspected as much." Tach bent and flicked a crumb from the top of his patent leather pump with the edge of his handkerchief. When he straightened, he had gathered his courage. "Hiram, are you all right?"

The word exploded in a sharp puff. "*Why*?"

"You look unwell. Come to my room later, and I'll check you over."

"*No*. Thank you, but no. I'm fine. Just tired." A smile creased the broad face as if it had been abruptly painted on by a cartoon animator.

Tachyon expelled a pent-up breath, shook his head as he watched Hiram bustle away to greet Senator Daniel Moynihan. The alien circulated, smiling, shaking hands—it still struck him as an odd custom even after all these years. On Takis there were two extremes: limited contact because between telepaths casual touching was repugnant; or between close friends and relatives the full embrace. Either choice caused problems on Earth. The light touch seemed snobby, and the full embrace raised homophobic reactions in the males of this planet. So Tachyon mused, and watched his gloved hand being swallowed again and again by the eager clasping fingers of the humans who engulfed him.

On a sofa set beneath one of the windows a man sat surrounded by three laughing women. The youngest sat on his knee. Behind him her sister leaned in, and twined her arms about his neck. Next to him on the sofa was a pretty gray-haired woman. Her dark eyes were affectionate as they rested on his face. There was a warmth in the scene that seemed to touch the emptiness that Tachyon felt in his own life.

"Come on, Daddy," pleaded the youngest. "Just one little speech." Her voice altered slightly, gaining in sonority and depth. "What is it that you would impart to me? If it be aught toward the general good, set honor in one eye, and death i'th'other, and I will look on both indifferently; for, let the gods so speed me as I love the name of honor more than I fear death."

"No, no, no." The man punctuated each word with a shake of the head.

"Julius Caesar might not be the best choice for a political convention," said Tachyon softly. Four sets of dark eyes regarded him; then the man lowered his gaze and his fingers combed nervously through his gray-shot beard. "Pardon my intrusion, but I could not help overhearing. I am Tachyon."

"We sort of guessed," said the girl behind the sofa. She surveyed the Takisian's brilliant outfit of green and pink, and tossed a droll look to her sister.

"Josh Davidson." The man indicated the woman beside him. "My wife, Rebecca, and my daughters, Sheila and Edie."

"Charmed." Tachyon brushed his lips across the back of three hands.

Edie chuckled, her gaze flickering between her father and sister. Emotions swirled about the little party. There was something just beneath the surface that Tachyon was missing, but deliberately missing. People had their secrets, and just because Tachyon could read them didn't mean he had the right. Another lesson learned after forty years on Earth was the necessity of filtering. The cacophony of untrained human minds would soon have driven him mad if he hadn't lived huddled behind his shields.

"Now I recognize you," said Tachyon. "You were brilliant last winter in *Doll's House*."

"Thank you."

"Are you a delegate?"

"Oh, god, no." The woman laughed. "No, my daughter, Sheila, is our representation."

"Daddy's a bit of a cynic where politics are concerned," said the older sister. "We were lucky to get him down here at all."

"Keeping an eye on you, young lady."

"He thinks I'm still ten," she confided with a wink to the Takisian.

"A prerogative of fathers." Davidson was staring so intently up at him that Tachyon wondered if this particular father was also sending him a warning—*touch my daughters and lose your nuts*. For his own amusement Tach decided to push it. He turned his blazing smile on the lovely Davidson daughters. "Perhaps I might buy the ladies Davidson lunch tomorrow?"

"Sir," said Sheila severely, but her eyes were dancing. "Your reputation precedes you."

Tach laid a hand over his heart, and faltered, "Oh, my fame, my lamentable fame."

"You love it," said Davidson, and there was a funny faraway expression in his expressive eyes.

"A condition that we perhaps share, Mr. Davidson?"

"No, oh, no, I think not."

There were polite murmurs all around, and Tach moved on. He felt eyes boring into the middle of his back, but didn't look back. It wouldn't do to encourage either of those lovely girls. He was only doomed to disappoint them.

5:00 P.M.

Gregg had taken most of the other candidates for puppets as a matter of course. It was easy enough. All Gregg needed was to touch them for a few seconds. A lingering handshake was enough, long enough for Puppetman to cross the bridge of the touch and crawl into the other person's mind, there to prowl in the caverns of hidden desires and emotions, bringing all the filth to life.

Once the link was established, Gregg no longer needed the physical contact. As long as the puppet was within a few hundred yards, Puppetman could make the leap mentally. Gregg artfully used Puppetman during the campaign to make the other candidates stumble over a question or seem too forceful and blunt in stating their positions. He'd done that until Gimli had started interfering late in the primaries and Puppetman became too erratic and dangerous to use.

Even though he'd had the opportunity, he'd left Jesse Jackson alone. The reverend was charismatic and forceful, a powerful speaker. Gregg even admired the reverend; certainly no one else in the campaign was so unabashedly straightforward, so unafraid of making bold statements. Jackson was an idealist, not a pragmatist like the rest. That was one strike against him.

And Gregg knew from experience that prejudice was also real, that it was easy for the average person to mouth sympathy but not to act on it.

The joker prejudice was real. The black prejudice was real. With or without Puppetman, Jackson would not become president even if he managed to get the nomination.

Not this year. Not yet.

It was something Gregg dared not say in public, but he also knew that Jackson was well aware of the fact, no matter what the man might say. So Gregg had let Jackson go his own way. In a way, it had made for a more interesting primary campaign.

Now, with Puppetman wailing inside and far too unreliable to let loose again, Gregg was forced to admit that it might have been a mistake. It would have made things much easier now.

The Reverend Jackson sat across the room from Gregg in a voluminous leather armchair, his legs crossed over impeccably pressed black pants, his expensive silk tie knotted tightly around his throat. Around the Jackson campaign suite, his aides pretended not to watch. Two of Jackson's sons flanked the reverend on wooden chairs.

"Barnett is making a mockery of the Joker's Rights plank," Gregg was saying. "He's diluting the impact by dragging in every special interest group he can think of. The trouble is that alone, I can't stop him."

Jackson pursed his lips, tapped them with a forefinger. "You come asking for my help now, Senator, but once the platform fight is over, it will be business as usual. As much as I disagree with the Reverend Barnett on basic issues, I understand the political reality. The Joker's Rights plank is your child, Senator. Without that plank's passage, you'll hardly appear to be a very effective leader for the country. After all, it's your own fundamental issue and you can't even make your own party listen."

Jackson looked almost pleased at the prospect.

I can take care of that. Just let me out . . . Puppetman was angry, irritated. The power pushed at its restraints, wanting to lash out at the self-confident Jackson.

Leave me alone. Just for a few minutes. Let me get through this.

Gregg shoved the power back down, leaning back in his seat to cover the momentary inner conflict. Jackson was watching him, very carefully, very intently. The man had a predator's eyes, mesmerizing and dangerous. Gregg could feel sweat starting on his brow, and he knew Jackson noticed it as well.

"I'm not concerned with the nomination at the moment," Gregg said, ignoring Puppetman. "I'm concerned with helping the jokers, who have experienced the same prejudice as your own people."

Jackson nodded. An aide brought a tray over to the coffee table between them. "Iced tea? No? Very well." Jackson took a sip from his own glass and set it down again. Gregg could see the man thinking, gauging, wondering.

And with me you could truly know. You could control those feelings . . .

Be quiet.

You need me, Greggie. You do.

Intent on keeping Puppetman down, he missed the next few words. ". . . rumor is that you've been pushing your people very hard, Senator. You have even angered some of them. I've heard tales about instability, about a repeat of '76."

Gregg flushed, started to retort heatedly, and then realized he was being goaded. This was exactly the reaction Jackson was trying to provoke. He forced himself to smile. "We're all used to a certain amount of mudslinging, Reverend. And yes, I've been pushing hard. I always push when I believe in something strongly."

"And the accusation makes you angry." Jackson smiled and waved a hand. "Oh, I know the feeling, Senator. In fact, I have the very same reaction when people question my work for civil rights. I'd expect it." He steepled his hands under his chin and leaned forward, elbows on knees. "Just what is it you want, Senator?"

"A Joker's Rights plank. Nothing more."

"And how do you propose to buy my support?"

"I had hoped you would agree purely for the sake of the jokers. On humanitarian grounds."

"I feel deeply for the jokers, believe me, Senator. But I also know that a plank in a platform is just so many words. A platform commits no one to anything. I will fight for the rights of all oppressed people, with or without planks. I did not promise my people planks. I promised them I would do my best to win at this convention, and I am doing just that. I do not *need* a plank; you do."

Jackson reached for the glass again. He sipped, waiting and watching.

"All right," Gregg said at last. "I've talked with deVaughn and Logan on this. If you keep your delegates in line, we'll release our Alabama delegates after the first vote with the strong recommendation they go to you."

"Alabama isn't important to you. You took, what, 10% of the delegates there?"

"That 10% could be yours. You were second to Barnett in Alabama. More importantly, it might indicate that momentum in the South was moving away from Barnett, which would benefit you."

"And you, as well," Jackson pointed out. He shrugged. "I was also second in Mississippi."

Son of a bitch. "I'll have to confirm this, but I can probably release my delegates there as well."

Jackson paused. He looked over at his sons, then back to Gregg. "I need to think about this," he said.

You're letting it slip away, damn it! He's only going to ask for more. I could have made him agree without any concessions. You're a fool, Greggie.

"We don't have time," Gregg said sharply. He regretted the words instantly. Jackson's eyes narrowed, and Gregg hurried to smooth over the gaffe. "I'm sorry, Reverend. It's just . . . it's just that to the jokers out there, the platform *isn't* words. The plank will be a symbol for them, a symbol that their voices have been heard. We all stand to gain, all of us who support them."

"Senator, you have a fine humanitarian record. But . . ."

Let me have him . . . ! "Reverend, sometimes my passion gets out of hand. Again, I apologize."

Jackson still frowned, but the anger was gone from his eyes.

You almost blew it.

Shut up. It was your interference. Let me handle it.

You have to let me out. Soon.

Soon. I promise. Just be quiet.

"All right," the Reverend was saying. "I think I can arrange things with my people. Senator, you have my support."

Jackson held out his hand. Gregg could feel his fingers trembling as he took it. *Mine! Mine!* The power shuddered inside, screaming and clawing and throwing itself at the bars. It took all Gregg's effort to hold Puppetman back as he shook hands with Jackson, and he broke the contact quickly.

"Senator, are you all right?"

Gregg smiled wanly at Jackson. "I'm fine," he said. "Thank you, Reverend. Just a little bit hungry, that's all."

6:00 P.M.

"Where I was raised, a person does not seat themselves uninvited at another person's table."

Tachyon shuffled through the seven pink message slips—all from Hiram—and thrust them into a pocket. "Where you were raised, a person also does not fail to acknowledge and thank another person for a gift. I know, I was there when you first learned to lisp out *tank-oo* when I would bring you candy."

The fury flaming in Fleur's brown eyes was so intense that Tachyon flinched, and half raised a hand in defense.

"Leave me *alone!*"

"I cannot."

"Why?" She wrung her hands, the fingers twisting desperately through one another. "Why are you torturing me? Wasn't killing my mother enough?"

"In all fairness, I think your father and I must share the blame. I broke her mind, but he allowed her to be tortured in that sanatorium. If he had left her with me, I might have found a way to repair the broken shards."

"If that was the choice, then I'm glad she died. Better that than being your whore."

"Your mother was *never* a whore. You dishonor her and yourself by that remark. You can't really feel that way."

"Well, I do, and why should I feel any differently? I never knew her. *You* saw to that."

"*I* didn't throw her out of the house."

"She could have gone to her parents."

"She *loved* me."

"I can't imagine why."

"Give me a chance, I could show you."

And as soon as the glib, flirtatious comment passed his lips Tachyon knew he had done a very stupid thing. As if to hold back the words, he pressed his fingers to his lips, but it was too late. Far, far too late.

Forty years too late?

Fleur rose from her chair like a wrathful goddess, and dealt him a ringing slap. Her nail caught on his lower lip, splitting it, and he tasted the sharp, coppery taste of blood. All conversation ceased in Pompano's. The silence made his skin crawl, and Tachyon chewed down the humiliation that filled his mouth like a foul taste. The *tick* of her high heels, as she stormed from the restaurant, beat into his ringing head.

Carefully, he held up two fingers before his face. Counted them. Dabbed at the cup with her discarded napkin. It smelled faintly of her perfume. His jaw tightened into a stubborn line.

8:00 P.M.

"Muscular dystrophy. Is it up or down on MS, Charles?"

"Christ!" Devaughn's voice, roaring through Jack's cellular phone, seemed more surly than ever. "I guess we can't be against Jerry's Kids, can we?"

The convention band staggered into the last bars of "Mame." Louis Armstrong could have played it better in his sleep. Jack was on the convention floor, standing on a scarred, gray folding chair, surrounded by his throng of Californians.

"Up or down, Charles?" Jack demanded.

"Up. Shit. Up." Jack could clearly hear deVaughn's fist banging on a desktop. "Shit-shit-shit. Shit-fuck-cunt. That bitch. That fucking WASP slut."

"I want to wring Fleur van Renssaeler's neck."

"You'll have to stand in line behind *me*, buddy."

"They're calling the vote." Emil Rodriguez tugged on Jack's sleeve. Jack hung up his portable phone and gave the thumbs-up sign to his horde of delegates. He tried to picture thousands of Americans in wheelchairs and leg braces cheering and reshuffling their political alignment, but his imagination failed.

Rodriguez, a short, bull-chested man, looked up at Jack with fury in his eyes.

"This sucks, man," he spat.

Jack got down from the chair and lit up a smoke. "You said it, *ese*."

Jim Wright gaveled for order. Jack looked at the dissolving huddles of delegates and considered the chaos that had descended on Atlanta today. The violent demonstrations, the platform fight, Sara Moregenstern's bizarre interruption of the press conference that morning.

Secret ace? he thought.

And then he thought, *Which one*?

For hours the convention had been tearing itself to bits over the Joker's Rights plank. The platform committee had passed it with a strong dissent from Barnett's crowd: Barnett had moved the issue onto the floor while no one was looking, and then the sweaty brawl started in earnest. Barnett's people stood united against the plank, Hartmann for, and Jackson made a principled stand with Hartmann. The others had just tried to delay things till they could work out how much mileage they could get out of declaring one way or another. The thing might have breezed through if it hadn't been for the violence surrounding the joker camp that afternoon; the middle-of-the-road candidates hung on for as long as possible, wondering if there was going to be an anti-joker backlash, but eventually the delegates began sideling toward the Hartmann point of view.

It was then that the Barnett campaign made their master stroke. Since they realized they couldn't stop the plank from passing, they began their attempts to dilute it.

Why should the party be only in favor of *Joker's* Rights, they asked. Shouldn't the party declare in favor of the rights of people with other handicaps?

Soon there was an up-or-down vote on whether victims of multiple sclerosis should be included in the civil rights plank. While Hartmann's managers, knowing perfectly well they were being sandbagged, cursed and threw furniture, the motion passed unanimously: no Democrat was going to be caught dead opposing people with an incurable illness.

Other diseases followed: amyotrophic lateral sclerosis, guillain-barre syndrome, spina bifida, post-polio syndrome—the vote on that one was close, mainly because no one had ever heard of it—and now Jerry's Kids. Barnett was succeeding in making the whole Joker's Rights issue look ridiculous.

Barnett's delegate head from Texas, a blue-haired woman in a white cowboy hat, red lacquered boots, and a matching red skirt and vest with a swaying white Buffalo Bob fringe, was on her feet making another motion. Jack told his phone to dial HQ and climbed on his chair again.

"Jesus Christ," said Rodriguez. "It's AIDS."

A panicked yelp went up from the convention. Barnett had made his master stroke. The eyes of every viewer panicked by retrovirus homophobic hysteria would be glued to the set, ready to see if the Democrats would endorse the pollution of their bodily fluids by lurking sodomites and junkies drooling contamination from every orifice. Furthermore, Barnett had convincingly linked AIDS with xenovirus Takis-A.

"Up or down, Charles?" Jack asked wearily.

"Fuck the queers!" Devaughn raged. "The hell with this!"

Jack grinned and gave his people the thumbs-down.

The retrovirus lost in a landslide. The convention had had enough of Barnett's tactics. The distractions had provided amusement for a while, and had succeeded in their principle duty of making Hartmann's convictions look silly, but now they were getting tiresome.

The Texas lady received instructions from on high and called for no more votes. Hartmann's people quietly moved that all other persons suffering from diseases were to be included in the civil rights plank. The motion passed unanimously.

The platform was moved and passed. Jim Wright gaveled the long day to a weary end. Hats and signs and flying ace gliders soared into the air from thankful delegates.

Jack told his delegates to be ready bright and early the next morning. By the end of Wednesday there were going to be at least two ballots, and they would say a lot about where the convention was headed.

He lit another Camel and watched the thousands of delegates funneling out the exits. The band serenaded their retreat with "Don't Cry for Me, Argentina."

For once Jack didn't react to the hated song. He was thinking about a secret ace.

9:00 P.M.

Billy Ray called Gregg from the Marriott's lobby. "Senator, you still interested in meeting with Barnett? Lady Black just told me he's on his way back to the hotel from a meeting."

It had been a horrible day. The afternoon and evening were worse than the morning. Amy, John, and finally deVaughn had tried vainly to arrange a conference with Barnett. They'd gotten as far as Fleur, who told them flatly that Barnett wasn't interested in speaking with Gregg. The struggle on the floor had reflected that uncooperative attitude.

Either Barnett or Fleur van Renssaeler had turned out to be a savvy political strategist. It had taken all of Gregg's influence to keep any kind of Joker's Rights plank in the platform at all, and without the support of Jackson, it would have been impossible. The plank finally adopted was a toothless, emasculated version of the original, fettered with conditions and clouded language. The kindest thing that could be said of it was that it *was* a Joker's Rights plank, the first. The networks might call it a "minor triumph" for Hartmann and the jokers; the angry crowds out in the streets knew it meant nothing.

With the platform set, the reasons for meeting Barnett were gone. *All but one.* The interior voice was emphatic. *Do it.*

"Senator? If we just happen to be in the hall or something when he—"

Worst of all, he'd had to deal with Puppetman's increasing desperation since the incident outside. He'd tried, but had never managed to submerge the power again. Puppetman was there, alongside him.

People were noticing. Jackson certainly had. Ellen was staring at him when she thought he wasn't looking; Amy, Braun, deVaughn all were handling him with obvious kid gloves. If he wanted this nomination, he had to do something about Puppetman. He couldn't afford to have his attention divided so strongly.

"Thanks, Billy. It sounds good. We have a few minutes? I'd like to freshen up."

"Sure. I'll be up to get you."

Gregg hung up and went into the bathroom. He stared at the mirror. "You're out of control," he whispered. Gimli's cold amusement answered him.

The day's efforts had cost him—the image that gazed back at him looked exhausted. *Barnett's for me,* Puppetman insisted again, and Gregg almost expected to see his lips move with the words. *Once we take him as a puppet, we can maneuver him the way we did Gephardt and Babbit. Just a nudge here and there . . .*

We were going to try that before, at one of the debates, Gregg reminded him. *He always stayed away from us, never let us shake his hand or touch him at all. This is crazy.*

Puppetman scoffed. *This time he will. You have to trust me. You can't win without my help.*

But Gimli—

We must try. If you stop fighting me, we can do it.

All right. All right.

Billy Ray insisted on talking for the few minutes it took to go down to Barnett's floor. Gregg let the monologue run unabated; he heard nothing of it. When the elevator doors opened, Ray stepped out, flashing his ID, to speak with the guards posted there. Gregg went to the edge of the balcony and stared down at the glittering lobby. A glider had landed on the carpet beside him: Mistral. He picked the toy up and gave it a gentle toss. It looped and then settled into a steady descent. Someone a few floors down saw it and gave a boozy cheer.

Five minutes later, an elevator chimed. Gregg turned to see Lady Black step out, followed by Fleur and Leo Barnett. Gregg put on a smile and strode forward. "Reverend Barnett, you're very well protected by your staff."

Lady Black had stepped aside, but Fleur remained between Gregg and Barnett, scowling and giving Gregg no choice but to stop or run into her. He moved to one side and held out his hand to Barnett.

Puppetman hunched, ready to leap.

Barnett was bluffly handsome, a fair-haired vision of the

Southern preacher. A faint smile lurked in his full lips, and the soft twang of his origins inhabited his resonant voice. "Senator Hartmann, I'm sorry. Sometimes my staff seems to think I need their protection as well as the Lord's. You understand." He looked at the proffered hand, and that faint smile crossed his mouth again. "And I'd gladly shake your hand, Senator, but unfortunately mine's rather sore at the moment. A little mishap downstairs in the lobby."

Puppetman cursed. Gregg pulled his hand back.

"Tell him that it was a joker, Reverend," Fleur snapped coldly. "Tell him how you shook the sinner's hand and how he tried to crush it. I still think you should go to the hospital. A fracture—"

"It's only a bruise, sister. Please . . ." Barnett smiled at Gregg as if sharing some private joke. "I'm sure the Senator has had similar experiences. Handshaking's the bane of politicians."

"That it is," Gregg said. He was so damned tired of smiling. He nodded to the stonefaced Fleur. "And I'm especially sorry it was a joker."

"A joker with one of *your* campaign buttons," Fleur sniffed.

"Which my people, like yours, give out by the thousands," Gregg countered, a little too sharply. He turned to Barnett. "There are enough misunderstandings already. I wanted to give you and your staff my congratulations on a hard fight over the platform, and to say that I'm glad we could finally come to a compromise."

That made Barnett's lips twitch, and Gregg knew he'd touched a nerve. "*I* did not agree to the modified plank," Barnett said. "There were, well, weak-hearted souls among my delegates who saw fit to accept it over my protest. It was a mistake, and—I must confess my own vanity—I'm sick over it. But the Lord also makes use of defeats, Senator. He's shown me that I was wrong trying to play these political games. I'm finding that this convention is hardly the place for someone like me."

For a moment, Gregg felt an uplift of optimism. If Barnett were to withdraw his nomination, even if he instructed his delegates to vote for Dukakis or Jackson . . . But Barnett was smiling again, taking out the well-worn Bible stuffed in his suit jacket's pocket and patting its gilded covers. "I am a man of God, Senator. For the remainder of this convention, I intend to do what I know best: I will pray. I will lock the doors of this world and open the doors of my soul."

Gregg's face must have shown his confusion. "Today was hardly a defeat for you, Reverend, and hardly a victory for me. I'd like to work with you to make a new path, one both we and our party can follow. Isolating yourself isn't the answer."

Barnett nodded seriously, as if weighing Gregg's argument in his mind. "It might be that you're right, Senator. If so, then I have to trust that God·will make it known to me. Still, I fully expect to spend the rest of this convention in prayer and not in playing the convention power games. Fleur's well-equipped to handle all that for the time being. I'm a stubborn fool sometimes. I don't really believe in compromise, I've no delusion that there is more than one right path.' The God I know and the God I've seen in the Bible doesn't compromise. God never came to 'understandings,' God never made 'concessions to political realities.'" Barnett glanced at Gregg, concern lining his high forehead. "I don't mean to offend you, Senator, but I have to say what I believe."

"Yet I believe in the very same God, Reverend. We're only men, not God Himself. We do the best we can; we're not enemies. It's human pride that keeps us apart. The least we can do as leaders is shake hands and try to resolve our differences." Gregg lathed his words with earnest conviction. "For the good of all. That would seem to be a truly Christian act." Gregg gave a bluff, self-deprecating chuckle and put out his hand once more. "I promise not to squeeze."

Puppetman quivered in anticipation. For a moment, he was certain that it had worked. Barnett hesitated, rocking on his toes. Then the preacher thoughtfully clasped his hands together around his Bible.

"The act I'd like to see us share, Senator, is prayer. Let me make an invitation to you. Join me in my vigil. Let's leave the politics to the delegates and kneel together for the next several days."

"Reverend . . ." Gregg began. He shook his head. *Why? Why does he avoid us every time?*

Barnett nodded, almost sadly. "I thought not," he said. "We walk very different paths, Senator." He began walking toward his room, clutching the Bible in his right hand.

Gregg let his hand drop to his side. "You don't shake

hands with enemies, Reverend?" Gregg's voice was harsh, tinged with Puppetman's vitriol. Fleur, following behind Barnett, flushed angrily. Barnett simply favored Gregg with another of his sorrowful, secretive smiles.

"People expect Biblical quotes from a man of God, Senator," he said. "It's not surprising, since the Bible often has just the right word for the occasion. One comes to mind now, from 1 Timothy: 'The Spirit distinctly says that in later times some will turn away from the faith and will heed deceitful spirits and things taught by demons through plausible liars— men with seared consciences.' Now that's a bit of hyperbole, Senator, but I think that—unbeknownst, perhaps—a demon taints your words. We're not enemies, Senator. At least I don't think so. And even if we were, I'd still pray that you'd come into the light and cleanse yourself. There's always hope for redemption. Always."

Barnett gave Gregg an unblinking, long stare. There was a distinct click as he turned the deadbolt behind him.

The brandy kept hitting the cut on his lip, and each time it drew a yelp. And a smirk from the bartender. Tachyon considered telling her to fuck off; then he realized what a picture he must present. The mark of Sara's nails from last night's fiasco lay like red furrows dug in the white skin of his cheek. His lower lip was split and slightly swollen from Fleur's nail. What a singularly unsuccessful lothario he was. No wonder the young woman behind the bar smirked. Women. They always stuck together.

"Hi. Mind if I join you?"

Josh Davidson slid onto the stool next to him. Tach turned to greet him with genuine pleasure. "No, not at all."

"When a man sits huddled on a stool at a bar, it generally means he wants to be alone, but I thought I'd take a chance."

"I'm glad you did. Buy you a drink?"

"Sure."

An awkward silence fell between the two men, punctuated only by Davidson's order. Suddenly they shifted to face one another, and both said in chorus,

"I've admired—"

"I've always admired you—"

They laughed, and Tachyon said, "Well, isn't that convenient? We obviously have good taste." Tach paused and sipped brandy. "Why are you down here?"

Davidson shrugged. "Curiosity."

"About what?"

"The political process. Can a man make a difference?"

"Oh, yes, I'm convinced of it."

"But you come from a culture that puts a premium on individual effort," said Davidson, rolling his glass between his palms.

"I take it you don't agree?"

"I don't know. It seems a questionable proposition to allow one man's vision, opinion, to shape policy."

"But in this political system it never happens. Even in my aristocratic culture the absolute despot is a fantasy. There are always competing interests."

"Yes, so how do you choose between them?"

Frowning, Tachyon said, "You make the decision."

"That sounds so easy. But what right do you have to substitute your judgment for . . . for . . ."

"The will of the people?" suggested the Takisian.

"Yes."

Tachyon steepled his fingers before his mouth, threw back his head and regarded the wine glasses hanging like crystal stalactites from their rack. "A representative owes the People not only his industry, but his judgment, and he betrays them if he sacrifices it to their opinion . . . Edmund Burke."

Davidson's laughter was sharp and clear. Tachyon stiffened. "Doctor, you astound me."

Tachyon didn't reply. He knew he astounded people. He had astounded people since the moment of his arrival on this planet. *August 23, 1946*. Ideal, where had the time gone? Forty-two years. He had lived almost as long on this world as on his own. *Home.*

"Hello? Where are you?" Dark, thoughtful eyes, soft with concern.

"On a world that doesn't exist for me anymore." Homesickness lay like a jagged lump in the back of Tach's throat.

So minutes, hours, days, weeks, months, and years,
Passed over to the end they were created,
Would bring white hairs unto a quiet grave.
Ah, what a life were this! how sweet! how lovely!

Gives not the hawthorn bush a sweeter shade
To shepherds, looking on their silly sheep,
Than doth a rich embroidered canopy
To kings that fear their subjects' treachery?"

The men's eyes locked. "Doesn't that describe Takis?" asked Davidson softly.

"And Earth. Treachery may be the one constant in an inconstant universe." Tach rose abruptly. "Pray excuse me. You were right, I do need to be alone."

11:00 P.M.

The day had been a total washout. Spector sprawled on the bed, two pillows propping him up. He had the TV remote control in one hand and a bottle of whiskey in the other. It was his bedtime ritual, and helped him feel less out of place.

He wasn't going to get to Hartmann in this building, not unless he was lucky beyond belief. And he'd used up his luck in getting this far. He didn't have access to the areas of the hotel that Hartmann would be in, except during press conferences. And he'd noticed that politicians rarely looked you in the eye unless you asked them a question. He wasn't dumb enough to draw that kind of attention to himself.

He sipped at his drink and played channel roulette. Atlanta had gotten pounded again, this time by the Cardinals. The news was full of political bullshit, of course. Was Hartmann porking this stupid reporter bitch? Did Leo Barnett really think God spoke to him? Spector wished he'd gotten contracts to kill them all. Politicians were mostly people who'd had too little morals and ethics to stay lawyers.

He'd eventually settled on an old movie. It was a period piece, set in France during the revolution. There was a guy in it who talked like Odie Cologne from the King Leonardo cartoons. Spector thought the actor had a double role, but hadn't been paying close enough attention to be sure. None of the colors looked like anything that occurred in nature. Just pastels that blurred and bled into each other anytime someone moved. Ted Turner's movies looked about as good as his baseball team.

It had been weird running into Tony, even weirder finding out that he was a honcho for Hartmann. Tony was a good guy and Spector liked him, but he'd always been something of a bleeding heart.

The actor was in deep shit now, headed for the guillotine. He didn't seem particularly upset about it. Spector would have gone kicking and screaming. He knew what it was like to die.

He could use Tony to get at Hartmann, if there was no other way. Spector had always prided himself on the fact that he never fucked over his friends. He'd never had many, so it wasn't that hard to do. But the job came first.

The actor had just sent a little blonde number up to the big blade with a kiss and now it was his turn. "It's a far, far better thing I do, than I have ever done before. It's a far, far better rest I go to, than I have ever known." The actor stood before the guillotine, noble, unafraid. Naturally, the camera pans up so nobody can see his head flop into the basket.

"What a fucking sap," Spector said, as he zapped the TV off. He downed another slug of whiskey and turned off the lights.

CHAPTER THREE

Wednesday
July 20, 1988

7:00 A.M.

The heavy thrum of the engines ran through every nerve. Tachyon stared gloomily out the plane's window, until returned to the present by a dig in the ribs from his seat companion. The stewardess indicated the covered tray with her eyes, and raised her eyebrows.

"Thank you, no. But I would like a drink. A screwdriver. Put that orange juice to good use." He smiled at her. She didn't respond. In fact she gave him a look that clearly said *you lush*.

He returned to his moody contemplation of the boiling thunderheads two thousand feet below. The stewardess returned with his drink, and Tach dug into his pocket for money. He came up with an inch-thick pile of pink message slips. *Tachyon, call me, goddamn it! Hiram*. He got the woman paid, and stared again at Hiram's insulting and uncommunicative message.

What the fuck did Worchester want, and what the fuck had Davidson meant? Did he mean to imply that Tachyon was a shepherd, and the jokers "silly sheep?" Or was the reference to a king meant for him? Or had it held a more personal meaning? Davidson had looked odd. Or was it just an irritating affectation on the part of a professional actor who couldn't carry on a conversation without a scriptwriter?

123

"Silly sheep. Goddamn him." Tach pulled out a handker-chief, and gave his nose a quick blow.

I'm going home to bury one of my lost sheep. Oh, Chrysalis.

He propped his head on his hand.

9:00 A.M.

He'd had to wait almost forty-five minutes to get seated. The atrium coffee shop was a blur of activity. Waitpersons bounced around from table to table like pinballs. Spector sat by himself in a small booth, ignoring the babble of everyone around him. He looked slowly around the room. There were lots of red-rimmed eyes and pained expressions. Spector figured most of them had gotten fucked-up or fucked or both last night. He hadn't managed much sleep himself until the early morning hours.

A waitress stopped at his table and made a face that might have been a smile the first thousand or so times she'd done it. She pulled out her pad and pencil and raised her eyebrows expectantly. "What can I get for you this morning, sir?" The words came out in swift, staccato fashion. So much for Southern hospitality.

"Just coffee for now." Spector smiled slowly. He wanted food, too, but figured he was going to get his money's worth out of this bitch. The waitress gave him a dirty look and shot away from the table.

Spector leaned back in his chair and forced his surround-ings to go out of focus. He had to come up with a plan to get at Hartmann. The pain was chewing at him big-time this morning, making it hard to think. Maybe he could get some inside dope from Tony. Find out where and when the senator would be most exposed. It would have to be crowded enough that nobody would realize exactly what had happened. At least, not for a while.

The waitress swept back over and set his coffee down hard, slopping it over into the saucer. "Sorry," she said, clearly not meaning it. "Will there be anything else?"

Spector waited a long moment before replying. "I'll need just a few more minutes."

The waitress rolled her eyes and walked away.

Spector picked up his cup and took a large swallow. The

coffee burned his mouth and throat going down. No problem; it would heal before he decided what to order. He'd never have blisters on his tongue again.

Spector glanced over at the line of people waiting to be seated. A trim, bearded, older man walked past the crowd and looked slowly around the room. The man saw Spector and began walking purposefully over to his table. Spector tensed his legs, ready to bolt up if necessary. The man looked familiar, somehow. He stopped at the other side of the table and smiled.

"Pardon me, it's rather crowded in here this morning. Do you mind if I join you? My name is Josh Davidson."

Spector was about to tell him to fuck off when he remembered that Davidson was one of his favorite actors. All the tension went out of him when Davidson smiled again.

"No, please, sit down, Mr. Davidson." Spector handed the actor his menu and looked for the waitress. He was damned if Josh Davidson was going to have to wait for service if he could do anything about it.

"Thank you so much," Davidson said, carefully seating himself. He pulled a folded newspaper out from under his arm and opened it up.

Spector spotted the waitress and was about to signal her when a large man emerged from the crowd. Hiram Worchester smoothed the creases in his lapels and looked from table to table.

"Mind if I read a section?" Spector reached for the front page, which Davidson had set aside.

"Be my guest."

Spector grabbed the paper and opened it quickly. He peeped up over the top. Fatman was still looking about. *If he's looking for Davidson, I'm sunk*, he thought. As satisfying as it might be to croak the blimpy bastard, he couldn't jeopardize the job. A waiter walked over to Worchester and nodded deferentially.

"I have to leave, Mr. Davidson," Spector said. "Not really feeling too well. Mind if I keep your front page?"

"Not at all. It's the least I can do."

Spector stood and walked slowly toward the door, keeping the newspaper raised in front of him. It looked stupid, but was better than having Worchester recognize him.

The waitress walked past him as he left. "Good riddance,"

she said, just loud enough for him to hear. Spector was too preoccupied to even care.

11:00 A.M.

Tachyon leaned against the side of the pew, and licked sweat from his upper lip. He was afraid he was going to faint from the stifling heat, and the four enormous fans in the back of Our Lady of Perpetual Misery did little to stir the heavy, moist air. He considered removing his velvet coat, but that would reveal the sweat-darkened circles beneath his armpits, and what an offensive state in which to say farewell to Chrysalis. He was supposed to verbalize that farewell. Sum up in brilliant, poignant words what Chrysalis had meant to Jokertown. And he had no idea what he was going to say. He hadn't really known Chrysalis, and on some level he hadn't really liked her. But one could scarcely say that in a eulogy.

Staring at her flower-draped casket, Tach wondered if Chrysalis's ghost was hovering nearby, listening to the hurried mumbling as the Living Rosary Society told their beads and offered prayers for the repose of her soul.

The procession began, led by a joker altar boy with a bronze helix hung with the joker Jesus. He was followed by two others swinging censors that sent clouds of incense into the already highly redolent air. Tach coughed, and covered his mouth with his handkerchief.

"I hate all this Catholic mumbo jumbo. She was raised a Baptist and she should a'died a Baptist."

Tach turned his head slowly and regarded the man seated next to him in the pew. He was a big man with a weathered face that was florid beneath his tan. The black suit coat strained across his belly, and tendrils of sweat left shiny lines on his jowls. There didn't seem to be anything to say so Tach didn't.

"I'm Joe Jory, Debra Jo's daddy."

"How do you do," Tach mumbled, as Father Squid, resplendent in his finest surplice, walked past with ponderous dignity.

The priest reached the altar, set his missal in place, then turned to the crowd and raised his arms wide saying in his sad, soft voice,

"Let us pray."

Throughout the mass, Jory and Tachyon struggled along,

always a beat behind the standing, kneeling, sitting worshipers. Last year it had been the same situation at Des's funeral—and in that moment Tachyon knew what he was going to say in the eulogy. He stopped trying to make sense of the alien ceremony, and simply sat with head bowed, tears slipping slowly from beneath closed lids as he composed his thoughts.

The little joker altar boy nudged his shoulder, and Tach returned from his reverie. A hamper containing tiny loaves of bread. The Takisian broke off a bite, and passed on the hamper. The bread seemed to swell in his dry mouth, and he choked trying to get it down. With a quick surreptitious glance to either side he unlimbered his flask, and gulped down a sip of brandy.

Father Squid beckoned, and Tach took his place at the lectern. Pulling out his handkerchief he wiped his face, drew a deep breath and began.

"Exactly one year ago on the twentieth day of July, 1987, we gathered in this church to bury Xavier Desmond. I spoke his eulogy, as I shall speak Chrysalis's. And I am honored to do so, but the melancholy truth is that I am weary of burying my friends. Jokertown is a poorer place because of their passing, and my life—and yours—is diminished by their loss." Tach paused and stared down at his hands where they gripped the lectern. He forced himself to relax.

"A eulogy is a speech in praise of a person, but I am finding this one to be very difficult. I called myself Chrysalis's friend. I saw her frequently. I even traveled around the world with her. But I realize now that *I didn't really know her*. I knew she called herself Chrysalis and that she lived in Jokertown, but I didn't know her natal name or where she'd been born. I knew she played at being British, but I never knew why. I knew she liked to drink amaretto, but I never knew what made her laugh. I knew she liked secrets, liked to be in control, liked to appear cool and untouched, but I never knew what made her that way.

"I thought about all of this on the plane from Atlanta and decided that if I couldn't speak in praise of *her*, at least I could speak in praise of her deeds. A year ago, when war raged in our streets and our children were in danger, Chrysalis offered her place—her palace—as a refuge and fortress. It was dangerous for her, but danger never disturbed Chrysalis.

"She was a joker who refused to act like a joker. The

crystal lady never wore a mask. You took her as you found her, or you could just be damned. In this way, perhaps, she taught some nats tolerance and some jokers courage." Tears were streaming down his face. In order to speak past the lump in his throat he pushed his voice higher and louder.

"Because we worship our ancestors, Takisian funerals are even more important than births. We believe our dead stay close by to guide their foolish descendants, a belief that can be terrifying or comforting, depending on the personality of the ancestor. Chrysalis's presence, I think, will be more terrifying than comforting because she will require much of us.

"Someone murdered her. This should not go unpunished.

"Hate rises like a smothering tide in this country. We must resist it.

"Our neighbors are poor and hungry, frightened and destitute. We must feed and shelter and comfort and aid them.

"*She* will expect all of this from us."

Tachyon paused and scanned the congregation. His attention was drawn to the bank of votive candles burning near the lectern. Crossing to it, he lifted one of the tiny candles and returned to the lectern. The flame flickered hypnotically before his eyes.

"In one year Jokertown has lost two of its most important leaders. We are frightened and saddened and confused by the loss. But I say they are still here, still with us. Let us be worthy of them. Win honor in their memories. *Never* forget."

Bending, Tach pulled his knife from its boot sheath. He placed the candle on the lectern and positioned his forefinger directly over the flame. With a quick slash, he cut his finger and extinguished the flame with a drop of his blood.

"Farewell, Chrysalis."

Running into Fatman had rattled him a bit, but a couple swallows of whiskey had helped calm Spector down. He sat hunched over the edge of the bed, staring at the headline. "HARTMANN TO SPEAK IN PARK TODAY." The senator was going to make a public plea to the jokers to demonstrate in a non-violent manner. It was risky, what with all the lunatics wandering around. No one was crazier than a politician with his back to the wall, though. And Hartmann was really up against it. Spector turned on the TV and tuned it to a channel that showed the times and places of the day's events. After a few moments waiting, there it was. A one o'clock speech and nothing about any cancellation.

Spector chewed his lip and paged through the paper absentmindedly. He needed an angle. He'd need a way to blend into the crowd and still stand out enough to manage to catch Hartmann's eye.

A small, corner ad caught his attention. It was Keaton's Kostumes. MASKS, MAKEUP, COSTUMES, PARTY SUP-PLIES, and MORE it promised. A man in a costume held up the list and smiled in a stupid, exaggerated way. He looked like Marcel Marceau. Spector tossed the paper, wiped the ink stains off on his gray pants, and started laughing.

Jack passed through the enormous brass revolving door into the Marriott lobby, saw the swarms of press and Hart-mann delegates, and tried not to think of pigs at a trough. The campaign was doing its best to feed its people and get everyone back onto the floor in the short time allowed by the luncheon recess, and the Marriott had obliged with a vast buffet that was serving up pasta salad and rare roast beef by the ton. Jack could see Hiram Worchester perched on a sagging sofa near the lounge piano, a plate piled high with food balanced on either knee. The glass elevators were jammed full of press and delegates taking hookers up to their rooms for a little noon relief. The piano man was playing "Piano Man" once again. Jack had an oppressive feeling he knew precisely what song was going to come next.

Fortunately Jack didn't have to cluster around the buffet tables and gobble his lunch with the others while the pianist offered the inevitable salute to Eva Perón—Jack had a perma-nent reserved table at the Bello Mondo, secured by offering the maître d' a crisp new hundred-dollar bill every day.

A good meal and a few double whiskeys would come in about right. It had been a lousy morning anyway. CBS commentators had jabbered right through most of Jimmy Carter's seconding speech for Hartmann, and the other net-works had cut away for commercials. Chairman Jim Wright, who Jack figured wanted Hartmann to win, had cued the band to play "Stars and Stripes Forever" at the end of the speech, which got the audience up for a massive floor demonstration that those watching TV had entirely missed. Jack could have sworn he heard deVaughn's screams all the way from the Marriott.

Jack was beginning to believe, in a purely superstitious way, in the existence of a secret ace who was out to get Hartmann. Or maybe just Gremlins from the Kremlin.

"Jack! Mr. Braun!" An avuncular Father Christmas figure rolled toward him, a straw porkpie hat shadowing his long white hair and straggly beard. Louis Manxman, a reporter for the LA *Times*, who had been aboard Hartmann's campaign plane from the start. There was a purposeful look in the newsman's eye.

"Hi, Louis." Jack tucked his briefcase under one arm, jammed his hands into the pockets of his Banana Republic photojournalist's jacket, and tried to skate past. Manxman moved purposefully to block him and grinned up through metal-rimmed bifocals.

"I want the story on that test vote Monday night."

"Ancient history, Louis."

"The papers have been praising Danny Logan's masterful strategy, the way he put it together at the last minute. Even deVaughn didn't know what was happening—you shoulda seen his face when he realized. But I know Logan from way back, and it doesn't seem like his kinda move at all. I've talked to every delegate head I could find, and they all say their orders came from you, not Logan."

"Logan knew what I was doing." Jack tried to move left. Manxman moved to block.

"A source told me the old mick was passed out Monday night."

"He was celebrating." Moving right.

"Celebrating from breakfast on, from what I hear." Blocking.

Jack glared at him. "I'm a busy man, Louis. What the hell do you want, anyway?"

"Was it you or wasn't it?"

"I will not confirm or deny. Okay?"

"Why deny it? You're a Hollywood boy—you should relish the publicity. Don't be such a weenie."

Jack stopped for a moment and wondered if "weenie" was going to be the operative word for this convention.

The inevitable happened, and the man in the white

tuxedo pounded out the opening bars of "Don't Cry for Me, Argentina." Jack felt his temper fraying.

"I'm late for lunch, Louis. I won't confirm or deny. That's for the record; that's my statement. Got that?"

The Santa Claus look was gone. "Forty years too late to take the Fifth, Jack."

Anger snarled in Jack. He fixed the reporter in a cold stare and stepped forward as if to walk right through him.

They were nearing the white piano on its pedestal. The man in the white tuxedo was still ringing through his paean to South American fascism. Anger began to roil in Jack in the wake of fear and humiliation. He said goodbye to Amy, then stepped up to the piano. The man in the white tuxedo gave him an automatic smile.

There was a big fishbowl on the piano with a green drift of tip money in the bottom. Jack reached for the rim of the glass, exerted just slightly, and cracked off a hand-sized piece. His golden force field fluttered slightly. The piano man stared. Jack pulverized the glass in his hand, then reached forward, opened the front pocket of the man's jacket, and poured the glass inside.

"Don't Cry for Me, Argentina" died away.

"Play that song again," Jack said, "and I'll kill you."

Walking away, Jack felt he ought to be ashamed of this brand of cheap satisfaction.

Somehow he wasn't.

12:00 NOON

Troll was Chrysalis's only pallbearer. The massive security chief from the Jokertown clinic cradled the coffin in his arms as if it were a sleeping child, and led the procession into the churchyard. More prayers were said, and Father Squid blessed the grave with incense and holy water. Tachyon scooped up a handful of dirt, and dribbled it slowly onto the coffin. It gave back a hollow, scrabbling sound like claws on glass, and Tachyon shuddered.

The sun looked bloated and somehow diseased as it floated in the pall of a smoggy New York summer day. Tach longed for the end. The dead had been buried. Now Atlanta was beckoning. But there was still the receiving line to be endured, and thirty minutes of human handshakes. Tach decided to spare himself some of the grossities. He pulled out a pair of red kid gloves, and worked them over his slim, white hands.

"Hello, Father," said a familiar voice to his left.

"Good to see you again, Daniel."

Tachyon couldn't restrain himself. He flung himself into Brennan's arms, hugging the human with a fierce grip, and a show of naked emotion that he knew the man was only tolerating. With a sharply indrawn breath, Tach held Brennan at arm's length and eyed him critically.

"We must talk. Come."

They walked deeper into the graveyard until they were partly shielded by several intricate tombstones. Tachyon peered around a weeping angel at the woman who stared curiously after them.

"The beautiful blonde must be Jennifer."

"Yes," said Brennan.

"I'd say you're a lucky man, but that would seem less than apt when you're being framed for murder. Is that what brought you back?"

"Partly. Mostly I'm here to find who killed her."

"And how are you progressing?"

"Not too well."

"Any theories?"

"I thought Kien might have done it."

Tachyon shook his head. "That makes no sense. We had a deal that took you out of the city and ended the war. Why would he risk restarting the whole killing cycle?"

"Who knows? I'm just going to keep poking until something jumps."

Dryly Tach said, "Just make sure it doesn't jump on you. I wish I could aid you, but I must return to Atlanta. You will keep in touch?"

"No. Once I finish this, Jennifer and I are leaving New York, and this time it will be for good."

"If you won't keep in touch, at least be careful."

"That I can agree to."

1:00 P.M.

Piedmont Park was packed. Spector shouldered his way through the crowd toward the podium. He felt like an idiot in the tight black-and-white outfit. His skin was suffocating under the greasepaint. He'd barely made it to the park on time. The costume shop had been wall-to-wall bodies, mostly jokers. Luckily, the gathering in the park had emptied the streets. He'd left his clothes and other belongings in a locker. The key was tucked under the wrist of his leotard.

He was still a good hundred yards from the podium. They'd done a mike test, but so far, no Hartmann. A shadow moved slowly over the crowd. Spector looked up, shading his eyes from the glare, and saw the Turtle gliding noiselessly over them toward the stage, which was being prepared for the senator's speech. There was applause and a small cheer. The crowd was mostly jokers, although there were a few groups of nats clustered at the edges.

"Look, Mommy, a funny man." A young joker girl pointed at Spector. She was sitting in a beat-up stroller, holding a flower. Her arms and legs were rail-thin and knobbed up and down. They looked like they'd been broken twenty times each.

Spector gave a weak smile, hoping the greasepaint around his lips made it seem bigger than it was.

The girl's mother smiled back. Patterns of blotchy red pigment crept across her skin. As Spector watched, one of the circles closed into a small dot and erupted blood. The woman wiped it away in a quick, embarrassed motion. She took the flower from her daughter's hand and held it out to Spector.

Spector reached out and took it, being careful not to touch her flesh. Being a nat in a crowd of jokers, even dressed as a mime, gave him the creeps. He turned away.

"Do something funny," the little girl said. "Mommy, make him do something funny."

There was a murmur of approval from the crowd. Spector turned slowly and tried to think. Funny was something he'd never been accused of being. He tried balancing the flower on the tip of a finger. Amazingly, he was able to. There was dead silence. Sweat dripped over his painted brows and into his eyes. He was breathing hard. It was still very quiet.

A gloved hand flashed before Spector's face, snatching the flower. It placed the stem between painted lips and struck an affected pose. Laughter from the crowd. The other mime bowed low and raised up slowly.

Spector took a step back. The other mime quickly

grabbed him by the elbow and shook his head. More giggles from the crowd. This was the last thing Spector needed. Not only was he the center of attention, but he was still a long way from where he needed to be. Hartmann might start up any second and Spector wouldn't be able to get through in time.

The other mime looked down, made a face, and pointed at Spector's feet. Spector glanced down instinctively and saw nothing there, just as the mime's hand came up under his chin and popped his head back. This got the biggest laugh of all. The mime clutched at his sides and laughed noiselessly.

Spector rubbed his mouth; he'd bitten his tongue. He gritted his teeth under the painted-on smile.

The other mime placed a finger on the top of Spector's head and danced around him like a maypole. He stopped in front of Spector, tugged at his cheeks.

Spector had put up with enough. It was time to get this fucker out of his hair. He stepped in close and made eye contact. He locked in and set the pain free, grabbing the mime's shoulders as he began to fall over. Spector lowered him slowly, pulling the mime's hands together over his chest. The shithead's eyes were glazed over with death and surprise by the time he came to rest on the trampled grass. Spector stuck the flower in the corpse's hands and applauded melodramatically. The crowd laughed and cheered. Some patted him on the back; others looked at the mime, waiting for him to get up.

"My friends." The amplified voice came from the podium. The crowd turned. Spector angled his shoulders and began pushing through. "Today, we will have the privilege to hear from the only man who can lead us through these next difficult years. A man who preaches tolerance, not hatred. A man who unites, instead of being divisive. A man who will lead his people, not herd them. I give you the next president of the United States of America, Senator Gregg Hartmann."

The applause was deafening. There were weird screams and whistles, joker noises. Spector caught an elbow in the ear from a freak with arms that hung to his knees. He shook it off and kept moving in.

"Thank you." Hartmann paused while the applause and cheers played out. "Thank all of you very much."

Spector could see him now, but there was no way to lock eyes at this distance, even if Hartmann was looking right at him. The crowd was pressing in toward the podium. Spector rode the flood of human mistakes; used his narrow shoulders to cut through. Another minute or two and he'd be in position.

"It has been said that I am a pro-joker candidate." Hartmann raised his hands to still the applause before it could start. "That is not strictly true. I have always placed one idea above all others. That this country should exist as our founding fathers planned it. Equal rights for all, guaranteed, under the law of the land. No individual greater than the next. No one, however powerful, exempt from the law." Hartmann paused. The crowd applauded again.

Spector was about a hundred feet away in the center of the crowd. Hartmann was wearing a beige suit. A slight breeze stirred at his styled hair. Secret Service agents flanked the podium, their eyes hidden behind sunglasses. The senator's gaze swept the crowd but missed Spector. It would take total concentration to lock on for the instant they had eye contact. If that even happened.

"I need your help to win our party's nomination and become your next president." Hartmann extended his hands to the crowd. "Your presence here in Atlanta can help me only if you demonstrate in an orderly manner. Any acts of violence, whether provoked or not, will certainly be used against us. You have the opportunity to make a simple, but eloquent statement. A statement made by Gandhi and Martin Luther King Jr. That violence is an abhorrent act. That it will not be tolerated, by you, under any circumstance."

Hartmann's eyes were drifting across the crowd again, headed straight for him. Spector held his breath and concentrated, the pain howling in his head. Just a little more. Spector stood on his toes. Their eyes locked . . .

. . . there was a sound. A Secret Service man knocked Hartmann down. Gunfire. There were screams and people tried to move, but were packed too closely together. Spector looked at a hilltop. There were maybe a hundred men in Confederate uniforms. Puffs of smoke came from their guns, then the echo of the shots across the park.

Hartmann was gone. There wouldn't be another chance. Not here, anyway. Spector jumped in behind a joker who was as broad as three normal men. It didn't matter where he was going. It would be safer than here. The Turtle whooshed by overhead. There were a few more rounds and then the gunfire stopped. Spector stepped on something that cracked. There was a groan. He held onto the joker's leather belt, which had WIDE LOAD painted on in gold.

No shit, Spector thought. But this was one time he was glad to have a fat freak as company.

6:00 P.M.

From the end of the corridor, Mackie watched the tall, thin man with coffee-and-cream skin close and lock the room door. 1531, just as *der Mann* said. It came to him that *Amerika* was decadent, even as his departed comrades of the Red Army Fraction used to say. Where else in the world might a man see a nigger wrap himself in a suit that cost more money than Mackie Messer had ever owned at one time in his life, and stroll out upon the town with a white woman on his arm?

To himself he laughed at his target's apparent attempt at disguise. She looked just like one of the *Reeperbahnstraße* girls, armored against unaccustomed daylight. It was appropriate. Just a whore; just another fucking whore. Who had lured the Man and would pay.

They turned away from him, toward the elevators. He pushed off from the wall next to the fire extinguisher under glass. He couldn't do them here—he was already thinking *them*; it was only logical, he mustn't leave a witness—because this crazy bourgeois palace was hollow at the core, like the culture that built it, and anyone on one of a dozen levels could see everything that went on out on the catwalks surrounding the atrium. His move had to come on the quiet; *der Mann* had been very explicit.

But that was no problem. Mack the Knife was subtle, like. Like his song. He would follow, and know the time.

Maybe he'd ride the elevator with them. He licked his lips at the joke. That would be really *kriminell*. They'd never suspect him. They might not notice him even. Perhaps they were in love. Perhaps the black man had a hard-on.

He moved. A voice grabbed at him. "Hey, you. Not so fast."

He turned. A squat white man in a brown suit stood there with a wire hanging out of his ear. Hotel dick; Mackie had the gradations of *cop* burned into his autonomic nervous system by the time he was toddling the Sankt Pauli cobblestones. He had been as discrete as possible, staying back in the entry to the room where the ice machine lurked and clattered to itself, fading through the wall into a utility closet when people got too near. But there was a limit to how covert even Macheath could be, hanging out here over sixty meters of emptiness in this unsettling outside-in place.

The suit laid a hand on his arm. You couldn't do that, not to Mackie Messer.

"You're lucky," he said. He touched the man on the point of his cheekbone, *buzzed* a fingertip.

Blood started. The man cried out and doubled over, slapping a hand to his face. Mackie phased through the steel fire door and started running down the stairs. He didn't dare lose his quarry now. Women were always changing their minds; no knowing if she would be returning to this place.

Spector sat on the edge of the bed, feet tucked underneath him. He was almost surprised to find his room clean when he returned. It had been that long since he stayed in a hotel. He was alternately planning his next move and watching TV. Right now, the television had his attention. A local reporter, trying not to look out of his depth, was interviewing Hartmann in the lobby.

"Senator, do you feel Reverend Barnett had anything to do with this afternoon's disturbance?" The reporter held the microphone up to the senator, who paused before replying.

"No. I think that, whatever our differences, Leo Barnett would not stoop to such tactics. The reverend is an honorable man." Hartmann coughed. "But I do feel that those individuals who disrupted the meeting likely share many of his dangerously narrow views. It is precisely this kind of unreasoning bigotry that we must all struggle to eliminate. Leo Barnett wants to solve the problem by removing wild card victims from society. I want to overcome the hatred itself." Hartmann sat back in his seat, folded his hands and stared hard into the camera.

"The guy's fucking good," said Spector. "But it won't make any difference."

The camera cut back to the studio. A black woman reporter turned to her co-anchor. "Thanks to Howard for that interesting interview. Dan, what have the police discovered so far about the perpetrators of the disturbance?"

"Not much, I'm afraid. Several of them are in custody, captured by the Turtle, but the police are getting very little cooperation." The reporter tapped his thumbs together. "There are rumors that most of them are members of the Ku Klux Klan, but that's been unsubstantiated. Although the disturbance was obviously well-planned, none of the individuals involved claims to be the leader of the group. And so far, no clue as to where the authentic Confederate uniforms and muskets came from." The reporter frowned and turned back to the black woman.

"Well, I'm sure the authorities will keep us posted if any new information comes to light in this bizarre incident." The black woman shook her head. "Although dummy ammunition was used, several individuals were hurt in the panic that ensued." The video cut to earlier footage of the panic in the park, the cameraman was running with the rest during the panic, bouncing the picture all over. "At least one person, a street performer, was allegedly trampled to death. Ironically, he was believed to be playing dead at the time. His name is being withheld pending notification of next of kin."

"Fucking A," said Spector, punching the TV off. He was off the hook for that one, anyway. But that didn't get him any closer to Hartmann. He'd almost felt something holding him off for the instant that they locked eyes. No. Just imagination. To do that he'd have to have powers like the Astronomer or Tachyon. "Astronomer for president," he giggled. "That'd make even Reagan look good by comparison."

He popped up off the bed and walked slowly around the carpeted floor, considering his options. Killing Hartmann might be more than he was up to. He could take the money and go someplace else, another country maybe. Maybe work for a casino in Cuba. Nope. He'd always done what he was paid to do. Fucking middle-class ethics again. Didn't stop him from killing people, but made him live up to a contract.

He sighed and walked to the phone. Tony was his only shot, he'd known that ever since they met in the lobby. It was kismet, or something. Didn't stop him from feeling like shit, though. He punched in the number and waited. An unfamiliar female voice answered the phone.

"Could I speak to Tony Calderone, please?"

"He's not available right now. Could I take a message?" The woman sounded tired.

"Yes, tell him James called. He'll know who you mean. Tell him I'd like to firm up that dinner invitation he extended."

Spector was almost surprised at how cool and polite he sounded.

"Yes, James, uh, what was your last name?"

"Just James. He'll know who you mean."

"I'll give him the message."

"Thanks." Spector hung up the phone and sighed. Maybe he'd order a steak from room service and hope the Peaches were on TV again tonight. *If they're America's team,* he thought, *we're all in a shitload of trouble.*

8:00 P.M.

Spotlights dazzled Jack's eyes. The long lenses of television cameras were trained on him like shotguns. An eddy of stage fright turned his knees to liquid. He hadn't done this sort of thing in years.

He looked up into the lights, gave the world a crooked grin—reflexes coming back, good—and said his line:

"The thirty-first state, the Golden State, is proud to cast its three hundred fourteen votes for the cause of Joker's Rights and the next president, Senator Gregg Hartmann!"

A roar. Applause. Silly hats and flying ace gliders took to the air. Jack tried to look noble, cheerful, and triumphant till the spotlights moved off to the state chairman of Colorado.

Take that, Ronald Reagan, he thought. *I'll show you how to work a camera.*

He climbed down from the little red-white-and-blue podium that had been brought in for just this purpose. The guy from Colorado, not sure of his totals, was fumbling his line. Fortunately Colorado had gone for Dukakis and Jackson.

The first ballot gave Hartmann 1,622 votes, Barnett 998, with Jackson, Dukakis, and Gore splitting the rest. Nobody was close to winning.

Chaos descended on the floor while media commentators made wise judgments and hedged predictions about what would happen next. Rule 9(c) went out the window once the first ballot was cast and floor managers were promising uncommitted delegates the moon.

The second ballot was called early, thirty minutes after the first, just so campaign managers could have enough numbers to see how things were going. Hartmann gained about fifty votes, mainly at the expense of Dukakis and Gore.

The convention burst into a series of sweaty huddles while media commentators tried to make up their minds whether fifty votes signified a "trend" toward Hartmann, or just a "lean." Floor managers went into fits at the thought of delegates slipping through their fingers.

The pandemonium went on four hours. By the time a sleepy-eyed Jim Wright called for the third ballot just before midnight, the three commercial networks had died of inertia and gone back to their standard summer fare of reruns and Johnny Carson, and only PBS was covering the action for an audience of a few thousand hardcore political junkies.

Hartmann hit an even eighteen hundred. The trend was solidifying. Hats and gliders zoomed ceilingward. Jack picked up his podium and threw it about a hundred feet into the air, a tumbling star-spangled sign of triumph, then reached out and carefully caught it before it could brain somebody.

The celebrations in Jack's suite went on for hours. He was stumbling off to bed before he realized that he really should have called Bobbie. Even if she turned out to be the starlet with the cellulite obsession, Jack figured he could have given her enough healthful exercise to make her happy.

10:00 P.M.

—Peachtree, tiled and echoic. They walked arm in arm. Sara had drunk two glasses of wine. It was the first alcohol she had had for over a year. She had never drunk much liquor— except for the weeks after the tour.

Ricky was regaling her with the latest candidate jokes going the rounds. "How about this one: if Dukakis, Hartmann, and Brother Leo went boating together on Lake Lanier, and the boat's engine blew up and it sank, who'd be saved?"

"The nation," Sara said. "Last time I heard it, it was Reagan, Carter, and Anderson. But then, you're too young to remember."

"What goes around comes around, Rosie. But I was old enough to vote in '80, if barely."

"You probably think I'm a wicked old lady robbing the cradle." She frowned; where was *that* coming from? *Steady*, she told herself.

Ricky patted her hand. "I certainly hope so, Rosie." He

laughed then, to show it was a joke. She felt the tension come into her, just the same.

A thin current of sound was running down the corridor, between the rocks of their laughter. "What's that song?" she asked.

He raised a brow at her. "Don't you know it?" She did, but she'd needed something to say. "It's 'Mack the Knife.' Standby of every low-rent lounge singer in the northern hemisphere. The Muzak's broken in here, see, so they hired this white dude to walk around and whistle."

She laughed and squeezed his arm briefly. *Damn. What am I doing?* She looked around, almost as if seeking some external cause for her behavior.

Movement behind. Her tongue pushed out between suddenly dry lips; she made her face turn to the side, as if she was admiring the brash fashions draped on the headless silver-and-black-and-olive-green mannequins posing in a boutique window.

"Somebody's following us. No, don't look!"

"Give me some credit, Rosie. I'm a journalist, remember? I didn't sleep through your seminar."

He glanced to the side, then faced forward. "Just some kid in a leather jacket." A frown spoiled the smooth perfection of his forehead. "Looked like he had a hunchback. Poor son of a bitch."

She looked back again. "Now, quit that, or you're going to turn into a pillar of salt. You were the one who wanted subtlety."

"I don't like the way he looks," she said. "He—*feels*—wrong, somehow."

"The instincts of a seasoned ace reporter. *Well*-seasoned."

"Is that a crack about my age?"

"The wine you drank." He patted her hand. "That's the spirit. Whistling past a graveyard, like. Walk on. Keep your head up. Never let them see you're afraid. It unleashes all those primitive Nordic predatory instincts."

She fought her neck muscles, which were trying to rotate her head toward the leather boy. "You think he could be one of Barnett's little helpers?"

"Been known to happen during this convention, Rosie. Wouldn't that be an irony, to get jumped on suspicion of being Hartmann fans?"

This time she did look back. He was sauntering along, hands in pockets, first the white shoe, then the black. Ricky was right, one shoulder definitely rode higher than the other. There was something a little too elaborate about the way he wasn't paying attention to them.

At least he's small. But then, Ricky wasn't exactly Arnold Schwarzenegger. . . .

Once around a curve, Ricky grabbed her hand and they took off running, Sara wobbling on her ingenue heels, Ricky's Guccis slapping the rubber runner. The passageway wound round and around. She kept looking back, saw no sign of pursuit.

They slowed, Sara puffing for breath, Ricky gracious enough to pretend to be winded. "One more turn and we're back in the Hyatt," Ricky said. "Another potentially ugly confrontation avoided. That's how we eighties types handle things."

They turned the bend and there he was. Leaning with his back and his cheek against cool tile, sizing them up. He started to whistle: "Mack the Knife."

Sara grabbed Ricky's wrist and hauled him back around out of sight. "I'm not sure that's a good idea, Rosie," he said. "We should just bluff our way past."

"Don't you *see*?" The terror was upon her. It glowed in her eyes like white-hot wires. "How did he get in front of us?"

"Some kind of service passage. We're right near the hotel. If he causes trouble we can make a lot of noise and someone will come rescue us."

And then he came out of the wall at them, lunging like a shark.

Like a dancer Ricky swung Sara behind him. "What the hell do you think you're doing?"

"Party *party*," the boy said with a *Hans und Franz* accent, laughing, spraying spittle from loose lips. "Everybody get down tonight."

There was a buzzing in the air, oppressive as the humid night outside Peachtree Center's artificial chill. The boy swung a hand *karate*-fashion for the side of Ricky's neck.

Ricky wasn't a racquetball ace for nothing. Nothing wrong with his reflexes; he blocked with a spidery forearm.

The hand went through it. There was a savage shrilling

moment like a buzz saw hitting a knot in a plank, and then Ricky's forearm and splayed hand just sort of toppled.

Ricky stood staring at the red hoop of blood springing out the suit-coated stump. Sara screamed.

Ricky pointed his arm, hosing his own blood into his assailant's eyes. The boy fell back, sputtering and swiping at his face. Ricky hurled himself at him, windmill arms whirling.

"Rosie, *run!*"

Her legs would not move. Ricky was pummeling the boy with stump and inexpert fist. It looked like the worst of playground bullying; Ricky was a head taller, with a good six inches' reach—

That sound came again. She knew she would hear it every time she closed her eyes for the rest of her life. She smelled something like burned hair.

Ricky's arm fell off at the shoulder. His blood vomited over the wall, white with a mosaic sprinkling of blue and green and yellow.

He turned a martyr's face to her. "Rosie," he said, and his gums were shocks of blood, "*Please* run, for god's sake run—"

The hand passed playfully. His lower jaw was sheared away with the rest of his words. His tongue flopped at her unmoored, a ghastly parody of lust.

She turned and fled, the charnel-house sound pursuing.

As she rounded the corner the heel of her left shoe snapped. She went to her knee with an impact like a gunshot. She skidded twenty feet, bounced off a wall. She tried to struggle up. Her leg would not carry her; she fell heavily against the tile.

"Oh, Ricky," she sobbed. "I'm sorry." Sorry for blowing the escape he had bought her with his life; sorry for the strange guilty surge of relief down underneath the terror that she would not have to face the question that another night in his room would bring between them.

She began to push herself along with her hands, knees up, scooting sideways on her rump. *He* came around the corner, looking twelve-feet tall. Blood splashed his leather and his skin, unnaturally bright in the fluorescent light. He was smiling around teeth like a collapsing fence.

"*Der Mann* sends his regards."

Single-mindedly she sculled away from him. There was nothing in the world but the motions of a losing race.

—And voices, down the corridor, welling up from where the passage from the Hyatt dipped under Center Avenue. A party of delegates in Jackson buttons appeared, black, middle-aged, well dressed, talking happily amongst themselves about their candidate's last-minute upsurge at day's end.

The killer in leather raised his head. A brief pigeon of a woman in a salmon dress with a bow beneath capacious breasts looked up, saw him with the blood upon him and his victim strewn into the corridor bend behind. She jammed fists beneath her eyes and screamed like hell.

The boy's eyes blazed at Sara. "Remember Jenny Towler," he snarled. And walked through the wall.

11:00 P.M.

Mine!

Puppetman felt the searing, twisted menace approaching. Gregg turned as Mackie ghosted through the wall of his bedroom, a crooked smile set above his crooked shoulders. There was a splotchy brown red stain on his right hand up to the elbow that could only be one thing.

Mine!

"All the fucking hotel rooms look the same," Mackie said.

"Get the hell *out* of here," Gregg snapped.

Mackie's grin slid from his punched face. "I wanted to tell you," he said, the German accent broader than usual. "I offed the nigger, but the woman—"

Mine! He's mine!

Gregg was surprised that he was able to hear Mackie's voice over Puppetman at all. The power slammed relentlessly against Gregg's hold, again and again and again. Mackie's raw, violent insanity radiated wildly, leaking from the boy's pores with an odor of decomposing meat, and spreading out in front of Puppetman like a rotting banquet.

Gregg had to get Mackie away quickly or the tenuous hold he had on himself would be entirely gone.

"Out," Gregg repeated desperately. "Ellen's here."

Mackie's mouth twisted, a sneer. He fidgeted, restlessly shifting his weight from foot to foot. "Yeah. I know. In the other room watching goddamn TV. They were showing Chrysalis's funeral. I saw her but she didn't see me. I could've buzzed her easy." He licked his lips. His nervous stare flicked across Gregg's body like a whip as Puppetman hammered again at the bars. "I don't know where Morgenstern is," he said at last.

"Then go find her."

"I wanted to see you." Mackie whispered it like a lover, a voice of velvet sandpaper. The lust was honeyed syrup, golden and rich and sweet.

Puppetman screeched in need. The bars in Gregg's mind started to crumble. "Get *out* of here," he hissed between clenched teeth. "You didn't get Downs, now you tell me you can't find Sara. What the hell good are you to me? You're just a useless punk, with or without your ace."

He'd always been easy with Mackie, placating the kid, feeding his ego. Even with Puppetman controlling the hunchback's emotions, he'd been afraid of Mackie—using him was like juggling nitroglycerine: it looked easy, but he was aware that he would only get one mistake. Gregg thought he might have made it now. Mackie's face had gone grim and cold. The lust did a quicksilver change to something simpler and more dangerous. Mackie's right hand was beginning to vibrate unconsciously as a threatening whine shivered the air.

"No," Mackie said, shaking his head. "You don't know. You're the Man. I love—"

Gregg cut him off. If there was going to be an explosion, it might as well be a big one. "I told you to take out two people who are a danger to us. They're both walking around now while you're telling me how good you are and how much I mean to you."

Mackie blinked. Twitched. "You're not listening—"

"No, I'm not. And I won't listen until all the loose ends are taken care of. You understand that?"

Mackie took a halting step toward Gregg, his hand up. The fingers were a dangerous blur.

Gregg stared him down. It was absolutely the hardest thing he'd ever done. Puppetman was a berserk thing behind his eyes, gibbering and frothing with the closeness of Mackie and the emotional backwash spilling around him. Gregg knew that he had only seconds before Puppetman surfaced entirely, before the mental bonds reversed and *he* would be the one underneath. Yet while he held Puppetman, there were no controls on Mackie and no way to dampen the madness. If the ace took another step, if he swiped at Gregg with that hand . . .

Gregg shuddered with effort.

"Come to me afterward, Mackie," he whispered. "After it's all done, not before."

Mackie lowered his hand, his eyes. The red violence around him faded slightly.

"All right," he said softly. "You're the Man. Yes." He reached out with his hand, safely quiet now, and Gregg fought the impulse to back away and run. He concentrated on holding Puppetman for just a moment longer.

Mackie's dry fingertips traced Gregg's cheek with a strange tenderness, dragging across stubble.

Gregg closed his eyes.

When he opened them again, Mackie was already gone.

Drawing his fingers down the strings, Tachyon pulled a sigh of music from the violin. The Secret Service agent swung his head in that heavy slow way of a bull confronting an irritant. Tach nodded politely to him. The man brightened considerably, cast a furtive glance over his shoulder, and quickstepped to where the alien was sitting cross-legged on the floor outside Fleur's room. Sounds of revelry drifted down the hall from a nearby room party.

"Hi."

"Hello."

"My daughter's crazy about you, and she'll kill me if she finds out I met you and hadn't gotten your autograph. Would you mind?"

"No, I'd be delighted." Tach pulled a notebook from his pocket. "Her name?"

"Trina."

For Trina with love. He signed his name with a flourish.

"Uh, excuse me, but what are you doing out here?"

"I'm going to play the violin for the lady in that room."

"Oh, a little romance, huh?"

"I hope. I won't make any trouble, sir. May I stay?"

The agent shrugged. "Yeah, what the hell. But if people complain—"

"Not to worry."

Tach lifted his bow, tucked the violin beneath his chin. A few years ago he had arranged Chopin's Etude in A flat for solo violin. The notes fell from the strings like crystal beads, like water chuckling over stones. But beneath the joy was a strain of sadness.

The faces of women. Blythe, Angelface, Roulette, Fleur, Chrysalis. *Farewell, old friend.* The door to the hotel room was flung violently open. Tach stared up into her smoldering brown eyes. *Hello, my love?*

"What are you doing? Why won't you leave me alone? Please, please, just leave me alone!" Her hair flew about her face.

"I can't."

She was on her knees before him, hands gripping his shoulders. "Why not?"

"It makes no sense to me. How shall I explain it to you?"

"You've twisted and corrupted everything you've ever touched. Now you're trying to do it to me."

He didn't deny it. Couldn't deny it. "I think we could make each other well. Wash away the guilt."

"Only God has that power."

He tentatively touched a strand of hair with the tip of a finger. "You have her face. Can it be that you don't have her soul?"

"You *damn* fool! You've made her into something that *never* existed."

She jerked her head away. His fingers trailed across her cheek, and he felt moisture. The violent withdrawal carried her a few steps to his left. Fleur leaned her forehead against the wall, every line of her body etched in agony. Tach laid the bow across the strings. Played.

12:00 MIDNIGHT

In the latex clown's head mask, Gregg was simply another of the jokers trying to stay cool in the sticky Atlanta humidity. The temperature was stuck permanently in the low nineties; the breeze felt like a moving sauna. The mask was an oven, but he didn't dare take it off.

It had taken time to arrange his escape from the hotel. Ellen had finally gone to sleep, but there was no telling when she might wake. He hated taking the risk, but he had to do something about Puppetman.

The power had gained the strength of desperation. Gregg

was afraid that its struggles were already too visible to outsiders.

Discarded Flying Ace Gliders transformed into Fucking Flying Jokers crumpled underfoot as Gregg stepped over the gutter and into Piedmont Park. Shapes moved through the trees and around the grassy hillocks. Police swept the perimeter with regularity, trying to keep the jokers in and anyone else out, but it was easy enough for Gregg to slide past them in the darkness and enter the surreal world of the park.

Once inside, the city at his back was forgotten. A tent village had sprung up on one of the hillsides, spreading shouting laughter and light. A bonfire flickered close by; he could hear singing. The jokers passing in front of the fire threw long, shifting shadows across the grass. Deeper in the park behind the peaked tents, Gregg saw erratic phosphorescent brilliance—there were enough jokers whose skin glowed, flashed, or radiated that it had become a nightly custom for them to gather on a hilltop at full dark like human fireflies: a UPI photographer's shot of them had become one of the more memorable images of the convention-outside-the-convention.

Gregg navigated through the park under Puppetman's guidance, following the tug of mental strings from the puppets within the crowd. There were many of them in the park, mostly longtime J-Town residents whose neuroses and foibles were familiar and much-traveled territory for Puppetman. Often he'd ignore them for the thrill that came from twisting some new puppet to his will, but not tonight. Tonight he was after sustenance, and an easing of the power's needs, and he'd take the quick, easy path.

One of the threads led to Peanut.

Peanut: a puppet since the mid-seventies, one of those he'd used during the tragedy of the '76 convention. The joker was a sad, simpleminded man whose skin had been turned brittle, hard, and painful. He'd been Gimli's associate within the defunct JJS, and his right arm had been hewn off by Mackie Messer just over a year ago—Peanut had come between Mackie and the Nur al-Allah's sister, Kahina. Arrested with others in the organization after Gimli's death, Peanut had been quickly released after Gregg's office interceded on his behalf.

Peanut had always been troubled by his friend Gimli's deep hatred of Gregg. Peanut had *admired* the Hartmann he knew. After his release, he'd even worked as a volunteer for the NYC campaign staff, canvasing the Jokertown district during the primary.

Peanut was like an old lover. Gregg knew all the buttons to push.

No one paid much attention to Gregg. Most of the jokers went bare faced, flaunting their jokerhood, but enough of them still wore the masks that Gregg was not overly conspicuous. He lingered at the edge of the tents, on the fringes of the crowd around the bonfire. He sat against a tree bearing a wind-tattered "Free Snotman" poster.

Sweat rained from his face onto the headlands of his Black Dog T-shirt.

He could see Peanut off to his right. Gregg dropped the bars around Puppetman—the restraints faded far too fast, emphasizing just how feeble was his hold on the power. Puppetman lanced out toward Peanut, examining the colors of the joker's dim mind and looking for something . . . *tasty*.

The hues of Peanut's mind were simple and plain. It was easy to separate the strands and find the ones Puppetman could use. With Peanut, as with so many of the jokers he'd taken, those strands were linked to sex. Puppetman knew that—no matter how they might deny it—most jokers loathed their appearance. They hated the thing they saw in the mirror. Many found other jokers just as repulsive. Fortunato had been one of dozens who profited from that truth: there was a vigorous, thriving market in Jokertown for nat prostitutes willing to entertain joker customers.

Peanut suffered as much as anyone from the stigma. His body tissues were unpliable and ridged. His face looked as if he'd slathered mud over it and then baked it in the sun. At the joints of his limbs, the skin often cracked and split, leaving pus-filled, slow-healing sores and scabs. Peanut was ugly, and Peanut was just smart enough to realize how slow witted he was. For a nat, that was an unhappy combination. In Jokertown, especially, it was far worse.

For Peanut (Gregg knew) sex was a rare mingling of pain and pleasure. His erections *hurt* and the leathery skin there cracked and bled from the friction of sexual contact. For days afterward he'd suffer.

Yet the wild card hadn't dampened the urges or stopped him from craving the release the act brought; if anything, his drive was stronger than normal. Peanut was a regular customer of the cheapest J-town whores; when he couldn't afford even their business-like ministrations, he'd masturbate in his flop, quickly and guiltily.

Puppetman knew that, knew it well. There were many times that Puppetman thought the wild card had been designed strictly for his benefit.

Caressing Peanut's mind, he saw the pulsing yellow of lust and knew that it had been days for him. The urge was there, already strong. Puppetman reached out, slowly brightening the color and saturating it until there was room for little else. Gregg, watching, saw Peanut grimace. The joker rose and walked away from the fire. Gregg waited, then followed behind.

There were tints and shades within the golden primary: an orange wash of muted sadism; the azure desire for nats; a coral-green preference for oral stimulation. Puppetman had seen such facets in every puppet. Desire was always complicated and sometime contradictory. Normally such things remained subdued or even denied—stuff of fantasies and masturbatory visions, minor whorls in the flood. But Puppetman could make the tendencies flare, make them dominant passions. He could force someone to become a violent rapist or a humiliated slave; he could make them seduce a child or a friend's spouse.

It was a favorite trick.

Do whatever you want. Just make it quick. Remember Gimli . . .

Puppetman snarled at the reminder. He prodded brutally at Peanut's mind and waited to see what would happen.

Peanut wandered to the edge of the encampment where a stand of trees held darkness. He seemed agitated, his whole body turning as he glanced from side to side. Gregg watched from the cover of one of the tents as Peanut seemed to come to a decision and headed into the trees.

Gregg pursued.

He almost ran into the joker.

Peanut had stopped a few yards into the woods. Gregg could hear what had caused him to halt: the panting groans could be only one thing. Peanut was standing motionless, watching the hidden joker couple as they screwed. The colors of his mind were confused, uncertain.

Puppetman touched him again.

Feel it? You can't just stand there and watch. Look at her. Look at her legs wrapped around him. See how she moves her ass under him, lifting her hips so he drives in deeper, eager, and hot and wet. That could be you. You want her. You want to feel her legs tighten around your hips, you want to feel your cock deep in her warmth, you want to hear her sighing in your ear and telling you to fuck her, fuck her deep and hard and good until you explode inside her . . .

Peanut tugged at his belt buckle with his one hand. The joker's pants pooled around his ankles.

But she won't want you. Not Peanut. You're disgusting and ugly, all hard edges. You're stupid. She'd be disgusted; she'd feel dirty and violated . . .

Puppetman could feel the lust and anger building in concert. He orchestrated it, adding pressure until he felt it simmering. *You'd have to be the master. It's what you want, what she wants. I know you. I know what you've thought when you stroke yourself . . .* Puppetman was sighing himself, ready. Ready to feed at last.

Peanut squatted down, hunting in the underbrush. When he straightened, Gregg could see a thick branch clutched in his fist. The joker raised the weapon.

Go ahead. Hit him and take the bitch. You want it. You must . . .

And Gregg heard deep, mocking laughter.

Gimli. *Where are you, damn you!* Gregg cursed. *Where are you hiding?*

Why, right here, Greggie. Right here. Gimli laughed and in that moment, the dwarf's wall slammed up as it had every time these past few weeks. Puppetman howled in frustration as the strings to Peanut were suddenly, jarringly, severed.

"No!" The shout might have been Gregg, might have been Puppetman. Puppetman flung himself against the mental barrier, trying to break through before it was too late. Peanut, startled, turned to see the figure in the clown mask. The stick dropped from his hand as the pair on the ground struggled to their feet.

What's the matter, Greggie? Can't control your goddamn pet?

Puppetman, exhausted and weak, cowered inside. Gregg fled, panicky at being seen. He'd never been caught before, never been noticed. Branches whipped at him as he ran blindly. Peanut shouted after him in alarm.

But there was no escape from Gimli's voice. Gimli was always there—as Gregg shoved his way through the tent encampment, as he stumbled from the park back into the streets, as he found his way back to the Marriott.

How much longer can you hold him, Greggie? the dwarf taunted. *A day? Maybe two? Then the bastard's going to fucking eat YOU. Puppetman's going to tear loose and fucking eat you whole.*

Spector couldn't see them across the lobby, but he knew they were there. A knot of people, Hartmann and his entourage, were moving toward him. There wasn't much noise. Spector took a step out to meet them. People were looking in his direction without noticing him. His pulse quickened as they got closer. Cameras flashed around Hartmann. Hartmann held out his hand to Spector.

Spector reached out and noticed he was wearing white gloves and a black leotard. People began to laugh and point. Spector gritted his teeth and locked eyes with the senator. He could feel Hartmann's blood boiling with pain, his ragged breathing, his heart trip-hammering into oblivion. An instant of satisfaction, then it was over. He fell to the floor. Absolute silence. The camera flashes continued, strobing around them. Spector kicked him over with his foot. It was Tony. His face was horrible, caught in a last scream.

Hartmann laughed and Spector looked up. He was surrounded by Secret Service. They drew their guns and pointed them at Spector. The barrels looked impossibly large.

Spector was opening his mouth to say something when the first shot took his lower jaw off. He tried to back away, but more bullets knocked him off his feet. Pieces of him were being ripped away. One of his eyes went dark. He'd been shot before, but it had never been like this. He could feel the rain of slugs pushing his body across the floor. Several of his fingers were gone off one hand. He held up the other in front of his face. It was still perfectly white, not a drop of blood on it. His other eye went dark.

He screamed and rolled off the bed, then crawled underneath it. There was no sound of gunfire. He moved his lower jaw and hands. His eyes adjusted slowly to the dark. Spector slid out from under the bed and turned on the table lamp. He was alone in the room. The air-conditioner kicked on. He jumped.

"Fucking nightmare." He shook his head and pulled himself back up onto the bed. "Jesus, what a fucking nightmare."

He fumbled for the TV control and switched it on. It was another old movie. He recognized John Wayne. For some reason seeing the Duke calmed him down. He reached under the night table and pulled out his bottle of whiskey. There was barely half a swallow left. He picked up the phone to order another bottle from room service. Tomorrow he was going to find someplace else to stay. Somebody was going to miss the real Herbert Baird soon, and Spector didn't want to be staying in his room when the police came knocking. He could call the hotel from wherever it was he wound up staying to see if Tony had left a message. He wished like hell it was all over and he was back in Jersey.

CHAPTER FOUR

Thursday
July 21, 1988

1:00 A.M.

"You bastard!"

The bow fell from the strings with a discordant squeal. Hiram glared down at Tachyon. His eyes, buried in pasty rolls of fat, glared red.

"Hiram, it is late. We are all under a good deal of stress. So, I'm going to ignore that."

Worchester struggled visibly for control, then said, "I've left twenty-seven messages for you starting on Tuesday evening."

Tachyon clapped a hand to his forehead. "Oh, Ancestors, Hiram, forgive me. Today . . . yesterday," he amended, checking his watch. "I was in New York for the funeral—"

"Did you see Jay?" asked Worchester.

"Jay?"

"Ackroyd."

Memory kicked in—*Jay Ackroyd*—a small-time private investigator, part-time ace and full-time friend of Hiram's. He was some kind of projecting teleport who had used his power on Wild Card Day 1986 to rescue Tachyon out of a ticklish situation.

"Oh, him. No."

"Come with me. We have a major problem. One I think only you can solve. Thank God, it doesn't seem to be too late.

155

If it had been, you *really would* have something to feel guilty about."

Tachyon snapped shut the violin case and fell into step with Hiram.

"So what is this all about?"

Worchester kept his voice very low. "Chrysalis hired an assassin."

"*What?*"

The big man snapped his fingers in front of Tachyon's face. "Wake up, Tachyon."

"Blood and line, I can't believe this."

"Believe it. Jay is seldom wrong about things like this. Even if he's somehow mistaken, can we afford to take a chance?"

Cold lead seemed to have settled into the pit of Tach's stomach. "Have we any idea of the target?"

"Jay thinks it's Barnett, but for safety's sake I think we can't rule out anyone. Security must be increased on all of the candidates. Our problem is how to alert the Secret Service without revealing all that we know. My god, it would all be lost then."

Hiram's voice faded to a basso rumble. The words lost meaning, and Tach sat in a private hell staring at the knuckles of his right hand as they slowly turned white.

"*. . . he killed Chrysalis, and now he's going to kill me*."

"*You don't want to believe*."

"*Help me*."

"NO!"

"Jesus Christ! Have you heard a word I've been saying?" Sweat had formed dark rings beneath the ace's armpits. "What are we going to do?"

"I'll tell the Secret Service that I was randomly skimming in a crowd, and picked up the surface thoughts of the assassin. His intent, but not his target or his method."

"Yes, yes, good." A new worry intruded. "But will they believe you?"

"They'll believe me. You humans are all so impressed by my mental powers." He patted Worchester's arm. "Do not worry, Hiram. We will stop him."

It was sheer bravado. And Tach had a feeling that Hiram knew.

5:00 A.M.

"You sure this is where you want out, ma'am?" the uniformed driver asked, craning to peer through the window at the tent city sprung up like post-rain mushrooms in Piedmont Park. Day was really starting to happen, paling the flames of the occasional camp fire dying on the trodden grass.

"I'm sure," she said and stepped out. The air was already congealing with a colloid of heat and wet, and diesel fumes, and the smell of secretions, human and not quite. She shut the door. The cruiser pulled away.

She resisted the urge to shoot the car a bird. When she'd asked for police protection, they'd just stared at her.

Hoping to contain hysteria and speculation, the Atlanta police were stonewalling on the Peachtree murder. Even Ricky's name was being withheld, ostensibly pending notification of his mother in Philadelphia. Sara's involvement had not been announced either; perhaps in part as a buy-off gesture, the APD spokeswoman was telling the press that the murdered man's companion was being held under protective custody.

Sara knew full well that the Atlanta police were trying to damp dynamite in a mason jar—the explosion, when it came, was going to be that much worse for the attempt. All the same she was glad of it. Ricky's colleagues would learn his identity soon enough, and infer that she was the woman who'd been with him when he was slain.

She dreaded what would happen then. She didn't even have a stirring of temptation to use the inevitable interrogation to try to expose Hartmann. She knew how futile that would be; Tachyon had done his job too well.

She put on her broad-brimmed hat, hoisted the strap of her bag higher on her shoulder. The intrepid reporter—now free lance—walking among the wretched of the earth, not to mention the butt-ugly, gathering their stories of anguish and repression: an act good for a few hours in the middle of a crowd.

She was afraid to be alone.

Deathly afraid.

She began to limp up the hill.

9:00 A.M.

Gregg didn't think he'd slept much at all the night before. The last ballot hadn't been cast until early morning, and then there'd been a mild staff celebration in the green room—he'd broken the eighteen-hundred-vote barrier. The hope was that the momentum would swing him to 2,081 and the nomination by evening. "Three hundred votes. Piece of cake," deVaughn had said.

And Gregg didn't care. He didn't care.

Gregg stood at the window of his suite looking down at the crowds swirling below in the morning sunshine—Hartmann supporters, mostly, from the hats. He rubbed his eyes, sipping on black coffee in a Styrofoam cup. The coffee burned in his stomach; Puppetman burned in his head.

"Goddamn it, you have to feed me," Puppetman wailed, and with the voice came the presence's agony—that feeling of slow starvation.

"I can't." Gregg could feel that emptiness in his own stomach, a steady craving. "I want to, but we can't. You know that."

"We don't have a fucking choice, not any more." Puppetman clawed at him with mental talons. Gregg's fingers clenched the heavy curtains. The sight of people walking in the morning sunshine mocked Puppetman's hunger. He wanted them. He wanted to leap down like a panther and ravage them. His fingers whitened with the intensity of his grip.

"Back in New York—" Gregg began, but Puppetman cut him off.

"*Now!* We won't get to New York for another week. I can't wait that long. *You* can't wait that long."

"What the hell do you want me to do?" Gregg raged back in desperation. "It's not *me*, it's Gimli. We have to do something about *him*. Give me another day," Gregg pleaded.

"*Now!*"

"Please . . ." Gregg was nearly sobbing. His head throbbed with the pain of holding Puppetman back. He wanted to rip his skull open and gouge out the demanding power with his bare hands.

"*SOON*, then, goddamn it! Soon, or I'll make you crawl

again. I'll strip you naked and make you beat yourself off in front of the press. Do you hear me? I'll eat you if I can't have anyone else. Gimli's right in that."

Puppetman raked his mind again and Gregg gasped with the pain. "Leave me alone!" he shouted. His knotted fingers tore the curtains from the wall in a fury. They crashed to the ground in a thunder of rods and hooks. Gregg hurled his coffee cup across the room, splattering the plush furniture and burning his hand. "Just leave me alone!" he screamed, his fingers dragging at his face.

"Gregg!"

"Senator!"

Ellen had come from the bedroom. At the same time, Billy Ray burst in through the hall door. Both of them stared at Gregg and the wreckage of the room, Ellen with a stark horror on her face, and her hands folded protectively over her stomach. "My god, Gregg," she said. It was a whisper this time. "I heard you arguing . . . I thought there was somebody else here . . ." Her voice trailed off.

Gregg blinked stupidly, shocked. For the first time Gregg realized that Puppetman *had* spoken out loud. He'd been holding a goddamn out-loud conversation with Puppetman and hadn't known. The horror of it made him moan.

Ellen glanced at Ray.

Billy looked from Ellen to Gregg, stared for long seconds. Then he backed out of the suite, closing the door behind him.

Gregg was gasping in the middle of the room. He forced his breathing to slow. He tried to shrug, to pretend it had been nothing. "Ellen . . ." he began, but couldn't say anything.

He was suddenly crying, like a child frightened of the dark.

Ellen came to him with a brave smile, cradling his head on her shoulder and stroking his hair. "It's okay, Gregg," she murmured, but he could hear the terror in her voice. "It's okay now. Everything's all right. I love you, darling. You just have to rest." Words. Just words.

Gregg could hear Gimli's laughter and—for just a moment—he wondered why Ellen seemed to ignore it.

"The great state of Iowa! God's country! Corn country!" (Tachyon wondered how the man could keep up this kind of

enthusiasm after so many ballots.) "Casts four votes for Senator
Al Gore!"

The Omni Convention Center made Tachyon think of a
giant funnel. People, like tiny grains of spices, all clinging to
the precipitous sides while gravity tried to tumble them
willy-nilly into the level area of the basketball court. It was an
exaggeration of course, but the facility did give the alien
vertigo.

Dribbling powdered sugar down his coat front, Tachyon
hurriedly balanced his cruller on top of his coffee cup,
snatched up his fountain pen, and jotted down the number.
Then glanced at the running totals in five columns each
headed by an initial. Gore was definitely floundering. Only a
matter of time now. Hartmann had crawled painfully to
nineteen hundred. Tach drew the back of his hand across his
gritty, aching eyes. His session with the Secret Service had
lasted until five. By then it seemed pointless to go to bed.

"Your boy's in trouble," said Connie Chung, sliding into a
folding chair behind him. The headset with its antenna made
her look like a lopsided insect.

"*My boy*, as you put it, is doing just fine. Once Gore drops
out—"

"You're going to be in for a rude shock."

"What do you mean?" asked Tach, alarmed.

"He's faced with a choice between three Northern liberals
and a conservative Southerner. What do you think—"

"No," said Tach with loathing.

She brushed sugar from his chin. "You really are a baby at
this, Doctor. Watch and learn." She started away then looked
back and added, "Oh, by the way, Gore's called a press
conference for ten o'clock."

The phone rang during Jack's first Camel of the day. For
a moment he couldn't find his briefcase, then discovered it
under the coffee table. He picked up the receiver and
collapsed on the couch. His caller was Amy Sorenson.

"We're in trouble. Gregg wants your ass over here."

Jack stared at the ceiling through gummed eyes. "What's
the problem?"

"Gore's called a press conference for later this morning.
He's dropping out, and he's gonna tell his people to support
Barnett."

"That cocksucker! That yuppie cocksucker!" For once Jack wasn't conscious of using bad language in front of a woman. He jumped off the couch, knocking the coffee table halfway across the room. "He's going to be Barnett's veep, right?"

"Looks that way."

"Prince Albert in a fucking can."

"And some wild card talent carved up a member of the Fourth Estate in Peachtree Mall last night, so guess who's gonna be capitalizing on it. Just get over here."

The staff meeting couldn't resolve anything except to hold on and hope for defections. Gore's endorsement couldn't be anything but the result of some major payoff, and it might offend some of his followers who couldn't stomach Barnett.

Hartmann gained another 104 delegates on the fourth ballot, so Jack's worst fears weren't realized. But Barnett picked up nearly three hundred, and the momentum was definitely his. On his little two-inch Sony, Jack heard Dan Rather relate stories of party power brokers trying to form an "anyone but Hartmann" movement. Speculations about a dream Dukakis/Jackson ticket were spiced with pointed reminders that Jackson had more delegates, and perhaps the ticket should be Jackson/Dukakis. Analysts wondered whether Jackson was willing to eat crow in order to be vice president.

Apparently he wasn't. The ABH movement, as Rather began calling it, seemed to remain the fantasy of a few party hacks and the Barnett campaign staff, who regarded "Anyone but Hartmann" as the equivalent of "Why not the Firebreather?"

Anyone but Hartmann. Jack couldn't believe he was hearing this. Why the hell wasn't it *Anyone but Barnett*?

A secret ace, he thought. Maybe there's a secret ace.

The Gremlins from the Kremlin as an alternate hypothesis was definitely losing ground.

At first it went well. Sara could do this walking in her sleep, the mechanical interviews, stuff of every third Sunday supplement article and human interest story on the tank town ten o'clock news: *What's it like to be a joker in America?*

It wasn't good journalism. It was something she specifically despised: families-of-dead-shuttle-astronauts, how-does-it-feel-to-be-raped reporting. But of course this wasn't journalism at all; it was survival.

It all went fine until she was recognized.

The jokers camped in the park came from all over: California, Idaho, Vermont, even a few from Alaska and Hawaii. While the better-read of them would recognize her name—she was one of the premiere writers on wild card matters in the world, after all—she wasn't a broadcast journalist. Everybody knew Connie Chung's face, nobody knew hers. That had always satisfied her.

But there were a lot of her old buddies from J-town here, too. She hadn't even thought what their reaction to her would be until a furred, taloned hand took her shoulder and spun her away from the joker mother and two desperately disparate children she was unspooling inanities from, into a hot blast of spoiled-meat predator's breath.

"Just what do you think you're doing here?" a voice asked.

The first panicked reaction was still echoing in the corridors of Sara's brain, *it's him I wish I had a gun dear God Ricky Ricky*, when she recognized the person who'd accosted her. She was hard to mistake: six feet from the black moist nose at the end of her wedge-shaped head to the tip of her tail, round-eared, bandit-masked, black guard hairs over buff fur shading toward silver on her belly, like a Disneymation anthropomorphic ferret made real. The only thing she wore was a green vest studded with Hartmann buttons and bitter joker slogans: WHY BE NORMAL? and JJS! and TAKE A NAT TO LUNCH. Sara knew her well; she should have been just another teenaged Italian girl wearing a dowdy, blue-plaid skirt to St. Mary's. She'd been busted for the first time at fourteen, during a Free Doughboy demonstration.

"Mustelina," she said. "Hi. How are you?"

"What do you think you're doing here, bitch?" Sara recoiled from her vehemence. It was amazing how the Disney people always missed details like the two-inch fangs curving from her upper jaw.

"What do you mean?" The time she'd spent among jokers had inured her so she didn't flinch away from the girl's breath. Mustelina's joker had included a compulsive craving for live meat. Fortunately there were a lot of rats in Jokertown.

A crowd was accreting. Many of the jokers from the sticks were anonymous behind masks, but the J-town contingent tended to parade its jokerhood, wearing disfigurements like proud stigmata. She recognized Glowbug and Mr. Cheese and

Peanut with his hard-shelled stump and a strange look in his eye. They had been her friends. There was little friendship here now.

"You know real well what I mean. You sold us to Barnett."

She blinked, tears starting hot. "What are you talking about?"

"You're the one tried to smear Senator Gregg," a Southern voice said from behind a Kabuki mask with eyebrows halfway up a domed white forehead.

"You turned on Hartmann," Mustelina said. "You turned on us. You got a lot of nerve coming here like this."

"Yeah, traitor," somebody else called.

"Nat!"

"Fucking Jew bitch!"

She tried to back away. They hemmed her on all sides, the faces of grotesques by Goya and Hokusai and Bosch, hostile masks of feathers and plastic smooth as bone. *Why did I come here? These are* Hartmann's *people*.

Suddenly Mustelina was snatched right out of her face and thrown fifteen feet. She curled into a ball, rolled, came up bottling and popping like a string of firecrackers.

A vast white figure loomed over the incipient mob. It held out a chubby hand, pallid and shiny as uncooked dough.

"Come on, Thara," it lisped in the voice of a black child. "I'll take you where it'th thafe."

She clung to the hand. Doughboy started forward with his rolling gait and Sara at his side. The crowd gave back. He was nonviolent. He also weighed in at upwards of six hundred, and had the strength of three or four nat men. In his own way he was quite irresistible.

"I thaw you on Mechano's televithion," Doughboy said. "You were thaying terrible things about the Thenator. Everybody thaid you were a twaitor."

She looked up at him. His face was an unpitted moon. He smiled without lips or teeth.

"You are my friend, Thara. I knew you'd never do nothing wrong."

She hugged him. She also kept walking. This was an ideal place for Hartmann's marionette to hit her, it had belatedly occurred to her. For that matter, if it hadn't been for Doughboy's arrival, his work might just have been done for him. Some of the crowd was still trailing along behind.

"Will you bwing me some candy sometime, Mith Thara?" Doughboy asked. "Nobody brings me candy since Mithter Thyiner went away."

He stopped at the street and faced her. "When will Mithter Thyiner come back? Do you think he'll come back soon?"

"He's not coming back, honey," she said gently. "You know that." It had been a stroke, that January. Doughboy found him paralyzed on his mattress in their little Eldridge Street apartment, carried him through the streets weeping and begging for someone to help fix Mr. Shiner. He reached Jokertown Clinic before an ambulance with a heavy enough suspension to carry him could be found—nobody was going to try to separate him from his friend and guardian. By that time there was nothing even Dr. Tachyon could do.

Tears rolled from Doughboy's button eyes. "I mith him. I mith him tho."

She reached up. She wasn't tall enough. He bent over until she could wrap her arms around his neck.

"I know you do, honey," she said through her own tears. "Thank you for helping me. I'll bring you candy soon. I love you."

She kissed his cheek and walked quickly away without looking back.

11:00 A.M.

"Doctor!"

He studied the handsome dark face, the intense eyes actively scanning the lobby of the Marriott. Missing nothing.

Tach bowed slightly. "Reverend."

"Deserting the floor of the convention?"

"Too chaotic."

"And disappointing?" suggested Jesse Jackson softly.

"It *will* be all right." Tach cocked his head speculatively. "And you, entering the stronghold of the enemy?"

"Gregg Hartmann is not my enemy."

"Ah, then you would have no objection to dropping out, and handing your delegates to the senator?"

Jackson laughed. "Doctor, you beat me to the punch. May we talk?" He indicated a sofa near one wall of the upper lobby.

AP, Time, the *Sun Times,* and the *Post* began circling like

barracuda. Straight Arrow, the Mormon ace from Utah, and
Jackson's ace bodyguard, eyed them with an unblinking stare.
The news of Tachyon's bombshell had spread quickly through
the security forces. To Tachyon's knowledgeable eye the lobby
seemed filled with discretely armed men.

"Wouldn't your suite be more private?" asked the Takisian
dryly.

The flash of white teeth behind the mustache. "Private is
not what I'm after. Let 'em speculate."

Tachyon debated. Decided that perhaps he and the
Reverend Jackson could use one another. Some might speculate that Tachyon's support of Hartmann was wavering. Others
might decide that Jackson was about to endorse Hartmann.

They settled onto the sofa. The tall black man, the
diminutive alien with one leg tucked up beneath him.

"I want you to transfer your support to me," said Jackson
bluntly.

"Just like that?"

"Just like that. I'm the logical candidate to represent the
jokers and aces. Together we can build a new world."

"I've been here forty-two years, Reverend, and I'm still
waiting for that new world."

"You must not give in to cynicism, pessimism and despair,
doctor. I hadn't expected that from you. You're a fighter—like
me." Tachyon didn't speak, and Jackson went on. "We have the
same interests."

"Do we? I want to see my people protected. You want to
be president."

"Help me become president, and then I can protect your
people—my people too." He frowned at the far wall. "Doctor,
my foreparents came to America on slave ships. You came here
in a spaceship, but we're in the same boat now. If Barnett
becomes president we all suffer."

Tachyon shook his head more in confusion than negation.
"I don't know. Gregg Hartmann has been our friend for twenty
years. Why should I abandon him now?"

Help me.

Kill me.

Believe me.

He ruthlessly silenced the voices.

"Because he can't win. The senator is stalling. My people
are reporting "Anyone-but-Hartmann" coalitions springing up

all over the convention. If Gregg Hartmann can't stop Leo Barnett, Michael Dukakis certainly cannot."

"And you can?"

That self-confident grin that had galvanized a country. Like an arc light in its intensity. "Yes, I can." The smile faded, and he stared intently down at Tachyon. "I understand. I know abandonment, and people being mean to you, and saying you're nothing and nobody and can never be anything. *I understand.*" His hand gripped the Takisian's shoulder.

Tachyon laid his hand over Jackson's. The same perfectly manicured nails, the same long slender fingers, but white on black. "Why is it when you and Barnett are reputed to serve the same god, your gods are so different?"

"A good question, Doctor. A very good question."

A Flying Ace glider sighed softly onto the tile at Tachyon's feet. He picked it up, stroked the molded white scarf with a forefinger. Jackson stared at the painted black face. His hand rose reflexively, and he drew his fingers down his cheek.

"Is your reluctance to back me entirely due to your loyalty, or is it because I'm black?"

Tach's head snapped up. "Burning Sky, no." He rose. "Believe me, Reverend, if I should ever decide to transfer my support from Gregg Hartmann you would be my first choice. You see, you have a charisma that is almost Takisian in its magnitude."

Jackson smiled. "And I take it that's a compliment?"

"Of the highest, Reverend, of the highest."

12:00 NOON

Gregg's room-service lunch sat untouched and cold on the coffee table of the suite. The Sony blared unheeded, and Tachyon sat like some damn wooden god on the couch. Dangerously near the surface, Gregg could hear Puppetman's voice, mingled with Gimli's mocking laughter. It took all of his concentration not to lose himself in the subliminal chatter and say something that would reveal the conflict underneath.

Worst of all, Gregg was afraid that Puppetman might start speaking out loud again.

He paced restlessly in front of the windows. The entire time he could feel Tachyon's violet gaze on him: judging, appraising, cool. Gregg knew he was talking too much, but the

motion and the monologue seemed to help keep Puppetman
down.

"Barnett's up another hundred votes in the last ballot.
One-hundred votes! We've gained what—twenty, twenty-five?
Someone's got to start plugging the holes, Doctor. Hell,
Charles said he'd talked to Gore's staff and was told Gore was
planning to stay in. That was just last night, for chris'sakes.
Barnett must have promised him the damn VP spot in return
for the delegates. We've got half the press yapping about an
'Anyone but Hartmann' movement, which means some of the
on-the-fence delegates are going to start believing it. Barnett's
already benefited from that garbage; Dukakis is back there
smiling and shaking hands and waiting for the deadlock or a
deal."

"I know all this, Senator," Tachyon said. There was a trace
of impatience in his voice as he folded delicate hands on his
lap.

"Then let's start *doing* something about it, damn it." The
alien's cool haughtiness made Gregg's temper flare, and Puppetman rose with the irritation. *No, idiot,* he told the power.
Not with him here, of all people. Please.

"I'm doing what I can," Tachyon said with clipped, precise
words. "Browbeating those who support you isn't likely to get
you anywhere, Senator. Especially not among your friends."

Gregg had no "friends," no confidants—unless he counted
Puppetman. He suspected Tachyon was the same. They called
each other "friend," but it was mostly the residue of a
political/social relationship that went back to the mid-sixties,
when Gregg was a councilman and, later, mayor of New York.
Gregg had performed favors for Tachyon, Tachyon had done
the same for him. They both affected the politics of the liberal,
the left. That far they were friends.

Tachyon was an ace. Gregg was afraid of aces, especially
aces who could read minds. He knew that if Tachyon suspected the truth, the alien would not hesitate even one
moment in revealing Gregg to the public.

So much for friendship. The thought made Gregg angrier
yet.

"Then let's talk frankly. As friends," Gregg shot back.
"The talk is all over the convention. You've been chasing Fleur
van Renssaeler like some horny teenager. There are things
here more important than your gonads, Doctor."

Gregg had never dared to speak to Tachyon that way before, not to a person with such a formidable mind power, not with Puppetman lurking in his head. Tachyon flushed a deep red. He rose to his feet with swift offended dignity. "Senator—" he began, but Gregg wheeled around with a chopping motion of his hand.

"No, Doctor. No." Gregg's anger was a glowing coal stuck in his chest. He wanted to use his fists on the prissily dressed man and see that fine, aristocratic nose flatten and splatter blood over the frilly satin shirt. Gregg gritted his teeth to keep from shouting in fury, from backhanding Tachyon's arrogant face. He ached to kick the man in his goddamn alien balls. It wasn't only Tachyon. It was the whole frigging day—the way his momentum had come to a wheezing halt on the convention floor, the eternal gnawing of Puppetman, the chortling of Gimli, Mackie's failures in New York and here since Chrysalis's death, Ellen: everything.

For just a moment, he wondered if Puppetman hadn't fanned the embers. The thought cooled him. He grimaced.

"I need you. You can pretend to be just a correspondent, but everyone knows better. You're a very, very visible supporter," he told Tachyon. "Everyone is extremely aware of your help with my campaign and our stand on the wild card issues. How does it look to the rest of the convention if the good doctor is obviously more concerned about getting laid than with making sure his candidate is nominated? Priorities, Doctor. Priorities."

Tachyon took a deep breath in through his nose, lifting his chin. "I don't need to be lectured like some errant child. Not by you, Senator, and especially not after I've spent the entire morning working for you. I find your accusations extremely distasteful."

"How distasteful will it be if Barnett is the next president, Doctor? He may pretend to be compassionate, but we all know what will happen. Do you think you'll still have funding for your clinic? Is what will happen to the jokers then worth a few minutes of grunting passion between a woman's legs?"

"Senator—" Tachyon uttered in outrage.

Gregg laughed, and the sound had a manic, cutting edge. He was sweating, his Brooks Brothers shirt ringed under the arms. "Doctor, I'm sorry. I apologize for offending you. I'm being blunt because I'm concerned. For me, yes, but also for the jokers. If we lose here, everyone affected by the wild card loses too. You understand that, I know."

Tachyon's lips were a thin, bloodless line. The angry flush lurked on his high cheekbones. "I understand better than anyone, Senator. It would do you good to remember that."

He spun on his toes in a graceful ballet turn and strode quickly to the door. Gregg thought that he'd stop and say more, but Tachyon simply walked out, nodding to Billy Ray stationed outside.

"Not even a fucking exit line," someone said in Gregg's voice.

Gregg wasn't sure who it was that spoke.

1:00 P.M.

A scuffle had broken out between a member of the New York delegation and an old woman from Florida. The two women had gone from shoves to the teeth-bared and hands-in-claws stage. Hiram, blood suffusing his face, eyes almost popping with fury, flung chairs aside and rolled toward them. At the tiered wedding-cake podium Jim Wright was banging desperately and ineffectually. He gaped as the head broke clean off the gavel, and went sailing away into the crowd.

Tachyon, end-running through the milling throng, saw Hiram clench his fist, then an indescribable expression washed across the ace's face, leaving his expression as blank as a beach after a retreating wave. The plump manicured hand fell open and hung limply at his side.

The old bat was wearing a Barnett button and a large wooden cross. For an instant the Takisian hesitated; then, seeing the sharp toe of the Florida delegate's shoe lifting for a kick, he threw caution to the wind, and mind-controlled the both of them.

The press arrived.

Security arrived.

Fleur arrived.

"*How dare you!* Let her go!" Fleur dropped her arm protectively over the Barnett delegate's shoulder.

Tach noted that Hiram had a grip on the New York madam. He bowed jerkily. "With pleasure, just don't let her hit me."

"OH MY GOD! HE CRAWLED IN MY MIND! HE POLLUTED ME! ALIEN—"

"Madam, I make it a point never to pollute ladies of your age and situation with my precious alien fluids. Or my precious alien time."

"Bastard!" Fleur swept the sobbing woman away.

Hiram drew a hand across his brow. "Not tactful, Tachy."

"I'm not feeling very tactful. This is a disaster."

"This overcrowding makes fights inevitable," said Hiram.

They settled into some empty chairs. Even Tach's knees were practically at his chin, so closely packed were the chairs. With a furtive glance for security or cameras the Takisian unlimbered his flask. Hiram gulped down an enormous swallow of brandy, choked, and suddenly Tach was shivering in distress as tears started rolling down Worchester's fat cheeks to mat in the heavy black beard. Sobs shook the massive body.

Tachyon threw his arms around Hiram, patting, rocking, soothing. A string of nonsense words, endearments and reassurances poured from his lips. His own voice was jumping.

The emotional storm passed, and Tach offered his handkerchief. Hiram touched his brow, lips with tentative fingers.

"Sorry. Sorry."

"It is quite all right. We are all under such strain."

"Tachyon, *he has to win!*"

The alien glanced from the wild, staring eyes to Hiram's hands closed vise-like around Tach's arms. The human's knuckles were turning white from the pressure. Tachyon lightly touched one hand, and said very softly and very gently.

"Hiram, please, you're hurting me."

Worchester released him like a sprung trap. "Sorry. Sorry. Tachyon, we have to do whatever it takes, don't we? This is too important to leave to chance . . . to the good will of others. This is one time when the end may justify any means. Yes?"

Eyes closed Tachyon remembered Syria. Jokers being stoned to death in the streets before the bored or avid eyes of the nat passersby. South Africa. A time, not so very long ago, when it wasn't considered a crime to rape a joker woman—just a lapse in taste.

"Yes, Hiram. Maybe you're right."

Patting the restaurateur absently on the shoulder Tach went in search of Charles Devaughn. What he was considering . . . no, committed to doing . . . was insane. Certainly unfair. But when had a Takisian ever been concerned with fair play? No sense approaching committed Barnett delegates. That would only arouse suspicion, and the affects might not last. But the uncommitteds . . . if they had a change of heart after some fervent politicking from Devaughn and the oh-so-persuasive and the oh-so-charismatic Dr. Tachyon. . . . And Michael Dukakis? He could afford to lose a few. His only hope now was to be selected as the vice-presidential candidate. . . .

It just seemed to sail down out of nowhere and into her hand. She barely had to move or will and she was holding it. She walked down Harris studying it: a plastic J.J. Flash Flying Ace glider, with holes carefully burned through its body and wings with a hot wire or rod. The face had been pen-blacked to oblivion with careful malice.

A couple of little black kids were wandering past in the other direction, staring at all the funny people. "What's you got there, lady?" asked the one in the Run DMC T-shirt.

She looked at the thing in her hand without comprehension. "A fucking Flying Joker," she said.

The room wasn't as nice as the one he'd had at the Marriott. There were old wooden blinds instead of curtains; the bedsprings creaked, and the pastel paint was peeling around the baseboards. The motel was forty-five minutes from downtown and he'd had to slip the desk clerk a fifty to get the room. Still, Spector felt much more comfortable here. There was an all-night liquor store down the block and a burger place across the street. He was finishing up a greasy doublemeat-doublecheese and trying to come up with some kind of believable lies to tell Tony. He still had his Marriott room key, so getting into the hotel would be no trouble.

They'd talk about old times mostly. At least, that was what he hoped. His life before drawing the black queen was a hopeless blur. He didn't think about his past much, and considered the future only slightly more. Mostly he thought about death. Not because he liked it, but it was hard not to. Death put everything else into insignificant perspective. If all the politicians and lawyers and corporate hotshots understood the reaper the way he did, they'd never bother to get out of bed in the morning.

Spector picked up the phone, an old beige rotary model, and dialed the Marriott. After about twenty rings there was an answer. "Marriott Marquis." The voice was curt and whiny. Probably the little jerkoff who'd been at the desk when he checked in.

"Yes. Any messages for 1031?"

They put him on hold without so much as a "one moment" or "let me check." Spector drummed his fingertips on his thigh. They were probably making him wait on purpose. Worse, they might have figured out what happened to Baird and were tracing the call. That would take at least a minute or two. He'd wait a few more seconds.

"Yes. Mr. Calderone says to meet him in the lobby at six this evening." Click.

"Fuck you, too," Spector said, rapping the mouthpiece on the edge of the nightstand. He tossed the receiver into the cradle and headed for the bathroom. Why was it ritzy hotels hired assholes? The little clerk was moving up the list. His chances of living out the week were even slimmer than Hartmann's.

3:00 P.M.

The CNN glass press booth hung like a vision of heaven at the top of the center. Tachyon labored wearily up the steps. Mentally preparing for another round of talks with journalists. A strata of society that shared a good many traits with carrion birds, he decided bitterly. *Must* have a story. The more tragic, horrifying, terrifying the better. *Hartmann's star, so bright at the beginning of this long campaign trail, seems to be sadly dimming in the white-hot fires of this Democratic convention.* The unctuous commentator mouthing the silly metaphor. But it seemed to be becoming a self-fulfilling prophesy.

The door to the press booth opened. Fleur emerged. The stairway suddenly became unbearably claustrophobic. They were going to meet face to face. It was unavoidable. Tachyon steeled himself. Suddenly Fleur's high heel slipped from beneath her, and she pitched headlong down the stairs. Calf muscles burning with strain, Tach vaulted up the steps, and caught her just before her dark head connected with the concrete. Her chignon had jerked loose, and strands of sable hair hung about her face. He righted her, and a few more hairpins fell pattering to the floor.

"Are you all right?"

"Yes, yes." She pressed a hand to her forehead, looking about in confusion. "I could have been killed." His arms were still around her. She glanced down, raised hesitant eyes to his face. "You're still holding me."

"My apologies." He began to withdraw. She laid her hand on his shoulder holding him in place. Tachyon felt her thigh, firm beneath the silk skirt, weld itself to his. His cock stirred.

"You could have let me fall. It would have been natural after . . . after the way I've treated you."

"I would never let you . . . fall."

Fingers, as soft as butterflies, explored his face, traced across his lips. "You saved my life."

"You exaggerate."

Fleur pressed her body to his. Tach groaned softly as his penis stiffened to rigid and aching attention. Suddenly she cupped his face between her hands and kissed him. All vestiges of control vanished. Tongue probing deep into her mouth, he gripped her buttocks. Their panting breaths set an odd counterpoint to the roll call droning up from the floor. Tach's hands played frenziedly across her body.

Fleur broke away. Struggled to rebutton her blouse. Tachyon gripped her trembling fingers.

"Here, let me."

"Take me to your room."

He looked up, fingers frozen on a button. She lifted his hand, bit down hard on a forefinger.

Help me.

A cry from his soul? Or a random thought from Fleur? He ignored the plaintive voice.

"We can't be seen leaving together," whispered Fleur.

He handed her his room key. "I'll follow . . . soon."

Jack's phone bleeped again. It had been ringing all through his lunch at the Bello Mondo and the other patrons were beginning to get annoyed. The Speaker of the U.S. House of Representatives, in fact, was scowling at him from the next table. Jack offered Jim Wright of Texas an apologetic look, opened his case, and took out the handset.

"This is Tachyon. I am calling from the press room. I must leave, and I require someone here with your kind of charisma."

"What for, exactly?"

"I will inform you when you arrive. Please hurry."

"Hey. Don't give me this Takisian-royalty-in-a-hurry crap." But Tachyon had hung up.

Jack contemplated grinding the telephone to dust.

Instead he finished his last bite of dessert, overpaid, and fed the maître d' his C-note.

The distance from the Marriott to the Convention Center was precisely one unfiltered Camel in length. Jack's neck prickled. He and Fleur van Renssaeler jostled in a door leading to the Convention Center. Psychos—his third wife had been a real nut case—made him nervous. Despite the way Fleur spooked him, Jack gave her a jaunty wave and grin, received a close-lipped smile in return. He saw a Marriott room key in her hand and figured she was heading to the hotel to give some reporter a blow job straight from God, maybe convert him to Barnett's cause.

Tachyon was waiting just beneath the ABC skybox, wearing his cavalier coat with the slashes and turnbacks, the riding breeches and boots. The alien's face was strained. When he saw Jack, the violet eyes flashed.

"What took you so long?"

"Hi, to you, too."

"It's imperative that you speak to the press immediately." Waving his plumed hat under Jack's nose.

"Fine." Jack tipped another cigarette out of the pack. "What am I supposed to be talking to them about?"

"This 'Anyone-but-Hartmann' business. If the media keeps harping on this, it will become a self-fulfilling prophesy."

"Okay." Jack grinned as he lit the Camel. "Is Connie Chung in there? And if she's married, is her husband here?"

"This is no time for—" Tachyon began waving the hat again, then abruptly swallowed his words. Color blossomed on his cheeks. At the sight, a cold, despairing certainty settled into Jack's mind.

"It's Fleur, right? That was your hotel key she waved at me."

"She did not wave—" The alien swallowed his words

again. Tachyon drew himself up to his full princely height—with the heels, about eight inches below Jack's—and glared with furious violet eyes. "I will not have my personal life questioned. This is no affair of yours."

"Darn right it's no affair of mine. I turned her down a few days ago."

Tachyon showed his teeth. "How dare you! Do you know who you're speaking to?"

Jack took a measured breath of smoke. "I'm talking to someone who's being led around by his dick, which is pretty funny, considering how long it's been since you last got it up."

Tachyon flushed red with anger. Cold fear touched Jack's spine at the thought that he'd gone too far, that this was someone who had been raised to kill at the slightest insult, who had in fact once sworn to murder Jack and might decide that he'd ignored the vow for too long . . .

But instead Tachyon just brushed past him, heading out of the Convention Center. Jack followed, his long legs keeping pace easily with the alien's quick step.

"Tach, okay, that wasn't fair," he said. "The point is, Fleur *did* make a pass at me the other day."

"I don't believe you." Tachyon spoke through clenched teeth, his boot heels tapping rapidly on the concrete.

"She's trying to embarrass the campaign. You know how much the whole Sara Morgenstern business cost us. There might be half-a-dozen network cameramen behind a two-way mirror watching you when you screw."

"In . . . *my* . . . bedroom?" Tachyon's measured answer came out as a half shriek.

"It's *still* a setup. Will you listen?" He grabbed Tachyon's arm. "It's a fucking—"

"Leave me alone!" Wrenching his arm free.

"She's a psycho. She's not her mother. Understand? She's not Blythe."

Tachyon stopped walking and spun to face Jack. His face was drained of color. "Do *not*," he said, "let that name past your lips ever again. You have not earned that right."

Jack stared at him, his annoyance turning to boiling anger. "This is for your own good," he said. He stuck his cigarette in his mouth and picked Tachyon up and put him under his arm. He started walking for the Omni Hotel while the alien kicked and struggled.

"Blood and bone! Let me down!"

"I'm going to find a cold shower and put you in it," Jack said. "Consider it your penance for throwing that bomb at me in Paris. If you want to get laid after that, I know a Miss Peachtree who will be glad—"

Jack stopped moving. He put Tachyon down. He marched up the ramp to the stair leading to the skybox. He dropped the cigarette to the concrete floor, ground it under his heel, and stepped in.

Then he blinked, took a long breath, and tried not to collapse. Tachyon had just shredded his mind like a newspaper torn by a high wind.

Reporters waited, scattered around tables and looking bored. Some were staring at him. Summoning nerve from someplace he didn't know he had, Jack gave them a smile and wave, and stepped forward to say his piece.

4:00 P.M.

"Would you like a drink?"

"No." Her arms were folded protectively across her breasts.

He hefted the bottle. Alcohol was sometimes an inhibitor. He quickly replaced the bottle. Hugged his elbows. Stared at the floor. They were separated by feet. It might have been light years. Never had he felt so gauche.

The hiss of silk brought his head up. Fleur's skirt puddled on the floor about her feet. She studied the far wall with frowning abstraction as she swiftly unbuttoned her blouse, unsnapped her bra. The heavy breasts swung free. She was larger bosomed than her mother had been. Tachyon couldn't decide if he liked it. His mouth was dry from nerves. He watched her buttocks dimple as she climbed into the bed.

"Wait," he forced out.

"Let's do this." As a come-on line it lacked something.

He jammed his hands into his pockets. Took a quick turn about the room. He noted his erection was back.

"I'm scared."

Propping her elbows on her knees, hands hanging loosely between her legs in front of her dark snatch, Fleur said dryly, "That's my line."

"Help me a little."

"How?"

"Undress me. Be loving with me."

She swung off the bed, and took hold of the lace cravat at his throat. Unbuttoned his shirt, and pushed it off his shoulders. Tach, standing with closed eyes, could feel her hair brushing at his skin. The scent of vanilla and spice washed across him—Shalimar. Blythe's scent. It brought it all back so strongly. That hot summer day in '48, the crackle of petticoats as he embraced Blythe, the smell and taste of Shalimar as his lips explored her neck.

Fleur slithered down the length of him like a worshiper at some ancient altar. Her lips were pressed to his belly as she opened his pants, and pulled them down over his hips. His erection throbbed in time to his beating heart. In a frenzy he kicked off his shoes, and struggled to free himself from the confining material of his pants. Fleur laughed, husky and low, as he lost his balance and sprawled on the floor. Kissing, clutching, panting, punctuating the desperate flow of endearments with deep groans, they lurched toward the bed. A single bead of sperm squeezed from the head of his cock. Terrified that he would lose it Tachyon spread her legs, murmuring Takisian obscenities like a pagan litany. The lips of her labia closed about him.

The touch of her mind. Roulette. Poison, death, terror, madness.

He began to lose it. The iron leaching from his penis. Suddenly other hands tangled in his long hair. A sweet husky voice encouraging him.

The muted click of the beaded curtains blowing gently in a hot breeze. The scratchy recording of "La Traviata" throwing sound, like shards of light, throughout the apartment. Blythe in his arms.

He drove deep within her. Gave a shrill cry of triumph. *Blythe. Blythe. Blythe.*

6:00 P.M.

Night was coming. She was sure of it. Sitting beneath a potted plant's notched ear in the Marriott lobby she could feel it slouching rough-beast-like toward downtown Atlanta.

When it came, it would thin the crowd. Remove, one by one, the forest of walking, talking trees in which she hid. Until there was no cover. It was simple mathematics: if safety was numbers, subtraction equaled death.

Night was the natural environment of Hartmann's hunchbacked puppet. She knew that. As she knew night would soon or late be born.

She had to find an indivisible one to protect her. Or the creature that clung to the fur of night's black belly would have her.

Tachyon had failed her. So had Ricky—though his failure had been of the noble variety, and had bought her twenty-four hours of air time. She had to find someone with the strength to shield her, someone who would accept the only coin she had to pay with. Before day's placenta burst.

She knew just the man.

The band was playing "Stars Fell on Alabama," which Jack hoped to hell wasn't some kind of political signal. After eleven futile ballots, almost anything could be taken for an omen by weary and desperate delegates. Jack hoped the song was only a crowd soother after the day's seventh fistfight on the floor, this last between a Jackson delegate defecting to Hartmann and a floor manager who was trying to change his mind. There was a motion on the floor to give up and go home for the day, something that was perfectly in tune with the delegates' premature weariness. Jack moved through his crowd to find Rodriguez.

"Listen, *ese*. We've stayed solid for Hartmann so far."

"Right."

"Everybody's going to come after us tonight. One crack in the façade of solid California and people are going to figure it's open season."

Sweat was pouring down Jack's face. There were sopping stains under the arms of his tailored shirt. At some point that afternoon the air-conditioners had given up.

"Call a meeting after dinner. Nine o'clock. Everyone attends."

Rodriguez looked at him. "What's the meeting *about*?"

"Who gives a damn? We'll figure out something. We just need to count heads, make sure none of the other guys' people are talking to ours. If we keep our delegates busy, we can keep them out of other people's camp."

Rodriguez gave a grin. "What you gonna do after that, man? Bed checks?"

"Something like that." Rodriguez's grin faded. Jack spoke quickly. "We're all blocked together at the Marriott. I want you to put someone you trust on each floor, check people in and out, make a list, get IDs. We can't stop the wrong people from visiting ours, but we can make sure they're seen when they do."

Rodriguez looked dubious. "You've seen all the hookers outside. We're supposed to get their *names*?"

"Just do it," Jack snapped.

Damn. His temper was unraveling along with everyone else's.

"Barnett's people are trying to compromise us," he said, lowering his voice. "One of their bimbos for Christ is fucking Tachyon even as we speak."

Rodriguez looked horrified. "Okay," he said. "I'll see to it."

Jim Wright looked relieved as he gaveled the convention to an early close, leaving the networks frantically trying to schedule hours of prime-time reruns.

Jack's temper growled in his mind as he crowded out the door. The whole thing had gone on too long, two days of balloting following two days of procedural fights, and all in the middle of a sweltering Georgia summer. Fleur van Renssaeler was off fucking Tachyon, hoping to accomplish god-knew-what, and Tach had left Jack to face the media unprepared.

Not only that, Connie Chung was clearly prepared to stay faithful to her husband.

At least he had his table waiting at the Bello Mondo, and a whole night before him. It had been a week since he'd last got laid. He had nothing better to do tonight than rectify that oversight.

There was another message from Bobbie waiting for him at the desk, but there was no answer when he returned her call. He showered, changed, endured the horrors of the glass elevator as he descended from his room to the Bello Mondo.

The waiter, recognizing him, brought his double whiskey without being asked. And then Sara Morgenstern, looking like someone had recently connected her to a car battery, sat opposite him. She was clutching a shoulder bag to her chest as if it were all she owned.

"Mind if I join you?"

He looked at her. She wore clothes well, even the rumpled blue-and-white prom dress she had on at the moment, but her white-blonde hair was disordered and there was an unsteady look in her sunken eyes.

"I don't want to hear about it, Sara," Jack said.

"Can I borrow one of your cigarettes? I'm feeling a little—out of sorts. I saw a murder last night."

"The one in the mall?"

Sara's hands trembled as they extracted a Camel. "It was an ace," she said. "A weird twisted teenage kid. He cut Ricky to pieces. Right in front of me."

Jack decided he didn't want this woman's company for even a second. "Sara," he said.

She looked up at him. There was too much makeup around her eyes, he noticed, trying to hide the effects of a sleepless night.

"The point is," she said, trying to smile, "I don't want to be alone tonight."

Which maybe changes matters, Jack thought. He reached into his jacket for his lighter and lit her cigarette. She inhaled and began coughing uncontrollably. Tears sprang to her eyes. "Jesus," she said. "What are these?"

"The kind I learned to smoke in the Army."

"I used to smoke Carltons in college. I really shouldn't start again. Oh, hell." She stubbed the cigarette out as if driving a dagger into her worst enemy.

"Have a drink. It lasts longer." Jack signalled the waiter.

At least, he thought nobly, he'd be taking this loose cannon out of play for a few hours, maybe a whole night.

All this and get laid, too.

He looked at Sara and an idea came to him.

Maybe he could take her out of play for a lot longer than he first thought.

The North Expressway was jammed, but Tony jockeyed the black Regal through it effortlessly. Spector was glad they weren't eating at the Marriott. There was considerably less chance of someone recognizing him away from the hotel. Tony had on a tailored, dark-blue suit and matching tie. Spector was in gray. His suit still smelled like the store.

"Where are we headed?" Spector asked.

"LaGrotta." Tony whipped across two lanes of traffic to take the Peachtree exit. "If I get us there alive. You'll love this place. Some of the best Italian food in town. Not New York, of course, but you go with what's available."

"Yeah, well, thanks for taking time out. I know you're real busy right now."

"I haven't seen you in ages, man. You get priority." Tony smiled. That smile had been turning women's hearts to goo and winning over men for as long as Spector had known Tony. He was a hard guy not to like.

"How did you wind up with Hartmann?" Spector wanted to keep Tony talking about himself. That way he wouldn't be asking many questions.

Tony shrugged. "One improbability leading to another. I got a loan and managed to talk my way into law school. Did some work in local politics. Just happened to be on the winning side a few times. Somebody in Gregg's camp noticed me and, well, I'm ethnic. That doesn't hurt."

"Plus, you're good. Always were. Good jump shot, good line for the girls." Spector smiled. "Hell, you could talk a good Catholic girl out of her clothes in less time than it took the rest of us to comb our hair."

"It's a sin to waste a God-given talent." Tony wagged his finger at Spector. "And you know how I avoid sin at all costs."

"Right." Spector glanced out the window. There were dark clouds gathering above the treetops with patches of gray below where the rain was already falling. "Looks like we might get wet."

"My friend, for a meal like this you'd swim the Hudson over to Teaneck." Tony made a contented sound. He looked over at Spector and kissed the tips of his fingers. "Trust me."

Thunder rumbled overhead. "I trust you, old buddy." Spector wished he could say it was a two-way street.

7:00 P.M.

He woke suddenly. Filled with a sense of total well-being. Or perhaps *filled* was not the proper description. Empty, floating, freed at last from two years of pressure and anxiety. Tach kicked free of the tangled sheets. The scent of sweat and sex hung heavy in the room. Realized with a thrill of disap-

pointment that the bed was empty. Sat up, then relaxed back
against the pillows at the flush of the toilet.

Fleur padded in, breasts swinging. She realized he was
awake, and her arms crossed over her chest.

"Don't, I like to look at you."

"You're a heathen."

"Yes. You're a courtesan."

She lifted the drapes, and looked out. "That's not very
nice."

"It was meant to be a compliment. Why haven't you
married?"

"How do you know I haven't?" She leaned back against
the window, one buttock cocked up on the narrow sill.

"I don't read married off you."

She stiffened. "Are you reading my mind?"

"No."

"You tried, the second time we did it."

"I would have tried the first time, but I was too busy
trying to make certain that I stayed . . . er . . . firm."

"Don't read my mind!"

"All right. It makes sex better for me, but all right."

"I think it's horrible that you can violate people that way."

"Fleur, may I remind you that I *didn't* read your mind. I
sensed your opposition, and I withdrew. I'm a very well-
mannered person, not to mention charming and handsome
and witty. . . ." There was no lightening of her somber
expression, and he trailed away into embarrassed silence. He
fumbled his flask off the bedside table, and took a swig. "Your
mother wanted so much for you. Husband, children, home,
happiness."

"I don't want to talk about her."

"Why not?"

"It's old history." She slid into the bed, her hand reaching
for his cock. "I want you in bed with me, not with her."

Spector loosened his belt a notch. He'd had a salad and
lamb stew. *Spezzatino de Montone* Tony had called it, sam-
pling a bite to make sure it was up to par. Tony had eaten a
chicken-and-almond dish with buttered rice on the side.
They'd split a strudel with custard for dessert, and that had
done it for Spector. He wasn't used to eating this much and

could practically feel the food piling up at the back of his throat.

Tony sighed. "Did I tell you?"

"Just as good as advertised." Spector drained what was left of the wine in his glass.

"We've been so busy eating that I haven't had a chance to ask you who you're lobbying for."

Spector tensed. So far, they'd talked about the old neighborhood, girls, basketball, what had happened to people. Tony had been his only good friend during his school years. It wasn't that people hated Spector, they just didn't notice him. Tony was Mr. Charisma. They were unlikely friends, but close all the same. Tony's question reminded him that he was here to kill Hartmann. It was an unavoidable fact. "Well, let's just say my employers don't share all the same views as your senator." Spector didn't want to lie, but he sure as hell didn't want to tell the truth either. Better to compromise.

Tony nodded and rounded up a few stray crumbs of strudel with his fork. "You don't want to talk about it, that's fine. You got any feelings about the wild card victims, I mean personally?"

"It's a tough break." Spector knew that as well as anyone, having drawn the black queen himself. Only Tachyon had been stupid enough to bring him back. "But there's lots of tough breaks. Some people just get a few more than others."

"Don't you think jokers are getting kicked around, though?" Tony was looking hard at Spector. He had a stake in this, somehow. Something that went beyond political attitudes.

"Sure. But what are you going to do about it." Spector picked up the bottle of Pinot Nero and poured himself another glass.

"Make sure their rights are protected, just like any other American citizen. That's what I want. That's why I'm working for Hartmann." Tony sat silently for a moment. "Don't think that's too much to ask, do you?"

Spector shook his head. "No. I've been around a lot of jokers. But it's different with them. Blacks, Italians, whoever else, they all still look like people. It's not their own fault, but plenty of jokers look like they should be in a zoo. Most people react with their guts, not their brains." Spector knew, he'd always gone with his instincts. If he hadn't gotten the virus himself, he'd probably hate the jokers like the rest.

Tony tossed his napkin on the table and signalled the waiter to bring the bill. "You got time to take a little ride with me?"

"Sure," Spector said, downing his wine. "What have you got in mind?"

"Just going to visit some friends of mine. Good friends. I'd like you to meet them." Tony smiled again. Spector couldn't say no.

"Maybe after we're done, you can introduce me to your boss. I'd like to meet him." Spector was uncomfortable, and it wasn't entirely due to his bloated stomach.

"We might just be able to do that," Tony said. "But first things first."

Right, Spector thought, *first things first*.

All his old skills had returned. His aspect was truly upon him. Tachyon grinned down at his penis thrusting aggressively from the copper hairs of his brush. Laughing, he dove between her legs, nipping at her thighs, licking, teasing. Only one thing remained. To join completely with her. To join with her mind. He would do it when they climaxed, he decided. That would forever put the terror of Roulette behind him. Wriggling up her body, he sucked in one dusky nipple. Penetrated her.

Her thoughts were sharp, as jagged as glass. *"You look just like your mother, and she was a slut . . . slut . . . SLUT.*

A hateful voice. He hadn't heard it in thirty-eight years. Even filtered through the layers of Fleur's memories, Henry van Renssaeler still had the power to disgust.

"You better prove how much you love me."

"I love you, Daddy. I love you."

The soft cadences of Leo Barnett.

"Open your heart to Jesus, and all your sins will be forgiven you."

The rest followed in swift, hurtful images. Fleur's realization of how he was using his power on the uncommitted delegates. The faked fall. The pretended passion. The disgust and dislocation as she tried to come to grips with the fact that she was in bed with her *mother's* lover. Even as she clutched at his sweat-slick body, she was pretending that he was *Leo Barnett*.

Fury took him, and Tachyon was closer to striking a woman than he had ever been in his life. He took his revenge by finishing the act with her, slaking his body's desires with hired meat. When it was over, he rolled out of the bed, and gathering up her clothes, tossed them on top of her. She stared at him, alarm shadowing the brown eyes.

"Get out."

"You read my mind—"

"Yes."

"You *violated* me."

"Yes."

She was scrabbling into her clothes, wadding up her hose, and cramming them into her purse, smoothing the tangled hair. Pausing at the door, she flung at him, "I accomplished what I set out to do. I kept you away from the convention."

"And you deserve something for your trouble." Tachyon dug out a pair of twenties, and slapped them into her hand. "Jack was right. You're not your mother. You are a slut."

She slammed the door behind her.

The air-conditioning was icy on his bare skin. Tach poured himself a drink, and took several deep breaths trying to slow his racing heart. Then as he lifted the glass to his lips, the door hit the wall with a report like a firing pistol.

Brandy sloshed across his chest and belly. "Oh, Ideal!"

"Expecting someone?" remarked Polyakov dryly as he eyed Tachyon's erection.

But there was a narrowness to the eyes, a tension to the jaw that made Tachyon think that the Russian's mind was anywhere but on Tachyon's sex life.

"If you could return your brains from your secondary head to your primary head, may we discuss a very serious problem?"

"Very funny." Tach padded to the dresser, and poured a fresh drink. Blaise settled cross-legged on the bed, and stared down at his hands. George stood solid and lumpish in the center of the room. "So what is this great and serious problem?"

"We were arrested."

"*WHAT!*" Tach turned like a slow-coiling snake on Blaise. "What did you do?"

"Nothing," he whined.

"Oh, no, just played master puppeteer with a joker, a Klansman, a neo-Nazi and a policeman," snapped Polyakov. Tach shook his head like a baffled pony. George continued grimly on, "You would think when he has a subtle and invisible power he would have the brains not to advertise when he is using it."

Something flickered between man and boy. Suspicious, Tach lanced out with his telepathy, but all he caught was the brittle edges of the passing thoughts. The flavor of conspiracy.

"They were all standing out there waving their dicks at each other. I was just giving them the opportunity to prove how tough they were. That stupid, ugly joker was trying to wimp out—"

"SHUT UP!" Even Tachyon jumped at the fury and command in the Russian's voice. Polyakov turned his back on the red-faced boy. "The preambulations of an adolescent, superpowered Caligula are not the problem. The problem is Henry Chaiken."

"Fascinating. And who by the Ideal is Henry Chaiken?"

"An AP reporter who used to be stationed overseas. He recognized me as Victor Demyenov, reporter for *Tass*."

"Blood and Ancestors." Tach's knees felt weak, and he felt for the edge of the bed, sat down hard.

"Naturally the police—"

Frustrated with the slow unraveling of the story, Tachyon snatched the memory from his grandson's mind.

The street flanking Piedmont Park. Glancing down to see the dusty footprints left by his tennis shoes on the hood of the car. The circle of sweating faces surrounding the little tableau. Mouths stretched with excitement, eyes glistening. Shrugging off George's clutching hands.

"*Come on. Come on! Put your money down. Not on an ugly joker he's going to get creamed.*"

The cop giving a convulsive jerk as Blaise twitched the cord binding the human to the quarter-Takisian child.

"*He's not going to help the joker. He hates them too. I know. I'm in his head.*"

"Soon after an army of police arrived, and Blaise discov-

ered the limit to his power," continued Polyakov, not realizing
that Tachyon had read it all.

A chill, like an icy finger, traced down his back as Tach
considered that at the end Blaise had been controlling nine
people. Tachyon's limit was three for full control, and that took
a tremendous toll on mind and body. *Nine*. And he was only
thirteen. *And I've been training him*. His eyes met the flat
implacable gaze of the sullen boy.

"Chaiken was an interested spectator to all of this, and he
found it interesting that my current identification did not
match his memory of me. I gave them a story about changing
my name as I changed my life, but if they are not complete
fools they will check."

"Your papers?"

"Are very good, but a question to the wrong place. A
photo shown to the wrong man. . . ." Polyakov shrugged
expressively.

"You have to get out of here. Out of the country. If you
need money I'll give it to you—"

"No. I came here to do a thing. I will not leave."

"What about *me*!"

"You don't matter any more than I do. What I do I do out
of a perhaps pathetic belief in an ideal. A familiar concept to
you, Tachyon. You curse with it, believe in it. We're not so
very different. We both have our honor. Unfortunately, it is
always purchased with blood."

There was again that fleeting glance between the Russian
and Blaise. Tachyon slipped beneath the teenager's imperfect
shields.

"You may not use Blaise. I forbid it!"

An infinitesimal arch of the eyebrows. Polyakov's mouth
twisted in a slight, bitter smile.

"I'll do whatever Uncle George wants," shrilled Blaise.

"I will kill you first," said Tachyon, eyes locking with the
Russian's.

"I'm not your enemy, Dancer. He is." A pudgy forefinger
thrust at the ceiling, and the Hartmann suite seven floors above.

8:00 P.M.

Standing with the fronds of a fern falling across his face
like bangs, Mackie Messer watched Sara and the big fuck leave
the restaurant.

She'd been keeping him at bay all day, keeping to the crowds, never letting him have a shot at her alone. He'd thought surely she'd go to the room she shared with the nigger to take a shower; women were crazy about keeping clean. He'd never seen *Psycho*, so he didn't realize that was the last thing a woman of Sara's generation would do in circumstances like these.

The memory of offing the natty nigger made his lips smile. It had felt good, his hand on bone. But the rush had faded. He was hungry. He hadn't spotted Sara till midmorning, over in the joker park. He hadn't even had a chance to phase into some restaurant's kitchen and rip off a bite to eat. Hunger was feeding the frustrated anger that had been building in him all day.

The bitch. I have to kill her. I can't let the Man down. He was going to have to do something soon, something violent, to let out all that feeling.

And now she and her new boyfriend headed for the elevators, arm in arm. Going upstairs to fuck; women were all alike.

He followed, weaving among delegates who didn't deign to notice a twisted boy, got to the elevator stand in time to see them go into one and the doors close. He laughed out loud: "Yeah. Baby, baby."

All he had to do now was see what floor they got off on. Then he'd find them.

He licked his lips. *I hope they're doing it when I catch them.* He thought of the man's big cock going into Sara, and his hard hand going into *him*, and almost creamed his jeans.

Drinks, exhaustion, and a heavy meal had done their work on Sara. Her knees had gone rubbery, and she leaned on Jack as they shot upward in the glass elevator. Jack closed his eyes against a surge of vertigo. Then he thought of the bottle of Valiums in his luggage and gave an inward smile.

Sara was clearly on her last legs. She'd be out like a light within hours, and some time toward morning Jack was going to creep out of bed, find the Valiums, crumble a couple of them in a glass of room-service orange juice, and feed them to her with breakfast.

That, he thought, should keep the loose cannon from rolling around for most, if not all, of Friday.

Jack led Sara along the curving atrium balcony, then down a short hallway to his suite. "Piano Man" echoed up from the floor of the atrium. Sara stepped through the door and stood there, her heavy shoulder bag pulling her off balance. Jack put the DO NOT DISTURB sign on the door, closed and locked it, and put his arms around Sara from behind. Despite the alcohol her body was taut as a watchspring. He brushed the disordered hair from her neck and began to kiss her nape. For a while Sara didn't react, then she gave a sigh and turned toward him. He kissed her on the lips. She took her time about responding, finally put her arms around his neck, opened her mouth, let his tongue flicker against hers.

"There," Jack said, grinning. "It's better when you help." Which was the line that Bacall gave Bogart in *To Have and Have Not*.

Sara didn't smile. "I've got to go to the bathroom. I'll be right back, okay?"

Jack watched her walk unsteadily toward the toilet. A sinking feeling was beginning to envelope him. This was playing too much like his second marriage.

He took off his jacket and poured himself a whiskey. He could hear water running in the bathroom, then silence. Maybe she was fixing her hair or makeup. Maybe she was sitting on the commode, reliving the death of her friend.

Jack lit a cigarette and thought about the first time he'd seen violent death, when his company was caught in a German counterattack down Highway 90 between Avellino and Benevento, and he remembered that the experience hadn't made him feel very sexy, either.

Damn, he thought. This had the potential to be a very depressing night.

The bathroom door opened and Sara gave him a brave smile as she came into the room. She'd fixed her hair and makeup and looked quite different from the scarecrow who'd sat opposite him at dinner.

Jack stubbed out the cigarette and walked toward her. He was about to take her in his arms when a young hunchback in a leather jacket walked right through the wall behind her, grinned, and lunged forward with a hand thrust out like a spear.

Without thought, Jack picked Sara up, made a half turn, and tossed her gently onto the sofa behind him. The air burned with Jack's golden light. There was the shrieking sound of a buzz saw hitting a spike buried in a tree, a sound that brought Jack's hackles erect and sent a surge of adrenaline pouring through his body. Jack turned back to the intruder and saw a look of shock on his young, pale face. Jack flipped a fist at the little man, a gentle backhand strike, and in a flare of yellow light the leather boy was flung against the bathroom wall with a bone-breaking crash. The boy dropped to the floor like a rag doll.

Sara screamed as she turned and saw the assassin. Jack jumped involuntarily.

"I got him, Sara," Jack said. She kept on screaming. He heard the sounds of her struggling to her feet.

Jack stepped forward toward the leather boy and leaned over him. The boy's eyes snapped open and his hands sliced out, flashing as if they were knives, and when they connected with Jack there was a flare of golden light, the screaming buzz saw noise, and bits of Jack's clothing flying like the fur of a fighting cat.

Jack didn't even feel the blows.

He picked up the boy by his leather jacket and held him at arm's length. The hunchback, as if he couldn't believe what was happening, kept hacking at Jack's arm, cutting the pale-blue Givenchy shirt to ribbons.

Apparently, the little guy hadn't ever come up against an invincible opponent before.

"Kill him!" Sara's voice. "Jack, kill him *now*!"

Jack thought not. He wanted to knock this character out and find out who he was working for. He aimed a slow open-hand slap at the boy's head, one that would maybe put him out for a few hours.

The slap went through the hunchback's head without connecting. His other hand, holding the boy's jacket bunched up under his chin, was suddenly holding nothing at all. A dazed, triumphant grin passed across the boy's face as he drifted—drifted slowly, not dropped—toward the floor.

"Jack!" Sara wailed. "Jack, oh JesusJesusJesus . . ."

An edge of fear grated across Jack's nerves. He flicked out punches, one-two, and both passed through the boy without touching him.

The boy's feet touched the floor. His grin twisted and he

dove forward, his body passing right through Jack, heading for Sara.

Jack spun and went after him. Sara was stumbling backward toward the door, holding her shoulder bag out protectively. The boy's hands sliced forward, hacking the bag in half with a ripping noise, like heavy cardboard torn by a buck knife.

Jack grabbed the hunchback's leather collar and jerked back with all his strength. The boy went insubstantial before his feet quite left the floor, but Jack had managed to impart a certain momentum and the boy sailed upward and back. Jack saw the pale face redden with fury as it disappeared through the ceiling. The lower part of his body remained visible as it shot back, then down.

"JesusJesus!" Sara was clawing at the hall door, trying to unlock it. "Oh, fuck!"

Jack had worked it out. The boy had to become substantial in order to use his buzzsaw hands. He was most vulnerable when he tried to kill.

It had been so much easier when all he had to do was grab cars full of fugitive Nazis and turn them upside down.

Sara got the door open and disappeared screaming into the hall. The leather boy soared back, his head appearing now, and Jack swiped at him a few times just in case he tried to turn himself solid again.

The hunchback kept sailing, went through the wall into Jack's back bedroom. "Hell," Jack said. He contemplated going through the wall after him and decided against it—he might get hung up partway through. He ran for the bedroom door and smashed through it in a bright flash of light. He saw the leather boy solid and on his feet, racing for the wall that led to the corridor outside. The assassin went insubstantial and dove through the wall head-first.

"Hell," Jack said again, reversed himself, ran for the hallway door.

The boy was just ahead of him. Sara wasn't visible, had probably run out onto the atrium balcony by now.

"Don't Cry for Me, Argentina" soared up from the ground floor.

Jack accelerated, swung a fist, missed the back of the boy's neck by inches. The momentum of the punch threw Jack off course and caromed him off the wall, and the boy drew ahead.

He must have heard Jack behind him, because as he reached the atrium balcony he turned, grinning his crazed grin. One buzz saw hand, just for demonstration purposes, sliced a chunk of concrete out of the balcony wall.

Jack was still moving forward with considerable momentum. He planted his feet in front of the kid and used his forward motion to torque his upper body forward, his right hand punching out toward the hunchback's chest with every ounce of strength he possessed.

The assassin went insubstantial.

The power of Jack's punch carried him over the balcony rail in a blaze of golden light.

She ran out the door and down the hallway because the stairwell had been closing in around her, about to grow an arm that would slice her in two. The terror was a solid lump in her throat.

She had no idea where she was going. A distant part of her mind observed that just now panic was her friend. Because she had no place to go, logically, and panic was better than despair.

I should just go back and offer my throat, she thought wildly. But her legs kept pumping.

And the wall did sprout a hand, and it did fasten about her wrist.

She screamed. It was as if her heart was exploding and the sound came out her mouth. She slumped in terror.

"Get up," a voice said, soft but peremptory. Accented. She looked up into the face of the old man who had accosted her after she bolted Tachyon's breakfast. Instead of his Mickey Mouse shirt he wore a lime-green leisure suit.

"Get up," he said again. "You know now what I told you is true."

She let him haul her to her feet, nodded. There were no words in her. She had lost her shoes.

"Then come with me. I'll take you to a place of safety."

She came.

As the Marriott atrium yawned out below, Jack had all the time in the world to think of how stupid he'd just been.

He tumbled, arms and legs flailing. Balconies spun past. Vertigo and terror tugged at his belly.

He gave a yell, just to give people below a chance to clear out.

"Don't Cry for Me, Argentina" floated upward toward him.

It occurred to him to do something to stop the tumbling.

Jack stuck out his arms and legs like a skydiver and tried to stabilize and slow his fall. His stomach lurched again as his body took a wild swing, but then the technique took effect. His vertigo lessened. The ruins of his Givenchy shirt fluttered out behind him like a flag, the remains of the sleeve snapping out little sonic booms close to one ear. His punch had carried him clear out into the atrium, there didn't seem to be a chance of guiding his fall so that he'd hit a balcony rather than fall all the way to the floor.

He tried real hard to think.

There were guy wires strung up here and there, carrying bits of colored cloth that were supposed to provide little abstract flags of brightness against the intimidating saurian rib-cage structure of the atrium. Jack tried to angle his fall toward one of these. Possibly it would break his fall.

Jack gave a yell again as his effort to guide his fall resulted in his pitching over headfirst. He flailed and stabilized, and then he wished he could think of something brave and inspiring to say. Not that anyone would hear it against the sound of the piano anyway.

He missed his intended guy wire by twenty feet. He began concentrating on trying to land where there weren't any people. He gave another shout.

Flying ace gliders danced and swooped below him, bright mocking spots of color.

People below must have heard, since they were trying to get out of the way. There was a patch of white down there that seemed to make a good aiming point. He tried to angle his fall toward it.

He could see individual people now. A blonde-haired black hooker, trying to run, but wearing such high heels that she could only hop like a sparrow. A man in a white tuxedo was staring upward as if he didn't believe his eyes. Hiram Worchester was jumping up and down and waving a fist.

Earl Sanderson floated past him, wings spread, heading for the light. Jack felt a sudden wash of sadness.

Too late, he thought, and then wondered what he meant by that.

Suddenly the sound of the wind in Jack's ears seemed to diminish. He felt a lurch in his belly, like when an elevator begins to move. The ground wasn't coming up any faster.

He was lighter, he realized. Hiram had just made him lighter, but hadn't been able to stop his fall entirely.

The patch of white, he saw, was the grand piano. He was about to plunge into it.

At least, he thought, he wouldn't have to listen to that stupid Argentina song again.

Spector could tell they were headed into Atlanta's jokertown. *The* Jokertown was in New York, but most other major cities had a ghetto for their freaks, too. The buildings were crumbling, burned-out, or otherwise beat to pieces. Most of the cars on the street were stripped or immobile junkers. There were slogans spray-painted on walls, "KILL THE FREAKS" or "MONSTER MASH." Obviously not put there by the neighborhood jokers. Atlanta's jokertown wasn't big enough to keep crazy nats from making a quick trip in to tear things up or kick some joker ass.

Spector heard a rumble that wasn't thunder and looked behind. There was a pink-and-white '57 Chevy tailing them. The muffler was shot and the car was making a lot of noise. Spector couldn't see well enough to know for sure, but figured there were some cracker punks inside.

"Don't worry about it," said Tony, pulling up against the curb beyond a dead Rambler.

"Who's worried?" Spector wasn't just talking. He'd killed more street punks than he could count. He opened the car door and looked over at Tony.

"Follow me." Tony walked around the car and trotted up a set of concrete stairs to a well-lit doorway. He pressed the doorbell and waited.

Spector walked up slowly behind him, keeping an eye on the street. The Chevy had cruised past them and turned the corner. He could still hear it over on the next street.

The door opened. A joker woman in a plain blue dress smiled at them. She was covered with something that looked like yellow rubber hair. "Tony!" She grabbed Calderone and gave him a hug. "We didn't expect to see you this trip, busy as you are."

"Never miss a chance for a visit, Shelly, you know that." The woman took a step back and tugged Tony in by his shirtsleeve. Spector followed.

"Shelly, this is Jim Spector, an old friend of mine from Jersey." Shelly looked puzzled for a moment and Spector was afraid she'd placed his name. But an instant later she held out her hand. Spector took it. Her rubbery hair felt creepy, and her flesh gave too much as he squeezed it.

"Nice to meet you, Jim," she said, pulling away. She turned back to Tony. "Why didn't you tell me you were coming? And bringing company, too. I'd have cleaned up the place."

Tony shook his head. "Shelly, my place never looks this good."

Spector looked around. The room was surprisingly clean. The furniture was inexpensive, but was dusted and polished. A black man was sitting on the couch watching a movie. This family, like almost all joker families, had nothing to do with blood relations. Their deformities were what brought them together.

"This is Armand." Armand turned around when Tony said his name. His jaws were hinged wrong, making his mouth a vertical pink slit. He had no lips or nostrils that Spector could see. Armand shook Tony's hand and then reached out to Spector.

"Nice to meet you," Spector said, taking the man's hand. It felt normal, at least.

"Kids in the den?" Tony asked, taking a step toward the next room.

"Yes. Playing cards, I think. Would either of you like some coffee?" She looked at Tony and then at Spector.

Tony looked over at Spector, who shook his head. "No thanks, Shelly, we just had a big meal." Tony gave her a pat on the shoulder and went into the next room. Spector smiled weakly and followed.

They were sitting at a card table. The little girl, older by a few years, was pretty except for her arms. Up and down them were rows of what looked like rose thorns. The boy sat across from her, holding his cards in his prehensile feet. He had no arms, but his head was several times larger than normal. It was supported by a metal brace attached to the back of the wheelchair.

"Hi, Uncle Tony," they said together. Both seemed more interested in their cards.

"Hey, squirts." He sat down at the table with them. "I want you to meet a friend of mine. His name is Jim."

"Hi, kids," Spector said. He felt completely out of place and would have been more comfortable with a broom handle up his ass.

"I'm Tina," said the little girl, turning over a card.

"Jeffrey." The boy didn't turn to look at him. It looked like it wouldn't be easy to do, anyway. He flipped over his card and laughed. His jack took her eight. He put both cards on the bottom of the deck. Jeffrey's stack was a bit bigger than Tina's.

"Playing war?" Spector asked.

"Joker war," corrected Tina.

Tony looked up. "It's the same, except that jokers beat everything. And a black queen kills the other person's card." Tony smiled. Spector couldn't imagine why the fuck his friend was so happy.

Jeffrey took another trick. "I think he's got your number, Tina," Spector said.

Tina wrinkled her nose and gave him her best killing look. Spector took a step backward, pretending to be scared. Jeffrey didn't seem as miserable as he obviously should be. Spector wanted to kill him and save the kid a lifetime of hell, but that wasn't, as they say, in the cards.

"Mommy says we can watch a movie later," Tina said. She turned her cards over and let Jeffrey collect them. "*The Manchurian Candidate* is going to be on."

Tony sighed. "Politics, mind-control, and assassination. Not the kind of thing kids should be watching. I'll talk to Shelly and . . ."

"Don't do that Uncle Tony," Tina pleaded. She looked over at Spector. "Mister, don't let him do it. Mommy promised."

Spector shrugged. "Don't want to have to get rough with you, old friend."

Tony threw up his hands. "Democracy at work," he said, walking back toward the living room.

"Yay," said Tina.

"My queen kills your last ace." Jeffrey fanned the cards with his toes. "I win."

"Congratulations, kids," Spector said. "Sometimes that's what it takes. Just remember that."

After the crash, after he'd landed right in the middle of the piano and then driven through the floor to the function space on the lower level, the thing that surprised Jack was that he started to float upward again through the hole he'd just made.

Hiram had made him lighter than air. Crap.

Before he could float out into space again, Jack grabbed some of the twisted rebar that had been supporting the atrium floor. He hung upside down. Flashbulbs dazzled him. A TV floodlight drilled between his eyes. The pianist was lurching about like a drunk. From out of the burning light he could see Hiram peering at him out of his doughy face.

"There's an assassin loose!" he yelled. "Little guy in a leather jacket! He's a wild card!"

"Where?" Hiram goggled at him.

"The senator's floor!"

Hiram turned dead-white. He spun and ran, arms and legs pumping. The crowd dissolved into pandemonium.

"Hiram!" Jack yelled. "Worchester, goddamn it!"

He was still lighter-than-air. And he was the only one who knew what the assassin looked like, and how to stop him.

The pianist danced before him in his white tuxedo. He pointed at Jack. "He tried to kill me! He threatened me earlier!"

"Shut the hell up," said Jack.

The pianist turned white as his tux and faded away.

Hiram's shot of antigravity diminished in a few minutes, and Jack tried to run for an elevator. He was still very light and he bobbled like an astronaut on the moon. He kept jumping across the atrium without going near the elevators. Security people were in the process of barring all the doors, which wasn't going to do very much to stop someone who could walk through walls. Some stranger finally led Jack to the elevator by the hand.

As Jack shot upward, he tried not to think of the skinny hunchback sitting up on top, slicing the cables with buzz saw hands. The security was concentrating on the hallway leading to Hartmann's apartment and HQ. Billy Ray was prominent in his white suit, flexing his muscles in front of a battery of gray-suited Secret Service. Some of them were carrying their Uzis in plain sight.

Shaking pulverized concrete dust out of his ruined clothes, Jack walked up to Ray and gave him a description of the assassin, including the fact he could make himself insubstantial. Ray took his job seriously for once and didn't give Jack a single sneer. He passed on the information with his radio and asked Jack to step into another room for a debriefing. Jack asked if he could change first—his clothes were ribbons. Ray nodded.

Jack headed back to his room. As he stepped through the open door, he realized that he hadn't bothered to tell anyone that this was where the fight had taken place.

He headed for his bedroom and his foot hit something lying on the carpet. He looked down and saw part of Sara's shoulder bag. He bent down and shook it open. One-third of a laptop computer slid out, along with scraps of paper that fluttered to the floor.

Jack reached down and picked up the papers. There were several sheets stapled together and cut neatly off near the top, a press handout giving Leo Barnett's appearances for the days leading up to the campaign.

Another was the top of a yellow legal sheet written in scrawled blue ballpoint. "Secret Ace," it said, underlined several times.

Below were just doodles, a row of crosses, a tombstone.

The next sheet was a photocopy on old-fashioned slick photocopy paper. It was obviously some official document.

DEPARTMENT OF DEFENSE, it said. DOD#864-558-2048(b)

BLOOD SERUM TEST
XENOVIRUS TAKIS-A

The rest was sliced off.

Jack stared at it for a long moment.

The secret ace, he thought, might not be secret much longer.

10:00 P.M.

Spector was relieved when it was time to leave. Everyone said their goodbyes, except Armand, who didn't look like he could say anything. Tony slipped Shelly an envelope as they stood in the doorway. Spector figured there was a check in it. Shelly waved goodbye and closed the door. Spector and Tony headed down the stairs toward the car.

"You see what they're like if you give them half a chance," Tony said. "Oh, son of a bitch." He was looking at the car. Someone had spray painted "BARNETT. FOR PRESIDENT!" in six-inch yellow letters on the Regal.

Spector didn't say anything, but figured that the Hartmann stickers on Tony's car had made it too much of a temptation for the jerks with the spray paint. "What do you bet it was those shitheads in the Chevy?"

"Good guess." The voice came from behind them. Spector and Tony spun around. There were seven of them, clad in sweat-stained T-shirts and denim jeans. The largest had on a brown leather flight jacket. "We don't much like being called shitheads, though. I think we need to teach you some manners." There were grunts of approval from the others.

Spector had seen and heard it all before, but this time it was different. He couldn't just kill these punks, or Tony would figure out he was an ace. Seven to two was lousy odds. They were going to take a beating.

The boy in the jacket slipped on some brass knucks and walked straight toward Tony. The others spread out and moved in. Tony was in a crouch, fists raised. Spector moved over next to him. Hopefully, he could keep the guy with the knucks busy. It'd hurt, but he'd heal in a hurry. Tony wouldn't. At least none of them were showing knives or guns.

The leader took a wild swing at Tony and got a hard, straight right to the jaw as a reward. The kid was knocked back a step, but the others swarmed in. Spector caught one of the punks in the throat with a flailing elbow, but this wasn't his kind of fighting. They quickly hammered him to the sidewalk, and started kicking him in the stomach. Spector rolled into a ball and protected his head. They kept on kicking the shit out of him for a few moments, then stopped.

"Let's teach these joker-pokers a real lesson now." The kid

spoke with the bravado only a pea-brained street punk can manage.

Spector rolled over and looked up. Tony was lying next to him, blood coming from his mouth and nose; eyes closed. He was out. The kid in the jacket pulled out a switchblade and clicked it open. Spector knew game time was over. He blinked a few times to clear his head before killing the kid.

There was a gunshot from the window behind them. The kid went down with a funny look on his face, his switchblade spinning off into the darkness. The other punks scattered before Spector could get up. The kid had gotten over the initial shock of being shot and was now screaming on the sidewalk. His right arm was a bloody mess between the shoulder and elbow.

Spector struggled up and kicked the kid in the mouth. "You shut up or I'll rip your tongue out, shithead." The kid stopped yelling, but still made pathetic mewling noises.

Armand came down the stairs holding a rifle. Shelly was a step behind, a rubbery hand over her mouth. Tina had her face pressed to the window and was peering down at the sidewalk. Porch lights, those that worked anyway, were coming on up and down the street. Several neighbors were headed toward them. Spector carefully rolled his friend over. Tony had a bad cut on his forehead, and several of his front teeth were chipped or split.

"Is he all right?" Shelly dabbed at the blood on Tony's face with her sleeve.

"He'll be okay, I think," Spector said, opening the back door and grabbing Tony by the armpits. "Help me lift him in. We need to get him to a hospital." Armand grabbed Tony's legs and they hoisted him into the back seat. Spector turned to Shelly. "You know where the nearest hospital is?"

Shelly nodded.

"Then get in the front seat and tell me where to go." Spector fished out Tony's car keys, closed the door, and walked around to the driver's side.

Armand grabbed him by the elbow and motioned to the kid with his head.

Spector coughed. "Tony would tell you to hand him over to the cops and hope for the best. Personally though, I'd cut his throat and feed him to the neighborhood dogs."

Armand's face changed, but Spector couldn't be sure it

was a smile. He slid into the driver's seat and cranked the Regal up.

"Buckle up, Shelly," Spector said, fastening his seatbelt. She did as she was told. Tony groaned as Spector punched the accelerator. They screamed off into the night.

CHAPTER FIVE

Friday
July 22, 1988

6:00 A.M.

The darkness should have been soothing. Instead, the air-conditioner droned like some slumbering evil beast and demons capered in the dim reaches of the ceiling. Gregg could feel his hands trembling. He tottered on the edge of an anxiety attack. The panic threatened to overwhelm him and set him screaming.

"Gregg?" Ellen whispered alongside him. Her soft hand touched his chest. "It's only six. You should be sleeping."

"Can't." He could barely even choke out the word, afraid that if he opened his mouth again he might start screaming.

Her hand stroked his cheek, and slowly the panic receded, though the shade of it remained behind. He lay there stiffly, feeling Puppetman crawl inside at the touch, like a slug just underneath his skin. "I'll be glad when this convention is over, no matter what," Ellen said.

"I'm blowing it, Ellen." Gregg closed his eyes, taking a long, slow breath that did nothing to calm him. The apparitions continued to dance behind his eyelids. "It's all falling apart around me, the whole thing."

"Gregg . . . Love . . . " Ellen's arms came around him, her body snuggling close, and she hugged him. "Stop. You're just letting the stress get to you, that's all. Maybe if you saw Tachyon, he could prescribe—"

"No," he interrupted vehemently. "There's nothing a doctor can do." Ellen drew back at his sharp tone, then returned.

"I love you," she said, empty of any other comfort.

"I know." He sighed. "I know. It's a damn good thing. God, you've been so understanding, the way I've been acting . . ." For a moment, he was on the verge of confessing, of just letting the whole madness spill out just to have an end to it. Then Puppetman wriggled inside, a reminder, and he carefully pushed the power back down.

You can't say it, it told him. *I won't let you*.

"You're worrying too much. The nomination will come or it won't. If not this year, you'll be in a good position for '92. We can wait. We'll have time to let the baby grow up a little." He could feel her smiling bravely—her own little obsession. "You'll have enough to keep you busy with our son or daughter. A little part of us."

Ellen took his hand and placed it on the swell of her stomach just below her navel. "Feel it?" she asked. "It's been kicking up a storm lately. Getting more active every day, stronger. It's waking up now. There, feel that? Say hello to daddy, little one," she crooned.

Gregg suddenly wished that she was right, that it was over. Ellen had brought up the subject after the hectic months of the tour; he'd been surprised at how easily he'd agreed. It seemed right, a symbol of normalcy after the violence and hatred. It had taken months; he'd been so pleased when they'd found Ellen was finally pregnant. Despite everything, he'd wanted the child as much as she did. He'd enjoyed playing the proud, prospective father. Even the power within had seemed to share the happiness.

A little part of us.

Now he could hardly remember that at all. The pride and love and hope had been driven away by Puppetman's needs.

There was a faint fluttering beneath his fingertips. Ellen laughed with the baby's movements.

Let the baby grow up a little.

And Gregg nearly pulled his hand away as if burned. The suspicion was like a physical blow. He *knew*, and with the knowledge, Puppetman howled inside.

The difficulties with Puppetman had started slowly and intermittently only a few months ago. The Gimli-presence had been faint and weak and unformed then, easily pushed away.

Getting more active every day, stronger.

"Oh, my god," Gregg whispered. The fetus kicked again, softly. He let the power slip out, just a touch. He looked inside Ellen, at the primal colors of the fetus.

There, wrapped around the child's emotional matrix like some strangling vine, there were other hues. Very familiar tints and shades.

Gimli had said it: *No, not dead. Just changed. It took me a long time to get back . . .*

"I can't believe it myself, sometimes," Ellen laughed. "It's so incredible to feel it, to know that this life—our child—is grow-

ing inside me."

Gregg lay wide-eyed, staring at her stomach and his hand. "Yes," he told her. "Yes, it's incredible."

"I wonder who it'll look like?" Ellen patted Gregg's hand. "I'll bet it'll take after you," she said.

It can't be true, he told himself. *Please don't let it be true.*

But he knew it was.

7:00 A.M.

"Jesus Christ, stop plucking at me! I don't need this shit!" Jack gripped the Takisian's hands, and flung them away like a man flicking water. "Jesus."

Tach firmly quashed the irritation he felt rising like gorge in the back of his throat, but still said in slightly aggrieved tones, "I was concerned. You could have been killed."

The snap of a lighter as Jack lit a Camel. "Well, find another way to show it. By the way, you look like shit."

"Thank you so very much. I didn't sleep last night."

"Hey, ditto."

"Jack, what happened? It was all so garbled on the news reports. I'm standing there brushing my teeth when I see you plummeting into the piano." He cocked his head to one side, and considered. "Which is, I suppose, the only fortuitous thing to come out of this mess."

"Fortuitous, hell. I was *aiming* for that damn piano."

Then in a few staccato sentences the ace outlined the rest of the evening; Sara's clumsy come-on, Jack's plan for taking the journalist out of the way, the arrival of the horrifying hunchback, the fight. Cognac-flavored vomit hit the back of Tachyon's throat, and he bolted for the bathroom.

"*Now* what?" Jack called.

Tach emerged wiping his mouth on a wet washcloth. "Sara, where is she now?"

"Hell, I don't know. She went out of that room like a missile, and I can't say I blame her. I haven't seen her since."

Tachyon pressed his hands to his face. "Mothers of my mother forgive me. I didn't believe her."

"What?"

"She came to me Monday night. Tried to tell me she was in danger. I wouldn't listen." The import of what he had just said struck him, and Tach lurched back into the bathroom.

He was down to stomach juices. The acid burned on its way up. Like the acid eating away at his trust, his certainty.

Hartmann is an ace.

Help me.

You'll be sorry.

Arms embracing the toilet, the ceramic rim cool against his burning cheek Tach murmured, "Help me."

Jack lifted him to his feet and asked, "How? What is it you need? What the hell's going on? Why did you bring up a secret ace on Monday? Talk to me, Tachy."

"Not now, Jack. Not now. I must find Sara."

8:00 A.M.

Billy Ray knocked and poked his head through the open door. "Security says the stairs are clean, Senator. You two ready?"

"We're coming now," Gregg told him. He finished knotting his tie and adjusted it around his neck.

Puppetman prowled like a sleek cat just under the surface, waiting. Ellen came from the bedroom and gave Gregg a worried, concerned glance. Gregg smiled back reassuringly, hating the act. "I'm fine," he said. "Much better this morning since I talked with you. Back to normal." He put his arms around her and patted her belly. "After all, the kid might just have a president for a daddy, right?"

Ellen leaned against him. She hugged him wordlessly.

"He still kicking this morning, darling?"

"He? And just what makes you so sure it's a boy?" Ellen teased him, hugging him again.

Gregg shrugged. *Because my child's a goddamn dwarf joker who's supposed to be dead. Because I've heard him talking to me.* "Just a hunch, love."

Ellen chuckled against his chest. "Well, *he's* been mostly quiet. I think he's asleep."

The breath went out of Gregg in a sigh. He closed his eyes momentarily. "Good," he said. "Good. Let's go, then. Amy and John are probably waiting." He waved to Billy.

The morning staff briefings were held in the campaign headquarters one floor below. Gregg had always taken the stairs down—while he could have commandeered an elevator, it hardly seemed worth it. Now he was glad for the routine. He knew exactly what he needed to do.

You're sure? You're sure this will end it? The power was vibrating with intensity. Puppetman's voice was insistent.

I don't know. If it doesn't, we'll find another way. I promise. Now that we know, we can plan. Just wait and be ready.

The stairwell was an ugly contrast to the halls: stained concrete landings connected by steep metal stairs. They nodded to Alex James, stationed there as usual. Echoes rebounded as Billy held the door open and let Ellen pass. Gregg caught the door and motioned to Billy to precede him.

I don't want to do this. I don't, Gregg thought.

We don't have a choice. Puppetman. Eager.

He searched in his head for Gimli and found nothing.

He let Puppetman loose.

As Ellen approached the stairs, the power lanced from Gregg in a rush, fearing that if he hesitated at all Gimli would stop him again. He invaded her long-open mind and found what he wanted.

It was all there, as he knew it would be: A faint, swirling vertigo as Ellen looked down the stairs; an uneasy feeling of imbalance from the unaccustomed forward weight of her stomach. Puppetman wrenched brutally at both responses, dampening everything else in her mind. When the inevitable quick panic followed, he amplified that as well.

It took less than a second. It was worse than he'd thought it would be.

Ellen tottered, screamed in fright. Her hand grasped far too late for the handrail.

Puppetman leaped for Billy Ray in that instant. He truncated the adrenaline surge as Billy saw Ellen lose her balance on that first step, slowing the ace's superb reflexes. Gregg himself could have done nothing even if he'd wished, trapped behind Ray. Billy made a valiant leap for Ellen; his fingertips grazed her flailing arm and then closed on empty air.

Ellen fell. It seemed to take a very long time.

Gregg pushed past the horrified Ray, whose hand was still futilely outstretched. Ellen lay crumpled against the wall on the next landing, her eyes closed and a deep gash streaming blood down one side of her head. As Gregg reached her, her eyes opened, clouded with pain. She tried to sit up as Gregg cradled her and Ray shouted for James to call an ambulance.

Ellen moaned, clutching suddenly at her stomach. There was bright blood between her legs. Her eyes widened.

"Gregg," she breathed. "Oh, Gregg . . ."

"I'm sorry, Ellen. My god, I'm sorry."

Then she began to cry with tremendous gasping sobs. He cried with her, mourning for the child that might have been, while another part of him celebrated.

For that instant, he hated Puppetman.

9:00 A.M.

The breakfast crowd was thinning out. The people who came here—some black, some white, all working class—had to get to their jobs. Spector was a hell of a lot more comfortable eating here than at the Marriott. There were too many people he was tempted to kill there, and after last night's attack he was in a particularly foul mood. He'd been working his way through the morning newspaper, but so far hadn't seen anything about Tony getting sent to the hospital by a group of anti-joker thugs.

He'd let Shelly check Tony into the hospital. He didn't want to be around when the cops showed and started asking questions. No point in pushing his luck. Shelly had given him a strange look when he took off, but he knew she wouldn't talk. She was satisfied that he was on their side and that would be enough.

Spector finished the last of his hash browns and bacon.

The coffee was hot and they kept his cup filled, so he didn't feel like going anywhere just yet. He was beginning to lose his enthusiasm for this job, anyway. Maybe he should just pay Tony a visit and skip town.

He'd sort it out later. Right now he was going to relax and mind his own business.

The press were lined up six deep in the waiting room. Gregg caught a glimpse of them every time the doors opened: a wash of portable video lights, a flurry of electronic flashes, a babble of shouted questions. The news of Ellen's fall had spread rapidly. Before the ambulance had arrived at the hospital, they were waiting.

Billy Ray leaned against the wall, scowling. "I can have security move them if you want, Senator. They're like a flock of buzzards. Ghouls."

"It's okay, Billy. They're just doing their job. Don't worry about them."

"Senator, I was so close, I tell you." Billy clenched his hand in front of his face, his mouth twisted. "I should have got her. It's my damn fault."

"Billy, don't. It's not your fault. It's no one's fault."

Gregg sat head in hands on a couch outside the surgical clinic. It was a careful pose: The Distraught Husband. Inside, Puppetman was exuberant. He rode Ellen's pain, relishing it. Even under the haze of the anesthetic, he could make her writhe inwardly. Her worry for the baby was a cold, primal dark blue; Puppetman made the emotion an achingly saturated sapphire, fading slowly into the orange-red of her injuries.

But better—far, *far* better—was Gimli. The Gimli-thing that had fastened itself on his child was in torment, and there were no drugs to blunt that pain, nothing to stop Puppetman from doubling and redoubling it. Gregg could feel Gimli suffocating, choking, screaming inside Ellen's womb.

And Puppetman laughed. He laughed as the baby died because Gimli died with it. He laughed because at last the insanity was over.

The infant's slow, horrible death was tasty. It was good.

Gregg felt it all numbly. He was being split in half.

The part of him that was Gregg hated this, was appalled and disgusted by Puppetman's exuberant response. *That* Gregg wanted to weep rather than laugh.

You shouldn't feel relief. It's your child dying, man, a part of you. You wanted it and you've lost it. And Ellen . . . She loves you, even without Puppetman, and you betrayed her. How can you not be sad, you son of a bitch?

But Puppetman only scoffed. *Gimli had it. It wasn't your child, not any longer. It's better that it dies. It's better that it nourishes us.*

In his head, Gregg could hear Gimli sobbing. It was an eerie sound. Puppetman chuckled at the anguish and desolation in it.

Gimli's cry turned abruptly to a rising, hopeless shriek. As his voice rose in pitch, it began to fade, as if Gimli were falling away into a deep, dark pit.

Then there was nothing. Puppetman groaned orgasmically.

The door to the surgery swung open. A doctor in sweaty scrub greens emerged. She nodded to Gregg and Ray, grimacing. She walked slowly toward them as Gregg rose.

"I'm Dr. Levin," she said. "Your wife is resting now, Senator. That was a terrible fall for a woman in her condition. We've stopped the internal bleeding and stitched up the scalp wound, but she's going to be badly bruised. I'll want to x-ray her hip later; the pelvis isn't broken, but I want to make sure there's no fracture. We'll need to keep her a day or two at least for observation, but I think—eventually—she'll be fine."

Levin paused, and Gregg knew she was waiting for a question. *The* question. "And the baby?" Gregg asked.

The doctor tightened her lips. "We couldn't do anything for him—a boy, by the way. We were dealing with a prolapsed umbilical and the placenta had torn away from the uterus wall. The child was without oxygen for several minutes. With that and the other injuries . . ." Another grimace. She rubbed at her hand, took a deep breath, and looked at him with sympathetic dark eyes. "It was probably better this way. I'm sorry."

Billy pounded the door with a fist, tearing a jagged splintery hole in the wood and gouging long scratches down his arm. Ray began cursing softly and continuously. Puppetman turned to feed on the guilt, but Gregg forced the power below the surface once more; for the first time in weeks, the power subsided docilely. Gregg faced the wall for a moment. With Puppetman satisfied, the other part of him grieved.

He swallowed hard, choked it back. When he turned, the doctor wavered in a sheen of genuine tears.

"I'd like to see Ellen now," he said. His voice sounded wonderfully drained, superbly exhausted, and far too little of it was an act.

Dr. Levin gave him a wan smile of understanding. "Certainly, Senator. If you'll follow me—"

10:00 A.M.

The first thing Jack thought when he heard about Ellen was: *Yes. The secret ace.*

"Where's the senator now?"

"At the hospital."

"And where's Ray?"

"With him."

Maybe Ray could keep the freak away, then. Jack had other things to do.

Sara's tattered notes seemed like a cold weight in Jack's breast pocket. He looked around, saw campaign workers milling around the HQ, pointlessly and silently, like survivors of a disaster. Which, of course, they probably were.

The secret ace had gone after Hartmann first, Jack figured, because Hartmann had more delegate votes. That was the only way to explain all the things that had gone wrong, from the networks cutting to commercial breaks during Carter's seconding speech to the riot before the platform fight to Ellen's miscarriage.

The thought of which, on reflection, made Jack burn with anger. The secret ace was picking not just on a candidate, but on civilians the candidate was close to.

Sara Morgenstern, who knew the ace's identity, had disappeared. Jack, along with the Secret Service, had been trying to find her all night long.

Devaughn was gone from HQ, and so was Amy. Jack went to the phone, ordered a thousand and one roses delivered to Ellen's room on his credit card, then he headed next door to the media center. He found an unused VCR, picked up some videocassettes of the other candidates as well as their campaign biographies, and took them to his room.

Maybe Gregg Hartmann's candidacy was finished. Jack couldn't tell, and couldn't change things one way or another.

He only knew one thing for certain. He was going to have to call Rodriguez and tell him to take charge of the delegation and vote his proxy for Hartmann on every ballot. Jack had other things to do. He was going hunting for the secret ace.

Even though a hotel is a fortress armored against the outside world, the outside gets in anyway, in subtle ways. Trying to flow through the crush of delegates and press toads, Mackie could tell it was morning, from the light that managed to battle inside, from a taste of the Chilled Sliced Processed Air Product extruded by the AC. Maybe it was just that as a Hamburg harbor rat he had an instinctive dread of morning, and could smell it when it lurked outside.

His hands were jammed in pockets, his head jammed in memories. Sometimes, when he was young and had fucked up again, the fog of booze would lift enough to permit his mother to fix him with a stern, bleary look and say, *Detlev, you disappoint me so*, instead of just shrieking and hitting him with whatever came to hand. He hated that the most. The shrieking he could ignore, the blows he could weather by tucking his head painfully between uneven shoulders and turning away. But the disappointment went right through him, there was no defense against that.

Every particle of his *life* had been a disappointment to somebody. Except when his hands were steel, were knives. When the blood ran: no disappointment there, oh no, laughter inside: *yeah*.

Until the last two days. Two chances: two failures. All he had to show was an incidental nigger in a suit worth more than Mackie's entire body. He thought at least the big glowing gold weenie was meat when he crashed the rail last night, but then this morning he saw on the news that he crashed through a piano and wasn't hurt.

He was glad about the piano, anyway. Son of a bitch never played his song.

Ahead of him he saw a pair of dark well-filled suits crowding a man with a garment bag over his shoulder, back toward the wall, out of the clotted traffic flow. They were leaning into him in that way pigs have when they know they have your ass. Mackie snagged a shred of conversation:

"No, really, I was wearing my pass just a moment ago. In

all this crush, somebody must have brushed against me,
knocked it off—"

That made Mackie smile. *He* had no need of badges. No
need to squirm in the grip, unreeling lies as obvious as a
whore's smile to amuse the pigs and make them give each
sideways smirks. He was still Mackie, *MacHeath the Knife* as
big as legend. Not a bug like this nat crasher.

He phased and sideled softly, through the crowd and
through the wall, toward his rendezvous with love and disappointment.

John Werthen had arranged for the makeshift press
conference in the gymnasium/auditorium of the hospital. As
Amy accompanied Gregg around the back of the small stage
there, he felt a sudden distress pulse from her. "John, you ass,"
she whispered, then glanced at Gregg guiltily. The auditorium
had been used for a Lamaze class the night before. Charts of
the stages of labor, cervix dilation, and positions of the fetus
were stacked in one corner. They almost seemed a mockery.

You had to do it, he reminded himself quickly. *You didn't
have a choice.*

"I'm sorry, sir," Amy said. "I'll have someone get rid of
them."

"I'm all right," he said. "Don't worry about it."

The tragic death of the Hartmann infant had become The
Story of the convention. Wildfire rumors flared through the
convention—Hartmann was pulling out; Hartmann had decided to take the VP spot behind Dukakis or Jackson or even
Barnett; Hartmann had actually been the intended victim of
Nur terrorists; a simultaneous attempt had been made on the
lives of all the candidates; a joker was somehow involved in
Ellen's fall; no, the baby had been a joker; Carnifex had pushed
Ellen or he'd just watched her fall without moving; Barnett
was calling it the hand of God; Barnett had called Hartmann
and they had prayed together.

There was a morbid glee to it all. The circus atmosphere
had been plunged into something halfway between horror and
fascination.

The auditorium was almost unnaturally quiet. "Senator, if
you're ready . . . " Amy said. Her eyes were red and puffy;
she'd been crying off and on since she'd arrived at the hospital.
Puppetman had made certain of it. She looked at Gregg and

tears brimmed again. He hugged her silently as Puppetman
lapped at the sorrow.

It was easy. It was all so easy with Puppetman.

Amy held the curtains open for him and he walked out
into the familiar glare of lights. The floor was a solid mass of
people: reporters in front; behind them, Hartmann supporters
from the convention intermingled with jokers and hospital
staff. Amy and John had argued for restricting admission
strictly to the press, but Gregg had overruled them. A large
contingent of jokers had besieged the hospital, and Gregg
insisted that they be allowed to attend as well. Security
blocked the doors after capacity was reached; behind the
windows, Gregg could see that the corridors were also wall-
to-wall.

Let them in, Gregg had told Ray. *The jokers are our
people. We all know why they're concerned. If they're clean,
give 'em passes until we're out of room. I trust you, Billy. I
know nothing will happen.*

Ray had been almost pitifully grateful at that. That had
tasted good, too.

Gregg walked slowly to the podium and bowed his head,
gripping either side of the lectern. He took a deep breath and
heard it echo against the hard tile walls. Puppetman could feel
the sympathy beating against him. He reveled in it. Gregg
could see the puppets interspersed with them: Peanut, File,
Mothmouth, Glowbug, a dozen others just in the first few
ranks. Gregg knew from long experience that a crowd was an
easily swayed beast. Control enough of them and the rest
would follow along.

This would be easy. This would be cake.

He hated it.

Gregg raised his head, solemn. "I . . . I really don't
know what—" He stopped deliberately and closed his eyes:
Hartmann Composing Himself. Out in the audience, he heard
a subdued sob. He tugged gently at the dozens of mental
strings and felt the puppets move. He let his voice tremble just
slightly when he resumed.

". . . don't know what to say to you all. The doctors have
given you their report. Umm, I'd like to say Ellen is doing
fine, but that's not really the truth. Let's just say that she's
doing as well as can be expected at the moment. Her physical
injuries will heal; the rest, well—" Again a pause; he ducked

his head for a moment. "The rest is going to take a lot of time. I've heard that there's already a roomful of flowers and cards that some of you have sent, and she asked me to thank you. She'll need all the support and prayers and love you can give her."

He gestured at Amy. "I was going to let Ms. Sorenson— my aide—read you my statement. I'd already drafted it, telling all of you that I was withdrawing my name from nomination due to . . . to the unfortunate accident today. I even read it to Ellen. Afterward, she asked me to give the paper to her, and I did. This is what she gave me back."

They waited, obedient. Puppetman tightened his fingers around the strings.

Gregg reached into his pocket. His hand came out fisted; he turned his hand over and opened his fingers. Scraps of paper fluttered to the wooden floor.

"She told me that she'd already lost a son," he said quietly. "She said she wasn't about to lose the rest."

Puppetman pulled the strings tight, opening the minds of the puppets among them. The murmurs of the audience rose, peaked, broke. From the back of the gymnasium where the jokers watched, the applause began, swelling and moving through the audience until most of them were on their feet, clapping hands together, laughing and crying at the same time. The room was suddenly noisy and wild like a camp revival meeting, everyone swaying and shouting and weeping, grieving and celebrating at once. He could see Peanut, his lone arm waving back and forth, his mouth a black wound in the scaly, hard face as he jumped up and down. The excitement triggered Glowbug's joker: his pulsing radiance rivaled the electronic flashes.

The cameras swiveled about, panning the odd celebration. Reporters whispered urgently into microphones. Gregg stood there, posed, his empty hand out over the torn-up paper. He let his hand drop to his side and lifted his head as if hearing the acclimation for the first time. He shook his head in feigned bemusement.

Puppetman exulted. Gregg channeled a portion of the stolen response into himself. He gasped at the pure, undiluted strength of it. He raised his hands for quiet as Puppetman loosened the strings slightly—it took long seconds before he could be heard at all over them.

His voice was choked. "Thank you. Thank you all. I think maybe *Ellen* deserves to be your nominee; she's worked as hard or harder at this, even when she was tired from the pregnancy or a little sick in the mornings. If the convention doesn't want me, maybe we'll place her name in nomination instead."

That brought more applause and outright cheering, sprinkled with sobbing laughter. All the while, Gregg gave them a wan, strained smile that had nothing of Puppetman in it. Part of him seemed to be simply, scornfully, observing.

"I just wanted all of you to know that we're still in this fight despite everything. I know Ellen is watching this from her room and she wants me to thank you for your sympathy and your continued support. Now, I'd like to get back to her myself. Ms. Sorenson will answer any other questions you might have. Once again, thank you all. Amy—"

Gregg raised his hands in salute; Puppetman yanked hard. They cheered him, tears streaming down their faces.

He had it all back.

It was his, now. He knew it.

Most of him rejoiced.

2:00 P.M.

The sound of a soap filtered through the cardboard and cottage-cheese stucco walls of the cheap motel room. On the screen of the room television a pretty young joker woman with bright-blue skin was trying to guess the password from Henry Winkler's clues. Wrapped in a cheap, stiff housecoat her mysterious benefactor had bought on sale at Kmart, Sara sat on the end of the bed and stared at the screen as if the images on it mattered.

She was still trying to pull together the broken glass pieces the news flash had left in her belly. *The wife of Senator Gregg Hartmann has miscarried in the wake of her tragic fall.* . . . The senator was bravely containing his grief as he fought for political survival on the convention floor. Just the sort of persevering spirit America needed to carry her into the nineties, or so the commentator's tone seemed to say. Or had that just been the blood in Sara's ears.

Bastard. Monster. *He sacrificed his wife, his unborn child, to save his political hide.*

An image of Ellen Hartmann's face surfaced through the shrouds she laid over her memories of the W.H.O. tour. A wan, brave smile, knowing, forbearing . . . infinitely tragic. Now she lay broken and near death, the child she had so desired lost.

Sara was never the strident kind of feminist who saw every human interaction in terms of grand collectives, political synecdoche wherein a man was Men and a woman, Women. Yet this struck her deeply, offended her on some primal level. *Angered* her: for herself, for Ellen, for all of Hartmann's victims, yes, but especially the women.

For Andrea.

There was a thing the man who had hurried her from the hotel last night as the police cars wailed their red-and-blue way to the latest battle scene, had suggested when they talked in the early hours of this morning. She had promised to consider it before he left about whatever errands he had to tend to—not even reporter's curiosity made her really want to know. Because his suggestion was natural enough, she supposed, for a self-confessed Soviet spymaster. But it shocked a Midwestern girl, transplanted into the neurasthenic garden of the New York intellectual set, even one who prided herself on her case-hardening in the streets and back rooms of Jokertown.

But still, but still. . . . Gregg Hartmann had to be stopped. Gregg Hartmann had to *pay.*

But Sara Morgenstern didn't want to die. To follow Andi oh-so-ungently into that night she could not believe was good. That was the covert *caveat* of George Steele's suggestion, neither hidden nor overtly stated.

But what, what chance do I have with that—thing—after me? The laughing, twisted leather boy, who hummed to himself and walked through walls. She could not hide forever. And when *he* found her. . . .

—She shook her head, whipstinging her cheeks with the ends of her hair, blinded by hot sudden tears.

Onscreen the blue woman cleaned up in the End Game. Sara hoped it made her happy.

3:00 P.M.

"Stop it." The steady angry flipping of the magazine's pages ceased.

"Why?" Blaise's tone was challenging.

Tach reined in his temper. Poured another brandy. "I am trying to think, and it is irritating me."

"You always stop using contractions when you're pissed."

"Blaise, please."

Propping the phone beneath his chin, Tach called Sara's room. The distant ringing echoed mournfully over and over again.

Tach drummed his fingers on the table, touched the disconnect button and phoned the desk. Blaise's magazine flew across the room like a terrified bird. "This is *boring* sitting here watching you be *stupid*! I want to go out."

"You have forfeited that right."

"I don't want to be here when the CIA comes to get you." The boy's grin was ugly.

"*Goddamn you*."

Fist upraised, Tachyon charged across the room. The knock at the door arrested him before he could strike the child.

Hiram and Jay Ackroyd were in the hall. Hiram looked like death. Ackroyd's face was puffy and swollen, and a lot of colors that a face shouldn't be. Tachyon's stomach formed into a small, tight ball, and tried to retreat into his spinal cord. He stepped reluctantly back to let them enter.

Hiram waddled to the window. For the first time in all the years he had known him, Tachyon realized that the ace was not using his gravity power to reduce his own weight. Worchester's footfalls were ponderous in the suite. Ackroyd seated himself on the sofa, and laid a garment bag across his knees. The silence stretched like cobwebs between the three men and the boy.

Ackroyd jerked his head toward the door. "Lose the kid."

"Hey!" Blaise burst out.

"Blaise, go."

He gave his grandfather a smirk. "I thought I'd forfeited the right."

"*GO*, damn you!"

"Shit, just when things were getting interesting." Blaise held up his hands, palms out. "Hey, no problem. I'm gone."

The door closed behind him, and the silence resumed. Nerves fraying, Tachyon flung out a hand. "Hiram, what the devil is this?" There was no reply from the ace.

Ackroyd said, "You gotta run a blood test, Doc. Right now."

Tachyon smirked and indicated the room. "What? Here?"

The detective grimaced. "Don't be dense, and don't be cute. I'm too fucking tired and I hurt too much to deal with it." The man's fingers trembled slightly as he unzipped the bag. "This is Senator Hartmann's jacket from Syria."

Tachyon stared in blind terror at the black stain on the cloth.

This was it. He could no longer postpone the discovery by reason of convoluted Takisian honor. Sara's accusations would be proved or disproved in old blood.

"How did you come to possess this?"

"That's a long story," Ackroyd said wearily, "and none of us have the time. Let's just say I got it . . . from Chrysalis. It was . . . well . . . sort of a legacy."

Tachyon cleared an obstruction from his throat, and asked cautiously, "And just what do you think I am going to find?"

"The presence of Xenovirus Takis-A."

Moving like an automaton, Tachyon crossed to the dresser, poured a drink, threw it back. "I see a jacket. Anyone could buy a jacket, doctor it with virus positive blood—"

"That's what I thought." Hiram's voice was a rusty grinding sound. "But he's," a jerk of the head toward Ackroyd, "been through too much. The link from Syria to this hotel room is clear. It's the sen—it's Hartmann's jacket."

Tachyon pivoted slowly to face Worchester. "Do *you* want me to do this thing?"

"Do we have any choice?"

"No. I don't suppose we have."

All the way to the Marriott, Puppetman nudged at the gnawing guilt inside Billy Ray. It was a delicious snack, soured and spiced with frustration. Gregg could feel Ray reliving the moment of Ellen's fall again and again, and he knew that every time Billy felt his fingers graze Ellen's hand. Ray sat in the front seat of the limo and watched the traffic far too carefully, blinking too often behind his mirrored sunglasses. Gregg could feel Carnifex aching to strike out at something, someone.

So simple, Puppetman chortled. *He'd do anything if he thought it might make up for his mistake.*

Remember that, Gregg told him. *Tonight, maybe.*

Now that it was over, Gregg was beginning to feel more normal. The numbness and feeling of being split in half was receding. Part of him still hated what he'd done, but after all what choice had he had?

None. None at all.

There was nothing else we could do, right?

Absolutely. Nothing else.

Puppetman was smug.

When Billy opened the door of the campaign staff room for Gregg, a cardboard Peregrine floated out. Someone had whited-out her costume and penned in pubic hair and enormous nipples on the bare breasts. "Flying Fuck" was stenciled on the side.

The place was a happy chaos. Gregg could see Jack Braun in one of the bedrooms with Charles Devaughn and Logan. Half the Ohio delegation seemed to be in the living room of the suite, dipping into the booze stashed behind the wet bar and waiting for their own meeting with Devaughn. Junior staffers were riding the phone lines while volunteers bustled in and out. Room service trays littered the floor near the door, the carpet was sticky with spilled soda. The place smelled like a week-old pizza.

Gregg watched the mood shift as soon as he entered. Puppetman felt the hysterical jubilation darken as the noise level dropped to nothing. Everyone turned to look at Gregg. Devaughn broke away from Jack and Logan. His well-groomed figure cut a wedge through the crowded room. "Senator," he purred. "We're all very sorry. How's Ellen?"

Puppetman could feel very little actual sorrow or concern inside his campaign manager—Devaughn felt nothing unless it directly impacted him, and *then* everything was a crisis—but Gregg nodded. "She's doing a good job of pretending that she's a lot better than she is. This has been a blow to all of us, but especially to her. I'm not going to stay here too long, Charles. I need to get back to the hospital soon. I just wanted to touch bases. I know I haven't been much help to you people . . . "

"You're mistaken there, Senator. That press conference at the hospital—" Devaughn shook his head. The yuppie-cut hair stayed perfectly in place. "John's meeting with Florida, Georgia, and Mississippi right now; it looks like we might be able to swing a lot of the Southern Gore delegates away from Barnett.

They're heavily into the strength of the family unit and that type of thing; we've got a lot of sympathy pull to use there." Devaughn didn't even notice the callousness of the remark, though aides around them audibly gasped. "Christ, man . . . " one of them exclaimed.

Devaughn simply plowed on. "I've been talking with Jack and the West looks solid, too." Devaughn couldn't keep the grin from his face. "We've got it, Senator," he said eagerly. "We're within 150-200 votes of the majority, and the swing our way is getting deeper. Two more ballots, three at the most. Barnett's drifting and going nowhere, and we're picking up everyone's defectors. It's all over but the VP decision. You'd better start making your final decision on that."

Some of the workers around them gave a cheer at the declaration. Gregg allowed himself a small half-smile. Jack had followed Devaughn over and was standing beside him. He grimaced at the display and Puppetman felt a faint spill of distaste.

"I'm sorry, Gregg," he said, giving Devaughn a hard glare. "Really. No one would have blamed you for dropping out. I think I would have given it up in the same situation. I know there's nothing anyone can say to make it hurt less."

"Thanks, Jack." Gregg clasped the ace on the shoulder. He heaved a great sigh and shrugged self-conciously. "Whether you believe it or not, hearing that *does* mean something. Listen, you're one of the main reasons I dropped back here. Ellen's asking to see both you and Tachyon. I think she wants to make certain I've got good people around me for protection."

Gregg felt a twinge from Billy Ray at that: more guilt. Just for the pleasure it would give Puppetman and because for the first time in weeks he could do such things without worry, he tweaked the guilt and let Puppetman savor it. Ray's intake of breath was audible.

"Tachy's over at the Omni, I think," Jack said.

"Then could I ask a favor? Would you find him and drag him back to the Marriott? We'll go over together, if it's all right with you two."

It had been easy enough to arrange. Ellen was a long-time puppet and extremely pliable. It would add to the favorable press the accident had given him. He could see the photo now: Senator Hartmann, Golden Boy, and Dr. Tachyon at Mrs.

Hartmann's bedside. From the slight twist to Braun's mouth, it was obvious the ace had come to much the same conclusion, but he shrugged.

"I guess. Let me go see if I can round up Tachy."

"Good," Gregg said. "I'll wait for you in my room."

4:00 P.M.

Jack hadn't found Tachyon at the Omni, and decided to go on to the hospital without him. Jack didn't have the heart to tell the candidate that Tachyon was probably back at the Marriott screwing Fleur van Rensselaer.

Hartmann stared silently at the back of Billy Ray's head as the limousine inched its way through bumper-to-bumper traffic on its way to the hospital.

Jack thought about the secret ace. If the fragment of Sara's photocopy clue was anything to go by, the unknown ace had to be a veteran who had somehow got his blood test suppressed. This left out Jesse Jackson, who, being a seminary student, had a draft deferment. The other candidates were all veterans, but the way Jack figured, the most likely suspect was Leo Barnett.

Barnett was a populist charismatic preacher who claimed to interpret the word of God, whose flock had mostly voted for Reagan in the last two elections, but who had followed him blindly into Democratic ranks. He preached against the wild card and wild card violence, but he didn't have the votes to take the nomination unless so much chaos broke out at the convention that a backlash gave him the nomination.

Maybe Barnett had been off in his tower praying for disasters to befall Gregg Hartmann. Maybe the angels had obliged him.

Or maybe it hadn't been the angels who had obliged.

There was another possible clue in Sara's "secret ace" paper, the doodles that included a row of crosses. Maybe Sara made those crosses when thinking about the Reverend Leo Barnett.

Jack held off making a judgment until he saw the videotapes. Dukakis impressed him as hardworking, intelligent, and fairly dull. Hardly the sort to employ twisted aces to chop up his enemies. But Barnett was riveting.

In the videos, he prowled the stage like a wary panther, wiping away buckets of sweat with a succession of huge

handkerchiefs, his voice ranging from a mild, just-folks West
Virginia twang to a lacerating, scornful jeremiad shriek. And
he was clearly no brainless ranting Holy Roller. His ice-blue
eyes burned with fearsome intelligence. His messages were so
well-constructed, so well-reasoned—at least within their apoc-
alyptic framework—that his communications skills had to be
the envy of any of the other candidates' speechwriters.

And Barnett was—Jack hated to admit this—sexy. He was
still under forty, and his blond Redford good looks and
dimpled chin obviously had his female audience in thrall.
There was one incredibly revealing scene, Barnett straddling a
prostrate young semi-deb who had been possessed by the
Spirit, Barnett shouting into his phallic microphone while the
girl babbled in tongues, and writhed and grunted in what to
Jack's jaded Hollywood mind seemed clearly to be a series of
staggering sexual climaxes. . . . And Jack, looking into the
preacher's intent face and ferocious predator eyes, *knew* that
Barnett *knew* he was bringing the girl off just with the power
of his presence and voice, and that Barnett rejoiced in the
twisted sexual glory of it all. . . .

Jack remembered a night in 1948, sitting after a Broadway
debut in a Sixth Avenue coffee shop with David Harstein, the
member of the Four Aces whose pheromone power hadn't, at
that point, been revealed to the public. Unknown to them, a
meeting of the Communist Party USA was being held down
the street. The meeting ended and several of the party
members showed up in the coffee shop and recognized Jack
and Harstein. What started out as autograph-seeking turned
into a combative political debate, as the comrades, fired-up
from their meeting, demanded ideological concurrence from
the two celebrities. Hunting Nazis and overthrowing Juan
Peron was all very well, but when were the Four Aces going to
proclaim solidarity with the workers? What about assisting
anti-Dutch forces in Java and Mao's army in China? Why
hadn't the Aces fought alongside the ELAS in Greece? What
about assisting the Russians in purging Eastern Europe of
unsound elements?

All the downside of celebrity, in short.

Jack had been all for saying goodnight and moving on, but
Harstein had a better idea. His pheromones had already
flooded the small coffee shop, making everyone amenable to
his suggestions. Shortly thereafter the comrades, including

several hulking dock workers and a couple horn-rimmed intellectuals, were standing on the counter doing Andrews Sisters impersonations. The late-night crowd was entertained with "Rum and Coca-Cola," "Boogie-Woogie Bugle Boy," and "Don't Sit Under the Apple Tree."

Jack thought about how easily Harstein had controlled the hostile crowd as he watched the last Barnett video, the one shot in Jokertown. Barnett moved amid the devastated landscape of a gang battle in New York, calling down the powers of heaven to heal Quasiman, who rose from the dead . . . and seeing that, Jack knew in his bones the identity of the secret ace.

Barnett could make things happen. How the talent worked, Jack couldn't say. Barnett had to be able to affect things at a distance: make TV producers cut to commercial when he needed it, compel candidates like Hart and Biden to self-destruct, make his followers love him and give him money, maybe erase the wild card from his own military record, erase Tachyon's impotence and give him a letch for Fleur, maybe even give long-distance orgasms to the faithful. The twisted leather boy with the buzz saw hands could be someone Barnett had promised to heal of the curse of his wild card, provided he did the Lord's bidding first.

Jesus, Jack wondered. Had anyone really looked at these videos? Had anyone at all been able to tell how important they were? They were like a flaming Biblical hand in the sky, its index finger pointing at Leo Barnett.

Barnett. The secret ace had to be Barnett.

And now Jack gnawed his lower lip and looked at Hartmann, wondering whether or not to tell him. Hartmann was still staring with a peculiar intensity at Billy Ray, who sat riding shotgun in front of him. Was he blaming Ray for what happened to Ellen? Jack wondered. Ray, from what others had told Jack, was certainly blaming himself.

Jack started to say something to Hartmann, then choked the words down. Somehow he couldn't interrupt Hartmann's thoughts, not after the events of the day.

He'd talk to Tach about it first, he thought. *Show* Tachyon the clues, the videos. Between the two of them, they'd be able to figure out a response.

All this long-distance mind-control stuff was more in Tachyon's bailiwick, anyway.

5:00 P.M.

Spector sat in the hospital reception area and paged through a copy of *Reader's Digest*. The couch was made of hard, red vinyl and had been repaired with silver duct tape. A dying fluorescent light flickered and buzzed overhead. The hospital stank. Not just the usual smell of antiseptic and disease, but jokers. The deformed had a stink all their own. But it was probably the only place in town that had bed space for them.

A young, rail-thin nurse with tired eyes walked over. "You can see him now. Room 205." She walked away without looking up from her clipboard.

Spector stood, stretched, and walked down the scuffed linoleum hallway. He'd decided not to fill the contract. There was no way in the world he was going to help Barnett and his shithead followers into the White House. He'd keep the money, of course. It'd stake him to a new start somewhere else. He'd go back to Teaneck first and get his things together, then take off. Maybe just spin a globe and go wherever his finger landed, like in the movies. There were bound to be plenty of places where his talents would be marketable. If his current employer wanted to try to track him down, they were welcome to give it their best shot. He wasn't really worried about it. But first he wanted to check on Tony and make sure he was going to be okay. After that, he was bouncing back to Jersey on the next plane.

He rapped the door to 205 open and poked his head in. Tony opened his eyes and smiled. It wasn't the same with so many broken teeth. "Come on in."

Spector sat down in a chair next to the window. Tony had gauze over one eye and an ugly mouse under the other. They'd taken stitches along his cheekbone and in his forehead. His lips were puffy and discolored.

"Want me to spring you?"

"Maybe tomorrow. The doctors said I had a couple of seizures secondary to the concussion. Nothing serious, but that's why they won't be transferring me out until this evening. I'll be staying at the same hospital as . . ." He closed his eyes.

Spector nodded. "Hurt to talk?"

"Hurts to blink, even. You okay?" Tony lifted himself up. "Those guys take it easy on you, or something?"

"I'm fine. They always want to mess you pretty boys up. Figure us ugly guys got enough trouble already." Spector shook his head. "You're going to make some dentist very happy. He's going to look at your mouth and see a new home entertainment system."

Tony was quiet for a moment. "You heard about Ellen?"

"Yeah." The news about Mrs. Hartmann's miscarriage had been the day's top news story. "A shitty break. Sorry."

"From a personal standpoint, I am, too. But this is going to put the man over the top at the convention." Tony reached up and scratched his nose, then winced. "I guess that sounds kind of cold. But it's going to help so many people that I think the trade off is worth it."

Spector glanced at the digital clock on the bedside table. "I've got to get going, Tony. Things to do. I may not get a chance to see you again for a while, but I can always look you up on Pennsylvania Avenue."

"Can you do me a favor before you leave?"

"Sure, name it."

"All my writing stuff is at the Marriott. I know we're getting the nomination tonight and I have to finish off the acceptance speech. There's a black briefcase on my bed. It's got everything I'll need, my laptop, CD player." Tony edged his shoulders up the bed, sitting up as straight as possible. "With Ellen's accident and the story about some assassin hanging around, there's nobody else to get it for me. I kind of got lost in the shuffle."

"Uh, I don't think they're just going to let me waltz up to your room to pick up your shit." Spector felt bad about crawfishing, but really didn't want to go back to the Marriott. He might see Barnett and have to kill the bastard.

"No problem. I'll write you out a note. Show it to the security people at the entrance and they'll take care of it. I can call the nurse at the front desk here, have her give you my room key."

Spector couldn't say no, much as he wanted to. "Okay. It may take awhile. Traffic is a bitch out there."

Tony smiled. Even with split, purple lips, the guy still came across like a winner. He took Spector's hand and shook it. "The team's still working."

"Right," Spector said, handing him a pen and a piece of paper. "I couldn't let you go outside looking like that. You'd need a mask to cover up all those stitches."

Tony grabbed him by the elbow. "That's it, Jim. Masks. That's the angle I'll work with. Something that really show-cases Joker's Rights." He let go of Spector and raised his hands. "America, wear a mask for one day. See what it's like to be treated as something less than human."

Spector stood quietly for a moment. "I think it needs a little work."

"No problem. Now that I've got the angle, the words will come." Tony began writing.

"I'll get your stuff back as soon as I can." Spector didn't shake his head until he was out of the room.

6:00 P.M.

Projected on the screen of the electron microscope, the wild card lay in its distinctive crystal pattern.

"Jesus," breathed Ackroyd. "It's beautiful."

Tachyon scraped back his bangs. "Yes, I suppose it is." He grimaced. "Trust us Takisians to create a virus to match our aesthetic ideal."

He swung around on the lab stool just as Hiram began to slide down the wall.

"*Ackroyd!*"

They each grabbed an arm, but it was like trying to stop an avalanche. All three ended up seated on the floor. Hiram ran a hand across his eyes and muttered, "Sorry, must have blacked out for an instant."

Unlimbering his flask, Tach held it to Hiram's lips. Worchester gulped down brandy, then his head fell to the side as if his neck were too fragile to support its weight. An enormous, ugly scab crusted on his neck. Tach touched it with a cautious forefinger, and Hiram straightened abruptly.

"Hey, can I have a sip of that?" Jay pointed with his chin to the flask. "It's been a hell of a week." The detective's Adam's apple worked as he gulped down the brandy. Ackroyd gusted a sigh, and wiped his mouth.

"There can be no doubt?" Hiram's eyes pleaded with Tachyon.

"None."

"But just because he's an ace . . . well, that proves nothing. He'd have been mad to admit to the virus. He might be a latent."

An uneasy silence fell over the three men. Tachyon, squatting on his heels, gazed thoughtfully up at the ceiling. Three floors above him Ellen Hartmann rested in her hospital room. Dreaming of her lost child. Never dreaming that her husband was a secret ace, and possibly a ruthless killer. Or had she known all along?

Jay cleared his throat and asked, "So what do we do now?"

"A very good question," sighed Tachyon.

"You mean you don't know?"

"Contrary to popular belief I do not have the solution to every problem."

"We've got to have more proof than this," said Hiram, pushing to his feet.

Ackroyd jerked a thumb over his shoulder toward the screen of the microscope. "What more proof do you want?"

"We don't know if he's done anything wrong!"

"He had Chrysalis *killed!*"

The two men were nose to nose, breathing in sharp angry pants.

"I demand *evidence* of wrong doing." Hiram pounded his fist into his palm.

"*That's* evidence," Ackroyd howled, pointing again to the screen.

Tachyon shouted, "*Stop it! Stop it!*"

Hiram's hands closed on Tachyon's shoulders. "You go to him. Talk to him. There may be some logical explanation. Think of all the good he's done—"

"Oh, yeah." Sarcasm lay like acid on the words. Ackroyd took another long pull at the flask.

"Think of what we stand to lose," Hiram cried.

"So he'll just lie to Tachyon. Where the hell does that get us?"

"He cannot lie to me." Hiram's hands dropped from his shoulders, and the big ace fell back a step. Tach drew himself up to his full, if inconsequential, height. Dignity and command wrapped like a cloak about him. "If I go to him, you know what I will do." Hiram's eyes were filled with dumb misery, but he nodded slowly. "Will you accept the truth of what I read in his mind?"

"Yes."

"Even though it is inadmissible in a court of law?"

"Yes."

The alien whirled on Jay. "As for you, Mr. Ackroyd, take the jacket. Destroy it."

"Hey, that's our only proof!"

"Proof? Are you really suggesting that we publicize this? *Think* . . . what we hold could spell the ruin of every wild card in America."

"But he killed Chrysalis, and if we don't nail him Elmo takes the fall."

Tachyon dragged his fingers through his hair, nails digging deep into his scalp. "*Damn you, damn you, damn you.*"

"Look, it's not my fault. But I'm damned if I'm going to agree to some sleazy little deal that lets Chrysalis's murderer walk."

"I swear to you upon my honor and blood that I will not let Elmo suffer."

"Yeah? What are you going to do?"

"I don't know yet!" Tachyon turned off the microscope with a vicious jab, carried the slide to the basin and washed the blood-stained fibers down the drain.

Hiram fell into step next to him as the alien headed for the door. Tach laid a hand on his chest.

"No, Hiram. I must do this alone."

"And if he's got Buzz Saw Boy waiting for you?" asked Jay.

"That is the risk I must take."

7:00 P.M.

Spector thumbed the plastic SPECIAL VISITORS badge on his lapel and laughed quietly to himself. Earlier in the week, he would have killed until he was waist deep in bodies to get one of these. Now, he didn't need it anymore. Life was fucking like that.

Hartmann's floor was surprisingly quiet. He'd expected wall-to-wall aides and Secret Service. Spector pulled out Tony's room key and counted off the room numbers in his head. He figured it was time to get out of the country. Australia, maybe, or some other place where they spoke something that resembled English. He stopped in front of

Tony's door and inserted the key. As he pushed in, he felt someone pulling it open from the other side.

Spector took a step back. A joker wearing Secret Service gear looked at his visitor's badge and motioned him in. The joker was tall and wiry, and gave Spector the once over when he stepped inside. His scaly, prominent brow ridge and some ugly lumps on his forehead were the only visible signs of his jokerhood. Spector figured there were more, but he wasn't interested enough to ask.

"Who are you?" the joker asked in a perfunctory manner.

"I'm a friend of Tony Calderone. He sent me over to pick up his writing materials." Spector pointed to a black briefcase on the bed. "I think that's it."

"I see. Would you put your hands on your head, sir?" Spector did as he was told and the joker frisked him quickly, but thoroughly. Spector tensed. If this guy looked at him too long, he might get recognized. He was sure the feds had a file on him with Demise in big letters at the top. "This is news to me, so I'm going to check with Calderone." The joker moved to the phone, flipped through a notebook to find the number, and punched it in. He was careful not to turn his back, but showed no sign of placing Spector's face. "Tony Calderone, please." Short pause. "Tony. This is Colin. There's a guy here who says he's picking up your writing equipment. You did. Describe him for me. Okay. Yeah. I'm sorry, we just forgot." Colin hung up. "You Jim?"

"Yeah. Are you done with me?"

The joker raised a hand to signal silence and put a finger to his earpiece. "Yeah, I'm still in Calderone's room. There's a guy here who's going to deliver his writing kit to the hospital. Why didn't someone remind me I'd forgotten?" Long pause. "No, the hotel people say no one stayed in Baird's room again last night. Okay, I'll check it again later, but I think we're wasting our time. Talk to you later." The joker sighed and headed for the door. "Let yourself out," he said to Spector. "Don't forget to tell Tony I'm sorry."

Spector nodded stiffly and didn't breathe until the door closed. They knew about Baird. Not that it mattered now, with him leaving town. Still, the sooner he got the fuck out of here, the happier he'd be. He sat on the bed and flipped open the briefcase. Little computer and compact disc player, plenty of other crap, just like Tony'd said. He snapped it shut and

headed to the bathroom for a drink of water. The city was
baking again today, with no relief in sight. He set the briefcase
down next to the toilet and was reaching for the tap when he
heard the voices.

Whoever they were, neither one of them sounded very
happy. Spector put his ear to the wall. His stomach turned
over when he figured out who was arguing. Tachyon. He'd
recognize that fucker's prissy little voice anywhere. And he
was chewing on Hartmann. Spector sat down on the toilet and
hoped no one came into the room while he was listening in.

The dizzying drop to the Marriott lobby lay before him.
Tach noticed in a detached and clinical sort of way that his
hands were gripping the balustrade so tightly that his knuckles
had gone white.

*Just climb out there. Past the safety wires. Let go. A long
fall into peace. A chance to finally rest. To not be responsible.*

Tears burned his already aching eyes, but the despair
passed quickly. He was a prince of the house Ilkazam, and his
line did not breed cowards.

Squaring his shoulders he faced the door of Hartmann's
suite. *Perhaps as Hiram believes there is some logical explanation.*

But Digger Jay claimed witnessed Hartmann watching
with pleasure as a hunchback ace with hands like buzz saws
eviscerated Kahina in the office of the Crystal Palace.

And last night that same hunchback had attempted to kill
Sara and Jack.

*He killed Andi, he killed Chrysalis, and now he's going to
kill me . . . me . . . me . . . ME.*

The rap of his knuckles on the door sounded loud in the
hall. From below the sound of merrymaking drifted upward.
Gregg was going over the top, top, top!

And I'm out of time, time, time.

Carnifex opened the door. He seemed shrunken somehow. Misery lurked in his green eyes.

"I need to see the senator, Billy."

The ace indicated with his free hand. Tachyon entered the
suite. Gregg was seated in a chair by the window rolling a
drink between his palms.

"Celebrating?"

The senator glanced up in surprise. "Well, not just yet,

but soon I expect. Where have you been? I sent Jack to look for you. I wanted you to visit Ellen with me."

Tachyon stared at that smooth face. The laugh lines about the eyes. The sensitive mouth that had tightened in anger as the senator had been confronted with barbarism in Syria and South Africa. Tachyon's power quivered like a live thing, but he held it in check, terrified to penetrate the mind behind that familiar, friendly face.

Tachyon stirred slightly. His continued silence seemed to be angering Hartmann.

"What the hell is wrong with you? I'm about to get the nomination."

"Send Ray away."

"What?"

"Send him away."

Hartmann rolled expressive eyes toward the ace. Clearly a *humor him* expression. The agent nodded and left.

"Now Tachy, what's this all about? Drink?" He hefted the bottle.

"You are an ace."

Gregg barked out a laugh. "Really, Doctor, you've been working too hard—"

"I tested the blood on the jacket you wore in Syria."

For a brief instant the man went rigid. But the face he presented to Tachyon was bland.

"I deny it. Categorically."

"It is written in your blood."

"The wrong jacket. The wrong blood. A plot by my enemies."

"The wrong blood." Tachyon rolled the words about his mouth, tasting them. "Yes, you did deal in the wrong blood when you had Chrysalis killed."

"I had *nothing* to do with Chrysalis's death."

"You left too many loose ends, Senator. Digger, Sara. It's unraveling, all of it."

"No one will ever believe them. Or you."

"*I* have the blood test."

"And *you'll* never publish it." Hartmann grinned, reading the answer in Tachyon's face. "Even assuming it were true, which it's not." He refilled his glass, and lounged back on the sofa exuding confidence.

"A touch of my power, and you'll lie naked before me,"

warned Tachyon. "I can see you. Read the truth of what you are."

Naked panic twisted the politician's face. He leaped up from the sofa, bourbon darkening the carpet as the glass fell from his hand. "This is insane, you've lost your mind. Ray. RAY!"

Tachyon hit him. Hard. Two swift body blows to Hartmann's gut. Anger gripped the alien like a physical force. He was trembling with rage and betrayal. Gregg tottered backward, clutching his stomach, mouth working as he gasped for breath.

Tachyon's power lanced out, gripped the human, brought him upright. He could see the terror in the human's eyes as he stood helpless in the grip of the Takisian's mental imperative.

He stepped into a place of putrescence. Slitted eyes burning with rage and hatred regarded him. A *thing* beyond all imaginings. *Puppetman*. It howled and fought, twisting as Tachyon, with the precision of a surgeon, laid back the years like flaps of rotting skin. Read a tale of death and pain and terror.

The frenzied greedy feeding as the baby and Gimli fell away into darkness. Sucking at Ellen's pain and fear. Rising lust as a joker, freed of all restraint, fell upon a woman and brutally raped her. A blood feast in Berlin as the maddened and unpredictable puppet Mackie Messer shredded his former companions. Hot-wet and salty. Mackie's emotions as he had sucked on Gregg's cock. Bribing and then murdering the technician who had blood tested him. The crunch of bone as Roger Pellman slammed a rock into Andrea Whitman's face. Tasty. Tasty. An orgasmic sensation. Bloated and distended the thing fed upon the helpless, the lonely, the afraid.

So strong were the emotions and memories that Tachyon felt an answering heat in his own groin even while his stomach heaved with disgust. He screamed in fury that this thing, this monster could draw upon his own darkest nature.

Puppetman laughed, a swirling, nauseous mass of violet and red. Tachyon formed himself into a silver and crystal blade. Flew at the monster. Beat it back into its den. Threw up bars of flame. It was the most terrifying and powerful construct the Takisian had ever encountered.

Withdrawing into his own body Tachyon became aware of

the stench of his own sweat, the violent trembling that shook his body. Hartmann sprawled on the sofa.

"You will never be president. *Never!*"

Gregg rose slowly, the action filled with menace. Loomed over the tiny alien. "You can't stop me. How can you stop me . . . *us*, little man?"

The Takisian retort rose without thought, but Tachyon suppressed it before it could pass his teeth, *Kill you.* No, the last thing he could do. Sudden death would lead to autopsy, and autopsy to . . . ruin.

Spinning on his heel he left the room.

Spector pushed his fist against the wall until he could hear his knuckles begin to crack. He gripped the knob to the adjoining door and tried to turn it. No luck. He took a deep breath, picked up the briefcase, and walked back into the bedroom. He set the briefcase down on the bed and rubbed the bridge of his nose.

Hartmann was playing them all for suckers. Tony had gotten the shit kicked out of him for nothing. The jokers in the park were supporting a fraud. The fucker was an ace, and a crazy one at that. He was a damned kingpin, just like the Astronomer, manipulating people into doing his dirty work while keeping his own hands clean. Spector gritted his teeth. He'd fallen for Hartmann's line, too. And he didn't like getting caught with his pants down. Rage boiled the pain up inside him. He had to do something, what he'd been hired to do in the first place.

Tachyon would probably be useless. He was so choked on his own fucking sense of self-importance that he'd figure withdrawing his support was enough. What a pathetic, little jerk. Treating the symptom instead of the disease, as usual, and leaving someone else to do the really hard work.

Spector was too pissed off to tell how long it had been since Tachyon left the senator's room, but he could still hear Hartmann moving around next door. Now was the time to nail him, before any more Secret Service showed up. He straightened the shoulders on his jacket, stepped out into the hall, and paced over to Hartmann's door. His hand was on the knob when he heard someone call out.

"Who are *you*?"

Spector pulled his hand away from Hartmann's door like

he'd taken an electric shock and turned to the sound of the voice. It was Jack Braun, and the Golden Boy looked suspicious and unhappy. Spector didn't think, he ran. He could hear heavy footfalls as Braun came after him.

Spector sprinted down the hallway and yanked open the door to the stairwell. Something grabbed his forearm as he stepped through. A tall, blond Secret Service agent tried to spin him against the wall. Spector knocked off the man's glasses and locked eyes. Why wouldn't these Hitler youth refugees let him alone? Golden Boy came through the doorway just as the dead agent hit the floor.

Jack sat downstairs at Hartmann HQ and ate pizza, waiting for Tachyon to finish his meeting with Hartmann. The mood was generally jubilant. Hartmann was less than a hundred votes from the 2,082 necessary to win, and it looked as if all the efforts of a platoon of secret aces might not be able to stop his progress. Flying ace gliders soared across the room. Amy Sorenson was laughing as she chatted in the corner with Louis Manxman. Even Charles deVaughn was occasionally allowing moments of cheerfulness to break through his scowling self-involvement.

Still, Jack worried. He needed to talk to Tachyon. Barnett was going to have to resort to desperate measures, and Hartmann's guardians needed to be prepared. He finished his pizza and headed across the room to where Amy was talking to the journalist. "Excuse me," he said, "but has the senator finished with Tachyon yet?"

Amy looked up at him with a relaxed smile. "Tachyon? He might still be up there. Don't know."

"Thanks." Amy seemed surprised at his curtness. Jack turned and trotted toward the door, passing Billy Ray, who, napkin in hand, was trying to get tomato sauce and cheese off his white suit.

Jack took the elevator up to Hartmann's floor. An undistinguished-looking man with an acne-scarred face was trying the knob to Hartmann's door. Alarms began going off in Jack's mind. He started moving faster.

"Hey," Jack said. "Who are *you*?"

The man looked up in surprise, then bolted.

Jack's own surprise nearly halted him in his tracks before

he remembered he ought to chase. He dug his toes into the carpet and charged.

This one, he thought, wasn't going to get away. The man was heading for the only stairway on this corridor, and Alex James was posted there. Between Alex and Jack, this character was not about to make his escape.

The intruder ran full tilt into the metal stairwell door, throwing it open with a booming crash that echoed even in the silent hallway. The door slammed shut. Over the whimper of wind in his ears, Jack heard the sounds of a scuffle.

Then he heard a scream.

The marrow-chilling wail, the ultimate sound of terror and despair, turned Jack's nerves to fire.

The scream bubbled away.

Jack lunged forward like a base runner diving for second and hit the door bar with both hands. The door thundered open, then slammed to a stop: Jack bounced headfirst off the metal as it stopped his dive. He growled as he ripped the door off its hinges, his power bathing the hallway in lucid golden light.

Alex James was lying on the landing, his face still set in a rictus of his final shriek, hand on the butt of his pistol. A chill danced up Jack's spine as he saw the face, and for the first time he realized the assassin might be a wild card.

Too bad for *him*, Jack thought.

No playing with this one. He wasn't letting this assassin get away like the hunchback.

Footsteps rattled on the stairway as the assassin spun around the metal guardrail at the bottom of the first flight. Jack caught a glimpse of a pale, scarred face and wild hair as the intruder ran down steps four or five at a time. Jack didn't bother to follow him down the stairs—instead he just vaulted the rail and dropped straight to the bottom of the second flight.

The assassin was right under him as he dropped—Jack kicked out as he came down, and his lashing foot caught the assassin in the side, hurling him off a wall and down onto the landing. Jack dropped to an easy crouch and spun to face the assassin. The man, face drawn with shock and pain, was picking himself up off the stained concrete.

Triumph roared like a hot wind through Jack's heart. Jack jumped in front of the assassin, planted both feet, and shot out a punch.

The man saw it coming and tried to jerk his head out of the way, but Jack's punch caught him in the side of the jaw. A spray of blood spattered the rough concrete wall. The assassin bounced off two different walls and pitched full length down the third flight of stairs, landing on his side. Jack's feet broke traction and shot backward. His upper body fell forward onto the palms of his hands.

Jack picked himself up, heart hammering, and shook blood from his knuckles. The assassin wasn't moving. Jack stepped cautiously toward the killer.

Something crunched under one foot. Jack lifted his heel and saw it was one of the assassin's teeth.

Streams of blood poured down the stairs from the killer's mutilated face. The crushed jaw was hanging by a strip of skin.

Jack winced. He really needed time to get used to the results of serious violence, and he hadn't had it. He hadn't been in a fight since the *Stacked Deck* put down in Paris.

He knelt by the man and looked at the blood-spattered face. Maybe he'd seen the man before.

The killer's eyes opened and stared into Jack's.

Death reached out from the man's eyes and seized Jack by the heart.

There was blood everywhere, and all of it was his. Spector grabbed his dislocated jaw, took several deep breaths, and jammed it back up into the socket. He blinked away the tears, but not the searing pain. Spector stood slowly and leaned against the concrete wall.

Golden Boy wasn't moving and didn't seem to be breathing either. Spector hadn't really figured he could hurt Braun much less kill him, but was happy to be wrong. This was no time to be impressed with himself. He had to move. The fight had been quick, but noisy, and more Secret Service would show up any minute.

He slipped off his shoes with his free hand and started down the steps. One flight. Two flights. He wouldn't be far enough away until he lost count. They could test the blood from the landing and find out he was an ace. A killer ace. He pressed the edges of his torn cheek together with his thumb and forefinger. The flesh began to knit itself together. Was it ten flights now? How many floors would that be?

A door opened in the stairwell above him. Spector moved

to the far wall and hugged it as he descended. He knew there was someone above him, looking up and down for a hand on the rail or someone looking back. He wasn't going to make that mistake. But what was his next move? He still had the key to 1031. It was risky, but he couldn't think of anything else.

His sides were killing him. Golden Boy had broken a couple of his ribs, too. Spector was breathing okay, though; at least his lungs hadn't been punctured.

He stopped at the landing on the tenth floor and took off his coat. His jaw had stayed connected to his skull, that was something, but he wouldn't be talking for a while. Spector used his coat lining to wipe the blood from his face and neck. Some of it was already crusting over and he had to scrape it off with his fingernails.

There were voices and rapid footfalls from above. Spector couldn't tell how far away they were or even if they were headed down. He was a dead duck here, though. That much was a sure thing. He spit into his palms and rubbed his hands over his face, trying to get any remaining bloodstains off. His jaw still felt like there was a circus strongman trying to pull it off.

Spector slipped his shoes back on and opened the door, then stepped out into the hall and made sure it shut quietly behind him. He folded his coat over his arm so that no blood was showing and walked slowly toward the open-air atrium.

The lobby area was more crowded than the hallway, but no one seemed to be paying any attention to him. He coughed as a bit of dried blood came loose in the back of his throat. A man at the railing turned and gave him a glance, then looked back up into the airshaft.

"Golden Boy," the man said, drunkenly, and pointed with an unsteady hand. Spector stared straight ahead and quickened his pace. He caught the movement of the corner of his eye. A Golden Boy glider spiraled slowly toward the ground floor. Spector knew it would hurt to smile, so he didn't try. He'd killed Braun and the Astronomer. Who else in the world could have done that? If he could get close enough to Hartmann it wouldn't matter that the senator was an ace. Spector would take him out, too.

He turned down his hallway and walked to the door of 1031. He'd gotten away again. It was almost like somebody was on his side. Maybe God was trying to make up for all those years of shit. *Keep it up*, Spector thought. He slipped his key into the slot, waited for the green light, and went in.

"The airline ticket was made out in the name *George Kerby.*"

Ackroyd's voice went very shrill on the final two words. Tachyon pulled his computer key out of the door, and pocketed it. As he stepped in, he heard Hiram rumble, "Tickets in the name of a ghost."

From Ackroyd. "Yeah, a ghost. A specter."

"*James* Spector!" Hiram said.

"And both George Kerbys came back from the dead," Jay said. "She hired that son of a bitch Demise."

Their backs were to him. They hadn't noticed his quiet entrance.

"We have to let them know," Hiram said. He crossed the room, picked up the phone, and punched for the operator. "Connect me to the Secret Service."

At last they noticed him. Hiram staring at him with dread, Ackroyd with shuttered, snake-like eyes.

"It . . . it's not true, is it?" Hiram said desperately. "Tell me that it's all some hideous mistake, Gregg can't be . . . "

Pity filled him for the loss of dreams, and shattering of faith. "Hiram," Tach said softly. "My poor, poor Hiram. I saw his mind. I *touched* the Puppetman." The horror of it returned again, and Tachyon shuddered. "It is a thousand times worse than we could ever have imagined."

The strength drained from his legs, and Tach sat on the carpet, buried his head in his hands, and began to weep. Through his misery he heard Hiram say, "*God forgive me.*"

What has He to forgive you for? I should have seen. Twenty years! I should have realized. I should have known!

Wracking sobs made his chest ache. Tachyon realized he was spiraling into hysterics. Grimly he reached for control, and the sobs began to subside.

"What are we going to do?" asked Hiram.

"Blow the whistle," Jay said.

Tachyon bounded to his feet. "No!" he said. "Are you mad, Ackroyd? The public must *never* learn the truth."

"Hartmann's a monster," Jay objected.

"No one knows that better than I," said Tachyon. "I swam in the sewer of his mind. I felt the vileness that lives inside him, the Puppetman. It *touched* me. You can't imagine what that was like."

"I'm not a telepath," Jay said. "So sue me. I'm still not going to help you whitewash Hartmann."

"You do not understand," Tachyon said. "For close to two years Leo Barnett has been filling the public ear with dire warnings about wild card violence, inflaming their fears and their mistrust of aces. Now you propose we tell them that he was right all along, that a monstrous secret ace has indeed subverted their government. How do you think they will react?"

Jay shrugged. "Okay, so Barnett gets elected, big deal. So we have a right-wing dork in the White House for four years. We managed to survive Reagan for eight."

Tachyon was stunned by this stupidity. "You cannot know the half of what I found in Hartmann's mind. The murders, the rapes, the atrocities, and him always at the center of his web, the Puppetman pulling his strings. I warn you, if the full story ever becomes known, the public revulsion will touch off a reign of terror that will make the persecutions of the fifties look like nothing." The alien gesticulated wildly. "He killed his own unborn child, and feasted on the pain and terror of its death. And his puppets . . . aces, jokers, politicians, religious leaders, police, anyone foolish enough to touch him. If their names become known—"

"*Tachyon*," Hiram Worchester interrupted. His voice was low, but anguish sobbed in every syllable.

Tachyon glanced guiltily at Hiram.

"Tell me," Hiram said. "These . . . puppets. Was . . . was I . . . one of . . . " He couldn't finish, choking on the words.

Tachyon nodded. A small quick nod. A single tear rolled down his cheek. He turned away.

Behind him Tach heard Hiram say, "In a grotesque way, it's almost funny," but he did not laugh. "Jay, he's right. This must be our secret."

When he turned around Tach found Ackroyd looking from Hiram to himself, and back again. The detective's eyes were bitter. "Do what you want," he said, "just don't expect me to vote for the fucker. Even if I *was* registered."

Suddenly Tach realized this was too important. He could not rely upon only their unsupported word. "We must take a vow," Tachyon said. "A solemn oath, to do everything in our power to stop Hartmann, and to take this secret to our graves."

"Oh, gimme a break," Jay groaned.

"Hiram, that glass," the alien snapped. Hiram handed him the half-finished drink, and Tachyon upended the contents on the carpet. He bent, slid the long knife out of his boot sheath, and held it up in front of the fascinated and aghast humans. "We must pledge by blood and bone," he said.

His grip on the hilt was slick with sweat, but he slashed hard across his left wrist. He was pleased that his only reaction was a soft almost inaudible intake of breath. Perhaps Earth had not softened him as much as he feared. Tach held the wound over the glass until there was an inch of blood on the bottom, then bound his wrist in a handkerchief and passed the knife to Ackroyd.

The detective just looked at it. "You got to be kidding."

"No."

"How about I just piss in it instead?" Jay suggested.

"The blood is the bond."

Hiram stepped forward. "I'll do it," he said, taking the knife. He shrugged out of his white linen coat, rolled up his sleeve, and made the cut. The pain made him inhale sharply, but his hand did not hesitate.

"So deep," Tachyon muttered. The cut was deep enough to be dangerous. Was Hiram so devastated by the betrayal that suicide seemed an option? Hiram winced and held his hand above the glass. The red line crept upwards.

Tachyon bent a stern eye on Ackroyd.

Jay sighed deeply. "So if you two are Huck and Tom, I guess that makes me Nigger Jim," he said. "Remind me to have my head examined when all of this is over." He took the knife, and yelped as the blade bit into the skin.

Accepting the snifter from the sweating Jay, Tachyon swirled the glass to mix the bloods one with the other, then lifted it above his head and chanted in Takisian. "By Blood and Bone, I so vow," he finished. He threw back his head, and drained a third of the glass in one long gulp.

Tachyon thrust the glass at Hiram. Both the humans looked nauseated.

"By Blood and Bone," Hiram intoned, and took his ritual swallow.

"Am I allowed to add some tabasco, maybe a little vodka?" Jay asked when Hiram gave him what was left.

Ackroyd's wisecracks were beginning to wear a little thin. "You are not," said Tachyon stiffly.

"Pity," Jay said. "Always liked Bloody Marys." He lifted the glass, muttered, "Blood and Bone," and drank the last of the blood. "Yum," he said afterwards.

"It is done," Tachyon said. "Now, we must make plans."

"I'm going back to the Omni," Hiram announced. "I was among Gregg's earliest supporters, and I daresay I am not without influence in the New York delegation. I may be able to have some impact. We *must* deny him the nomination, at all costs."

"Agreed," said Tachyon.

"I wish I knew more about Dukakis . . . " Hiram began.

"Not Dukakis," the alien said. "Jesse Jackson. He has been courting us all along. I'll speak to him." He clasped hands with Hiram. "We can do it, my friend."

"Real good," Jay said. "So Greggie doesn't get to be president. Big deal. What about all his victims? Kahina, Chrysalis, the rest of them."

Tachyon glanced over. "Not Chrysalis," he said, not believing he had forgotten to tell them this.

"What?" Jay croaked.

"He threatened Chrysalis, yes," the alien said. "He made her and Digger watch while his creature tortured and killed Kahina, but he never acted on that threat. When he heard of her death on Monday morning, he was as surprised as anyone."

"No fucking way," Jay said. "You got it wrong."

Nostrils tightening in fury Tachyon pulled himself up to his full height. "I am a Psi Lord of Takis, trained by the finest mentats of House Ilkazam," he said. "His mind was *mine*. I did not get it *wrong*."

"He sent Mackie after Digger!" Jay argued.

"And he commanded Oddity to retrieve the incriminating jacket, and destroy it. Most assuredly. *After* he heard that Chrysalis was dead, he took steps to protect himself. But he had no hand in ordering that death." Tachyon put a hand on Jay's shoulder. "I'm sorry, my friend."

"Then who the fuck did it?" Jay demanded.

"We have no time to argue about this now," Hiram said impatiently. "The woman's dead, nothing will—"

"Quiet," Jay said urgently.

A newsflash flickered across the screen. " . . . latest tragedy to strike the convention," a solemn announcer was saying. "Senator Hartmann is unharmed, repeat, *unharmed*, but reliable reports indicate that the ace assassin took the lives of two other men in his attempt to reach the senator. We are still waiting for final confirmation, but unofficial sources indicate that the killer's victims were Alex James, a Secret Service agent assigned to Senator Hartmann—" A photograph of the dead man appeared on the screen, above the announcer's shoulder. "—and the chairman of Hartmann's California delegation, ace Jack Braun. The controversial Braun, who starred in feature films and TV's *Tarzan*, was better known as Golden Boy. He was considered by some to be the strongest man in the world. Braun first came to public attention . . . "

Jack's picture appeared on screen as the announcer went on and on. He was in his old fatigues, smiling crookedly, surrounded by a golden glow. He looked young, alive, invincible.

"Oh, Jack," Tachyon said. For thirty years he had prayed for Jack's death. Even plotted it in angry alcoholic dreams. Now it had come and another little part of Tisianne died.

"He *can't* be dead," Hiram said furiously. "I just saved his damnable life last night!" The television set floated off the carpet. Scraped against the ceiling. "He can*not* be dead!" Hiram insisted, and all of a sudden the TV was falling. It hit the floor, and the picture tube exploded.

"He will not have died in vain," Tachyon said. Did it mean anything? He didn't think so. He just spoke to assure himself that he was still alive. Tach touched Hiram on the arm. "Come," he said.

The pain was greater than anything Jack had ever imagined. It burned through him from head to toe, searing every nerve, every muscle, every square millimeter of skin. His brain had gone nova. His heart was an exploding turbopump. His eyes felt as if they were melting. Every cell in his body was on fire, every strand of DNA in revolt against its inherited code.

The black queen, Jack realized. Somehow he'd just drawn the black queen.

He could feel his body shutting down in protest against the agony. Bit by bit, organ by organ, like someone throwing all the circuit breakers in a big building.

The pain ended.

He saw himself crumpled on the landing, his face set in an expression of dumb shock. The assassin, barely able to move, managed to get his jacket off and wrap it around his head, stopping the flow of blood from his mangled jaw. "Hey," Jack said. He tried to grab the guy. "Stop!" Somehow the assassin crawled away.

"Yo. Farm boy."

Jack looked up in surprise at the sound of Earl Sanderson's voice. Earl looked younger than when Jack had seen him last, the young athlete just graduated from Rutgers, and was dressed in his old Army Air Corps fatigues with the insignia taken off, his leather flying jacket with the patch of the 332nd Fighter Group, the black beret, and long silk scarf. The Black Eagle—scholar, athlete, civil rights attorney, ace . . . and maybe Jack's best friend.

"Hi, Earl," Jack said.

"Man, you're *slow*," Earl said. "We're supposed to be flying out of here by now."

"I can't fly, Earl. I'm not like you."

"Slow, farm boy." Earl was grinning. "Slow."

Jack was mildly surprised when they both began to fly. The Marriott Marquis was gone and they were in the sky, heading toward the sun. The sun began to get brighter and brighter.

"Hey, Earl," Jack said. "What's going on here?"

"You'll work it out sooner or later, farm boy."

The sun was almost blinding, the yellow light turning whiter and whiter, all color leached away. Jack saw other people there, guys from the 5th Division and Korea, his parents, his older brother. The were all flying, rising into the sky. Blythe van Renssaeler neared him and gave him a shy smile.

"Damn. He's asystolic," she said. "Flat line."

"Huh?" Jack looked at her.

Archibald Holmes strode confidently toward him, dressed in a white linen suit. He lit a cigarette and put it in its holder.

"Hi, Mr. Holmes."

"Okay," Holmes said. "I got the ET down his throat. Where's the bag?"

"Why does he keep glowing on and off like that?" Blythe asked.

"Can't help it, really," Jack shrugged.

"Start O_2," said Holmes. "I'm going to shoot some epinephrine down the endotrachial tube. I'll want a milligram of atropine in a minute."

Jack looked around and saw that Earl was holding hands with a long-legged woman with blonde hair tousled over one eye and broad, padded shoulders.

"You must be Lena Goldoni," he said. "I've seen your pictures."

"We've got fibrillation," said Lena.

"*Slow*," Earl said, shaking his head. "Farm boys are so *slow*." His scarf was rippling in an invisible wind.

Jack realized he was here with almost all the old Four Aces crowd, everyone except David Harstein, and he began to wonder if he should apologize for what he'd done to them, how he'd destroyed them all. But they all seemed so happy to see him he decided not to mention it.

More people were clustering around him. Some of them he'd forgotten he'd known. Even Chester the Chimp, who'd played opposite Jack in *Tarzan of the Apes*, was there, riding on someone's shoulders.

"Give him three-hundred joules," said the ape. "Stop CPR. Clear! *Clear*, Goddamn it! Get your hand off that metal rail, will you, Lois?"

The light was getting brighter and brighter. Circling around them, the rays seemed almost palpable, like the walls of a tunnel. Jack felt his speed increase as he shot toward the source of the light. He began to hear people singing, a million voices raised in joy.

The light grew nearer, not just white light but the White Light. Jack's heart lifted. He began to understand what it was that Earl wanted him to know.

"Three-hundred-sixty!" shrieked the ape. "Clear! Clear!"

Jack stretched out his arms and prepared to dive into the heart of the White Light. Suddenly he seemed to hesitate in his progress. He was slowing down. Desperately he tried to speed up. He longed to fly farther.

He realized the White Light was looking at him.

"What a *weenie*," the White Light said. "Get that weenie *outta* here."

Jack coughed and opened his eyes and saw people crouched over him, men and women he recognized from Gregg Hartmann's Secret Service detail, working with emergency medical equipment that was part of their standard issue. He felt an ache in his solar plexus and he couldn't stop coughing. Jack looked up over their heads, saw blood-flecked concrete walls and steep stair risers.

"Normal sinus rhythm," one said. "We got pulse. We got pressure." He spoke in Archibald Holmes's voice. A couple of the others cheered.

A tall brown-haired woman was speaking into a walkie-talkie. "Ambulance on its way." The voice was Blythe's.

"I blew it," Jack tried to say. He couldn't talk over the endotrachial tube they'd slid down his throat. "I blew it *again*." He was too weak too feel much emotion over it.

The ambulance crew arrived and carried him away.

8:00 P.M.

He had himself well in hand. The emotional devastation of an hour ago was passed. Jack was dead. The friendship, the man he had known as Gregg Hartmann was dead. Chrysalis was dead. Very well. So be it. He was in control now. He would do what had to be done.

But these officious twits were arguing with him. Mouths moving, gums and tongues red against black and white faces.

"I'm telling you the reverend is *busy*. You don't have an appointment," said the black aide patiently, as if explaining addition to a retarded child.

"He will see me. I am Tachyon," explained the alien in the same patient, condescending tone.

"Go and phone. Use appropriate channels," said Straight Arrow calmly.

"I don't have *time* for appropriate channels," snapped Tachyon. His control was unraveling like line reeling from a fly fishing rod.

"It's late," put in the aide.

The door to the suite was partially ajar. Tachyon measured the gap between the two far bigger men. It would accommodate him. Wriggling like a fish he darted between them, and through the door.

"HEY!"

Shouts. A wall of people advancing upon him. Phones shrilling. A television pouring its electronic inanities into the crowded suite.

"Get out of my way! GET OUT OF MY WAY! WHERE IS HE? I MUST SEE HIM!" His voice ringing shrilly in his own ears.

"You can't just waltz in here—" bawled Straight Arrow.

People had gripped him by arms and legs, lifting him completely off the ground. Tach screamed with fury, and writhed in their grasps. Mind-controlling people frantically, he felt the holds on him loosen, then jerk tight again as new people stepped forward to replace those he had dropped slumbering to the floor.

The connecting door to the bedroom flew open, banging violently into the far wall. Jesse Jackson, reading glasses clutched in his hand, glared at his supporters, and roared, "LET HIM GO!"

The two oldest Jackson sons pushed back the irate staffers. The very pretty and very self-possessed Jackie Jackson helped Tachyon smooth his coat. Slowly order was restored. Jesse Jackson beckoned to Tachyon, and he joined him in the bedroom. The door closed, blocking off the worst of the noise, and the curious gawking faces.

"Here." Tachyon opened his eyes. Jackson had thrust a hotel glass filled with scotch under his nose. "You believe in making an entrance, don't you, Doctor? You couldn't have just called and asked to see me?"

Tach pressed a hand to his eyes. "I didn't think." Squaring his shoulders he pushed up and off the wall that had been supporting him. "Call a press conference, Reverend. You have just become the new, best hope for the wild cards."

Jackson seemed bereft of words. He slapped his hand against his thigh then took several quick turns about the cramped room.

"Why?" His tone and expression were equally grim.

"Upon reflection I have become convinced of the strength of your arguments."

"Bull. You roar in here like a madman. You're shaking like

a leaf. . . . " Desperately Tachyon clasped his hands, trying
to still the betraying tremors. "What's happened?"

The Takisian flung out a hand in a sharp jagged gesture.
"Do you want what I am offering you, or not?"

"Yes. But I want to know why."

"No."

"Yes. Look, Doctor, you're going to have to tell the press
something. You may as well practice on me."

The bed in the suite was an elaborate canopied affair.
Tachyon wrapped his hands about the neweled post, and
rested his forehead against the wood. In a flat monotone he
recited, "Gregg Hartmann's instabilities are well-documented.
Though everyone hoped that the tragedy of 1976 was forever
behind the senator I have determined that this morning's
events have badly shaken the candidate, and I cannot in good
conscience support the gentleman in his bid to secure the
presidential nomination of the Democratic Party." He dropped
his hands, and turned to face Jackson. "There, will that do?"

Jackson smoothed his mustache with a forefinger, "Yes, I
think it just might." His eyes were grave as he looked down at
the tiny alien. "Do you fully understand the consequences of
what you are doing?"

"Oh, yes." The words came out, carried on a breath.

"And that doesn't deter you?"

"I cannot let it." Tach headed for the door. Paused with
his hand on the knob, and looked back, "I am trusting you with
my people, Reverend. You had best not prove my faith
unfounded."

10:00 P.M.

"—instabilities are well-documented," the small man with
the long red hair was saying from the midst of the television
screen. In the background the letters JAC and SON winged
out either side of the grinning giant black man beside him. "I
fear that the tragic events of this morning have overwhelmed
Senator Gregg Hartmann."

"You fucker, you fucker!" Mackie Messer screamed, spew-
ing fried pork-rind crumbs at the screen. His skinny, twisted
little body was practically levitating above the taut hotel
bedspread, like a speck of superconductor caught in a mag-
netic field.

The pork rinds tasted mostly of salt and grease. Failure tasted like shit.

Der Mann hadn't sent him away. He had permitted him to stay, in a room as stolen as the pork rinds—funny how you could always find an empty room no matter how jammed a hotel was. At least if you could walk through walls.

It had been close. Mackie could tell. He could always tell when rejection was near. He had a lot of experience with it.

Tachyon looked directly into molten-silver glare. It seemed to push his eyes back deep in dark pits.

"I am no longer convinced of Senator Hartmann's abilities adequately to represent the Democratic Party, either as a presidential nominee or as president. Therefore I have decided to support the Reverend Jesse Jackson, who has demonstrated his commitment to jokers. . . . "

For a nigger! The alien bastard was throwing over the Man for a jungle savage! And Mackie, who could at least have killed the blonde cunt who was trouble for the Man, had fucked up.

He was worthless. He deserved the Man's rejection. Just as he deserved to be abandoned by his mother. With a sob he tore a pillow from the candy-wrapper embrace of the bedspread and stuffed it over his face as if that could keep the tears in him.

11:00 P.M.

The phone rang. Tachyon glanced at Jay's slumbering form, but the detective didn't even twitch. He was beyond mere sleep; it was an exhaustion so deep that it was almost unconsciousness. Tachyon stared at him in bitter envy. He was bone tired, but his restless mind would not allow him to rest. Knocking back the last inch of brandy in his tumbler, the alien reached out and snagged the phone.

"Hello. No, I'm not giving interviews—"

"Dr. Tachyon, this is the front desk. The Great and Powerful Turtle is hovering in front of the entrance, and he's calling for you."

"Tell him I am busy."

"But—"

Tachyon replaced the receiver, and resumed drinking.

A few minutes later the phone rang again.

"Look, goddamn it! Meet me! We've got to talk."

Tachyon pondered on where Tommy had parked the shell while he made the telephone call. "No, Tommy."

"You owe it to me."

"No."

He hung up the phone, and had another drink.

The glass blew in with the sound like a rocket detonating. With a yell of terror Tachyon wrapped his arms about his head as glittering slivers rained across carpet and furniture. Turtle was a vast black bulk blotting out the stars. There were shouts of confusion coming from the hall.

"You can hang up a phone. I thought I'd call in person."

"Oh, Tommy."

"Let's go, we've gotta talk."

"I can't."

Turtle's power seized him. Swung him out the shattered window, and held him suspended three hundred feet above the pavement. "You can."

Tachyon glanced down at the roofs of the cars flowing past beneath him. Swallowed his stomach. "All right. I can."

Turtle deposited him softly on the rounded back of the shell. Tach groped for a hand hold. He was too drunk to balance without it.

"Why, Tachy?"

"I had to."

"One more ballot, and we would have had it." Tachyon remained silent. "Look, goddamn it, talk to me!"

"I cannot."

"*You cannot.*" Tommy imitated in a whining, prissy little tone.

Anger stirred wearily. "Look, Tommy, what's the problem? Jackson holds every position that Hartmann held."

"Jackson can't become president."

"You don't know that."

"Jackson is a *black* guy who supports *jokers*!"

"I decided he was the best person to represent the wild card interest."

"*You*, you decided? Just like that. Well, what about the rest of us?"

"You have known me for twenty-five years. You must trust me."

"Trust you. Even though you betrayed us. You know what you've done. You've just given the nomination to Barnett."

"No I haven't! And you know me well enough to know that I have sound reasons for what I've done."

"Then tell me what the fuck they are!"

"No." Tach began to cry.

"Shit, you're drunk."

They were skimming the roof tops, spotlights stabbing at windows, and cornices. The curving roof of the Omni Convention Center came into view. In the darkness, thousands of lights flickered at the foot of the sprawling building. Tach, blinking away the moisture that clouded his eyes, realized that a sea of silent jokers, their masks and deformities highlighted by the flames of a thousand candles, stood in mute vigil.

"Look at them. Look at them good. What are you gonna tell them, Tach? Trust me? While the troops come to round them up."

"It will not come to that."

"And if it does?"

"It would not change the decision I have made tonight."

Turtle read it as arrogance, and it snapped his control. "JESUS CHRIST, WHO THE FUCK DO YOU THINK YOU ARE?" A number of curious masked faces were lifted toward them.

Tachyon's temper shredded. "I am Tisianne brant Ts'ara sek Halima sek Ragnar sek Omian of House Ilkazam, and when I do a thing it is for a good and sound reason. Do not question me!"

"I'm not your fucking serf!"

"No, but you are my *stirps*, formally adopted by me. You are blood and bone of my line, you and your heirs forever bound to my house. You forget yourself!" he hissed.

"Oh fuck you! Fuck you to hell! We're just playthings to you. That's all we've ever been. Lab rats in your great experiment."

They were over Piedmont Park now. Turtle dropped like a plummeting stone, and seizing Tachyon with his teke, he deposited him on the steps of a fountain.

"For the last time, Tachyon, answer me."

"I cannot."

The power lashed out. Caught Tachyon across the face. He fell backward down the steps, landing hard on his side.

Groaning, he struggled onto an elbow. He was blinded by the floods as Turtle swooped in low. Gingerly Tach explored his ribs. Decided they were merely cracked not broken. Turtle hovered for an instant then shot straight up, and vanished over the trees of the park.

Tachyon did not miss the message or the symbolism in that single blow. *December 1963. The steps of Jetboy's tomb. "You don't give a damn about anybody."*

"But I do. I'm doing this to protect you. Because I love you. He has a killer who can walk through walls. And I took a vow."

But Turtle had raised one terrifying specter—Barnett—as president. Tachyon had kept Hartmann from the presidency; he now had to stop Barnett. And for that he needed Jack.

By the time the ambulance got Jack to the hospital he was feeling okay, though weakened. Assuming he'd had a heart attack, they put him through a battery of tests. He was too tired to resist, but by the time they announced the results were negative and they were going to do a brain scan for sign of a something-something-cerebral-episode, Jack's strength had come flowing back, and he put his foot down. It was an ace power that had hurt him, he said, and he'd lived through it. There was nothing wrong with him physically. The whole thing happened in his head.

The doctors compromised by making Jack stay overnight for observation. Minutes after the nurses left, he was on the phone to Billy Ray, describing the man he'd seen and the nature and extent of his powers.

"He's working for Barnett," Jack said. "He and the other guy, the leather boy."

"I'll pass on your suspicions," Ray said. "The guy who got you, by the way, we figure that was James Spector, a.k.a. Demise. He's got a certain rep. Put on a pair of shades, though, and he can't lock eyes with you."

"Tell the *senator*, for Christ's Sakes. That's two aces aiming at him."

"The senator's got other things to think about, Jack boy. Tachyon and the jokers have defected to Jesse Jackson."

"*What?*" Jack sat bolt upright in bed.

"The fucking alien bastard."

"When did this *happen?*"

"About the same time a certain Golden Weenie was getting his ass kicked in the stairwell. Talk to you later, asshole."

Jack hung up the phone and stared for a long moment at the darkened television set propped in the corner.

The screen was the same blank color as James Spector's eyes. A cold flood lurched up Jack's spine.

And then he thought, the secret ace. The secret ace—hell, Leo Barnett, call the guy by his name—Barnett got Tachyon somehow. Probably through Fleur. Fleur got him alone and Barnett hit him with something.

Jack slid out of bed and found his blood-spattered clothes in the closet. He started drawing them on.

He was alone now. And he knew what he had to do.

Tachyon was pounding his fists on the nurses' station. It hurt like hell, but he couldn't seem to stop.

"How could you have let him leave? How could you? I need to see him. I must see him!"

"Doctor," said a slim black nurse gently. "I'm going to call Dr. English from the psych ward—"

"I do not . . . require . . . a . . . psychiatrist. I require . . . Mr. Braun."

"And he's . . . not . . . here," the nurse said with the same careful enunciation Tachyon had used.

A hand closed vise-like about his elbow. "Dancer, come away."

Tachyon whirled, the violent move pulling a groan from him. Polyakov kept his grip on the Takisian's elbow, fingers tightening painfully on the joint. Meekly, Tachyon allowed himself to be led away.

"We knew from the news reports that you had at last come to your senses," said George quietly as they walked out of the hospital.

"We?"

He waved down a cab. "Sara. I'm caring for her."

"Oh thank the Ideal. Take me to her—"

"What do you think I'm doing?" grunted Polyakov as he swung open the door of the cab.

CHAPTER SIX

Saturday
July 23, 1988

1:00 A.M.

They stood before a door at a Motel 6 on the outskirts of
Atlanta. Tachyon tried to think what he would say to the
woman he had so wronged, but all he could think about was
how tired he felt. He tried to figure out when he had last slept.
He had a bad feeling it had been Tuesday night.

Polyakov rapped once sharply on the door.

"Sara, it's George."

Tachyon tensed for the moment, and then Sara was there,
staring strained and white-faced up at him. She wore a
crumpled blue-and-white dress. The petticoats crackled as she
backed away, arms folded protectively across her breasts.
Polyakov was a stolid dark shadow behind him. Tachyon felt
his throat work several times as he tried to force out words.
Suddenly he advanced on her in a rush. Dropped to one knee,
and lifting the hem of her skirt, pressed it to his lips.

"Sara, forgive me."

She was making faint inarticulate mewing sounds. Her
fingertips brushed wraith-like across his hair as he knelt with
bowed head before her.

"What's he doing?" she finally asked pathetically.

"Making an overly dramatic Takisian gesture. In times of
stress, he reverts to this sort of extraordinary behavior,"
grunted the Russian. "I'll leave you two alone." The door

closed softly behind him, and they listened to his footsteps retreating down the hall.

She tugged at his shoulder. "Oh, get up, please."

The pain from his cracked ribs drew a grunt from him as Tach pushed to his feet. "Forgive me if I embarrassed you, but words were inadequate. I have wronged you horribly."

"Then . . . then . . ."

"Yes, you are not mad," he said answering her greatest fear. "I have confronted the monster." She began to cry. Gently he reached out with a fingertip, and wiped her cheeks.

"*Oh, Ricky.*"

Her shoulders were jutting blades as he pulled her into an embrace. "Hush, it is over now."

Throwing back her head she looked up at him. "Really? Truly?"

"Yes. His momentum is broken. He can never regain it."

Her lashes fluttered wearily down onto her cheeks. "Then I'm safe."

"Yes."

He kissed her, tasting the salt from her tears. Her white-gold hair lay across his shoulder as she rested her head against him. So tiny. She was one of the few women on this hot-and-heavy planet who made him feel tall. Elfin pale, approaching Takisian standards of beauty. And he remembered that he had wanted her. Three years ago when she had entered his life, begging him to save the pathetic joker Doughboy who had been wrongfully accused of murder. Now he was whole—or at least his body was. And he was lonely and lost and afraid, and so was she. . . . He transferred his kisses to her mouth.

He knew she could not be a virgin, but there was something so delightfully shy and awkward about her responses. He swung her up into his arms, and groaned again.

Her head snapped back, tendons etched in the thin neck. "You're hurt."

"It's nothing." He tottered to the bed, ignoring the pain. Laid her down.

He wondered at this sudden surge of libido when all about him his life lay in shattered ruins. Then he realized it was appropriate. The Takisian spirit was a dauntless one, and it would always seek to lure victory out of defeat, creation from despair. Tach paused, asked, "Do you want me?"

"Yes, oh, yes. I'm so grateful . . . so very grateful." She choked, and the tears matted in the hair at her temples.

Sliding his hands up her haunches Tach snagged the top of her panty hose, and pulled them down. And noticed that runs and holes had left them like a tattered cobweb beaten in a killing wind.

"Oh, my poor little one. My little, little one."

Suddenly he was sobbing. Agony shot through him as the paroxysms shook his sore ribs. Sara, looking terrified, pressed her palms to his cheeks.

"Oh, don't. Please don't. What's wrong?"

"I trusted him, and he betrayed me. Now," his arm flailed in the general direction of Piedmont Park, "they think *I've* betrayed them. I'm so tired. So tired."

Sara with gentle hands undressed him. Got him beneath the covers. Her naked flesh was as clammy as his. For a long time they merely hugged, shivering as their minds and bodies tried to relax. Tachyon had a hand cupped over one tiny breast. Sara lay in the curve of his arm lightly tracing the line of his lips with a forefinger.

"It's probably a good thing I'm not on Takis."

"Why?"

"I'd have been dead long ago. If a mere human, a groundling, can outmaneuver me at the Takisian game." He shook his head.

"Which is?"

"Intrigue. I've known Hartmann for twenty years. And I never suspected."

"He was very cunning. I've spent—" Her voice deepened and thickened with bitterness. "And ruined—my life pursuing him."

"And now you've succeeded. Was it worth it?"

"I don't know." She sighed, and he kissed her.

Tachyon barked out a short laugh, then muffled a groan. "I have no idea where my thirteen-year-old grandson is, isn't that incredible? I'm so damned busy strutting about the grand stage of life that I have no time to live. I wonder what it would be like to be just a person?"

"Boring. You'd hate it."

Easing up on an elbow, Tach stared down at her. "Do you think so?"

"Yes."

He laid back down. "I don't know. To have a wife, children, friends."

"You have friends."

"I think I lost most of them tonight."

Sara began to cry again. "I'm sorry. It's all my fault—"

Tachyon laid a hand over her mouth. "No, that's my line."

"Ricky loved me, and *he* had him cut to pieces. I never even slept with him."

The alien slid his hand down her stomach, matted his fingers in her mons. "Then let us honor the dead by celebrating living."

"Isn't that a little callous?"

"Hush, Sara, you think too much."

2:00 A.M.

Jack was sweating as he sat up in bed, his back propped against thick hotel pillows. A half-empty bottle of whiskey stood in his hand. He'd run through two packs of Camels.

The television was on, an old Boris Karloff suspense film. Karloff kept looking at Jack with James Spector's eyes. Jack turned the set off with remote control. The television kept staring at him, so he got out of the bed and turned the TV set to the wall.

He knew what he had to do. He didn't know if he had the nerve to do it.

He'd never done this kind of thing by himself before. There'd always been Mr. Holmes or Earl or someone to give him advice and make sure everything worked out all right.

The secret ace had already come close to killing him twice.

Third time, he wondered, the charm?

10:00 A.M.

Tachyon was seated in front of the room service tray buttering a slice of toast when Jay emerged from the bedroom. He wore one of Tachyon's suits, and though it was too short in the arms and legs, the man looked decidedly more elegant and well kept.

Blaise, stretched out across an armchair, looked up and

sniggered. Tachyon gave his grandson a stern look. "Blaise, did you enjoy your little ride on the luggage carousel?"

The boy looked sullen. "No. I felt stupid."

"Then by the Ideal you *will* mind your manners," Tachyon told him, "or I will have Mr. Ackroyd teleport you back to the Atlanta airport."

"I can't help it if he's funny," Blaise complained. "He looks like a fruit."

"Those are *my* clothes," Tachyon pointed out stiffly. "Myself, I think it's a dramatic improvement."

"I'm with the kid," Jay said. Blaise looked surprised. Then he grinned. Jay whipped up his finger in a quick-draw move. Blaise flinched. "Gotcha," Jay said. He smiled. So did Blaise.

Tachyon watched this in confusion. Apparently teleporting his wayward heir halfway across Atlanta had established a rapport. He remembered George once telling him that Blaise needed to fear someone before he could care for them. Tach felt depressed.

"He's enough of a rapscallion without your encouraging him," Tachyon muttered.

"Ah, he's okay," Jay said, pulling a chair over to the room service cart. "For a Takisian." He lifted the silver dome off his plate, and attacked the Eggs Benedict wolfishly.

Tachyon was patting his lips with a napkin and Jay was mopping up the last of the yoke with a piece of toast when the knock came at the door. Tachyon stood. "Who's there?"

"Carnifex. Open up, I don't have all day."

Tachyon glanced back at Jay. "Let him in," the detective said. "Ray's tough, but there's nothing he can do against you, me, and the Cisco Kid over there." He gestured toward Blaise.

The alien nodded and opened the door. Carnifex glanced around and stepped into the suite, wearing his skin-tight white uniform that outlined every muscle and tendon in his body. "Regs say we're supposed to stay out of the political bullshit," Ray told Tachyon with disdain. "Good for you. Otherwise I'd have to whip your ass. You been hanging around Braun too much, I guess. Some of it must have rubbed off."

Tachyon's mouth tightened. "Say what you came to say, Ray," he told the government ace. "Your opinions on political and moral issues interest me not in the slightest."

"Gregg wants to see you."

"The sentiment is not reciprocated."

"You'll see him," Ray said, with a crooked smile. "Gregg said to tell you he has a proposition he wants to discuss."

"I have nothing to discuss with the senator."

"Scared?" Ray wanted to know. "Don't worry, I'll hold your hand if you want." He shrugged. "Come or don't come, either way it's no skin off my nose. But if you don't, you're going to regret it." The ace in the white suit looked around the suite: at the windows Turtle had shattered, the television Hiram had dropped, the urine stain on the sofa. "Must have been a hell of a party," he said to Tachyon. "Somebody ought to teach you to clean up after yourself, Doc. This place is a mess."

He was going out the door when Ackroyd called out. "Hey, Carny."

Tachyon winced.

Ray turned around with a dangerous glint in his green eyes. "That's Carnifex, asshole."

"Carnifex Asshole," Jay repeated.

Tachyon winced again, and closed his eyes.

"I'll try and remember," Jay continued. "How many of those Good Humor suits you own?"

"Six or eight," Carnifex said suspiciously. "Why?"

"Must be hell to get the bloodstains out," Jay said.

Tachyon couldn't believe he was hearing this. As a child Ackroyd must have enjoyed kicking over ant hills, and investigating beehives.

Ray glared at the detective. "Stay out of my way, shamus," he said, "or you'll find out firsthand." He slammed the door behind him.

"Shamus," Jay said. "He actually called me shamus. God, I'm so mortified." He turned to Tachyon. "You gonna go?"

Tach straightened, and lifted his chin. "I must."

Jay sighed. "I was afraid you were going to say something like that."

Maybe he'd got some sleep, maybe he'd just passed out from time to time. He figured he better do what he had to before all motor coordination went to hell and he couldn't punch the numbers on his cellular phone.

"The Reverend Barnett, please."

"May I say who's calling?" The female voice spoke with a heavy Spanish accent.

"This is Jack Braun."

The accented voice was prim. "The Reverend Barnett is not available to anyone, Mr. Brown. He is in a prayer vigil expected to last until—"

"He'll talk to me!" Jack's voice rose to a near shout.

"Sir," with feigned patience, "the Reverend Barnett—"

"Tell him," Jack said, "that I can deliver California."

There was a long pause before the voice returned. "I will connect you to Miss van Renssaeler."

Little hangover stilettos entered Jack's eyes at the mention of the name.

At least he was getting closer to the reverend.

He's coming. Puppetman could sense Tachyon's arrival from Billy Ray's disgust. *We're making a mistake not trying to take him . . .*

No! Gregg was vehement. *He's too strong for us. If we attack him that way, he'll have an excuse to retaliate. My way's better.*

You're weak. You're feeling guilty.

The accusation was too close. Yes, he was feeling guilty. He'd known Tachyon for twenty years, after all. *Just shut up,* he told Puppetman. *Let me handle this.*

Sure. Sure. Who else has he told? Hiram knows. Maybe lots of others . . .

Shut up!

Gregg was facing out of the window as Billy—with obvious ill will—ushered Tachyon into the suite. "One traitor for you, Senator," Ray said as he held the door open. "Wonder how much they paid the little creep?" Ray shut the door behind Tachyon so closely that the alien had to step quickly into the room or have it strike his leg.

Gregg continued to shuffle through the pages of the folder he held in his hands, slowly and deliberately turning the pages. He waited until he heard Tachyon sniff in irritation. "Say whatever it is you want to say, Senator. I do not have a great deal of time to waste on you."

The words hurt, more than they should have. *I didn't do those things,* he wanted to say. *Puppetman did them.* But he couldn't say that because Puppetman was listening. He turned around to face the red-haired alien and tossed the folder on the coffee table in front of Tachyon. "Damned interesting reading matter, that," he said. "Go on, Doctor. Pick it up."

Tachyon glared, but he snatched up the folder with delicate fingers. He riffled through the pages stamped with Justice Department seals and shrugged. "What is it, Senator? Play out this farce and be done with it."

"It's simple enough, Doctor." Hartmann seated himself in one of the chairs, lounging back. He put his feet on the coffee table with studied nonchalance. "You invaded my mind and took ammunition to use against me. I don't like being stuck with an empty revolver in a duel. So I went looking for things about *you*. I wondered who was whispering about me in your ear. I wondered where the lies might have come from."

"They are *not* lies, Senator. I saw the disgusting, perverted filth in your head. We both know that."

Please, Puppetman begged at the insult. *Let me try. No!*

Gregg waved a hand. "*Someone* convinced you to rape my mind, Doctor. I know Hiram was partially involved, but Hiram really wants to believe in me. He's not the source. My guess was that it had to be Sara, and if it *was* Sara, she might have been working in concert with someone else. You see, I know Kahina—you remember poor Kahina, Doctor?—had talked with Sara. I know she and Gimli had had contact with another man, a Russian. I even had a photograph. And I have friends in high places, remember, Doctor? They checked a few other things out for me, checked backgrounds and chronologies. You'd be surprised at what they'd found, or then maybe, just maybe, you wouldn't."

Gregg shook his head. He gave Tachyon the famous crooked half-smile that had become the cartoonist's icon for Hartmann. "It's actually ironic, isn't it, Doctor? The HUAC folks were right all along. You always *were* a goddamn communist from outer space."

Tachyon had gone white. His body shook, his lips were pressed together into a hard line. Puppetman caught the overflow of emotions and chuckled. *Got him. We got him.*

"Bang," Gregg said. "You see, I've got a few bullets, too. One called Blaise, and one called Polyakov—and other names. Very high-caliber ammo."

"You can prove nothing," Tachyon blustered. "Your own people say Polyakov is dead. Kahina is dead. Gimli is dead.

Everyone you touch seems to be dead. All you have is hearsay and innuendo. No facts."

"Polyakov has been seen here, in Atlanta. The other facts would be easy enough to find," Gregg told him comfortably. "But I don't want to go to the trouble."

"And what is it you *do* want?"

"You know that as well as I do, Doctor. I want you to say you made a mistake. I want you to tell the press and the delegates that it was all a private misunderstanding between me and you, and that everything's patched up again. We're friends. We're pals. And you'd sure as hell be disappointed if everyone didn't vote for me. If you don't want to actively campaign for me, fine. Leave Atlanta after you make your statement to the press. But if you *don't* do that, I *will* start digging for those facts you're so casually dismissing. You might take the nomination away from me, Tachyon, but I'll make sure you get dragged down with me—you and that upstart grandson as well."

It had worked. Gregg was certain of it. Tachyon blustered wordlessly, his fists clenched around the folder so that the cardboard crumpled, bright spots of color on his cheeks. The prissy little wimp was about to goddamn *cry*, his eyes welling with tears.

We've won. Even if all he does is keep his mouth shut, we've won. We'll be okay. You see? Gregg told Puppetman.

And after this is over, we'll find a way to take him out. Finally and permanently.

Tachyon *was* crying, a line of wetness trailing down from both eyes. He drew himself up like a bantam rooster, his chest puffed up, and he glared at Hartmann. Gregg laughed, scornfully.

"We have a deal, then," Gregg said. "Good. I'll have Amy set up the press conference—"

"No," Tachyon said.

He hurled the folder at Gregg. Papers scattered like ghostly autumn leaves. "No!" Tachyon said again, and this time it was a defiant, weeping shout. "You may do as you wish, Senator, but *no*. You may go to hell. And as for your threats to take me with you, I don't care. I have been there before."

Tachyon turned to leave as Gregg shot to his feet. Puppetman howled inside, frantic. "You son of a bitch!" he screamed at Tachyon. "You stupid bastard! All I have to do is make one phone call and you're finished! You'll lose every-thing!"

Tachyon glared back at Gregg with smoldering violet eyes. "I lost everything important long ago," he told Gregg. "You can't threaten me with that."

Tachyon opened the door, sniffed loudly, and closed it with silent dignity behind him.

He awoke to the sound of the door opening. Spector was lying under his bed. He'd spent the night there, afraid to sleep in the open. He peered out through the inch-tall gap between the carpeted floor and the edge of the bedspread. A pair of brown buckle-down shoes walked past and clopped onto the tiled bathroom floor.

"Nobody in here again last night." It was a black woman's voice. "Wasting our goddamn time on this junk. Guess I'd better call the man and tell him."

"That's what they said to do," said a voice from the hall. "So, I'd do it if I were you."

The feet moved over next to the bed. Spector held his breath.

The woman lifted the receiver and punched in four numbers. Waited. "He's never at his desk. Always wanting to be with the delegates, or Secret Service." She cleared her throat. "Yes, sir, this is Charlene up in 1031. There was nobody here last night. Course, I'm sure. You know we smelled whiskey the first night he was in, but not since." A long pause. "Yes, sir. We'll keep an eye on the room." She hung up the phone. "Asshole."

There was laughter from the hallway.

The woman walked back toward the door. "You know, if we're going to do this spy shit, I think we should get paid extra for it. Don't see why we should bust our asses to make Mr. Hot-Shot Hastings shine." She closed the door.

Spector could hear the woman carrying on outside the room. Even a New Yorker would have trouble getting a word in edgewise with her.

He was dead tired. His jaw felt like it had been stuck back on with ten-penny nails. Moving would take more effort than he was willing to make right now. He closed his eyes and listened to the maids' cart squeak its way down the hall.

* * *

Breakfast of steak and coffee hadn't quite done the job of making Jack ready to face the Reverend Barnett and a stable of killer aces, but a couple last-minute shots of vodka had. They'd steadied his hands for shaving—not that he could have cut himself if he tried, since even the wicked cutthroat he used couldn't match his protective wild card—but he hated to do a sloppy job.

While he dressed, he watched the news. The day's first ballot had Hartmann down by two hundred. About thirty of Jack's own delegates had defected, some to Dukakis, some to Jackson. Barnett was up about forty votes total.

A new sense of urgency poured through Jack.

He dressed in his summer power suit of navy blue cotton, handmade by an old man in New Jersey he'd been going to for forty years, a light-blue Arrow shirt, black Italian wingtips, red tie—he never understood why power ties were supposed to be yellow now, since yellow ties always made him think of someone who'd been careless with his breakfast eggs. He put on heavy Hollywood shades, partly to hide his hangover, partly in case Demise was waiting for him somewhere, and took another welcome shot of vodka before he left. He'd buy some cigarettes in the lobby.

Barnett's limousine met him at the door. The traffic was impossible, complicated by marching jokers and Catholics for Barnett and Mutants for Zippy the Pinhead and shuttle buses disgorging journalists from the outlying hotels where they'd been quartered.

Fleur met him at the door to the Omni Hotel. His nerves did a little dance at the sight of her, but he managed to repress his urge to flee, and instead smiled and shook her hand. "I have an elevator waiting," she said.

"Fine." They stepped across the polished lobby floor.

"I apologize for any difficulty Consuela gave you. She's used to fielding calls from cranks."

"No problem."

"She's a refugee from the anti-Ladino persecutions in Guatemala, a poor young widow with three children. The reverend made it possible for her to stay in this country."

Jack turned to Fleur and smiled. "That's remarkable, that

a man as busy as the Reverend Barnett would take the time to help someone like that."

Fleur looked into his deep black shades. "The reverend's like that. He cares."

"Not just the reverend, I'm sure. You've been possessed by the spirit of charity yourself, I'm sure."

Fleur tried to look modest. "Well, I—"

"I mean, sacrificing your chastity just to cure old Tach of his problem."

She stared at him, goggle-eyed.

"By the way, just between us," Jack grinned, "*did* he ever manage to get it up?"

Jack, smiling, followed a white-lipped Fleur out of an elevator whose temperature seemed to have dropped about fifty degrees. Secret Service people, Lady Black among them, prowled the long corridor leading to Barnett's suite. Jack hoped she didn't recognize him.

He passed by a busy suite filled with tables and campaign workers. Most of them seemed to be women, many of them young and attractive.

They came to a door, and Fleur knocked. Leo Barnett, looking younger than his thirty-eight years, opened the door and stuck out his hand.

"Welcome, Mr. Braun," he said.

Jack stared at the hand, wondering if Barnett could take his mind by touching him; and then, summoning nerve from somewhere, he reached out and took the hand.

He was shaking again. Tachyon paused, the glass almost to his lips, and considered. How many drinks did this make for the morning? Two? Three? He set the glass aside with overly broad gestures. Patted it firmly as if to keep it in place, to keep it from flying back to his hand, crossed to the ravaged room service breakfast tray, and took a bite of cold toast.

His stomach revolted. Gasping, cold sweat breaking at his hairline, the alien staggered into the bathroom, and sluiced water over his face. From the bedroom he could hear Blaise and Ackroyd talking, laughing.

Crossing to the bedroom Tachyon opened the door. The conversation broke off. Jay looking up inquiringly, Blaise with a brooding light in those strange purple/black eyes.

"Mr. Ackroyd, come in here, please. I need to talk to you."

Jay shrugged, tried to pull down the pants that hiked up above his ankles. Followed Tachyon into the sitting room. "What did Hartmann want?" he asked as he poked at the room service tray.

"Mr. Ackroyd, I require a favor of you."

"Sure, name it."

Tachyon lifted a hand. "Do not be so quick to commit yourself. Having me in your debt may not be enough to outweigh what I will ask of you."

"Jesus Christ, get to the point, Tachyon. All this flowery Takisian bullshit." Jay sank his teeth into an orange slice, and tore away the meat.

"Hartmann is blackmailing me. I have refused to meet his demands, but I require time. A day, two at the most, and it will be over. Hartmann will have lost the nomination." Tach's voice ran down, and he stared blankly into an eternity of blasted hopes. Gave himself a shake and resumed. "You can give me that time."

"The point? The point?"

"You must remove a man from Atlanta. The more conventional means are closed to us."

Suspicion bloomed in the detective's eyes. "Why? Who is this guy?"

The abandoned drink came easily to his hand, the beaded glass cool against his palm. Tach drained the brandy in a long swallow. "Long ago I was saved from death by a man who has alternately been a devil and an angel to me."

Ackroyd threw his hands into the air. "Shit."

"This is difficult for me," Tachyon flared. He rolled the glass between his hands, then burst out, "In 1957 I was recruited by the KGB." He smiled sadly at Ackroyd's expression. "It wasn't all that difficult. I would have done anything for a drink. At any rate, years passed. I proved to be less useful than originally hoped. They cut me loose, and I thought I was free. Then last year the man who ran me those many long years ago re-entered my life and called the debt. He's here. In Atlanta."

"Why?"

"Hartmann. He suspected the existence of the monster. Now Hartmann has found out about him, and our connection."

"Connection?"

"He is Blaise's tutor."

"Oh hell." Ackroyd dropped into a chair.

"This is the bludgeon with which Hartmann seeks to cow me. I'm probably going to jail, Mr. Ackroyd. But I'll see him stopped before I go."

"You want me to pop this guy away."

"Yes. Already the FBI and the Secret Service have been alerted. They are combing Atlanta for George."

"Are you still a commie?"

Tachyon laid fastidious fingers against the lace at his throat. One slender copper eyebrow arched arrogantly. "*I*? Consider, Mr. Ackroyd."

The detective eyed the slim peacock figure dressed in green, orange, and gold. "Yeah, I get your drift." He slapped his hands onto his thighs, and pushed up from the chair. "Well, hey, it's all ancient history to me. Let's go pop this commie somewhere."

Tachyon opened the door to the bedroom. "Blaise."

"You're taking him? I mean, he knows?"

"Of course. Come child, I want you to have a chance to say farewell to George."

Here Jack had come in his power suit, hoping to impress the well-dressed conservative preacher he'd seen on the tapes; and instead Leo Barnett looked about as formal as Jimmy Carter slopping around the house in Plains. Barnett was dressed in worn jeans, a checked shirt, and black Keds. His razor-cut blond hair was slightly disordered. He shambled back into his room and stuck his hands in his pockets.

"Would you like breakfast? I believe there's plenty left on the buffet."

Jack looked around the room where Barnett had spent his prayer vigil. It was an ordinary hotel suite, with a little kitchenette, a wet bar, a big TV, even a hooded fireplace with some rolled-newspaper logs. All the light was artificial: the curtains were drawn, as per Secret Service instructions. A picture of Barnett's fiancée stood on one table, a Macintosh II sat on a table, and there was a silver steam table on wheels near the door, presumably with breakfast under its covers.

"I've eaten, thanks," Jack said.

"Coffee, then?"

Jack considered the state of his nerves and his hangover. What the hell, maybe he'd already blown it in the elevator. "I don't suppose a Bloody Mary would be possible . . . ?"

Barnett didn't seem in the least surprised. "I expect we can find one somewhere," he said. He turned to Fleur. "Could you try and oblige Mr. Braun? Perhaps the press room downstairs would be the place to start."

"Certainly, Leo." Her tones were set at about three degrees Kelvin.

Barnett smiled at her warmly. "Thank you so much, Fleur."

Jack's gaze bounced from Barnett to Fleur to Barnett again. Slut for the Lord? he thought again; and then, I wonder if his fiancée knows?

"Have a seat, Mr. Braun."

Jack picked an armchair and settled into it. He reached into his pocket for a Camel. Barnett drew another armchair close to Jack's right side and sat in it, hunched forward slightly, his attitude expectant.

"How can I help you, Mr. Braun?"

"Well." Jack took a deep breath and summoned what nerve he could. He tried to remember the acting lessons he'd taken forty years before. "See, Reverend," he said, "I've almost died twice in the last couple days. I went off a balcony, and that was maybe enough to kill me if Hiram Worchester hadn't made me lighter than air, and last night this ace called Demise actually seemed to have stopped my heart for a while . . ." His voice trailed off. "The thing is," he said insistently, "I wonder if somebody's trying to tell me something."

Barnett gave a little wry smile, then nodded. "You haven't had much occasion to give thought to the eternal, have you?"

"No. I guess not."

"Life has always been right here on Earth for you. You've had eternal youth. An indestructible body. I assume you don't have to worry about money." He gave Jack a frankly admiring glance. "I remember *Tarzan* very fondly, by the way. I don't think I ever missed an episode. I remember swinging from a rope down by the swimming hole back home, trying to give that yell you used to do."

"I never did the yell, actually," Jack said. "It was dubbed in, a lot of different voices kind of strung together electronically."

Barnett seemed a bit disappointed. "Well. I guess you

don't think about that when you're ten years old." He grinned again. "Whatever happened to the chimp, by the way?"

"He's in the San Diego Zoo." Which was the answer Jack always gave to that question, though it was completely untrue. Chester the Chimp, shortly after entering adolescence, had been shot dead after trying to tear off his trainer's arm. Most people, Jack had learned, preferred the chimp to have a happy ending—an attitude Jack had no sympathy with, having himself always disliked the surly little scene-stealing beast.

Barnett seemed to recollect himself. "I'm sorry, Mr. Braun," he said. "I'm afraid I've let myself distract you."

"That's okay. I'm not sure what I was going to say, anyway."

"Many people don't have the terms for talking about the eternal." Barnett gave a quick, self-deprecating grin. "Fortunately, we preachers are more or less equipped for the job."

"Yeah. Well. That's why I'm here."

Jack was having a hard time reconciling this laid-back Barnett with the ferocious preacher he'd seen in the video tapes, the blond panther stalking his own congregation, the predator Jack was certain was a secret, murderous ace. Could this be the same man?

Jack cleared his throat. "You ever seen *Picture of Dorian Gray*? A great old Albert Lewin picture from the forties. George Sanders, Hurd Hatfield, Angela Lansbury." He cleared his throat again. The endotrachial tube had left it irritated, and his smoking wasn't helping it. "Donna Reed, I think," he said, trying to remember. "Yeah, Donna Reed. Anyway, it's about this young man who has his portrait painted, and his soul goes into the portrait. He starts living a real, I dunno, wicked life, whatever you want to call it, but he never has to face any of the consequences. He just stays young, and the portrait gets old and . . . dissipated? Is that the word?"

Barnett nodded.

"Anyway, at the end, the picture gets destroyed, and Dorian Gray gets all old and evil all at once and drops dead." He grinned. "Special effects, you know? Anyway, I've been thinking a lot about that. I've been thinking, you know, I've stayed young for forty years, and I haven't led a precisely unstained life, and what if it wears off? What if I get old all of a sudden, like Dorian Gray. Or what if *some crazy ace kills me*?"

Jack realized he was shouting. His heart lurched at the further realization that he wasn't acting any more, that all this trauma was genuine. He cleared his throat again and settled into his seat.

Barnett leaned toward Jack, put a hand on his arm. "You'd be surprised how many visits I've had from people in your situation, Mr. Braun. Perhaps their presentiments were not as . . . *spectacular* as yours, but I've seen a lot of people resembling you. Successful, outwardly contented men and women who gave no thought to the eternal until they were touched by it. Perhaps a warning heart attack, perhaps a loved one killed in an accident or a parent suffering a fatal illness . . ." He smiled. "I don't believe any of these warnings are accidental, Mr. Braun."

"Jack." He stubbed out his cigarette. He'd almost lost it there, he thought.

"Jack, yes. I *believe* there is purpose to these warnings, Jack. I believe the Almighty has ways of reminding us of His existence. I believe that in these narrow escapes you've had, there is a revelation of God's purpose."

Jack looked through his dark shades into Barnett's twinkling blue eyes. "Yeah?" he said.

There was a burning intensity in Barnett's china-blue eyes. "The Lord says, 'Look unto me, and be ye saved, all ends of the Earth: For I am God, and there is none else.'"

Look unto *me*, Jack thought: did Barnett mean God or himself? The preacher spoke on.

"Your wild card gave you a false belief in your own immortality, and the Lord has seen a way to warn you of its falsity, remind you whence true immortality lies, and spare you to do His work."

There was a knock on the door. As the sound pulled him out of his track, Barnett seemed to jolt slightly. He looked at the door.

"Come in."

Fleur entered with a Bloody Mary in a one frigid hand. "Mr. Braun's drink."

Jack smiled at her. "Call me Jack. Please."

She glared at him while Jack took the drink from her hand

and looked into it under the rims of his shades to see if perhaps she'd spit in it.

"Thank-you so much, Fleur." Barnett didn't smile quite as warmly this time. His words were a dismissal, and Fleur obeyed.

Jack sipped his drink. It was excellent: apparently someone in the press room knew how to keep the journalists happy.

"Is it good?" Barnett seemed genuinely curious.

"It's fine." Jack took a bigger swallow.

"I've never . . ." Barnett waved a hand. "Well, that doesn't matter." Surprise rang through Jack at Barnett's wistful tone, precisely that of a small boy whose mother won't let him outside to play in the rain.

Maybe, Jack thought, Barnett really hadn't had any choice in his life. Maybe they'd all been made for him. Maybe the only time he ever did anything he wasn't supposed to was when he ran away to the Marine Corps.

Hell, he thought savagely. Nobody *makes* you run for president.

Barnett leaned back in his armchair, steepling his fingertips under his chin. His attention had returned fully to Jack. Jack looked at the preacher carefully from behind his big shades.

"I'd like to tell you about a dream of mine, Jack," Barnett said. His voice was soft, gentle. "The Lord put it into my mind some years ago. In this dream, I found myself in a giant orchard. Everywhere I looked there were fruit trees, all rich with God's abundance. There were all sorts of fruit in the orchard, Jack, cherries and oranges and apples and persimmons and plums—every conceivable variety all filling God's vast cornucopia. The orchard was so beautiful that my heart just swelled up with joy and gladness. And then—" Barnett looked up to the ceiling, as if he was seeing something there. Jack found his eyes following the preacher's, then caught himself. Stage craft, he thought. He took a healthy swallow of his Bloody Mary.

"And then a cloud came over the sun," Barnett continued, "and a dark rain began to fall from the cloud. The rain fell here and there in the orchard, and wherever it touched, the fruit was blighted. I could see all the oranges and lemons turning black and falling from the tree; I could see leaves withering and dying. And more than that, I could see the blight growing even after the rain passed, I could see the darkness reaching out to try to taint the healthy trees. And then I heard a voice."

The preacher's voice changed, deepened, became stern. A chill surged up Jack's spine at the completeness of the transformation. "'*I give this orchard into thy keeping. Unto thee I give the task of destroying this blight.*'"

Barnett's voice and manner changed again. He was fervent, exultant. His powerful voice rang in the small room. "I *knew* the fruits of the orchard were God's children, made in His image. I *knew* the rain cloud was Satan. I *knew* the blight was the wild card. And I threw myself down on my face. 'Lord!' I prayed. 'Lord, I am not strong enough. I am not worthy for this task.' And the Lord said, 'I will *give* thee strength!'" Barnett was screaming now. "'I will *make* thy heart as steel! I will *make* thy tongue as sharp as a sword, and of thy breath a whirlwind!' And I *knew* I had to do as the Lord asked of me."

Barnett jumped out of his chair, paced back and forth as he talked. Like God was jerking his chain, Jack thought.

"I *knew* I had the power to heal the wild card! I *knew* that the Lord's work had to be done, that His orchard had to be pruned!" He waved a finger at Jack. "Not as my critics would charge!" he said. "I would not prune wickedly, or arbitrarily, or maliciously. My critics say I want to put jokers in concentration camps!" He gave a laugh. "I want to put them in *hospitals*. I want to *cure* their affliction, and keep it from spreading to their children. I think it is *sinful* of the government to keep wild card research at such a low level of funding—I would multiply it tenfold! I would *wipe this plague from the Earth!*"

Barnett turned to Jack. To Jack's amazement there were tears in his eyes. "You're old enough to remember when tuberculosis was a plague upon the land," Barnett said. "You remember all the hundreds and thousands of tubercular sanatoriums that sprang up all over Arizona and New Mexico, where victims were kept from infecting others while science worked on a cure. *That's* what I want to do for the wild card.

"Jack!" Barnett was pleading. "The Lord has prolonged your life! The Lord has spared you from death! This can only be because He has a place for you in His plan. He wants you to *lead* the victims of this plague to their salvation. 'He was wounded for our transgressions, he was bruised for our iniquities: the chastisement of our peace was upon him; and with his stripes we are healed.' *Healed*, Jack!" Barnett's face was joyful, rapturous. He stood in front of Jack, raised his hands triumphantly. "Won't you *help* me, Jack! *Help* me bring the cure to God's afflicted! *Pray* with me now, Jack! 'Verily I say unto thee, Except a man be born again, he cannot see the Kingdom of God—but as many received Him, to them gave He power to become the sons of God, even to them that believe in His name.'"

Jack, to his astonishment, felt as if a giant hand had gripped him by the neck and flung him out of his chair. Suddenly he was on his knees in front of the preacher, his two hands raised and clasped between the hands of the Reverend Leo Barnett. Tears streamed down Barnett's face as he lifted his head and cried out in prayer.

"'Therefore if any man be in Christ, he is a new creature; old things are passed away; behold all things become new.'"

The man's power was almost palpable, Jack thought. This couldn't be all good showmanship and razzle-dazzle. Jack *knew* about showmanship; he'd never seen anything like this.

He's an ace, Jack thought. My god, he really *is* an ace.

Maybe he'd never really believed it till this minute.

Barnett was an ace, and Jack was going to bring him down.

11:00 A.M.

Cal Redken sounded like the acne-scarred junk-food addict he was. In the background of all his conversations was the rustle of plastic wrappers; his words were slurred by the effort of sneaking around wads of Twinkies, Snickers, and Fritos. He sounded fat and slow and lazy.

Only the first of those was true.

Gregg had taken him as a puppet long ago, more from reflex than desire. He'd played with Redken's voracious appetite, mildly amused that he could make a man eat until he was literally, sickeningly, stuffed. But that had not fed Puppetman particularly well, and Gregg had rarely utilized his link. Redken was not Hiram—an ace with peculiar abilities and tastes. Redken was a competent, if sedentary, investigator. There was no one better at following the confusing labyrinth of bureaucracy. It had been Redken who'd put together—

overnight—the unproved web of conjecture with which Gregg had confronted Tachyon.

Now, he'd make sure the conjecture became fact.

The phone rang twice at the other end, followed by an audible gulp and "Redken."

"Cal, Gregg Hartmann here."

"Senator." Cellophane tore in the background; a new snack being opened. "You get my package all right?"

"Early this morning, Cal. Thanks."

"No sweat, Senator. Interesting stuff you had me looking up," he added reflectively. He took a bite of something, chewing noisily.

"That's what I want to talk with you about. We need to pursue this further. I need to know if we can bring charges against Tachyon."

"Senator"—swallow—"all we have now is circumstantial stuff: a Russian agent assigned to the right city in the right year, another coincidental crossing of paths in London last year, your contact in the JJS and her story, a few other tenuous links here and there. Nothing's solid. Not even close."

"It scared hell out of him, Cal. I saw it. I know something's there."

"That's still far from proving it."

"Then it has to get closer. You know what Video told us last year. Gimli and Kahina had definite Soviet connections. An agent met with them one night last year in New York, and Gimli called him Polyakov."

"Polyakov's dead, Senator. All our sources say the same thing; the KGB and the GRU believe it too. Maybe they're just using his name to confuse us."

"They're all wrong. Video still has the pictures in her mind. He matches Polyakov's description."

"So do a few thousand other people. There's a lot of fat, bald, old men. Plus, you're not going to get any court to accept a joker's wild card talent as evidence. A mental projection isn't a photograph."

"It's a start. Find her, look at what she has. Listen to her. Then keep digging."

Redken sighed. Plastic crackled like dry leaves, and his voice was suddenly muffled by something soft. "Okay, Senator. I'll do it. I'll try. How soon do you need this."

"A week ago. Yesterday at the latest."

Another sigh. "I get the idea. I'll call New York as soon as I'm off. Anything else?"

"*Soon*, Cal. I gotta have this soon."

"You're asking me to miss lunch."

"You do this for me and I'll buy you your own damn restaurant."

"You got a deal, Senator. Talk to you later."

The last word was obscured as Redken placed another bite of something in his mouth. The line clicked and went dead.

"Somebody's on us."

"What?" Tachyon slewed around in the cab, and stared out the back window.

Ackroyd laid a hand on his arm. "Easy. He's good. You'll never spot him that way. Cabby." The detective fished out his wallet. "There's an extra fifty in it for you if you can lose the gray Dodge. Back about three cars."

The man's black face split in a wide grin. "Sure thing, mister."

Tachyon followed Jay's mortified gaze as the detective fanned out a ten and three ones. Grumbling Tachyon pulled out his wallet, and stripped off the bills, tucked them into the driver's shirt pocket. And promptly landed in Ackroyd's lap as the cab accelerated abruptly into a hard left turn. Blaise, grinning delightedly, clung like a young monkey to the front seat.

"Just like Paris, *K'ijdad*."

"Huh?" asked Jay.

"Never mind. You know enough of my secrets," growled Tachyon.

Jay glanced behind. "Still on us. Damn, he's good."

"What are we going to do?" The fluttering in his stomach was back, and Tach could feel a fine shivering running through his hands.

Ackroyd ran a hand across his mouth. "There's probably not going to be time for any long good-byes."

The Motel 6 sign loomed ahead.

"Sara's there, too," said Tachyon.

"Jesus Christ. You got the whole New York Philharmonic there? Maybe the Dodgers?"

"This is no laughing matter."

"No shit. Punch it, buddy. Everything she's got."

The cab gunned down the street, turned with a squeal of tires into the parking lot. The threesome were out before the car had stopped rolling. Jay flung his remaining ten over his shoulder as they pelted for the room.

Sara was curled up on the bed, legs tucked beneath her, pillow clutched to her chest, listening to the television. Polyakov, a bemused expression on his round face, stepped back to avoid being trampled. Jay seized the edge of the door, and slammed it shut. Threw the deadbolt. Tachyon ran to Sara, and yanked her up off the bed. Blaise flung himself into the Russian's arms.

"No time to explain. Hartmann knows. There is someone after us." Tachyon seized Sara's dress at the neck, and pulled. It ripped with a loud rending sound. Sara screamed, and covered herself. She was wearing only her bra. "Into the shower, quick! Don't come out, and by the way, you rent by the hour." The alien was propelling her toward the bathroom door, unsnapping her bra as they went.

Heavy footfalls were coming down the hall at a run.

Polyakov's gray eyes were calm, fatalistic. "There's no time."

"Yes, there is. Jay will get you out of Atlanta. For the gods' sake, Blaise, *move!*"

The water thundered on. Polyakov gently sat the boy aside.

"Open up! Open the goddamn door!"

Tachyon recognized Billy Ray's voice.

"*Now!*" he hissed urgently to the detective. Ackroyd formed his fingers into a gun. Polyakov vanished. There was an audible *pop* as the air rushed back into the space formally occupied by a body.

Tachyon leaped across the room, seized the bottle of vodka on the dresser, ripped open his collar, and in a long, low dive threw himself onto the bed.

The door blew open, splinters flying across the room as Billy Ray bulled through. Jay shielded Blaise with his body, and Tach covered his face. The Justice Department ace had a gun, a .44 magnum. Tachyon stared down the barrel. It yawned like a cave's mouth.

"All right. Where is he? Where the fuck is he?"

"Huuuh?" asked Jay.

"Asshole!"

Ray stiff-armed the detective, and Ackroyd went down. Ray tore the closet door off its hinges, and flung down the clothes. Glanced beneath the bed, headed for the bathroom door. Tachyon crossed his fingers, and prayed to whatever ancestors might be lurking nearby.

"Get out of there. Now!"

Sara's voice floated over the rush of falling water. Clearly female. Heavily Southern. Tachyon prayed that he was the only one who heard the panic underlying the words.

"Wal, sugah, how many you boys gonna be?"

The shower curtain rasped back. Sara screamed. For a long moment there was silence from the bathroom. The sharp report of a slap. Ray re-entered the room the pale pink imprint of a palm already fading from his cheek, the front of his white uniform wet from the thundering water.

Breathing heavily, he said, "He was here. That goddamn Russian was here."

Jay looked to Tach. "Russian? I don't see any Russian. Do you see a Russian? And sweetcheeks in there sure don't sound Russian. Russian costs you extra." He grinned at the outraged ace.

"Why did you try to get away from me?"

Tachyon sighed, took a long pull on the bottle. "Because I was afraid you were the press, and I didn't want to be found visiting a prostitute."

"You always take a kid?" He gestured at Blaise with the .44.

"Could you put the gun away? It makes me nervous when you wave it around like that. Most fatal shootings are accidental, you know."

Ray glared at him. "This wouldn't be an accident. Answer the fucking question."

With a delicate clearing of the throat Tachyon said, "Well, that is the matter in a nutshell. It's time the boy learned." He glanced about the motel room. "This lacks the ambience that I could wish, but she is *very* good. I tried her myself last night. Of course, nothing can compare with the woman my father gave to me on my fourteenth birthday—"

Ray stormed back through the shattered door.

"Fourteen? No kidding?"

"Oh Ackroyd, *please!*"

12:00 NOON

"*You* call the press conference," Jack told him. "The press hasn't seen you for days. If *I* call them, they might not show up."

Barnett had agreed.

Jack watched the convention while the plans went forward. Hartmann had clearly lost all momentum. Totals changed on every ballot. The only steady factor was Barnett's slow advance, gaining with every step as the opposition began to disintegrate. Rodriguez looked poleaxed every time he announced California's changing delegate count. Jack's heart went out to him.

The press conference was arranged in one of the hotel's function spaces, the place Barnett used as a press office. Jack managed to down two more Bloody Marys before the business began.

Fleur spoke first, standing behind a podium crowned with a forest of network microphones. Jack and Barnett stood off to one side as Fleur went through a long round of mike tests.

She kept casting Jack sidelong glances throughout. Obviously she didn't trust him an inch.

Even hidden behind his Hollywood shades, Jack felt naked.

"Before the Reverend Barnett's announcement," Fleur said, "there will be another brief announcement from someone who may be a surprise to you. I'm referring to Mr. Jack Braun, the head of Senator Hartmann's California delegation, also known as Golden Boy."

Jack didn't smile or wave as he stepped to the podium. Microphones jabbed at him like a forest of spears. He took off his shades, folded them, smiled into the blinding camera light. He hoped the booze and sleeplessness hadn't made his eyes too red.

"I've just finished a two-hour interview with the Reverend Leo Barnett," Jack began. He could hear automatic cameras making zipping noises as they fired at him. He gripped the podium and tried not to feel the earthquake that rocked his nerves.

"This convention has seen a lot of strange events, a lot of violence," he said. "Some people have been killed. Two attempts have been made on Senator Hartmann's life, both by wild card aces, and I have fought both those aces personally. The Reverend Barnett has claimed all along that wild cards have been responsible for much of the chaos that has plagued this campaign. After the meeting today, I can only agree with him."

Jack's forty-year-old media reflexes told him that the TV cameras' long lenses were zooming in. Except for the sound of automatic cameras and snapping shutters, the room was absolutely quiet. Jack screwed his face into an expression of deep sincerity and gazed steadily out into the audience, just like when, years ago, he'd played Eddie Rickenbacker telling General Pershing he wanted to fly.

"There are secret aces at this convention," Jack said. "There is one in particular who has a very influential role. He's responsible for a lot of the chaos here, for at least some of the deaths. I believe he can influence people at a distance to cause them to act in ways contrary to the law and their own interests. Other aces, murderous aces, work for him. They have tried to destroy his opponents by violence."

Jack could sense Barnett and Fleur standing to one side, their heads together as they tried to figure out where he was taking this. Jack gave the cameras a grim Clint Eastwood smile.

"After my interview this morning, I've concluded that that secret ace . . ." Insert dramatic pause here, he thought. "Is the Reverend Leo Barnett."

Cameras began swinging crazily, trying to get Barnett's reaction. Jack raised his voice and shouted into the mike stand.

"Barnett's behind the assassination attempts!" he said. Triumph sang in his veins. "I defy Leo Barnett to prove he isn't an ace!"

Barnett gaped at him. Fleur van Renssaeler's face was dead white, her mouth moving in furious, silent anger.

Barnett shook his head slowly as if shaking off a punch, then stepped forward. Though he never intended to, Jack found himself backpedaling, surrendering the podium.

The preacher leaned over the microphones, hands in his pockets, and gave a shaky grin. "I don't know what Jack's up to, here," he said. "I came down for another reason entirely. But if it's what Jack wants, I'm willing to stand right here for however many hours it takes to assemble a team of doctors to give me the blood test." His grin widened. "I know I don't have the wild card, and anyone who says I do is a liar or . . ." He cast a sidelong glance at Jack. "Deeply misguided."

Jack stared back into the preacher's blue eyes and felt his triumph drain into his black Italian wingtips.

Somehow, he thought, he'd fucked up again.

Spector turned on the tap over the bathroom sink and took a mouthful of water. He swished it around for a few moments and spat it out. The water was stained brown from the dried blood. Spector took another mouthful and swallowed it. He was as thirsty as he was tired. It was always this way when he had to heal up after a major injury.

He tested his jaw. It moved up and down without too much trouble, but side to side hurt like hell. He could feel the bone popping in its socket. After a few months it might not be so bad. All in all, things could be much worse.

He heard a sound at the door. Spector knew he didn't have time to get back under the bed. He looked around the bathroom. The only place big enough was the shower. He stepped inside just as the door to his room shut. Somebody was talking softly to himself in the bedroom, and Spector had an idea who it was. When the noises approached the bathroom, Spector held his breath. Again. Much more of this and he'd turn blue permanently.

He focused the death-pain. It was always there, always ready. He saw pudgy fingers on the edge of the shower curtain.

The man tore the plastic curtain back, and opened his mouth to scream.

Spector locked eyes before the desk clerk could get anything out. He pushed him to the point of death, then stopped. Spector caught him by the collar as he slumped over. He leaned the man against the bathroom wall and emptied his victim's pockets. He took the keys and wallet, and ignored the rest. This guy probably knew just about everything there was to know about the hotel. If Spector could get him to tell the truth, he might find out a few things.

Spector bent down. He steadied the man with one hand and slapped him with the other. When he started to come around, when Spector was sure he could feel it, he popped the guy really hard a few times.

The man opened his eyes. Spector put a hand over the

pudgy mouth. "Quiet. If you call for help. If you answer my questions in anything but a whisper. If you don't answer my questions. I'll kill you. You understand?"

The man nodded. Spector slowly took his hand away. "Who are you?"

"My name's." He took a breath. "Hastings."

Spector checked the wallet. "So far, so good. What are you doing in here?"

Hastings stared wide-eyed around the room, he seemed to be looking through Spector for a way out. "Uh, the government people told us to be on the lookout for anyone we thought was suspicious. I just had a feeling about you."

"I don't much appreciate that," he checked the first name on the driver's license, "Maurice."

Hastings wiped his mouth. "You're not who you say you are. Not Baird. You're an ace."

Spector nodded. "You know, with your deductive skills and your gift for hunches you'd make a damn good P.I."

The man gave a half-smile, trying to acknowledge the compliment in spite of his fear. "Thanks."

Spector waited a few moments, then added. "I hate P.I.s." He was enjoying the hell out of this. He'd almost forgotten about this jerkoff, and now he had the fat bastard on a horn.

"Oh, god, please, don't kill me. I'll do anything." Hastings was shaking. He wiped his mouth again.

"Oh, I'm not going to kill you. Not if you give me what I want," Spector lied, trying to think of the best place to hide the body. "We'll start with an easy question. Where's the nearest unoccupied room on this floor?"

"We're full up. I swear."

Spector clucked his tongue. "Don't bullshit me. I know there's always a few left vacant for contingencies. You know what I'm going to do if you keep lying to me? I can make you do an airwalk from the tenth floor down to the lobby. The fall will only take a few seconds. Make quite a mess, though. Maybe I should just put you in the shower and liquefy you. Down the drain you go. No muss, no fuss."

"No, please." Hastings clasped his hands together. "I think 1019 is open. Just don't kill me. I'm sorry I bothered you. I can do whatever you need. Give the Secret Service some bad leads. Really."

Spector pulled a card out of Hastings' wallet. "This is your passkey?"

He chewed his lip for a second before replying. "Yes."

Spector leaned in close to Hastings and stared into his eyes. "You're not lying to me now?"

"No. May God strike me . . . It's the truth, I swear."

"Right. Get into the shower." Spector pulled back the curtain. "Do it now."

Hastings hustled his overweight body inside. "But why?"

Spector locked eyes again, and made it count this time. Hastings collapsed onto the tile. His body twitched and then was still. "That's why." He slowly closed the curtain. "Nobody fucks with me and gets away with it." It wasn't the best place to put a corpse, but as usual he'd had to improvise.

Spector checked himself in the mirror one more time. Now he had a crooked jaw to match his crooked smile. Maybe, when it was all over, he could buy a crooked house in the Bahamas. But not until Hartmann was done with. Then, he could worry about vacation time.

1:00 P.M.

"You *weenie*." There was a furious glare from Tachyon's violet eyes as he stalked by, medical bag in hand. Behind him, reporters were clustered three deep around Barnett, who had of course passed the blood test without registering the taint of any black rain from Satan.

"Oh, shut up," mumbled Jack, from deep in the heart of another Bloody Mary.

Tachyon spun on his heel, marched back, stood in front of Jack, his pointed chin thrust out. "You may have just given the nomination to Barnett! You realize that?"

"I thought that was you." Jack's formless anger centered on Tachyon. "I thought that was you, off banging Fleur and switching to Jackson when things got tough."

Tachyon colored. "The only thing you can do now is try to move California to Jackson."

Jack sneered at him. "Fuck you, asshole. At least *I'm* doing something."

Tachyon stared at him, swallowed a retort or two, then flounced away.

Jack, standing by himself at the back of the press room,

realized he was going to be mobbed by reporters as soon as
Barnett finished his speech. He headed back to the bar set up
in the back of the room, found a 500-milliliter flask of 151-proof
rum, and put it in his pocket.

He figured he'd probably be safest on the convention
floor, where he could hide behind the rest of his delegation.

2:00 P.M.

Gregg phoned from Ellen's hospital room. He stroked her
hair as the call went through, smiling at her pale, drawn face.
Ellen tried to smile back and failed. She looked lovely and
very vulnerable, and he could feel tears starting in his eyes,
looking at her.

God, I'm sorry, Ellen. I'm very, very sorry.

Someone picked up the phone and he tore his attention
away from her. "Cal? Hartmann."

"Senator." Redken sounded nervous. Gregg could tell
that he didn't want to talk. "How's things going?"

The fat s.o.b. If we were there . . . Puppetman rose,
angry. "That's what I wanted to know. I'd expected some action
by now, Cal."

That put the man immediately on the defensive. Gregg
could damn near see the flush on Redken's pimply face as he
blustered. He'd be reaching for a candy bar in consternation.
"Look, Senator, it isn't so easy." A wrapper snapped in the
background. "The bottom line on your Russian is that he's
dead. Dead a year and a half and fried to a crisp. The file is
closed according to *everyone* I've talked to, and no one in the
Justice Department, the CIA, or the FBI seems inclined to
open it. I'm getting tired of being told I'm nuts or a pain in the
ass or stupid."

Gregg could feel his own temper fraying. Redken was
stonewalling and making excuses, and in the meantime,
Tachyon was still here and still kissing up to Jackson.
Devaughn was scowling and cursing, and all the political favors
had been called in just to slow the reversed momentum.

Ellen smiled at Gregg quizzically from her bed, sleepy
from a shot of Demerol; Gregg brushed her hair back from her
forehead and shrugged back to her. He took a deep breath and
returned his attention to the phone.

"Video's got the damn pictures, Cal. I know she's a joker,

but the images are real. Didn't they convince someone to at least start looking? Didn't you get her deposition? What about the reporter who made Polyakov here in Atlanta. Doesn't anyone believe him?"

"No one can *find* Video, Senator. That's the problem. A reporter's supposed sighting isn't enough. No one's seen Video for several days. Without her, well, I don't know how much I can help you."

"That's not good enough," Gregg said flatly. "Not good enough at all."

Cal sighed, just on the verge of insolence. He put something in his mouth, chewing noisily. Puppetman stirred. *When we get back to Washington, he'll pay for this.* Gregg pushed the power back down harshly.

"I'm sorry, Senator," Redken was saying again. "I've done all I can do at the moment. We'll keep looking for Video. I'll keep following the paper trail, but it's damn cold and you know how slow that can be at the best of times. I'll hound Peters over at Intelligence and tell him again that his data's screwy. If I do get more, I'll make sure the right people jump. But it might be a few days before that happens."

Gregg's temper went entirely. "I don't *have* a goddamn few days, Cal. I may not even have this afternoon."

There was no answer to that, just the hiss of the satellite connection and Redken's chewing. "Look, get what you can as soon as you can," Gregg said at last. "And keep in mind that I'll remember just how well you do." He slammed the phone back into the cradle.

"Serious problems?" Ellen asked. She held out her hand to Gregg.

He took it. He let Puppetman lick at the pain that leaked around the edges of the Demerol. It seemed to salve his own frustration.

We have to do it ourselves, Gregg. There's no other way. It's safe now, with Gimli taken care of. Think of it.

Gregg was. And he knew exactly what he needed to do.

"Maybe," he said in answer to Ellen's question. "Or maybe not as serious as I'd thought. There's other ways to deal with the problem. It's time to start using them."

"I'm sorry you and Dr. Tachyon quarreled, Gregg. He's such a nice man, but so stubborn."

"Don't worry about it, darling," he said. "Tachyon is just a temporary problem."

4:00 P.M.

It was like being on Mercury. The air-conditioning of the Marriott beat on his back as he stepped through the doors. The Atlanta heat started the sweat rolling down his face. The sidewalk was crowded with Jackson supporters waving bright-red JESSE! signs. Just beyond them was the limo. Jackson clasped Tachyon's hand and lifted them up over their heads. Tachyon squirmed, dancing on his toes. The reverend was so much taller.

A ragged cheer went up, and they headed for the limo, smiling and shaking hands as the spectators crowded in around them. Jackson pressed the flesh with practiced ease. Tachyon looked at him enviously.

Ackroyd was waiting at the door of the car. "What now?"

"Jesse wants us to talk to the jokers outside the Omni," Tachyon explained. "He and I together. His positions on wild card issues are just as strong as Hartmann's, if they will only listen . . ." He gave a long, deep sigh. "Jay, if you have other leads to follow up, there's really no need for you to come along."

Jay shrugged. "Might as well," he said, "can't dance."

At least the limo was air-conditioned, Tachyon thought gratefully as they drove off.

Jackson's bodyguard, the ace called Straight Arrow, stared implacably across at him. Tach began to realize how hopeless, how *stupid* this was. They were not going to listen. Jesse would have a better chance without him. Tension made his voice jump as he blurted, "This is *not* going to work."

"Faith, Doctor," said Jackson.

He was wedged firmly between Jay Ackroyd and the reverend. He looked desperately from Jay to Jesse. "They hate me now."

The limo pulled up, and Jackson studied the ranks of silent jokers. "Only some. It's not as if you switched your support to Barnett. I'm not *that* unacceptable, am I?"

"Not to me." Tach gave the tall human's arm a squeeze. "And you will convince them. I know it."

"Well, help me a little."

"I will do my uttermost best."

Straight Arrow swung open the door of the black limousine, and Jackson and Tachyon stepped back out into the heat. The police had driven a wedge into the jokers. At the end of that long aisle was a flatbed truck equipped with a sound system. The heat was unbelievable, bouncing in waves off the pavement. As he watched, Tach saw Arachne's eight legs fold beneath her and she went down with a sigh. There was a flurry of movement as her nat daughter dropped down at her mother's side, and began fanning the unconscious woman with a folded newspaper.

"How can they hate them so?" Tachyon asked. The lilac eyes were wide with misery. "They are pitiful, and so brave. So very brave."

The crowd had noticed them. Uncertainty ran like a shiver through them, then large numbers began pushing forward against the lines of police as Jackson walked into their midst. Setting his jaw, Tachyon threw back his head, and followed. His eyes met Gills'. The joker's thick neck worked, the membranes over the gills fluttering. He hacked, and a gob of thick white mucus hit Tachyon in the face. The alien recoiled, then lunged forward, hand outstretched, pleading for understanding. But Gills had already turned his back on Tachyon.

He mopped away the spittle, and they moved deeper into the crowd. Up ahead Tach could hear the ring of Jesse's voice, but the words eluded him. He was too busy scanning the crowd, evaluating the faces of his friends and people. Disinterest, outright hatred, sympathy. A shadow fell across him. Turtle. But Tommy flew on.

A huge, pallid figure snapped the linked arms of two policemen. A brick wall wasn't going to stop six-hundred pounds of Doughboy. He rolled to a stop before the tiny alien.

"Doctor."

"Yes, dear." He couldn't bring himself to call the joker "Doughboy."

"They thaid Mith Thara's a twaitor, and now they thay you are too. I don't underthand."

"It's very confusing, child."

"Don't you love the thenator anymore?"

Tach covered his eyes with a hand. "I love all of you better."

"Funny way of showing it," howled a voice from the crowd.

"Traitor. *Traitor! TRAITOR!*"

The sound battered at him, and Tach dropped his face into his hands. Suddenly Jackson was there, an arm tight about his shoulders.

"Come on. You can *do* it. We walk through this crowd. We get up on that truck, and we speak. It's going to be all right."

"No, Reverend, I am afraid that some things can never be repaired."

But he had been reminded of his duty, so with a smile firmly in place Tach began moving down the line of people. Some of the most unbelievable things were held out to him—claws, tentacles, misshapen lumps covered with foul-smelling discharge. The sight of a normal human hand was such a relief that Tachyon almost ran to grip it.

A young man, dressed in a leather jacket despite the heat, raised heavy lids to regard him. Eyes as blank as a shark's.

Jokers clogged the street, silent and horrible. The heat and the light seemed to suffocate you, to wrap around your chest like a python, tightening by degrees. It reminded Mackie of Hamburg in summertime. He hated anything that reminded him of home. He hated the heat and the humidity, and wasn't too crazy about the light of day. Most of all he hated jokers.

Nonetheless he was happy. Redemption sang in his veins like a hit of good speed.

Der Mann was giving him another chance. He was Macheath again, slipping through the mob with his song bubbling mantric down in his throat.

In this mass of monsters, nothing was remarkable. Particularly Mackie. His lack of size let him avoid most contact. The awful heat sent sweat tentacles crawling down his ribs inside his jacket and aging T-shirt, but his personal stink was lost in the crowd.

Glancing impact, then, "Hey, there, motherfucker!"

The hand on his arm was feathered. "Watch who you're shoving! Who the fuck you think you are?"

"I'm Mack the Knife, you filthy creature!" Anger swelled like his cock. He started to bring a buzz.

No! Remember your job! He snarled something wordless

and phased out, leaving the monstrosity standing there holding air. The stupid look on what passed for its face made him laugh.

Insubstantial, he walked through a maggot clump of horrors pretending to be people, found an eddy big enough to phase his skinny body back in. The jokers paid him no mind. A chant had started, low and hostile. The words blurred in his mind. He didn't try to understand. Jokers had nothing to say. The beasts didn't even know he was walking through them! He was Mackie Messer, he was stone mystery and death. He was invincible.

Looming alongside his quarry was the tall nigger running for president—and wasn't *that* capitalist decadence, to let such people hold political office? Karl Marx said the black man was a slave, and *der alte Karl* knew what he was talking about. The man hanging tight on Tach's other side struck Mackie somehow familiar. Probably one of the alien's toadies from Jokertown.

Tachyon was moving down a line, shaking hands or whatever. The thought of all that joker touch made Mackie's skin creep. He circled, like the shark in his song, who wears his teeth in his face.

You must be extremely careful, the Man had said. *Tachyon is a mind reader. You must not let him sense your intention.*

Good enough. He was Mack the Knife. He knew how to do these things.

It would be simple to phase through the crowd, approach from behind, *buzz* his hand and jam it right through Doctor precious Tachyon's alien fucking heart. It would be *too* simple. He'd never done an alien before. Nor had he done anybody really *big*, really famous like Tachyon was.

He wanted to feel Tachyon's eyes in his. He wanted the little bastard to know who was killing him.

The jokers surged forward, carrying him right where he needed to go.

The world contracted to Tachyon and the touch.

The afternoon came to Jack in little coherent bursts interspersed with noise and pointless movement, like a film cut into pieces and spliced together at random. Delegates surged back and forth, vote totals changed by the half hour.

The only two constants were that Hartmann was losing votes and Barnett was gaining. Despite denials from Hartmann and Devaughn, everyone assumed that Jack's accusation of Barnett had been a last, desperate attempt by Hartmann's camp to regain its lost momentum. "Hey," Devaughn finally scowled as reporters pressed him. "Give the guy a break. Yesterday somebody stopped his heart—who knows how many brain cells he lost?"

Thanks, Charles, Jack thought. *Compassionate as always.*

The only conceivable remedy was another swig of over-proof.

Jim Wright, calling for vote after vote, looked as if his liver had just failed. Fistfights swirled on the floor. The band played whatever came into its collective head, anything from Stephen Foster to Jagger-Richards. A Starshine glider crashed in front of Jack and he stepped on it by mistake while trying to pick it up. He tried to throw the crumpled thing anyway, and it came apart as it left his hand.

Fucking flying joker, he thought.

As Jack finished the bottle, a kind of lucidity returned, an intense consciousness of the horror of it all. *Aw, shit,* Jack thought. *I've drunk myself sober.*

No choice, he decided, but to get another bottle. He lurched from his seat and headed across the pandemonium toward the nearest exit. As he left the auditorium, he saw a young woman with Hartmann buttons talking earnestly to a tall black man in hornrims.

"Sorry, Sheila," the man in glasses said. "Your old man's the nicest guy I've ever met, and I'm sorry to disappoint him, but if I don't switch to Jesse on this vote I can kiss my standing in the neighborhood goodbye."

Some kind of rally was going on right outside the auditorium. There was a flatbed truck covered with Jackson banners and a limo trying to get through the crowd toward it, the horn bleating. Swarming around everything were more jokers than Jack had ever seen in one place.

He tried moving through the crowd, but it was too dense. The people in the limo must have decided the same thing, because its doors opened and the passengers got out—Straight Arrow in his gray uniform, some little white guy Jack didn't recognize, Jesse Jackson, and Tachyon.

Great. Just the people Jack wanted to see.

The crowd roared. Media people jostled jokers to find camera setups. Police and Secret Service were trying to wedge their way to the truck without knocking anyone off their feet. Tachyon and the candidate were shaking hands as they progressed. Someone spit in Tach's face. Straight Arrow looked appalled, probably not at the saliva but at the fact it could as easily have been a bullet.

A shadow passed overhead and Jack looked up. The Turtle moved past in silence. Someone had painted HARTMANN! across his shell in big silver letters.

Jack looked down and saw, through a split-second gap in the crowd, the freak gliding through the crowd. The kid with buzz saw hands, just fifteen feet away.

Adrenaline crashed into Jack with the force of a hurricane. "*No!*" he yelled, and began to swim through the crowd with great sweeps of his arms, driving his way heedless of yells of protest.

The leather boy had disappeared. Jack craned to find him.

Then there he was, leaning forward under the arm of a policeman, his hand outstretched. Tachyon saw him and smiled.

"*No!*" Jack yelled again, but no one could hear him.

Tachyon took the hand.

Tachyon took his hand with something like relief. He clamped down hard.

"I'm Mackie Messer," he said, and laid on maximum buzz.

There was a shower of blood and bone and the buzzsaw sound that Jack remembered all too well. Tachyon screamed. So did a hundred other people. So, maybe, did Jack.

Jack charged forward, but the crowd was surging back, and he stumbled, almost fell, as people went down around him. A silver-eyed joker child was clutching his leg. Jack tried to shake the boy off, yelling in fury.

Tachyon staggered back, blood pulsing from his torn wrist. Straight Arrow had been watching the crowd around Jackson and was only now turning his head to comprehend the situation. The policeman under whose arm the leather boy had reached was the only one near enough to react. Half the cop's face was dripping with Tachyon's blood, and his actions were slowed by shock. He tried to grab the boy's leather jacket. If he'd had time to think, he'd have done almost anything but that.

The leather boy turned to face the cop and Jack's heart jumped into his throat. All the kid had to do was glance past the policeman and see Jack heading for him. But the freak didn't notice Jack—he was too busy smiling up at the cop, his tongue enjoying the taste of Takisian blood on his lower lip. He sliced off the cop's right arm at the shoulder.

The kid turned back to Tachyon, away from Jack. Jack shook off the joker kid and ran, his arm cocking back, his hand making a fist. If the kid was going to finish off Tach, he'd have to remain material, and Jack could hit him with all the force of a cannon.

The leather boy reached toward Tachyon. His hand movement was gentle, almost a caress. One more step and Jack was going to knock the hunchback's head about twenty blocks.

Jack let the punch go, and the freak disappeared with a *pop!* The punch spun him around as Jack screamed in rage. Tachyon's blood slipped under his feet but somehow he managed to stay upright.

"*Who did that!*" he shrieked.

Straight Arrow was standing there, a flaming arrow raised high in one hand, like a statue of Zeus throwing a thunderbolt. The Secret Service had knocked Jackson down and had piled on him. A lot of guns were out.

"Ackroyd," Straight Arrow said. The flame disappeared from his fingertips.

The crowd moaned as if in pain. Men with television cameras circled the police cordon, trying to get a better look. The eyes of the nation were sopping it all up.

Tachyon's eyes fluttered and he fell to the pavement. The cop was screaming. Jack could see that his wound was too high to tourniquet. Jack stepped up to him, drew back his fist, hit him gently on the temple. The policeman's head bounced like a punching bag and he went unconscious.

Straight Arrow stepped next to Jack. His shocked face was pale. He reached out a hand to the policeman's wounded shoulder. Flame pulsed hotly. Blood hissed, boiling away, as he cauterized the wound. The smell of burning flesh eddied up, and from Jack's layered memories came the screams of a man burning to death in a flaming tank somewhere under Cassino.

Maybe the cop's life could be saved if the man didn't die of shock in the next five minutes. Jack followed, feeling helpless, as Straight Arrow moved to Tachyon's side and picked up the wounded arm. Tachyon's face and ruffles were covered with blood. There were things grinding under Jack's feet that he didn't want to think about.

Straight Arrow cauterized Tach's wound with the same efficient pulse of flame he'd used on the cop. Jack turned away, not wanting to have to listen to the hiss of blood, smell the burning meat. He reached for his cigarettes. Rage danced through his nerves. He'd *had* the kid, would have crushed his murderous little head like an eggshell.

Jesse Jackson was getting to his feet. From his bewildered expression it was clear he hadn't seen a thing. Secret Service were trying to call for ambulances on their radios.

"Ackroyd." Straight Arrow rose from his crouch. "Where did you send him?"

Ackroyd was the nondescript-looking man Jack had seen leave the limousine with Tach and Jackson. He seemed as much in shock as anyone else.

"Yeah," he said. "Oh, Jesus." His hands wandered over his own body as if he had an itch he couldn't locate.

"You!" Jack roared. "Who the hell *are* you?"

Ackroyd looked at him uncomprehendingly.

"Jay Ackroyd," Straight Arrow said. "Private cop. They call him Popinjay."

"I *had* the bastard!" Jack shook his fist in rage, crushing his pack of cigarettes. "I could have turned him into JELL-O! Aw, fuck!" He threw down the pack of cigarettes and kicked it into the crowd.

"Where'd you send him, Ackroyd?"

"Popped him," Ackroyd said.

Straight Arrow grabbed him by the lapels and shook him. *"Where'd you send the assassin?"*

"Oh." Ackroyd licked his lips. "New York. The tombs."

Straight Arrow took his hands off the detective and straightened in satisfaction. "Good," he said.

Jack wanted to knock Ackroyd into the next country. *"He walks through walls!"* he yelled. "He's *out* by now!"

Straight Arrow's face fell.

Ambulance sirens wailed in the distance. Jack looked around the scene, the two wounded men, Jackson kneeling by

Tachyon, the Secret Service with their guns out, the crowd wailing and moaning in shock, TV cameras taking it all in . . .

He'd lost again, Jack realized. Another tragedy he couldn't stop. Everything was slipping through his fingers.

And no one was going to profit from any of this besides Leo Barnett.

He was in a room surrounded by big niggers and bars. For a moment Mackie thought he was dreaming. Then he became aware of the hot gobbets of alien meat clinging like melted plastic to his face and the front of his jacket.

His right hand held air. His left was stiffened into a blade, vibrating, ready to take Dr. Tachyon's head off his shoulder. But he was no longer in the brightness of the Atlanta street and there was no Tachyon.

"*Nein!*" he screamed, slamming the heels of his hands against his forehead. "*Nein, nein, nein!*"

He had failed again. It wasn't possible. But he had failed.

A hand clamped his shoulder. Nausea tsunami crashed from one side of his stomach to the other as he turned to find himself staring up at a gigantic black with a hairless dome of head and a gold ring in his ear.

"Hey, man," the giant said in a mild voice, "how fuck you get in here?"

Mackie screamed again, this time making no attempt at words. He made his hands do things, then, and then it was other people who were screaming, and when the screaming stopped he ran straight through the bars of the holding cell, down green echoing corridors that reeked of puke and sweat and fear, and downstairs and out into the grimy sunlight of New York.

He had to get back to Atlanta at once. To redeem himself in the eyes of his master, his love.

5:00 P.M.

The first thing Gregg did was shake Jesse's hand.

Puppetman raced outward from the touch, opening the man's mind eagerly. It was an exquisite mind, one that felt things deeply. That was, after all, the best kind. There was a wash of deep orange-red there now, a memory of something very painful and horrible. Gregg knew what that would be.

Jackson hadn't changed his jacket; it was still spattered from Tachyon's blood. The sight of it made Gregg uneasy, a fluttering of guilt returning that made Puppetman mock him, inside.

"Reverend, thank you for meeting with me on such short notice and after such a horrible afternoon. How . . . how is Dr. Tachyon?"

"Clinging to life. In critical condition. The doctors say there was too much damage to reattach the hand." Jackson's long, dark face frowned. "A terrible event, Senator. A very terrible event. I have not seen such cold, sick violence since the Reverend King was assassinated."

Puppetman watched Jackson's emotions carefully. There was horror and fear, and revulsion, but none of it was directed toward Gregg. Which told him that Tachyon was still remaining silent about Puppetman.

Good. Then it doesn't matter—yet—that Mackie didn't finish the job.

There was only a faint yellow ochre of distaste inside Jackson directed at Gregg, and Puppetman easily pushed that back down, scrubbing it with the respect he knew Jackson had for Gregg's stand on common issues.

"I'm sorry to hear that, Reverend," he said. "Please, take a seat. I've told my aide to contact your staff and have a change of clothes sent over. Would you like anything to drink?" Jackson declined with a wave of his hand and took a chair; Gregg sat on the couch opposite him. He steepled his hands in front of his face as if trying to decide what to say.

"This isn't a time I'd choose to say any of this," Gregg said at last. "Not after this afternoon. But maybe this *is* the best time. We need to end the violence here. We need to unify the convention and start to work on the real campaign against Bush."

"I know what you're going to say, Senator. You should know that my staff wants me to say 'no.'" Jackson seemed easy and comfortable despite the trauma of the afternoon. He sat crosslegged, his big hands cupped around a knee. The dark stains on his jacket made the image eerily surreal. Outwardly, he was cool, collected, almost indifferent.

Puppetman knew better. Inside the man was suddenly eager. He could see it; bright, electric blue, flashing like lightning. "They want me to say 'no' because they're convinced that with Dr. Tachyon's support, our Rainbow Coalition stands to win here," he continued. "No half-victories, Senator, but everything."

"I've had a friendship of nearly twenty years' standing with Dr. Tachyon," Gregg said. "He's a prideful and very stubborn man. The truth is that you and I are only taking votes away from each other and allowing Barnett to win. The truth is that if the presidential candidate isn't me, it also won't be you. I think we both know that, no matter what we'd like to believe. If I don't win here, Leo Barnett will be the candidate. The attack on Tachyon today has only strengthened his position."

Puppetman could feel Jackson's irritation with that. It was no secret that the two ministers didn't care for each other. Jackson was an idealist, on the far left fringes of the party as Barnett was to the right. Gregg let Puppetman caress that irritation until Jackson visibly scowled.

"Reverend, you don't know why Tachyon came to you," Gregg went on. "My staff wanted to release this to the press after Tachyon withdrew his support, but I didn't let them, in deference to those twenty years of friendship. Tachy . . . well, there's no graceful way to put this. In the last few days, the doctor has become involved in a relationship with Barnett's campaign manager, Fleur van Renssaeler. I don't know whether she seduced him or he her—it doesn't matter, I suppose. But when I confronted him with it, he exploded. Said the relationship was none of my business. I insisted that indeed it was—understandably, I think—and pressed harder." Gregg made a sour, chagrined face. "I probably said some things I shouldn't have said. Our argument was bitter and harsh. He walked out. The next I heard of him, he was making the announcement that he was withdrawing his support."

Gregg smiled sadly. "I can understand why he would turn to you, Reverend. We have our differences, but I think someone looking at our records and our public stands would find us very similar. We're both against prejudice and hatred of any kind; we'd both like to see all sides coming together to work in harmony. We've worked together on the platform fight; I know our ideals are the same."

In Jackson's mind, Puppetman pushed here, pulled there.

"That sounds like one of your campaign speeches, Senator." There was a faint smile on his face. "I've heard the rhetoric before."

"And rhetoric is cheap. I know. I also know that if you look at my voting record, if you look at what I've done as chairman of SCARE, at how I've reacted to any joker or civil rights legislation, then you'll see that we're not very far apart. I think we could work together well."

"Which brings us back to that question you haven't asked me yet, Senator."

He's very interested, even without me. Feel it? Taste it?

"You know what I'm offering." Gregg said it as a fact, not a question.

"You're offering the vice presidency," Jackson said, nodding. "You're saying 'Reverend Jackson, why don't you tell your delegates to vote for the Hartmann/Jackson ticket?' With my delegates and yours, we might win the nomination."

"With your voice, with your strength, with your power, *we*"—Gregg paused, stressing the word—"we win not just the nomination, we win the presidency."

Desire was bright, bright blue. Mottling it underneath were dark splotches of doubt. Puppetman scraped the darkness away, made them fade into nothingness. Jesse pursued his lips. "I could make the same offer to you, Senator . . ." he began, but Puppetman was still prodding, still working on his mind.

Jackson's voice faded.

He nodded.

He held out his hand.

"All right, Senator," he said as they shook. "You're right. It's time to build a bridge we can walk over. It's time to begin to bring all of us together."

Puppetman shouted in triumph. Gregg laughed helplessly.

He had it. This time he would have it. A little maneuvering yet to do, and it would be his.

The overproof rum hit Jack's stomach like a wave of welcome flame. He took another couple swallows, then capped the bottle and stuffed it in a pocket. He'd bought it after Tachyon had been carried off to the hospital and the Secret Service let him go.

There was still blood on his cuffs and shoes. He was trying not to think about how it got there, and he figured the overproof would help.

He stepped up to one of the back doors of the Omni.

Aw, hell, he thought. There was the big guard with the broken nose, Connally. Connally was already shaking his head, refusing admittance to a gray-haired man who was waving a pass in his face. Jack could almost recite the dialogue along with Connally and the delegate.

"Sorry. Nobody gets in this way."

"But I just *left* through this door. You saw me."

"Nobody gets in this way."

"Officer, I'm merely going to collect my daughter, who is a delegate. I do have a pass."

A chill finger caressed Jack's neck at the sound of the man's voice. He stopped, about ten feet behind the man, and stared at the back of his gray head. Where had he heard this before?

"Well," Connally said slowly. "I suppose it won't make that much difference. Even though nobody's supposed to come through here."

"It'll be okay," said the man.

Shaking his head, as if he didn't realize why he was doing this, Connally reached for his belt, produced a bunch of keys on a chain, and opened the door.

Surprise danced through Jack's head.

"Thank you, officer. That's very kind." The man stepped through the door.

Jack moved forward. Something here wasn't right. "Excuse me," he said.

Connally glared at him. "Where do you think you're going, asshole?"

Jack forced a smile. "I'm a delegate."

Connally closed the door and firmly locked it. "Nobody gets through this door. That's my instructions."

Jack peered through the glass door at the gray-headed man's retreating form. "You just let *him* through," he said.

Connally shrugged. "What if I did?"

"He's not even a delegate! *I'm* a delegate!"

Connally looked at him. "He's not an asshole. You are."

As Jack stared through the glass door he saw the gray-haired man glance back, a short take over his shoulder, his hand raised to give Connally a friendly wave. The man saw Jack, and the bearded face turned to stone before the man dropped his arm and headed on his way.

Jack's hackles rose. He'd seen that face recently, on the cover of *Time* magazine after an actor named Josh Davidson had done *King Lear* in Central Park.

More importantly, he'd seen that *look* before.

He remembered a bunch of dock workers dancing on a table, singing "Rum and Coca-Cola."

Sorry, Sheila, he remembered, *your old man's the nicest guy I've ever met.*

He knew Davidson's look, Jack thought again. He'd seen it once before, back in '50, when he'd walked out of the committee room after testifying before HUAC and walked right past where Earl and David and Blythe and Mr. Holmes were waiting, walked right past them without saying a word.

Suddenly Jack was running, dashing past the surprised Connally toward one of the doors he could use.

Josh Davidson, Jack knew, was a secret ace.

As Jack ran for the doors, the bottle of overproof slipped out of his pocket and smashed on the concrete. He didn't slow down.

So far as anyone knew, Jack was the only one of the Four Aces left alive. No one knew for sure, because one of the four was missing.

After serving three years on the island of Alcatraz for contempt of Congress, David Harstein had walked off the boat in 1953. A year later Congress passed the Special Conscription Act, and Harstein had been drafted. He never reported. No one had seen him since. There were rumors that he'd died, been murdered, defected to Moscow, changed his name and moved to Israel.

There hadn't been a single rumor to the effect that he'd had some plastic surgery, done a little weightlifting, put on some weight, grown a beard, taken voice lessons, and become a Broadway actor.

Your old man's the nicest guy I've ever met. Naturally. No one could dislike David Harstein, not once his pheromones got to them. No one could disagree with him. No one could avoid doing what he wanted them to do.

Jack waved his ID at the man at the door, then plunged through. He ran through the crowd of people in the direction he'd last seen Davidson, ignoring the stares of the other delegates. Over the heads of others, he saw Davidson heading into one of the tunnels that led to the floor. He followed, caught Davidson's arm, said, "Hey."

Davidson spun around, threw off Jack's hand. His eyes were like chips of obsidian. "I would rather not talk to you, Mr. Braun."

Jack started to retreat. He could feel the color draining out of his face. He took a grip on his nerves and stepped forward.

"I want to talk to you, Harstein," he said. "We've got almost forty years to catch up on."

Harstein took a step backward and clutched at his heart. Jack felt a surge of terror: maybe he'd just given the old geezer a heart attack. He reached out to hold Harstein upright, but the man coldly knocked Jack's hands away, then turned partly away and leaned on the wall.

"If it be now," he murmured, "'tis not to come; if it be not to come, it will be now; if it be not now, yet it will come."

"Readiness is all," said Jack, completing the quote. He'd played Laertes in high school.

Harstein looked sharply at Jack. "All these years, and *you* discover me. It's appropriate somehow."

"If you say so."

"Why are we having a conversation? Unless you mean to blow the whistle on me."

Jack took a long breath. "I'm not blowing the whistle on anybody, David," he said.

The actor's face was contemptuous. "An interesting step out of character."

"You're the expert on character."

"I'm the expert on prison, too. I spent three years there."

"I didn't send you to prison, David," Jack said. "They sent you away before I ever testified."

"Another interesting distinction." Davidson shrugged. "However, if it serves to salve your conscience . . ."

Tears stung Jack's eyes. He sagged against the wall. He couldn't use the defense he'd used on Hiram. Harstein *had* been there. He hadn't broken, and that's why they'd sent him to prison.

And what had happened to Blythe had been far worse.

It was as if Harstein had picked the thought out of his head.

"I went to see Blythe right after I got out of prison.

November 1953. I talked my way past the orderlies. I even
went into her cell. I told her everything was going to be all
right. I told her she was well. She wasn't. Three weeks later
she was dead."

"I'm sorry," Jack said.

"*Sorry.*" Harstein seemed to taste the word, rolling it
about in his mouth. "So easy to say, yet having so little effect.
We can make our lives sublime and, departing, leave behind
us footprints in the sands of time." His eyes met Jack's. "A
wind came up, Jack, and it blew away our footprints." He
stared at Jack for a long time, an implacable look from which all
emotions had been leached. "Leave me alone, Jack. I never
want to see you again."

David Harstein turned and walked away. Jack slid slowly
down the wall, terror and remorse shuddering through his
body. It was at least five minutes before he got control of
himself. When he stood up, he had huge sweat stains under
his arms.

Delegates passing through the tunnel looked at him with
pity or disgust, assuming he was drunk. They were wrong.

He was sober, perfectly sober. He had been so terrified
he'd burned every ounce of alcohol in his system.

Jack stepped back into the auditorium just as Jim Wright
announced the latest delegate totals. Hartmann's total was
going into the sewer.

7:00 P.M.

The hotel concourses were nearly deserted. Most of the
people were watching the main event over on the convention
floor. Spector walked into the snack bar, a bottle of Jack Black
tucked under his arm. He'd slept most of the day away, had to
get something to eat. The Marriott restaurants were out of the
question; after the fight with Golden Boy, there were sure to
be people looking for him. But he was weak from hunger and
had to get something.

He wandered around the aisles of junk food and souve-
nirs, picking out a couple of candy bars, a can of cashews, some
sausage sticks. A young black man was behind the register,
staring at a small black-and-white television. Spector set his
stuff on the counter and peeled off a bill.

"Be right with you, mister," said the clerk. "They're

supposed to show Tachyon's hand exploding after these commercials. Missed it live. Damn, I bet that was something to
see. Did you catch it?"

"Tachyon's hand blew up? What the hell are you talking
about?"

"You been by the pool all day or what?" said the clerk,
shaking his head. "Some ugly little dude shook the doctor's
hand and blew it clean off. They say . . . Wait a second.
Here we go." He turned the television around so Spector
could see, too.

The video was in slow motion. Tachyon was working the
crowd, shaking hands. "Who gets him?" Spector asked.

"Some little hunchback. See, there he is."

Spector opened his mouth. Shut it. It was the same little
twerp who'd been on the flight down with him. The hunchback took Tachyon's hand and blood went everywhere. The
cameraman was jostled by the panicked crowd and the video
ended.

"Is he still alive?" Spector had always wanted Tachyon
dead, but found himself hoping for the best. After all, killing
Tachyon was something he planned to do himself, someday.

"So far." The clerk turned the television off and rang
Spector up. "I guess he's tougher than he looks." He sacked
the junk food and handed it over with Spector's change. "You
don't go shaking hands with the devil, mister."

It's a bit too late for that, Spector thought, smiling. He
pocketed his change and headed back to the room.

"Hey. Jack."

"What is it, *ese*?"

"Orders from Devaughn."

"Yeah." Jack spoke without enthusiasm. He was hiding
from interviews in the middle of what remained of his loyal
delegates—the disloyal ones, a third of the total, were off
caucusing with their new managers.

"After the recess," Rodriguez said, "the Jackson camp is
gonna move to suspend the rules of the convention in order to
let Jesse speak. We're supposed to vote in favor."

Jack looked at Rodriguez in surprise. "We can't let a
candidate speak. Hell, they'll *all* wanna—"

"News is, Jackson's going to drop out." Rodriguez smiled

and tapped his nose. "I smell something, Jack. Betcha Jackson's cut a deal with the boss. Betcha he's gonna be veep."

Jack's mind worked through the idea. He hadn't been in charge of his own delegation since he'd gone off the balcony on Thursday: it was Rodriguez who had been riding herd on California and voting Jack's proxy for Hartmann. He had to respect Rodriguez's instincts here.

As for the Hartmann/Jackson ticket: why not? It was the same deal that Roosevelt and Garner had cut in '32, during the last stalled Democratic convention.

"Our totals and Jesse's," he said. "Are they—?"

"Not enough. Jesse's people are working on Dukakis now."

"Barnett will *have* to smell something." Or Fleur, he thought. Fleur had the sharper nose.

Maybe, Jack thought, it was Fleur who was the secret ace, not Barnett. He wondered if Fleur had been in the military.

"After this morning," Rodriguez being tactful, "there's no approaching them. Someone talked to Fleur whatsername: she says No. Doesn't even want to talk about it."

Jack rose to his feet, scowling toward the massive battleship-prow of the podium as Jim Wright called the convention to order and announced there would be another ballot. The damned vote would take forever: the managers had totally lost control of the delegates and each delegation would have to be polled man-by-man. The move to suspend the convention rules would come after the vote total was announced. And then *that* would have to be voted on—God, how long could this go on?

"Fuck! Fuck!" Rodriguez was shouting into his cellular phone. He slammed the thing into its cradle, then looked at Jack. "Dukakis will go along with it. He hasn't got anything to lose, and maybe he can pick up some of Jackson's delegates. But we can't change the rules without Barnett. We need a three-quarters vote."

"This sucks, *ese*."

"Barnett's going over the top if this Jackson stunt doesn't work." Rodriguez took a breath. "Okay. Here's what Devaughn wants. We're gonna start spreading the rumor that Jackson is dropping out, that all he wants to do is address the convention and make a plea on behalf of his constituency. Nobody's calling the shots with his individual delegates anymore. Maybe Barnett's troops won't pay attention when he tells them to vote no."

"Maybe."

Rodriguez shrugged. "The whole scheme's a maybe."

Jack felt his hands balling by his sides. There had to be some way to repair things, some way to repair the damage that the assassin aces had done—hell, that *Jack* had done.

He remembered longshoremen dancing on a countertop.

David Harstein, he thought wildly. Get Harstein on the platform. Use him to influence the entire convention to nominate Hartmann by acclamation.

No. Stupid. Everyone would notice. People watching on TV would wonder how come they weren't as enthusiastic as the people at the convention. And the air-conditioning might blow Harstein's pheromones away.

Harstein's power was subtle; it had to be used subtly. He could only influence a few people at a time.

Maybe, Jack thought, a few *important* people.

Maybe Barnett's campaign manager.

Jack thought of Fleur dancing on tabletops, flinging her underwear into the Omni atrium, calling Leo Barnett on the phone to tell him how good Tachyon was in bed . . . Jack gloried in this picture for a moment before the whole thing fell apart.

David Harstein hated his guts. Who was he to make plans for the man?

The hell with that. Harstein wanted Hartmann elected, right? If nothing else, Jack could resort to blackmail. He knew Harstein was a secret ace. He could threaten to reveal it.

He thought of himself weeping in the tunnel and his stomach turned over.

Jim Wright read Alabama's delegate total. All for Barnett.

That decided it. Jack was moving, walking from California to New York across the massive front of the podium.

Harstein was seated in the bleachers watching his daughter address the New York delegation. His look was both sad and proud. Jack slapped Harstein on the shoulder and pinned him to his seat.

The actor's eyes were veiled, cautious, watching. "I thought we had reached an understanding. You leave me alone. I leave you alone."

Jack spoke quickly. "Listen, it's important. In a few

minutes there's going to be a motion to suspend the rules of the convention in order to let Jackson speak. He's going to withdraw and give his support to our man."

"Good for Gregg Hartmann." Scowling. "What's that got to do with me?"

"The vote has to be damn near unanimous. Barnett has enough votes to block us. I figure we can talk to Fleur van Rensselaer and make her change her mind."

"*We*?" The pointed emphasis made Jack want to melt into the ground. "Is this your plan? Or have you told Hartmann about me?"

Jack shook his head. He was trying not to cringe. "Nobody knows but me. I won't say anything, but you've got to help me."

Harstein rubbed wearily at his forehead. "And you expect me to talk my way into Barnett's headquarters and change everybody's mind?" He seemed almost to be talking to himself. "What year do you think this is? 1947? This sort of thing didn't work then, and it isn't going to work now."

He was right. It was so obvious. How could Jack have been so stupid?

Jack caught himself just on the point of shrugging and walking away. Harstein's pheromones had already got Jack agreeing with him. What did he mean, *it didn't work then*? David had talked Franco right off his throne. Still, when he spoke, he didn't sound convincing even to himself.

"If we don't do this, Barnett's going to win. This will all be for nothing." Sweat poured down Jack's face. He felt as if his heart was going to explode any second. "All we have to do is change one mind. Fleur's."

Davidson looked away, thinking. Jack took a desperate lungful of air, tried to calm his trembling limbs.

"I've made a life," Davidson said. "I've got a family. I can't risk them. My counterfeit identity won't stand up to thorough investigation." He looked at Jack. "I'm an old man. I don't do that sort of thing anymore. Maybe it should never have been done."

Surprise sang in Jack's veins. He wants my understanding, he thought.

"You're doing that sort of thing now," Jack said. "You wouldn't be here if you weren't trying to influence people."

"Jack, you still don't get it, do you? I can't *help* but

influence people. I can't turn my power on or off. That's why I'm *not* a delegate. That's why I keep to myself. What right have I got to replace a man's opinion with mine? Is mine necessarily any better than his?" Harstein shook his head.

Jack fought against the ferocious urge to just agree with Harstein and walk away. "Our opinions," he said, fighting to get every word out, "are one hell of a lot better than the ravings of a man who threatens us. Your daughter—" He pointed at her and remembered her name, Sheila. "Sheila has the wild card. You've got a full dose, both chromosomes, and even if your wife didn't have the virus, you couldn't help but give Sheila a latent. And if she marries someone with another latent, their kids could end up with a full wild card."

Harstein said nothing. His eyes traveled to where his daughter stood among the other delegates. Sheila was looking back, her face worried. She knew, then, of her father's identity, guessed that Jack knew as well.

"Do you know what will happen to them if Barnett becomes president?" Jack went on. "They'll be confined to a nice hospital in some remote location, a hospital with a razor-wire fence. And you won't have grandchildren— Barnett'll see to that."

Harstein turned to Jack. The ice had returned. "Kindly don't mention my daughters again. Don't you ever *use* that line of argument with me. You don't give a damn for them, or me."

Harstein fell silent. Looked at his daughters again. Spoke softly. "We have seen the best of our time: machinations, hollowness, treachery, and all ruinous disorders, follow us disquietly to our graves." He looked at Jack. "That was an unfair argument. But it convinced me; I will do what I can." He hesitated. "I'm a little surprised. I thought you'd threaten to expose me. I'm glad to see I was wrong."

That's always an option, Jack thought. But didn't say it.

He didn't mind developing a reputation for decency for a change.

It took only a minute to walk from the Omni complex to the Omni Hotel next door. It was almost ten minutes before Jack and Harstein could get an elevator to Barnett's headquarters. A lot of Barnett's people were around: there was a lot of staring. Jack ignored them and did a lot of thinking.

Their convention IDs were enough to get them into the hotel, and probably into the operations room. Security would be greatest around the candidate, and Barnett's room was on another floor. Jack's problem would be staying in the operations room long enough to get next to Fleur and let Harstein's pheromones do their work.

Harstein's mention of blackmail had set Jack's mind working.

While waiting for the elevator, Jack got some hotel stationary from the front desk and penned a note, then wrote *Fleur van Renssaeler* on the back.

The note said: *I need five minutes of your time. If I don't get it, the world (and Reverend Barnett) will find out about your sins of the flesh with Tachyon.*

He considered signing it *Yours in Christ, Jack Braun* but decided that might be pushing things a little far.

The elevator doors opened and Jack stepped inside, surprising the hell out of two Barnett supporters of the little-blue-haired-lady variety. Jack smiled politely as he entered and pressed the button for Barnett HQ.

People waiting for the elevators did a lot of double takes as Jack stepped out, but nobody stopped him as he headed for the operations center. He walked right through the door, past a lot of young women on telephone banks, and failed to see any sign of Fleur. He grinned at the nearest worker.

"Where's the boss lady?" he said.

The girl stared. She was maybe seventeen, cute in an unformed blonde way. Her glasses slid down her nose. Her name, according to her name tag, was Beverly.

"I—" she said. "You're—"

Harstein bent close to her and said, "Go ahead. You can tell him." He smiled reassuringly.

"Ah—"

Harstein's expression was gentle. "It's really all right, Beverly," he said. "Mr. Braun's here on business, and I'm just tagging along."

Beverly pointed with a pencil. "I think Miss van Renssaeler is in her office," she said. "Two doors down. 718."

"Thank-you."

The room was beginning to buzz with alarm. People were glaring at Jack and dialing phones. He smiled at them all reassuringly, gave them a wave, and left. Harstein followed.

"I hope it's a small room," Harstein said. "You have no

idea what the advent of air-conditioning has done to my power."

Heads poked from the door as Jack strolled to 718 and knocked. He could hear televisions, and a phone ringing in the room. The phone cut off, and he heard steps coming to the door. It opened.

A silver-haired man stood there, his eyes widening in shock, then narrowing in anger. He flushed.

"Yes." Fleur's voice, on the phone. "I guess he's here. Thank you, Veronica."

"You are not welcome here," the silver-haired man said.

"I'd like to see Miss van Renssaeler," Jack said.

The man tried to slam the door. Jack held it open with his hand. "Please," he said.

The door jerked open. Fleur looked at Jack from over the rims of square-cut reading glasses. Her mouth was a grim slash. Two other men stood behind her, in various uneasy postures. Televisions turned to various networks babbled along one wall.

"I don't think we have anything to talk about, Mr. Braun," she said.

"We do," Jack said. "I'd like to apologize, for a start."

"Fine, you've done that," Fleur said. She started to close the door.

"I'd like to speak to you for just a few moments."

"I'm busy. You may write for an appointment, after the convention." The door closed to a few inches, and again Jack stopped it. Jack produced the envelope from his pocket.

"Okay," he said. "Here's my appointment request. I'd like you to read it now."

He lightly tossed the envelope inside and let Fleur close the door. He looked down the corridor to see two security men walking toward him, doubtless summoned by the phone ladies. Their expressions, in the face of a man who used to throw Russian tanks off Korean mountainsides, lacked confidence.

"Uh," the nearest one said.

Jack grinned at them. "No problem, officers. I'll be leaving as soon as Miss van Renssaeler gives me an appointment."

They looked at each other, then decided to wait. "We were told there was a problem," one of them said.

"Problem? No problem."

The guards did not seem reassured.

The door opened. "Five minutes," said Fleur. "And that's all you get." She turned to the men in the suite with her. "Reverend Pickens, Mr. Smart, Mr. Johnson, I hope you'll excuse me. Something's come up."

The men filed out past Jack, offering mixed distrust and relief. Jack stepped into the room, and Harstein followed.

"Who's this man?" Fleur said. "I didn't agree to see him."

"Josh Davidson, madam." Harstein gave a stage bow, sweeping low.

"He's an old friend of the family. He's with me."

"He can wait outside."

"Madam, I will not interfere in your business," Harstein said. "An old fellow like me finds it hard to wait in cold air-conditioned corridors. I won't be any harm. Have I not a moist eye, a dry hand, a yellow cheek, a white beard, a decreasing leg, an increasing belly? I'm an object of pity. Pray do not scorn and cast me out."

Fleur looked at him. The corners of her mouth twitched in reluctant amusement.

"This is against my better judgment," she said, "but you can stay."

Fortunately, her better judgment did not prevail.

9:00 P.M.

The Jackson motion came up, was seconded, passed overwhelmingly. Harstein kissed Fleur's hand goodbye, and he and Jack made their way to the elevators.

"We may have just made a president," Jack said. He felt pleasantly drunk, as if on champagne.

Harstein just kept walking for the elevator.

"Hey. We *won*."

"Things without all remedy should be without regard," said Harstein. "What's done is done." He looked at Jack. "And so, too, are we done. Never speak to me again, Jack, never come near me or my family. I'm warning you."

Jack's blood turned chill. "Whatever you say," he said.

He let Harstein take the first elevator by himself.

Sara had the proper plastic smile molded into her face when he stepped off the People Mover with his shiny new travel bag slung over the shoulder of his leisure suit. She looped her arms around his neck and hugged him with a fervor that surprised her.

"Uncle George!" she squealed. "Oh, it's so good to see you!"

Polyakov hugged her and patted her shoulder. "Not so shrill, child. Eardrums are brittle things at my age. Why didn't you meet me at the gate?" He took her arm and steered her into the traffic streaming toward the escalators that led to the baggage carousels.

"They're not letting anybody but passengers with tickets into the boarding area. Are you sure it's safe to just come in openly like this?"

Smiling, to all appearance chattering happily to the elderly relative she'd just been reunited with, she nodded toward the security checkpoint where the passengers were filing through the metal detectors like cows through the chute for their appointment with the hammer. A pair of young men stood to one side, eyeing the crowd as discreetly as anybody that beefy could. Their suits were dark, and tight under the left armpits. A little fleshtone wire trailed from each man's ear.

He smiled. "They're looking for dangerous Russian spies trying to get *out* of Atlanta, not back in."

"But the airport—"

"I could have taken a bus, I grant, especially since the good doctor's friend happened to transport me to the Port Authority in New York City." At the mention of Tachyon, Sara's face twisted briefly, as if she'd stepped on a tack. "But that would have been too slow, and anyway they're doubtless watching the bus terminals as well. Also, I detest buses."

They were on the moving stair now. "You heard what happened?" Sara asked.

"It was all over the televisions that infest the passenger waiting areas in LaGuardia—how lonely your capitalist lives must be, that you use your enormous production to surround yourselves so completely with synthetic company. An ace assassin making an attempt on the life of a potential presidential nominee, especially one as controversial and ethnic as Jackson—it's all raised quite the sensation."

That was how the police and media saw it, of course: the hunchbacked kid in leather had been trying to hit Jackson, and Dr. Tachyon had gotten in the way.

"How is it with Tachyon?" the Soviet asked.

She stumbled a little coming off the escalator. The hand that had caressed her, touched her last night as so few men had, was cooked meat and splintered bone now. The way that made her feel—

—The way it made her feel was something she would not confront now. *Nothing matters,* she told herself, *but staying alive long enough to see Andi avenged.*

"The doctor," he prodded gently, "how is he?"

"He's in what they call stable condition. They had to amputate, but he's recovering well. They have him in some hospital, the media aren't saying which one. The police have tied his assailant to Ricky's murder, and the fight with Jack Braun Thursday night. They know he can walk through walls. Lieutenant Herlihy has finally had to bite the bullet and admit he's got an ace killer on the loose. Not just a killer but a political assassin, and he's stalking the convention."

She didn't try to keep the bitter satisfaction from her voice. *If only the police had listened to me,* she thought, though what they could have done even if they had was none too clear. At least it would have meant somebody thought she was more than a hysterical woman who'd been spurned by her love object.

Somebody other than the man who called himself George Steele.

They walked toward the sliding robot doors to the humid outside. Sara had a car in the lot that she'd rented under an assumed name—now, of course, Atlanta's finest were falling all over themselves with eagerness to talk to her. Even if she'd had anything more to say to them, she had no illusions about their ability to protect her from that pale-eyed youth who hummed as he killed.

Polyakov shook his head. "The bad times are coming for wild cards in this country. Whatever we do here, that is true, I'm afraid. But it makes it that much more imperative we stop the madman Hartmann. You might have to take a more active role."

She stopped dead in the middle of the doors, which spasmed open and shut in mechanical frenzy. "No! I've already told you. I can't do that."

He took her by the arm and urged her out to the sidewalk. Diesel fumes and cabbies assailed them. They ignored both.

"Someone has to. Tachyon may not be able."

"Why not you? You're a killer ace, too. Why not use your power?"

He glanced around without moving his head. No one was nearby. "My. Our goal is to prevent World War III. How well would that end be served if an American presidential candidate was killed by a KGB ace?"

That was *his* goal. She turned and darted across the street, avoiding being run down more by luck than by design. He followed more cautiously.

He was puffing slightly when he caught up in the short-term parking. "It was clever of you to check your answering machine."

He was trying to gentle her like he would a frightened animal. She didn't care. "Clever of you to leave a message saying where you were coming in and when." She opened the driver's door of the rose-gray rental Corolla and slid in.

"That's my business," he said as she leaned across to unlock his door. He opened the rear door and put his bag in back. "I'm a professional spy. I'm paid to think of such things."

"Being a spy is not so much different from being a journalist," she said. "Just ask General Westmoreland." She turned the key with a savage twist and started the car.

"My right and my privilege to stand here," said Jesse Jackson, "has been won—won in my lifetime—by the blood and the sweat of the innocent."

From Jack's point of view, the candidate's figure was tiny, dwarfed by the massive white podium, but his ringing orator's voice filled the air. Jack heard the restless delegates grow hushed, expectant. Everyone, whether they liked Jackson or not, knew this was going to be important.

"I stand as a testament to the struggles of those who have gone before; as a legacy for those who will come after; as a tribute to the endurance, the patience, the courage of our forefathers and mothers; as an assurance that their prayers are being answered, their work has not been in vain, and hope is eternal . . ."

Those who have gone before. Jack thought about Earl, standing in his aviator's jacket on that platform, his baritone voice rolling out of the speakers. It should have been Earl there, he thought, and years ago.

"America is not one blanket, woven from one thread, one color, one cloth. When I was a child growing up in Greenville, South Carolina, and grandmama could not afford a blanket, she didn't complain, and we didn't freeze. Instead she took pieces of old cloth—patches—wool, silk, gaberdeen, crocker-sack—only patches, barely good enough to wipe off your shoes with. But they didn't stay that way very long. With sturdy hands and a strong cord, she sewed them together into a quilt, a thing of beauty and power and culture. Now, Democrats, we must build such a quilt.

"Farmers, you seek fair prices, and you are right—but you cannot stand alone, your patch isn't big enough. Workers, you fight for fair wages, you are right—but your patch of labor is not big enough. Jokers, you seek fair treatment, civil rights, a medical system sensitive to your needs—but your patch is not big enough . . ."

Years ago, in voice and diction lessons courtesy of Louis B. Mayer, Jack had learned the tricks of the rhetorician. He knew why preachers like Jackson and Barnett used those long cadences, those rhythmic, crafted emphases . . . Jack knew that the long sentences, the rhythms, could put the audience into a mild hypnotic trance, could make them more suscepti-ble to the preacher's message. What if it had been Barnett standing here? Jack wondered. What message would be rolling forth in those glittering images, those seductive rhythms?

"Don't despair!" Jackson shouted. "Be as wise as my grandmama. Pull the patches and pieces together, bound by a common thread. When we form a great quilt of unity and common ground, we'll have the power to bring about health care and housing and jobs and education, and hope . . .

"When I look out at this convention, I see the face of America: red, yellow, brown, black, and white. The real patchwork quilt that is our nation. The rainbow coalition. But we have not yet come together; no strong hand has yet bound us together with a strong cord. I address you tonight to tell you the name of the man who will unite our patches into something that will keep America from turning cold in this long, freezing night of Reaganomics . . ."

There was a murmur among the delegates. Not all, including Jackson's own followers, had been told this was a resignation speech. Some of them had just gotten their first clue.

"His foreparents came to America on immigrant ships," Jackson said. "A friend of mine, desperately wounded this afternoon as he stood beside me, came to this planet on a space ship. Mine came to America on slave ships. But whatever the original ships, we are in the same boat tonight."

From quilts, then, to boats. There was applause, whistles, a constant murmur. A woman was on her feet in the Illinois delegation: "*No, Jesse!*"

"This convention has been threatening to sink the boat," Jackson continued. "We have been running from one end of the boat to the other, from the progressive end to the conservative end, from the right side of the boat to the left side, and the boat may turn over—and Democrats, we may sink. It is time, therefore, to give the rudder to someone who can steer it safely to harbor. Tonight I salute this man—he has run a well-managed and a dignified campaign.

"No matter how tired or how tried, he always resisted the temptation to stoop to demagoguery. I have watched a good mind fast at work, with steel nerves, guiding his campaign out of the crowded field without appeal to the worst in us.

"I have watched his perspective grow as his environment has expanded. I've seen his toughness and tenacity, knew his commitment to public service."

Jackson paused, his intent eyes searching the convention, his hands grasping the platform. Wondering, maybe, what his new role as Kingmaker Jesse might bring.

"I urge the convention to unite behind this man, this new captain. I urge everyone here, all the delegates, my own not excepted, to vote for a new captain before our boat turns over and we sink for another four years. The name of the captain—"

Silence. Jack could hear his own heart beating. "*Senator!*" Jackson said.

Jack looked at Rodriguez in the next seat. "*Gregg!*" he said, in unison with Jackson.

Rodriguez looked back. There was wild joy in his eyes. "*Hartmann!*" he roared, along with Jack and Jesse and the crowd; and suddenly everyone went mad.

Mad for Gregg Hartmann.

Spector sat on the carpeted floor in front of the television. He had the volume turned way down; nobody was supposed to be in 1019, and he didn't want people snooping around this room, too. He'd bought a can of cashews and a pint of whiskey downstairs and had put away most of both during the balloting. He'd hoped that Hartmann would lose. A candidate who'd washed out wasn't likely to have the same kind of tight security as the nominee. As usual, things had gone all wrong.

The delegates were chanting, "Hartmann, Hartmann, Hartmann," until the name itself pissed him off. Jesse Jackson had pulled out of the race for some reason. All the commentators were talking about some kind of behind-the-scenes deal. In any case, Hartmann had gone over the top on the next ballot. Signs for each state were waving back and forth. There were balloons, confetti, and endless boring speeches.

Golden Boy was still alive. That made Spector even more nervous than he'd been before. Braun got a good enough look at him for an ID. The Judas Ace had looked plastered or sick when the TV cameras had shown him. Spector sighed. Usually when he killed them, they stayed dead.

Tomorrow he'd concentrate on finding a way to get at Hartmann. Right now, he didn't have the first idea how he'd go about it, but the senator wasn't leaving Atlanta alive. Of course, Spector might not either. He didn't bother trying to tell himself that there were some things worse than death. He knew better.

If he could find someone to help him, someone powerful, he might actually walk away in one piece. And he knew one person who might be inclined to help. It was a big risk, but what the fuck.

He turned off the TV, curled up into a ball around the almost empty bottle, and tried to get to sleep.

CHAPTER SEVEN

Sunday
July 24, 1988

7:00 A.M.

With one cheap towel wrapped around her dripping body from breasts to thighs and another wound around her hair, Sara emerged from the bathroom in a breath of steam. Motion was effort; she had rigor mortis to the depths of her soul.

"We can't rely on Tachyon anymore." She forced her words out like lumps of plasticine through a window screen. They weren't a question.

The man who called himself George Steele sat on the bed in trousers and undershirt, looking down at the backs of his hands. They were hairy, like his shoulders. He raised his head.

"We cannot."

"You know the plan we discussed earlier?"

His eyes narrowed. "Yes."

"I'll do it." She turned and went back into the bathroom to dry her hair.

9:00 A.M.

Hospitals were tasty and Puppetman was getting hungry.

Gregg leaned away from the Compaq Portable III and rubbed his eyes. He typed a quick message: *Tony, I'm taking a break. The speech looks good, and I'm sending my last edit.*

I'll leave the computer on and pick up the draft when I get back. Thanks.

He sent the file via modem to Calderone's portable and rubbed his eyes.

"Tired, love?" Ellen smiled at him from her hospital bed, half-asleep herself. "I think the next president of the United States ought to get some sleep. You had a long night last night, and Jack tells me you and Jesse stayed up till all hours planning the campaign."

"It was a glorious night, Ellen. Jesse's speech was a wonder. I'm sorry you weren't there. None of it was possible without you."

She smiled at that, tinged with sadness. She was still pale, her skin almost translucent, and her eyes were puffy and dark. The death of their child had marked her more permanently than he had thought possible. "I'm coming to hear your speech tonight. Nothing could stop me. Kiss me, next president of the United States."

"Picked up on that phrase, have we?"

"After last night's roll call? 'The great state of New York casts all its votes for the next president of the United States: Gregg Hartmann!' How many states are there?" She held her arms out.

Gregg leaned over the bed and kissed her softly on the lips. Puppetman nudged at him. *Give her to me.*

No. Leave her alone. We've put her through enough.

Getting sentimental, are we? The power mocked him, but didn't seem inclined to argue. *Then let's go elsewhere. I'm hungry.*

Gregg hugged Ellen. "Listen," he said. "I'm going to take a short walk. Thought I might see some of the patients, shake a few hands."

"Campaigning already," Ellen gave a mock sigh. "Mr. Next-President-of-the-United-States."

"Get used to it, love."

"You'll get tired of handshaking before it's all over, Gregg."

He gave her a strange grin. "I doubt it," he said.

Inside, Puppetman echoed him.

11:00 A.M.

Spector woke up groggy. There was a metallic taste in his mouth and he hurt all over. All his stuff was at the motel, so he couldn't shave or brush his teeth. He'd have to stop by there and clean up before making his visit. He sat on the corner of the bed and rubbed the grit from his eyes.

He picked up the phone book and thumbed through until he came to hospitals. He found the one Tony was in, hesitated for a moment, then punched in the numbers.

"Tony Calderone, please," he said to the switchboard operator. It rang several times before being answered.

"Calderone."

"Uh, yeah. This is Jim. I wanted to explain about the other day."

"Right. Colin said you were up in my room. Hope you didn't get mugged again." Tony sounded glad to hear from him.

"Nothing like that. Got sidetracked with business is all." Spector wanted to tell him everything, but knew Tony wouldn't believe it. He was too committed. "I just wanted you to know I was all right."

"Yeah, I was a little worried. Got the speech done. Best thing I ever wrote. Hope you get a chance to catch it." Tony paused. "You sure nothing's wrong?"

"Nothing getting back to Jersey won't cure." Spector twisted the phone cord. "It was really great seeing you again. I mean that."

"We'll do it again sooner than you think. In Washington." Tony sounded completely confident.

"Right." Spector knew that by the end of the day Tony would hate his guts forever. So much for his one friend. But he knew he couldn't walk away now. "Look, I have to get moving. Still got a thing or two to take care of before I go."

"Okay. Well, after things get settled you give me a call. In the meantime, look after yourself."

"So long." Spector set the phone lightly in its cradle. He couldn't let this sentimental crap take away his edge. He was going to need it.

Spector put the whiskey bottle in his coat pocket, he gave

the room a slow look before leaving. He knew he wouldn't be coming back.

12:00 NOON

Jack hadn't found Blaise on any of his intermittent searches, and he decided it was time to head for the hospital and tell Tachyon that Blaise was gone.

Hell. The kid would probably be right by his grandad's bedside.

Hartmann supporters were wandering about the Marriott lobby in various attitudes of inebriation or exhaustion. Yellow warning tape fluttered around the hole that Jack had driven into the floor. Jack saw the pert waitress he'd noticed before and gave her a wink. She grinned at him. He was sufficiently preoccupied with notions concerning the waitress that he didn't see Hiram until he almost tripped over the huge suitcase—almost a trunk—that the man had set next to him.

Hiram seemed as surprised as Jack. The big man's eyes were wide in alarm. Maybe the suitcase contained something valuable.

Hiram had a man with him, a thin joker with a little mustache and webs of skin over hollow eye sockets.

"Oh. Sorry." Jack stepped around the suitcase. He looked up at Hiram.

"Won't you be staying for the acceptance speech?"

"Ah. No. I've—uh—stayed longer in Atlanta than I meant to, anyway." Hiram's eyes gazed at Jack out of bruised sockets. He was a mess: his hair awry, his collar open to reveal the sore on his neck. Maybe he'd slept in his suit. He took Jack's arm and led him away, out of earshot of the thin joker. "Actually, I've been wanting to speak to you."

"I'd been hoping to see you, too." Jack ventured a smile. "I wanted to thank you for the other day. You maybe saved me from getting hurt, making me light that way."

"I'm glad I was able to be of assistance." Hiram glanced over his shoulder at the joker and gave a nervous smile. He turned back to Jack. "I wanted to tell you something," he said. His tone sent a little warning signal down Jack's spine. Whatever was coming, Jack knew he didn't really want to hear it.

"Sure," he said.

"I wanted to say that I understand now," Hiram said. His voice was leaden. "That you were right when you said that you didn't know till you've been tested."

"Oh," said Jack. He didn't want to hear this confession. Whatever Jack was, whatever he'd done, he didn't want anyone else's sins rattling around in his own head. He had trouble enough coping with his own.

"When I was attacking you the other day," Hiram went on, "I was really attacking myself. I was trying to deny my own betrayals."

"Yeah." Jack just wanted Hiram and his soap opera to leave. What kind of betrayal could someone like Hiram pull off, anyway? Buy second-rate cuts of veal for his restaurant?

Hiram looked at him, eyes bright, as if he was expecting some kind of wisdom from Jack, some way to handle this burden of self-knowledge. Jack didn't have much to give.

"You can't change the past, Hiram," Jack said. "You can maybe make the future a little better. We've done that, I think, with what we've done in the last week."

"*Hiram.*" The joker was looking at them with his blank eye sockets. Jack had the uneasy feeling he was being scrutinized. "It's time to go."

"Yes. Of course." Hiram was panting for breath, as if the conversation had somehow exhausted him.

"See you around, maybe," Jack said.

Hiram turned without a word and headed back to pick up the suitcase. Either it held nothing, or Hiram had made it light.

A giddy wave of paranoia struck Jack at the sight of Hiram hefting the huge suitcase and heading for the big revolving doors. Suppose *Blaise* . . .

But no. The suitcase was big, Jack realized, but not big enough to hold a teenage boy.

The events of the last few days had made him jumpy.

1:00 P.M.

Even with the medication, Puppetman could feel Tony Calderone's pain. It tasted spicy. He tweaked it, just for the pleasure. Tony grimaced and jumped slightly in his bed, joggling the laptop on his food tray. His face went visibly pale.

"You okay?" Gregg asked, ignoring Puppetman's interior laughter.

"Just a twinge, Senator. No big deal." His denial was belied by the sweat on his forehead. Puppetman giggled.

Now leave him alone. We have to work.

No problem, Greggie. It just feels so good to be free again. We've put it all together. It's all ours now.

"I've been thinking about the speech, Senator," Tony was saying. "I think I've come up with the catch phrase we've been looking for. I was looking through all the old speeches. You remember what you said in Roosevelt Park when you declared that you were running?"

That brought back memories—it hadn't been long after that speech that he'd had Kahina killed in front of Chrysalis and Downs to guarantee their silence about his ace. *That certainly worked well*, Gregg thought ironically.

But it did, Puppetman insisted. *It kept things quiet through the campaign. Tachyon found out too late. It's all taken care of now.*

I suppose . . . "What phrase where you thinking of, Tony?" Gregg asked the speechwriter.

Tony punched a key and read the words on the LCD screen. "'There are other masks than those Jokertown has made famous.' Your own line, too, if I recall, and a good one. 'Behind that mask is an infection that's all too human . . . I want to rip the mask off and expose the true ugliness behind, the ugliness of hatred.'" Tony tapped the screen. "That's a powerful image. I think it's time we built on it."

"Sounds fine to me. What have you got in mind?"

"I've been working along those lines since last night. And I've had another thought." Tony grinned, and Gregg felt an upwelling of pulsing yellow—Tony was proud of this one. He pushed the laptop aside and sat up straighter in the bed. His fingertips drummed on his thigh in excitement.

"What if we had everyone wearing masks: you, Jesse, everyone on stage and all our delegates out in the audience? Jokers, aces, and nats, every last one masked so you can't tell the difference. Then, when you hit the right line—" Tony closed his eyes, thinking. "I don't know, something along the lines of, 'It's time for all of us to remove our masks, the masks of prejudice, of hatred, of intolerance' but stronger, much stronger, and with a lot of buildup. And just as you say it, *boom*, everyone rips off their mask and tosses it in the air."

Gregg chuckled. He turned the scene over in his mind. "I like it. I think I like it a lot."

"It's hot. It's a guaranteed spot on every channel. Can you see it, all those masks in the air? Man, you talk about an *image*. It rivets the wild card issue in every voter's mind, and Bush is going to have a hell of a time getting drama like that at the Republican Convention."

Gregg slapped the bed sheets and stood up. "We'll run with it. You start working on the speech; I'll get together with Amy, John, and Devaughn and get this coordinated with our people. Tony, this is good. When you have a full draft, send it up to Ellen's room. I've got the modem on the Compaq set up."

"You got it, Senator," Tony grinned.

"The public's never going to forget what happens tonight, Tony. Get cracking; we don't have much time."

Gregg was grinning as he left the room. Tachyon was out of the picture, the nomination was wrapped up, and now the perfect image for the coming campaign. He was so pleased he didn't even listen to Puppetman's whining for just one last taste of Tony's pain.

3:00 P.M.

"Although there was a small portion of the carpus remaining, I chose to amputate a few inches farther back on the radius."

Dr. Robert Benson's method of delivery was dry in the extreme. *No bedside manner at all*, thought Tachyon, staring with sick horror at the ungainly lump of bandages swathing his right arm. *Perhaps he thinks I can take it being a physician myself . . . Well, he's wrong.*

His arm throbbed in time to the beating of his heart. Tach glanced up at the IV mechanically clicking fluids into his body. They had inserted the needle into the big vein on the back of his left hand. *Good, they noticed I was right-handed. . . . no stupid, no right hand to put it in*. He gagged.

"Feeling nauseous?" Benson held a basin under his chin. "That's natural, the aftereffects of the anesthesia."

"I . . . know. How . . . long . . . what time?"

"Oh, time. A little after three on Sunday."

"So . . . long."

"Yes, physically you're very run down, and the massive shock and blood loss," he shrugged.

"I'm hurting."

"I'll send in a nurse with another shot."

"I'm very allergic to codeine. Use morphine or—"

"Doctors make the worst patients. Always trying to take over their own treatment." But Benson smiled as he made a notation on the record. "Go back to sleep."

Tach felt his lower lip trembling. "My hand."

"From what I've seen of the news clips you're lucky to have gotten off so lightly."

"Doctor." Benson paused at the door, looked back. "Don't tell them."

Benson scratched his chin. "About the virus, you mean?"

"Yes."

"I won't."

Eyes closed, Tachyon evaluated his condition. The painful throat from the endotrachial tube, the overall sense of disorientation from the anesthesia, a painfully distended bladder, and, overriding all, the thundering pain from his mangled arm. The phantom fingers of his right hand twitched convulsively.

If he were at home, he could have a hand regrown in a matter of weeks. But would the wild card virus now twined lovingly in his DNA permit a normal growth? Or would it place some horror at the end of his arm?

It seemed the final and ultimate irony that he, who had killed his own kin attempting to prevent the release of the virus and spent forty years laboring among its victims as a means of atonement, should be forced to suffer so much.

"Just manifest and get it over with!" he cried aloud. Tears ran hotly into the hair at his temples, and matted in his sideburns.

The virus maintained its smug silence.

4:00 P.M.

When Jack stepped into Tachyon's hospital room, he saw the red-haired alien writhing on the bed, clutching his stump.

"Jesus," Jack muttered, and walked fast to the bed. "What just happened?"

"I keep reaching for things with my right hand." Limply.

"Call the nurse. Put your stump in a sling, help you remember."

"Yeah, yeah, yeah." Still cradling his stump.

Jack reached for a cigarette and lit up. "You want me to call the nurse, get you a shot?"

"No." Tachyon's mouth was a thin line.

Jack blew smoke at him. "People think *I'm* a macho asshole. They haven't dealt with Takisian princes, that's all." He glanced around the room. "Has Blaise been here today? I've been sort of looking for him. I want to make sure he's okay."

"I have not seen him." Worry crossed Tachyon's features.

"Someone saw him with Jay Ackroyd. That detective guy who zapped that freak away before I could pound him."

"And saved my life, from all reports," Tachyon pointed out. His left hand touched his stump. "If Blaise is unsupervised he could get into trouble."

"Precisely my thought."

Tachyon's manner turned imperious again. "Find my grandchild, Jack."

"I'll try."

Tachyon sat up, pointed with his good hand at the closet. "Get my clothes, will you?"

Jack looked at the alien in surprise. "Tach, don't worry. I'll find him."

"I must go to the convention."

Jack laughed nervously. "It's all over. You don't have to go anywhere."

Tachyon froze, his violet eyes wide. "What do you mean?"

Jack gave a sigh. "No one's told you, huh?"

"*What happened?*"

Jack hesitated. He didn't want to get into this. He took a long drag of smoke, tried to get it over with fast. "Gregg and Jesse cut a deal. Jackson withdrew and threw his support to Gregg. Gregg's got the nomination, Jackson will be veep."

"No." Tachyon's eyes dilated in horror. "No, no, no."

Impatience rattled through Jack's mind. "Will you stop worrying about Gregg's stability, for heaven's sake? He put this whole deal together. He's on top of things, okay? Even with all these aces gunning after him."

"*No! No! No!*" A jolt of horror ran through Jack as Tachyon raised his right arm high, then brought his stump smashing down on the railing of his bed. The stump smashed down again and again.

Jack dropped his cigarette and grabbed Tach's arms. He wrestled the thrashing alien back to the mattress, held him till he calmed down. "What the hell's the matter with you?"

Tachyon just glared at him.

The thought struck Jack with the force of a hurricane. Suddenly he felt as if he were blown off his feet, whirled away into darkness, carried off somewhere without light, without security, without hope.

"Gregg, right?" he said. "Gregg's the secret ace."

Tachyon just looked away.

"Talk to me, damn it!"

"I cannot."

Jack's knees felt as if they wouldn't support him. He lurched backward, groping for a chair, and sat down. His cigarette was smoldering on the floor and he picked it up, took a long drag. A tentative, fragile calm descended on him.

"Tell me, Tach," he said. "I need to know. I need to know if I fucked up again."

Tachyon closed his eyes. "It no longer matters, Jack."

"The one thing I do right. The one thing I do right in years, and—" Jack looked in surprise at the cigarette he had just crushed in his hand. He looked for some place to put it, found none, shrugged, dusted it off onto the floor.

"Tach," Jack said. "I need to know this. I got Gregg nominated, never mind how I did it. I need to know whether I did good or not."

Tachyon's eyes were still closed. Jack looked at him in rising anger.

"Are we going to have to play twenty questions here, Tach?"

Tachyon said nothing.

"Is Gregg a secret ace?"

No answer.

"Sara Morgenstern accused Gregg of being a killer. Is that true?"

Nothing.

"The little freak who tried to kill Sara. Does he work for Gregg?"

The last words were a shout. Tachyon just lay there, his eyes closed. Finally he spoke.

"Go away. It's over. There's nothing we can do."

Rage blazed in Jack's mind. He rose from his chair, lunged over the bed to shout in the alien's face. "You're so arrogant," he said. "You're such a goddamn prince. *You* say it's over, so it's over. *You* say that people should stop supporting Hartmann, and you give no reason, but they're supposed to go along with you because you're a Takisian prince and you know better than anyone else. Has it ever occurred to you that if you'd just fucking *condescended* to tell some of us lowly Earth scum about Gregg, we might have managed to put the brakes to his campaign without getting Barnett elected? Instead you just *ordered* me to deliver California to Jackson, and expected me to say, *Yeah, your lordship, whatever you say.*" Jack shook his fist in front of Tachyon's closed eyes. "Has it ever occurred to you that maybe you can *trust* a human being now and again? Has it?"

No answer.

"Damn you anyway!"

Tachyon said nothing. Jack turned and bolted the room like a runaway locomotive. His rage fueled his long stride out of the hospital, down the corridor, out into a blazing, humid afternoon that seemed to suck the anger right out of his body.

He headed vaguely toward the Omni. He really didn't have anywhere to go. He didn't know what to do about Hartmann, and Blaise could be on this particular street as well as anywhere.

If only the goddamn alien had trusted us, Jack thought.

Then it occurred to him that maybe it was he, Jack, years ago, who had taught Tachyon not to trust anyone, not with anything that mattered.

That thought depressed him all the way home.

The speech was set, protocol for the evening's speeches had been set with Devaughn and Jackson's staff, Gregg had called the other candidates personally and asked each of them to join him on the campaign road in their home states. Dukakis and Gore had been politely enthusiastic, congratulating him on the victory and promising their help to unify the party. Only Barnett had been cool, as Gregg had expected.

To hell with him. We'll take him as a puppet and play with him the next time we meet.

Ellen was sleeping. Calderone's latest version of the acceptance speech was in the Compaq waiting for him. He could hear Colin, the joker Secret Service who had replaced Alex James, scuffing his feet outside the room.

Gregg kissed Ellen, saw her eyes flutter open. "I'm going back to the hotel and meet with Logan and a few others," he whispered. Ellen nodded sleepily.

Gregg packed the Compaq into its bag and collected Colin at the door. "Heading back to the Marriott," Colin said into his walkie-talkie. "Bring the car around to the side entrance. Get some people on the elevators."

On the first floor, Gregg heard a familiar voice at the desk. "Please, mister. Listen, they're for the senator's wife . . ."

Peanut. Puppetman stirred.

"Just a minute, Colin . . ." Gregg headed for the lobby, Colin relaying the change of plans to the others.

Peanut was holding a rather bedraggled but huge bouquet of flowers, trying to give it to the guard behind the desk. The man shook his head repeatedly, grimacing.

"What's the problem, Marvin?"

He'd met Marvin while wandering the hospital this morning. Marvin was a slow moving and lazy security guard, the butt of a dozen jokes Gregg had heard over the last few days from the doctors, the nursing staff, and the orderlies. They'd shaken hands in passing: Puppetman had sensed immediately Marvin's distaste for his job. In fact, there didn't seem much that Marvin liked at all, jokers least of all.

"He wants me to take the flowers up to your wife's room," Marvin growled, pulling at the belt slung underneath the overhang of belly. Marvin didn't like politicians either, especially Democrats. He eyed Colin's blue-suited athletic figure with contempt. "Looks like he got them outta some damn trash can, if you ask me."

Peanut was looking forlornly at Gregg, the moist eyes trapped in folds of hard, furrowed skin, the flowers drooping in his lone hand. Puppetman could feel the undiluted admiration swelling from the slow-witted joker, underlaid with a surprisingly deep sorrow for what had happened to Ellen.

"I'm really sorry to cause trouble, Senator," Peanut said. He looked as if he were about to cry, glancing from Gregg to Marvin to the impassive gaze of Colin. "I thought maybe she might like them . . . I know they ain't much, but . . ."

"They're very pretty," Gregg told him. "You're Peanut, aren't you?"

Pride swelled in Peanut at the recognition. He tried to smile, and skin cracked around the mouth. He nodded, shyly.

Gregg held his hand out for the flowers. "Marvin's overdoing his job," he said without looking at the guard. "No one needs protection from compassion and caring." Puppetman felt Marvin's cold rage at that, and Puppetman licked at the emotion eagerly, saturating it. "Ellen will be proud to have your flowers, Peanut," Gregg continued, holding out his hand. "I'll make sure she gets them. In fact, there's a space at the foot of her bed where she'll see them when she wakes up. I'll tell the nurse to put them there."

Peanut handed the flowers to Gregg. The joker's mind was glowing with yellow-white pride, overflowing with azure hero-worship. "Thank you, Senator," he blurted out, ducking his head. "Thank you. You . . . well, everyone out there loves you. We all know you'll win."

Gregg gave the flowers to Colin. He hugged Peanut for a moment, then smiled at Marvin. "I'm sure Marvin will be glad to get you a taxi to wherever you're going, won't you, Marvin?"

Ah, the hatred. Marvin's gaze was daggered. "Sure," he said. "No problem." He bit off the end of each word. "I'll take real good care of him."

"Good. Thank you again, Peanut, and thank you from Ellen. She'll love them." He glanced at his watch. "And I really need to be running. Peanut, it was good to see you again. Colin—"

They walked away.

Puppetman rode with Marvin.

Gregg closed his eyes in the back of the limo as they rode to the Marriott, relishing Marvin's fury and Peanut's pain as, behind the dumpster in the back of the hospital, the security guard beat the crap out of the joker.

It was a nice little snack.

6:00 P.M.

Spector had gone to Piedmont Park after leaving the Marriott. He just wandered around, unnoticed, among the jokers. He'd never seen so many happy freaks in all his life. They were singing, and hugging, and kissing each other. Those that could kiss, anyway. They must have been partying all night, since at least half of the crowd had found some shade to take a nap in. If they'd known what he was going to do, or try to do, later on, they'd have torn him into a thousand pieces.

He'd eventually gotten bored of it and walked over to Oakland Cemetery. He strolled around among the marble monuments and weathered headstones, reading the inscriptions on them and hoping for inspiration. But none came. He was just killing time, and he knew it.

He caught a cab and went to his motel, cleaned up, and took another cab to the hospital. He'd finished off the bottle of whiskey and bought another. He'd had a few slugs from it already, hoping to calm his nerves.

He walked up to the main desk and motioned to the woman behind it. She nodded and walked over. She was middle aged, slightly overweight, and had mousy brown hair in a tight bun. "What room is Dr. Tachyon in?" He flashed her his fake press card.

"Can't you leave that poor man alone?" she said, shaking her head.

"Sorry, lady. Your job's compassion; mine's the news." Spector put the card away. "You let me know his room number, and I won't try to stop you feeling sorry for him. Fair enough?"

"435," she said, lowering her eyes.

"Thanks," he said, turning away. "It's in the public interest, believe me."

The hospital was so completely different from the one Tony had been in, they might have been on different planets. The walls and floors were spotless. There was almost none of the disinfectant smell you normally got in hospitals, and no stink of jokers at all. There were paintings on the walls and the woman on the p.a. system sounded like something from a wet dream.

He stopped outside the room, made sure no one was

looking, and took another quick slug of whiskey. He shook his arms like an athlete loosening up, took a deep breath, and stepped inside.

What he saw almost made him laugh. Tachyon was facing away from him. He was wearing a blue hospital robe slit up the back and his little white ass was showing. He was holding a bedpan with his one good hand, and his prick was dangling over it. Nothing was happening. At the end of his other arm was a gauze-covered stump. Spector couldn't manage to be afraid of this pathetic little thing. He closed the door.

The crippled alien didn't even turn to look at him. "Please, just another few minutes. I know I can manage something. Maybe if you run some water for me."

"Turn it on yourself, Doc."

Tachyon jumped and quickly covered himself. "By the Ideal, have you no shred . . ." He turned and saw Spector, then closed his mouth and stared wide-eyed. "You!"

Spector walked quickly over to the bed and took away the little box used to summon a nurse. "You won't be needing this."

Tachyon turned away from Spector and tried to pull himself toward the far corner of the bed.

"Careful, you'll pull your IV out." Spector pointed to the tube that ended in a needle in the Takisian's arm. "I'm here for your help."

Tachyon shook his head in horror. "No. James, you mustn't. I can't allow it."

"Can't fucking allow it?" Spector kept his voice quiet, but there was no concealing the contempt. "If anybody deserves to die, it's Hartmann. I need you to mind-control some people and get me close. I'll do the rest."

"James, please," Tachyon still wouldn't meet his eyes. "I beg you . . . don't do this. An autopsy . . . the scandal." Tachyon gathered himself before continuing. "They would run mad. Hunt down every wild card. Quarantine them."

Spector wasn't going to waste his breath arguing. He reached down, grabbed Tachyon's stump, and squeezed. He put a hand over the Takisian's mouth to muffle the scream. Tachyon bit into his palm, drawing blood. Spector let go. "Watch this, Doc." He held his hand in front of Tachyon's face and watched the wound close over.

"Ancestors," Tachyon gasped.

"Don't know everything about me after all, do you? Now

show some guts for a fucking change. Do the autopsy yourself. Or mind-control the people who do. Use your goddamn power for something other than getting little hero-worshiping bitches to suck your alien weenie." Spector turned Tachyon loose and took a step back.

Tachyon shook his head. "You don't understand. Need rest. Peace." The little alien seemed on the edge of hysteria. "Only rest will be the peace of the grave."

It was the wrong thing for Tachyon to say and it pushed Spector over the edge. He slapped the alien hard, but not as hard as he wanted to. "You feel that? Well that's nothing compared to what I have to live with every minute of every day. For the rest of my life." Spector leaned in. "I killed a little girl once. Just to see her mother's face when she found her. And I thought of you." It was a lie, but Spector wanted to give the knife as many turns as he could. "If you don't help me, there'll be lots more. You owe me, Doc. Christ, what you did to me. You'll owe me forever."

"I'm sorry," Tachyon said, pulling the pillow over his head with his one good hand. "But I can't."

"I should have known." Spector got up and headed for the door, looked at the TV and stopped. Someone was interviewing the joker Secret Service guy who'd been in Tony's room.

"Then, all those on the podium during Senator Hartmann's acceptance speech will be wearing masks?" The reporter asking the question was standing as far away from Colin as he could.

The joker cleared his throat. "Yes, those are the senator's wishes. He feels it would make a certain statement to the American public."

"You, too?" the reporter asked.

"Yes, I've had occasion to wear them in the past." Colin looked like he wanted to take the reporter's head off. "Old habits die hard. And like most of us, I'm a creature of habit."

Tachyon groaned behind him, but Spector barely noticed. So, Tony had sold his boss on the mask idea. A group of masked people on stage was a whole new ball game. He might not even need the little creep.

Spector walked over and handed him the bedpan. "When I'm done with Hartmann, I'm coming after you."

He heard piss hitting the pan as he left the room.

Spector laughed. "Don't say I never did anything for you."

* * *

Tach lay on his side, the mangled arm propped on a pile of pillows. There was the strong smell of urine, and the sheets were damp beneath his hip. He had been shaking so hard that he had put most of his load in the bed. He tried to marshal his scattered thoughts.

Oh, Ideal, James Spector, the man who could literally kill with a look. I should have mind-controlled him . . . captured him. But I was scared.

He thought of what his father would have said to that admission. It would not have been kind. Princes in the House Ilkazam did not admit to fear.

James was going to kill Hartmann, and then there would be an autopsy, and then the world would end.

Too bad about Troll and Father Squid and Arachne and Spots and Video and Finn and Elmo—no, Elmo would miss the backlash against the wild cards. He was going to Attica for a murder he didn't commit, and Tach knew what they did to jokers in Attica. Too bad about all of them.

And him too.

Blaise was gone. Jail loomed ahead, for the investigation Hartmann had launched would live on after him. Didn't they still execute people for espionage? *And I had to become an American citizen.* But he would never see jail, Spector would kill him first.

He could always phone the Secret Service. Warn them about Spector. But then Hartmann becomes president. But was that so bad? *I could monitor him, control him perhaps.* Stupid! *He'll only kill me. He's tried already. He won't rest now until he succeeds.*

But the wild cards would be safe.

No, too many people knew. Jay and Jack and Hiram, Digger, Sara, George, and Spector. Hartmann would try to have them all killed, and in self-defense they would speak. And if the backlash would be horrendous now it would be unimaginable once the man was president.

I don't know what to do! Ideal, what should I do?

Nothing. He was too tired. Too miserable. Too sick.

He closed his eyes, and grimly went searching for the anesthesia of sleep. The pain killers lay like a blurring fog across his mind, but the pain ate through them like acid.

"It's not so bad. It doesn't hurt so bad. It'll be all right."

And—surprisingly—Tach agreed with the soft voice. He forced open gummy lids, and stared up into Josh Davidson's face.

"Hello. How are you feeling?"

"Better now. I thought everyone had abandoned me."

"Sometimes people get reminded of the obligations and duties of friendship." Davidson's nose wrinkled at the sour odor of urine.

"I wet the bed," said Tach miserable and embarrassed.

"Then we should get the bed changed. Let me help you." Davidson lowered the rail, got an arm around Tachyon's waist, and a grip on the IV unit, and helped him into a chair. "Wait, I'll be right back."

He returned moments later with a nurse. She stripped and remade the bed. Davidson seemed impatient for her to leave. The door swung shut behind her. The actor seated himself across the small table, reached into his coat pocket, and took out a pocket chess set.

"I thought we might have a quick game." He palmed a pawn of each color, hid them behind his back, then offered two closed fists to Tachyon.

Tach started to reach out with his right hand. Both men froze and stared at the gauze-covered stump. "Left," Tachyon said.

Davidson's fingers uncurled, revealing a black pawn. "Here, wait, I'll set it up for you." There was a catch in the actor's mellifluous voice.

Davidson opened pawn to king-four. They played a few moves in silence. Then Tachyon looked up. "The Evans gambit. That's a very old-fashioned opening," he said, shifting slightly because the vinyl on the chair was sticking to his bare bottom. "I had a friend who always used that opening."

"Oh?"

"No one you would know."

"What happened to him?"

"I don't know. He's gone now. Long gone. Like all the rest."

"Maybe not," said Davidson. Tach laid the tip of his left forefinger on the knight. "You don't want to do that. The bishop would be better," the actor murmured.

The alien switched pieces, and . . .

"David! David! DavidDavidDavidDavidDavid."

The IV drip had ripped from his hand as he threw himself on the man opposite him. And his weakness betrayed him. He could not keep his feet. David Harstein caught him beneath the armpits, and they huddled on the floor.

The tweed coat was rough against his skin. Catching on the stubble that littered his cheeks. He was wailing like a three-year-old, but he couldn't stop. David's hand was softly stroking his curly hair.

"Hush. It's all right now."

And of course it was because such had been the Envoy's power.

"Oh, David, you've come back to me."

"Only for a little while, Tach." The Takisian stiffened. "I'm old, Tachy. Someday I'll die." They sat silent for a few moments then David shook off the mood and said, "Let's get you back to bed."

"No, no, this is fine. Talk to me. Tell me everything. Those beautiful, beautiful girls—yours?"

"Yeah, I'm pretty proud of them."

"Do they know?"

"Yes, my family's been a pillar for me. I was so bitter when I got out of prison. The government tried to *recruit* me for their covert ace operations." The mobile mouth twisted. "I ran, and David Harstein died, and Josh Davidson was born. I had a new identity, but all the old hate remained. Then I met Rebecca. She took away the hurt. They've never betrayed me." The man's dark eyes were thoughtful and distant.

"Jack is . . . What I mean is he has . . ."

"It's all right, Tach. Braun and I have found common ground, to quote our vice-presidential nominee. And Braun reminded me that maybe we do have an obligation." He paused considering for a long moment. "Last night, when we all thought you were going to die, I realized that just knowing you resided in the same world with me was a strange kind of anchor. A comfort. Rebecca reminded me that . . . well, that knowing I was alive might be a comfort to you."

"It is," Tachyon sighed, taking a tighter grip on David's lapel.

"I've spent thirty years admiring and envying those aces who had the courage to use their powers," Harstein mused.

"You had the courage."

"Yes, but not the wisdom."

"That is always the problem, is it not?"

"What are you thinking?" the Envoy asked as he studied that thin chiseled face.

"Which is the most important, David? Love, honor, courage, duty?"

"Love," said the actor promptly.

Tach patted his cheek. "Gentle one."

"And for you?"

"Honor and duty. I must get to the Omni, David. Will you help me?"

"Tachyon, you're in no condition."

"I know that, but needs must . . ."

"Will you tell me why?"

"I cannot. Will you help me?"

"What a question."

7:00 P.M.

Spector hid behind the bed and hoped what Colin had said about being a creature of habit was true. Hastings' body was still in the shower. You couldn't really smell it until you were in the bathroom. Obviously, the maids had only peeked in while making their rounds, or they would have found it. Spector checked his watch. It was right at 7:00 P.M. If the joker was late, or didn't show at all, he'd have to hustle to get over to the convention hall. He'd bought a mask of his own, but was afraid it might not match the others.

He heard soft footfalls stop in front of the door. Spector crouched down behind the bed. The door opened. Shut. He heard someone sniffing the air. Spector stuck his head up. The joker was reaching for his gun. Spector made eye contact and pushed hard. Colin's legs folded up underneath him and he made a strangled little noise, then he fell over dead.

Spector had tried to make it quick. The brief conversation he'd had with the joker didn't give him any cause to dislike the guy. He was just in the wrong place at the wrong time. As Spector kneeled next to the body, he noticed something that he'd missed before. Colin's hair had a pronounced oily sheen. It definitely wasn't hair dressing, and more likely was just a by-product of his being a joker. Spector had washed his own hair earlier in the day and it was dry as a bone. He rubbed his hands over the corpse's head, then through his own hair. After repeating the procedure a few times Spector's hair had the same look as Colin's. Also, unfortunately, the same litter-box smell.

Spector rifled the body. Colin was carrying ID, a gun, an earpiece, and even a mask. Spector thought back to the beginning of the week in the dusty mask factory. It seemed more like a month.

He pulled off the joker's clothes and then his own. A few minutes later he was ready. The suit was a little loose and the gun strap tugged uncomfortably at his shoulder, but he'd live with it. He went into the bathroom and put on the mask, then stepped back from the mirror and looked at himself. It was close to perfect. The oily hair really made the difference.

He carefully dragged the joker's body to the shower stall and dumped it on top of Hastings. He wouldn't want to be the maid who finally got to clean the place up.

The vacant hall behind the podium reverberated to a low-Richter earthquake. Outside in the basketball court the crowd was working itself into a final frenzy, with a lot of help from Hartmann's little gnomes.

The fools, Sara thought. Her breath ricocheted off the inside of the egret-feather mask and rattled in her ears. *It's like some kind of fairy tale: they're about to proclaim their new king, and never suspect that behind that smiling mask he's a demon from Hell*.

The stocky man in the blue coveralls with the NBC logo on the right breast and ROBO TEAM block-lettered across the back held up her VIP pass for her approval. It bore a fictitious name and a photograph. In the feeble light drizzling from far away, overhead, she could make out a face framed by white-blonde hair. The face wasn't hers. It was a joker face, the kind calculated to keep even the hardest-core ex-Special Forces jock in a Secret Service monkey suit from peeking beneath the mask to make sure the real thing matched the photo.

She had read enough le Carré not to be surprised. "George Steele" was a high-ranking KGB agent, after all; he would have his resources, and it was obvious this attempt to derail Hartmann was no spur-of-the-moment affair. She nodded. He pinned the pass to the front of her white dress.

"Now," he said, stooping to where an NBC minicam lay

tipped to its side, "are you certain you want to go through with this?"

The minicam opened. Its printed-circuit guts had been partially scooped out to make room for a compact Heckler & Koch P7 pistol. Dim highlights perched uncertainly on black steel.

He picked it up, pinched the slide back to examine the chamber, then jacked a round in. "You remember what I showed you? The three dots line up with the target sitting on them as if they were a table. The weapon will not fire unless you make sure to switch off the safety here at the side and squeeze the other safety at the back of the grip."

She nodded, impatient. "I remember. I used to shoot a .22 as a kid. Colt Woodsman. It belonged to my cousin."

"Nine millimeter does a fair amount of damage but has little shocking power. I suggest you keep firing until the target goes down."

Or until the Secret Service boys nail me. She held her hand out. He passed the pistol to her. She slipped it into her white patent-leather purse and carefully fastened the clasp.

"World peace depends upon your going through with this," he said.

Her eyes found his and held them. "Avenging Andi depends on my going through with this. And Sondra Fallin, and Kahina, and Chrysalis. And me."

He stood facing her as if feeling he should say something and unsure of what. She stood on tiptoe, gently kissed his cheek. He turned and quickly walked away.

She watched him go. *The poor thing. He thinks he's using me.*

Funny how naive a spy master can be.

The feeder hall was virtually deserted. Anyone who could possibly cram into the deep bowl of the Omni was inside cheering the conclusion of Jackson's vice-presidential speech. Tachyon heard the sound of the crowd as a vast deep-throated roaring. *A surging beast, and I'm walking in its maw,* he thought.

David had gently dressed him, but sliding that mangled arm through the sleeves of shirt and coat had drenched him in cold sweat. While David had talked them past the nurse, Tach had palmed pain killers from the evening medication tray. He had dry swallowed them in the taxi, but they hadn't taken effect yet, and he found he could hardly stand.

The agent on the door was eyeing the pair skeptically. The slender, dark older man, his arm tightly about the Takisian's waist. Tach presented his press pass.

"There's no room in there, Doctor." He eyed Harstein suspiciously. "Where's your pass?"

"I don't have one. He's the one who needs to get in."

"There are no seats available."

"That's all right. I'll stand."

"I can't let you, it's a fire hazard. Go over to the Congress Center. You can watch on the big-screen TV."

Tachyon fought down a wave of dizziness and nausea. Ran a hand across his clammy face, and felt the scratch of stubble against his palm.

"Please," he whispered, and cuddled his mutilated arm to his chest.

"I think it would be a very good idea if you let him in," said David softly. "How much harm can it do? He's one small man."

"Yeah," said the guard hesitantly.

"He left the hospital just to be here for this moment. I know you'd like to help him."

"Oh, all right. What the hell. Go on in."

Tachyon squeezed Harstein's shoulder hard with his left hand. "David, don't disappear again."

"I'll be waiting."

8:00 P.M.

Spector was sweating buckets. Getting onto the podium had been no problem. Making himself stay there was. The convention hall was huge, much bigger than he'd imagined, seeing it on TV. Thousands of people, millions if you counted the TV audience, would be looking in his direction. He peered at the lighted network booths and strained to see if he could recognize Connie Chung, or Dan Rather, or what's-his-name from CNN. It kept his mind occupied enough to keep his feet planted on the stage.

Jesse Jackson was speaking, his powerful voice rising and falling in his usual Southern preacher style. Jackson's nomination as VP was obviously the price Hartmann had paid to get him to drop out of the presidential contest.

Spector couldn't see any way to get at Hartmann while he was on stage. Better to wait until he was escorting the senator back to his hotel and let him have it then. He could run off to telephone an ambulance and slip away. Everyone would be too caught up in the moment to miss him. Then it would be back to Jersey and a little peace and quiet.

He just had to bide his time.

"It was all my idea. People are saying the campaign came up with it, but the whole thing was my call." Jack gave a theatrical sigh. "I was wrong, but it seemed like a good idea at the time."

The newscasters were filling time with celebrity interviews. Below the CBS skybooth, the convention was humming, awaiting the candidate. Half of them seemed to be masked.

Jack smiled ruefully into Walter Cronkite's crinkled eyes. "It all seemed to fit together. All the wild card violence—and remember, I was attacked twice myself—it all seemed aimed at hindering Senator Hartmann's candidacy and promoting the Reverend Barnett's. When I saw Barnett personally, I saw how charismatic he is. With people like Nur-al-Allah in the world—remember, he's another charismatic religious leader who happens to be a wild card—I just jumped to the wrong conclusion."

"So you are satisfied that there are no wild cards in the Barnett camp?"

Jack offered a practiced, cynical smile. "If they're there, they're well-hidden." He laughed, disingenuous. "They'd have to be, Walter."

Behind Cronkite a couple dozen video monitors showed the cameras panning the convention. People waved signs, danced, laughed behind their masks. Sweating men in headphones busied themselves over consoles.

Cronkite seemed in an easy, conversational mood, hardly the hard-ass reporter right now. Still, his question stung. "Do you think you should apologize to the Barnett campaign?"

Jack gave another patent smile. "I already have, Walter. I delivered a personal apology to Fleur van Renssaeler yesterday afternoon." He tightened the smile, looked into the camera. *Take that, Fleur*, he thought.

"So how do you feel now that Gregg Hartmann has finally won the nomination?"

Jack stared into the camera and felt his smile freeze. "I think," he said carefully, "that I messed up a few too many times to feel happy with much of anything, Walter."

Cronkite put an over-the-audio speaker in his ear, listened for a moment, then looked up and said, "I understand the candidate is about to speak. Thank you, Jack, and we'll switch now to Dan Rather and Bob Scheiffer."

The red light on the camera went off. The crowd was roaring, cheering, on their feet.

Jack wished with all his heart that he could cheer with them.

For a long moment Tachyon was disoriented. Then he spotted the California banner, and he knew where he was. The speakers podium thrust like the prow of a ship into the crowded hall. On its various tiers and levels stood the great and powerful.

Claw-like his hand closed on a man's shoulder, and he forced the reporter aside.

"Hey, asshole! Watch out."

"Move," Tach snarled, and pushed past him. Deeper into the crowd. Searching for a clear view.

". . . THE NEXT PRESIDENT OF THE UNITED STATES . . ." The words finally penetrated Tachyon's haze. ". . . GREGG HARTMANN!"

The fifteen-thousand people in the Omni erupted. The band blared out "Stars and Stripes Forever." Cheers, screams, whistles. Balloons floated down to be batted aside by wildly swinging Hartmann signs. Tachyon shuddered under the assault of sound and the proximity of so many people.

His aching eyes focused on the podium. Gregg grinning, waving, linking hands with Jackson. Ellen, wan and drawn in a wheelchair at his side, smiling. Suddenly what had been only a peripheral bit of information penetrated. *Eighty percent of the people in the Omni wore masks*. What had been a merely hopeless task had now become impossible. There was no way by ships or stars that he could locate James Spector in time to prevent the killing.

He wept while all around him the crowd screamed.

* * *

". . . the next president of the United States, Gregg Hartmann!"

The crowd went wild out in the Omni. Green-and-gold Hartmann signs waved back and forth as the band played. The nets on the ceiling rained balloons down on the cheering delegates.

Puppetman was nearly in orgasm. The pent-up emotions of the long week were being released in one huge celebration, and the sheer tidal force of it was staggering. Gregg took off his clown's mask and stepped forward onto the speaker's platform, raising his arms in victory; they shouted back to him fiercely, the noise almost deafening. He had to shout to Jesse to come forward with him. They clasped hands, raised them waving to the people, and the cheering redoubled, drowning out the band, making the Omni shake with the thunderous acclamation.

It was glorious. It was ecstasy.

The ovation went on for long minutes. Gregg waved, raised his hands, nodded. He saw Jack Braun up in the CBS booth with Cronkite, pointed and smiled, giving him a thumbs-up salute. He kissed Ellen, in a wheelchair at the rear of the podium. He grinned at Devaughn, at Logan, at everyone. Behind their masks, he knew they were all smiling back at him.

We did it! The power in him was drunk with the adulation. *It's all ours, everything.*

Gregg could only grin helplessly in agreement.

All ours.

When they finally quieted slightly, he stepped to the podium. He looked up at the packed stands, at the shoulder-to-shoulder mob on the floor. Many of them were in masks, joining with those on the platform.

"Thank you, every last one of you," he said huskily, and they roared again. He raised his hands; the cheering softened. It felt good, being able to do that.

"This has been the hardest struggle of my life," he continued. "But Ellen and I never gave up hope. We trusted in the judgment of all of you out there, and you haven't let us down."

The chant was sweeping across the convention floor:

"Hartmann! Hartmann!" A wave, a torrent, it swept them all up. *"Hartmann! Hartmann!"* Gregg shook his head in feigned modesty, letting it all wash over him and grinning down at them.

"Hartmann! Hartmann!"

And the grin suddenly went frozen on his face.

Somehow, Mackie was down there in the front ranks of the crowd, grinning like all the rest, a hunchbacked boy-man dressed all in black and leather. A chill rattled down Gregg's spine.

It's okay, Puppetman murmured inside his head. *It's okay. I can control him.* But Gregg shivered, and when he leaned toward the microphones again, his voice had lost some of its enthusiasm.

Forging across the floor between delirious delegates in white plastic straw-like hats with HARTMANN emblazoned on them, Mackie felt as if he were made of air. He never felt any different when he went insubstantial—phased out—but if he did this was how he might feel. As if he was just going to diffuse like a cloud at any moment.

He hadn't slept last night, wedged in between a pair of stinking winos on the bus from the New York Port Authority. The business-suit pervo, with a taste for the slightly bizarre, who'd picked him up in Times Square had obviously realized the kind of love he was looking for was expensive to come by in the age of AIDS hysteria; he was carrying quite a roll of cash in his pocket. Even after Mackie had peeled away the blood-stained hundred on the outside there was more than enough for a plane ticket. But he hadn't dared take a plane. They might be watching the airports for him; he'd let himself be seen three times now.

Der Mann would be very disappointed.

He was up there on the podium now. A tropism of love and contrition drew Mackie to him. He was not supposed to approach Hartmann in public. He would not. He just needed the nearness of him.

He pushed out from under the array of press boxes, hanging over the packed court like the Death Star. Eel-like he flowed between shouting men with strained shirt buttons and fat women in pastel dresses, every face shining with sweat and grease and greed for the spoils of the love feast of capitalism.

The spectacle would have disgusted and intimidated him had he any room in his mind for thoughts that weren't of Hartmann. Of love and duty and failure.

The podium rose before him like a blue Rhine castle. He didn't see the Man yet, but the man on stage was talking about him. He looked to the wings, trying to catch sight of Hartmann.

White motion took his eye. Tiers of VIP boxes rose either side of the podium like layers of a wedding cake. A diminutive figure in a white dress was excusing its way past seated dignitaries on the level to the left of and even with the podium. It wore a flamboyant bird mask of white feathers that gleamed like silver under the lights.

He started to think, *filthy joker cunt*. Then he realized what had drawn his attention.

The way she moved. He could always recognize a person by posture, the way she carried herself, the way her limbs and body acted together. He could always pick his mother, the bitch, out of a mob of Sankt Pauli whores by her walk.

Now he recognized Sara Morgenstern, who had greater claim on him than any woman since his mother died.

Joyous fury bubbling within him, he began to force his way through the mob. He would not fail his man again. Or her.

Hartmann was speaking. The crowd, chanting his name, would barely let him get a word in edgewise. Jack wandered around the CBS skybooth and tried to stay out of everyone's way.

The monitors showed a crowd going mad. Jack watched and wondered what he could do.

He could tell people. But he'd had a chance just now, and he couldn't.

He couldn't be the Judas Ace again. He couldn't start a new round of persecutions.

He reached for a cigarette, and then he saw the leather boy on one of the monitors.

He couldn't mistake the slight, hunchbacked figure, not even behind the mask. The puny body and arrogant, jerky walk was an unmistakable combination. "Hey!" Jack said. A surge of adrenaline almost knocked him off his feet. He jumped forward just as the freak walked off camera. "That's the killer!" He jabbed a finger at the monitor. "Right here! Where's that camera pointing?"

The director looked at him with fury in his eyes. "Will you get—"

"Call the Secret Service! That's the chainsaw killer! *He's on the convention floor!*"

"What—"

"Where's that camera pointed, goddamn it?"

"Uh—Camera Eight? That's on the right side of the podium . . ."

"Damn!" The freak was right under the candidates.

Jack looked around frantically. The commentators, deep into their zen, had yet to hear his panicked shouts.

"Camera Eight." This from the director. "Pan left and right. Ready Eight? Cut Eight."

Jack jumped up on the desk in front of Cronkite and lashed out with a foot. The safety glass on the front of the skybooth bulged outward, a network of cracks appearing around Jack's foot. A startled Cronkite wheeled back on his desk chair, barking out oaths sea-dog style, as Jack put his foot through the safety glass, then punched out to widen the hole.

The beams supporting the Omni Center's ceiling were just in front and overhead. Jack jumped, caught an I-beam with both hands. He moved hand-over-hand along the beam toward the podium. This was going to take forever. He swung back, forward, pushed himself off, flew from one supporting beam to the next.

He'd done this for years on NBC. The old Tarzan reflexes came back without thought.

There was sudden commotion. Hartmann's speech had been interrupted. He was too late.

As Gregg Hartmann strode forward through torrents of applause, Sara deliberately moistened her lips. *How confidently he walks. He thinks he's a god.*

But there were no gods any more. Just men and women, some with more power than any mortal could safely use.

The purse fell open beneath numbed fingers as if of its own accord. She reached a gloved hand inside. The metal and checked rubber of the grip were cool fire, burning her fingers.

"Andi," she whispered. She drew the pistol. Letting her purse dangle from her forearm by one strap she raised the weapon both-handed.

* * *

Mackie was practically running through the close-packed delegates, using cattle-prod buzzes of his elbows to well-padded rumps to clear a path, phasing out when he had to. He'd do Sara fucking Morgenstern on nationwide TV, fuck her right straight through the heart with his good right hand. *Der Mann* would be so proud.

He felt pressure in the armpits and then his feet paddled air as he was hoisted off the floor by the collar of his leather jacket. "Not so fuckin' fast, joker," a voice grated in his ear.

Squirming, he was turned around into a blast of booze-and-tobacco breath. His captor was a large man in a bone-white jumpsuit, with black hair hanging into his face. It was a strange sort of face. It looked as if it had been busted into its component parts and hastily super-glued back together. The nose was a mangled mass, the cheekbones mismatched, and the green eyes burned at different angles.

"You better not fuck with me, goddamn you!" Mackie screeched, half-blind with fury. "I'm goddamn not a joker! I'm Mack the Knife!"

The big man winced from the shower of angry spittle. "You look like Jack the Shit to me, Junior. Now let's you and me and my good right hand go somewhere for a little talk, nice and private like—"

Mackie lashed out with his own right hand.

His fingertips touched the knobbed right cheekbone with a noise and smell like a dentist's drill going into a tooth. They slashed through cheek and lip and bone, cutting away half the lower jaw at a slant. Nude teeth grinned at him a millisecond before washing out in a rush of blood. The big man dropped him and clapped both hands to the spurting ruin of his face.

Mackie turned back to the podium. A woman with orange-dyed hair stood in his path, her mouth a tunnel right down to her belly. He hacked her out of his way like an explorer taking a machete to an inconvenient branch.

Der Mann would have to understand. There was no time for subtlety any more.

She hadn't expected the screams so soon. She was betting her vengeance—since her life was forfeit anyway—that every eye in the Omni would be locked on the podium as Gregg began his speech. But no one in the VIP seats nearby showed any sign of being aware of her. The three dots of the sights rose before her eyes like fat white moons seeking auspicious alignment.

Peripheral vision betrayed her. There was a commotion amid the Mississippi delegation, right up front of the podium. For all her efforts to see nothing but Hartmann and the rising moons, her eyes flicked briefly in that direction.

She felt the strength puff from her like air from a burst balloon. *He* had come. The leather kid. Slashing a bloody swath through the crowd, straight for her.

Hartmann was speaking. Mesmerized, Tachyon watched the movement of the mouth and heard not a word. Overlaid upon the plain familiar features was another face—bloated, dissipated, evil—Puppetman leered down at him.

Sickened, he dropped his gaze. Stared blankly at his stump. His thoughts chased one another like swirling leaves.

Have to stop him.

How?

Have to do something.

What?

Must think.

Have to stop him.

How?

How?

How?

Screams cut into the words of the candidate, the cheers of the crowd. Thin, like a trickle of blood pushing into healthy tissue. Spreading now, becoming a hemorrhage. The reporters surrounding Tachyon sensed that something was happening. They began to lurch forward, carrying Tach with them. They came up against a wall of fleeing humanity. Delegates, mouths wide with terror, running for the exits.

The world narrowed to thrashing arms, the stench of fear. Tachyon's shields reeled under the onslaught of fifteen-thousand people reacting in either terror or confusion.

A burly man, the buttons that covered his chest chattering like castanets, caromed into the tiny alien. Tach screamed, a shrill tearing sound as the bandages covering his amputation caught on the man's belt buckle, and he was yanked after him. He lost his footing and went down, the bandage tearing free.

Feet pounded across Tachyon's back driving the breath from his chest. He felt his cracked ribs give. A red-hot poker had been driven into his chest. Driving deeper with every breath he took.

But it was nothing compared to the agony of his arm as terrified humans ran over him, their heels grinding the stump into the floor of the Omni.

I am going to die. Terror lay thick and choking on the back of his tongue. A tiny thread of fury shot through him. *No! I am damned if I will die in this humiliating fashion. Trampled by hysterical groundlings.*

It took all his concentration to think through the suffocating blanket of pain. Braun's mind was a familiar glow in the midst of madness. His power lashed out, nestled close like a homing bird returning to a place of safety. He read the confusion and hesitation in the big ace's mind.

Jack, save me!
Tach?
Help me! Help me!

He couldn't hold the contact any longer. With a sigh he dropped away.

But Jack was coming.

A freight-train weight smashed into Mackie from behind. It drove his right hand, held like a spearhead at the end of his stiffened arm, right into the chest of a man with a pink shirt and beige tie. Irresistible, the mass forced him onward, down. His hand exploded out of the man's ribcage in a welter of blood. He hit the floor. His head rebounded off hardwood, and he felt something snap in his chest.

Squealing with rage and pain, he put a *buzz* all over his body. His attacker yowled and rolled away. He jumped to his feet.

"You fucker, you fucker, I'll cut your dick off and make you eat it!" He was screaming in German now, but it didn't matter; his hands would do all the talking that mattered.

Through a screen of tears he saw a fist swelling toward his face. Something tugged his mind, an eyeblink of doubt, of distraction. Belatedly he started to phase.

The blow caught him on the chin, snapping his head back. . . .

And then passed harmlessly through.

* * *

Gregg had stopped speaking, though with the cheering and chanting, no one seemed to have noticed as yet. Looking down, he saw Carnifex bull his way toward Mackie, making a visible wake in the crowd. Mackie, with some second sense, noticed the ace at the same time and turned, snarling. The hands were buzzing now. Someone next to Mackie screamed and pointed, and then everyone was trying to make space around the hunchback as Carnifex shouted and charged.

Puppetman shouted with him, exultant. *Good. The boy's no use anymore. Let Carnifex kill him.*

Mackie will carve him up, Gregg told the power.

They're both puppets. We can control this game.

It was a strange blend of ecstasy and fear. It tasted so good.

Yes, get rid of Mackie. That wasn't going to be easy. Mackie swung, and a line of blood followed, ruining the front of Carnifex's spotless uniform even as the ace swung a fist and knocked Mackie backward off his feet. Already the blinding, pulsing red of pain and terror was swelling in Carnifex's mind. The ace in white was backing up a step, watching Mackie's hands as the kid levered himself off the floor, grinning despite his smashed, ruined mouth.

Puppetman reached out. He found the fear in Carnifex and clamped down on it brutally. Then he reached for Mackie, looking for the switch in that crazed mind that would render him vulnerable.

There, Puppetman said in satisfaction. *There.*

A gunshot sounded loud in Gregg's ear. In that moment, Puppetman startled with him, losing Mackie for a precious instant as the packed auditorium erupted in horrified screams, as panic and terror drifted through the air like a thick fog. "My god, they're killing each other!" someone cried.

"*Stop!*" Gregg shouted into the microphones, but his voice was lost in the uproar.

Have to do it, she realized, *now. Before he gets here.* She willed into her arms the strength to straighten, to raise the blunt black pistol.

Bleating in terror, a tall, gangly man with gray hair fringing a narrow promontory of skull came boiling out of his

chair like a stork frightened from a canebrake. A flying elbow
hit the gun and spun it out of Sara's grasp.

She shrieked in despair as it cartwheeled over the front of
the box and into the crowd.

Gunfire crashed from the podium, and Gregg Hartmann
vanished under a wave of Secret Service suits.

Spector jumped when something shattered the glass up in
the media booth. It froze him for an instant and agents were
already swarming over Hartmann and the other big wheels,
pushing them into the wings or knocking them to the floor. He
ran several steps toward the senator, but two other men had
him face down behind the podium.

The screams were deafening. Spector couldn't think with
all the racket. Gunshots. He saw several agents firing toward
a target in the crowd. Golden Boy was swinging on the girders
overhead toward the area where the men were shooting.
Spector piled on top of Hartmann. The senator grunted, but
didn't turn over to face him. In a moment or two he would look
over his shoulder, and Spector would be waiting.

Jack swung from beam to beam like a desperate pendu-
lum. He couldn't tell what was going on up on the platform.
He could see Billy Ray's white suit, Secret Service with guns,
delegates stampeding—no Hartmann, no hunchback. There
was just the unmistakable impression of violence being done.

He flung himself to a beam above his own California
delegation, then stopped.

Gregg Hartmann was the secret ace, a killer. Why should
he care what happened to the man?

While he hesitated, he heard a scream resonate in his
mind. Tachyon was down in the stampede, being trampled.

He hesitated again. The cry came again. He saw there was
no one directly below him, then dropped.

He danced back. His chin felt as if someone had hit him
with a hammer and his neck muscles groaned. If he'd taken the
full force of the blow, it would have snapped his neck. *Who* is
this?

His vision cleared. He staggered as if he'd been punched
again. It was the black-haired man with the spare-parts face.
Leering at him with his deaths head grin. The front of his

jumpsuit was red-splashed now, as by a spastic eating spaghetti in red sauce. The blood-geyser had dwindled to a trickle.

"S'ow you a thing or two, you little son o' a hnitch!" the big man bellowed. He swung a haymaker at Mackie.

Terror yammered in his brain. *I can't beat this monster!*

Fighting down the fear Mackie phased, just ahead of impact that would have pulped his forebrain. The big man's momentum carried him right through him. He recovered with a tiger's quickness, spinning around with his hands coming up to strike or defend.

Mackie was right after him, anger overwhelming persistent fear. He aimed a stroke at the temple. *Let's see how he does with his head cut in half*.

The big man snapped up a hand in a knife-edge block. Fingers tumbled like clothespins from a sack as Mackie sliced through it. The black-haired man threw himself backwards into the crowd, just managing to keep from catching the buzz saw hand in his skull.

His breath tore at the right side of his chest like talons. He must have cracked a rib when that big fucker tackled him.

He phased through the curtain wall at the foot of the podium, into the hidden moat that separated the delegates from the stand. From the corner where the square-sectioned column of the podium proper met the facing of the elevated dais a muscular young man with a wire trailing from one ear gaped at him and hauled a tiny machine-pistol from inside his dark suit coat. Mackie met his eyes and grinned, unaware that his nose was bleeding and his smile a ghastly clown's.

The Secret Service man's finger convulsed on the trigger. A spray of nine-millimeter bullets passed through where Mackie *wasn't* and ripped into the crowd behind. The fresh screams of the shot almost made Mackie come.

He cut the Secret Service man's neatly pressed legs out from under him, right below the knee. The agent toppled shrieking into the moat, leaving blood splashed across the front of the dais and his lower legs standing. Briefly.

White ziggurat steps flanked the podium, too large to serve as stairs. Mackie began to clamber up them.

A blow from behind sprawled him across the second. Dazed, he felt himself picked up and flung like a doll. He smashed into the outer wall of the moat.

He was broken inside. "*Mutti*," he groaned. "Mommy."

It was the black-haired man, who had clubbed him down with his mangled hand and thrown him with the good one. Who was snarling at him from the foot of the podium, peeling what lips Mackie had left him, back from his teeth.

Who gathered himself and leapt like a tiger on a staked kid.

In desperation, Mackie thrust himself from the wall, bringing up a hand. Bringing on that buzz.

His hand met resistance. Fluids drenched his face, hot and sticky.

The big man crashed through the retaining wall trailing loops of gut like greasy purple-gray pennons.

Lying on her stomach on the VIP box's floor, Sara had a perfect shot at Hartmann. He was buried for the moment beneath a pile of Secret Service bodies, but they were concentrating on what was happening in the audience. No one was sparing the dignitaries' seats any attention at all. When they let him up, she'd have him dead to rights.

Except she'd lost her gun.

She drummed a fist on the floor of the box with a deliberate self-hating cadence.

Gregg had no chance to recover.

Two Secret Service people hit him like blitzing linemen, shoving him down on the floor with guttural, wordless yells, their guns out. Colin, the joker, piled directly on top of him, almost knocking his breath away. "Stay down, Senator!" Puppetman snarled at the interference.

He could still hear the buzz saw whine of Mackie's hands, tangled with the crowd's screams, as Carnifex plowed into the boy. But he couldn't see, couldn't pull the strings easily because he didn't know what was happening.

Let me go! Just let me have them! That's the only chance.

Gregg let loose all hold of Puppetman, lying there underneath the guards as the power reached out, savage.

He mind-raped Carnifex, slicing out the pain and the fear, pumping the adrenaline so high that he could almost feel the ace's heart pounding in his own head. At the same time, he tried to dampen Mackie's insane rage, but that was like handling fire—it burned, it twisted in his grasp.

Smash him! Puppetman screamed to Carnifex. *Use that*

*damn strength and make the little man another bloodspot on
the floor.*

Then he felt Billy scream in agony despite the mindblock
and even as he gulped at the pain greedily, he knew Mackie
had won this battle. The weight on top of him was gone. Half
a dozen of the Secret Service were shouting on the podium as
Gregg struggled to get up, to see again. "He's cutting us to
pieces—"

Then there was more gunfire, loud, and too close.

With frantic palm strokes Mackie wiped his opponent's
blood from his eyes. The bitch was gone. *Damn, damn, damn.*
He had to find her, he could not fail again—

He looked up. Hartmann was nowhere in sight. Had
something happened to him, happened to the Man?

Weeping tears and blood, coughing up bloody snot, he
scrambled up, a broken toy on a giant's stairs. Unimpeded, up
onto the ramp that gave onto the dais from stage right.
Hartmann was lying there beneath half a dozen young men in
suits. He looked all right. Grateful tears filled Mackie's lower
eyelids.

He felt a hot breath on his cheek, heard a yell of agony
from behind him as the bullet went home. A dark-suited man
knelt beside the Senator on his knees, pointing a gun at him
with both hands.

He tried to phase. Doubt and fatigue clamped his mind.
I can't—

Yellow fire reached for him from the short muzzle.

Black fire exploded in his chest. He fell.

Strong arms dragged Spector off Hartmann and spun him
toward the crowd. "He's cutting us to pieces. Get your piece
out. We've got to nail him," said the Secret Service man who'd
pulled him upright.

It was true. A little hunchback was slicing men to pieces
with his buzzsaw-like hands. Spector popped the leather
restraint and hauled out his gun. What the hell, might as well
look the part; it could help him get free later. Spector kneeled
and fired. The gun had more kick than he'd expected and the
bullet took down a man well behind the fight. He steadied his
gun hand with his free arm and aimed, then squeezed off three
more rounds. The hunchback spun and went down.

Spector turned back toward Hartmann. "Are you all right, Senator?"

Hartmann looked up and Spector caught his eye.

Darkness pulled at Mackie with seductive arms. He fought it. There was something he had to do. Someone—

Terror burst inside him. His eyes came open.

He lay spread-eagled across a tier. The dais's facing hid the Senator from him. *Der Mann needs me!*

That need gave him strength. He made his limbs respond to his will. Made himself climb, despite the tendency of hands and Keds to slip in the red liquid that covered the ledge.

Der Mann lay where he had been before. But his neck was craned, and he was staring fixedly up at a tall, gaunt Secret Service agent. His expression seemed both elated and terrified.

Hatred for the skinny agent hit Mackie like amphetamines. *He's the one who shot me!* But worse than that, he was doing something to the senator. Mackie couldn't see what, but he *knew*.

He limped forward. His right foot dragged. Each step sent a white-hot poker through his belly. *He needs me. I won't— —fail—him—again.*

Spector felt something in Hartmann resist him for a moment, then it sucked him in like a whirlpool. His death-pain boiled into the senator's mind; every excruciating detail, the broken bones, the fiery blood, the choking, rushed out.

But something was wrong. Hartmann's mind wasn't reacting like any of the others. It was bloating, feasting on Spector's death. Spector pushed harder. Slowly, the other mind gave way under the pressure and began to fade.

So good so tasty but it hurts and it kills . . . it isn't real it can't be real it isn't possible . . .

But it was and Puppetman's voice had faded to a whisper and left completely and even the pain that leaked into Gregg from Puppetman was like a searing acid poured down his psyche so that he wanted to scream and plead and beg don't kill me don't kill me I don't want to die.

But he couldn't break that awful gaze, couldn't tear himself away from those strange, sad, pained, startled, hurt eyes, those eyes that weren't Colin's at all but someone else's . . .

. . . and he knew that he was going to die, that he would be next, that he would follow Puppetman into the void behind those eyes . . .

"You're killing me!" Gregg spat with all the strength he had left, hoping that those eyes would blink or look away or turn . . .

. . . and there was nothing left in his world but those eyes . . .

The dark-clad back loomed ahead of Mackie like a narrow cliff. Mackie swayed. He wanted to lie down and sleep for a long, long time.

Instead he raised his right hand, brought the buzz. He looked at his fingers, a pink blur. The sight gave him strength.

He swung his hand in a flat sweeping cut.

Spector could barely stay on his feet. His knees wobbled from the strain. He'd given Hartmann everything he had, and felt him go under. But the son of a bitch was staring at him, blinking. It simply wasn't possible.

Spector remembered the gun in his hand. He centered it on Hartmann's chest. He heard a sound like a giant bee, and hesitated. He felt a grinding pain in his neck. The convention hall spun, over and over, then rushed up and slammed him in the face. His ears were roaring, but none of the sounds seemed to make sense. There was a body lying on the floor not far from him. It was Colin; at least, it looked like the joker. But he didn't have a head. There were ribbons of tattered flesh on the neck where it had come off. All Spector could see were rushing feet.

It had to be a dream. Like the one he'd had before, only worse. He felt sick and paralyzed, but at the same time strangely euphoric. He'd just close his eyes and bring things back under control.

The head had rolled against the back of the podium. Feeling as if he were drifting on air Mackie limped toward it through roaring silence.

Painfully he leaned forward. His body felt like a dry twig that broke in a new place with every few degrees he bent.

He picked up the head, straightened slowly. He held the head up, to show to Gregg, to show to the herd of frightened sheep in white hats who trampled one another in their frenzy to flee him.

"I'm Mackie Messer," he croaked. "Mack the Knife. I'm special."

He brought the head to his face, kissed it full on the lips. The eyes opened.

Spector felt something on his mouth. He opened his eyes. The hunchback was staring down at him, a mocking smile on his lips. It wasn't a dream. The realization was like a fist in his chest, but he didn't have a chest anymore. The little fucker had sliced his head off. He was going to die. After all he'd lived through, he was going to fucking *die*! Again.

Spector fought through his panic and locked eyes with the hunchback. He channeled his pain and terror through his eyes and into the man who'd killed him. The world began to shake and blur. Spector felt the darkness closing in and tried to push it all into the hunchback. A familiar fear crept into Spector. He felt very alone.

The darkness was complete.

Mackie tried to pull his eyes away. The head's eyes held them with black-hole suction.

Something was shaking his soul to pieces. His body began to shake in sympathy, vibrating faster and faster, out of control. He felt his blood begin to boil, felt himself sweating steam from every pore.

He screamed.

The skin on the severed head's cheeks crisped and blackened from the friction of Mackie's fingers. The buzzing fingers met bone, began to shake the skull to pieces, to agitate the fluids within the rounded box of its cranium to the boiling point.

But the eyes—

The leather boy exploded. Sara dropped her head into her arms, felt wet impacts in her hair that would stay with her forever.

When she looked again, there was nothing left of hunchback or head but red-and-black splashes steaming all over the podium.

There was a dead moment.

Then Gregg was pushing aside his blanket of Secret Service agents, struggling to his feet. The crowd had flowed back from the podium like mercury from a fingertip. Now it washed forward again with a roar that went on and on.

That's it. He's president now. This guarantees it. The death of his ace assassin was no comfort. President Gregg Hartmann would have no need of German psychopaths to deal with his opponents.

If we even get that far. Steele had hinted that Soviets would launch a first-strike rather than see Hartmann inaugurated.

Her head was a dead weight. She let it drop, and let the grief pour out in hopeless tears.

Jack just tossed people out of the way till he found Tachyon, then picked the little man up and stuffed him securely under one arm. Gunshots cracked out; the stampeding crowd accelerated. There was wild but confused violence on the platform. Jack couldn't see a thing.

Jack bulled his way through the crowd, parting them like the Red Sea. Finally he and Tachyon stood in front of the massive white podium, but from his low angle they could see nothing.

Whatever had happened seemed to be over. Gregg Hartmann rose from the crush of Secret Service and brushed himself off as he walked uncertainly to the microphones.

"Damn," Jack said. "We're too late."

There were still people shouting and screaming in the hall; there was still panic as they stampeded for the exits or stared at the podium in frozen horror.

Yet the impression Gregg had was somehow one of silence, of a frozen moment like a still photograph. He could hear his own breath, gasping and very loud in his ears; he could feel very clearly the hands of the Secret Service man on either side of him. He could see Jesse Jackson being herded off the podium, Ellen blockaded by a cordon of uniformed security, dignitaries on the floor or standing with hands to faces or running blindly from the scene.

There was more blood and gore than Gregg had thought possible.

And a strange, echoing void inside his head.

Puppetman?

There was no answer.

Puppetman? he queried again.

Silence. Only silence.

Gregg took a shuddering breath. He allowed himself to be hauled to his feet, then shrugged away the restraining hands that wanted to pull him from the podium. "Senator, please—"

Gregg shook his head. "I'm fine. It's over." And it was very clear what he had to do now. The path was laid out before him, a gift. Puppetman was gone, and the loss was as if some great, dark burden had been lifted from him, a burden he hadn't even been aware that he was carrying. Gregg felt *good*. There was carnage and destruction all around him, and yet . . .

Later. Later we'll know.

He straightened his jacket, tugged at his tie. He arranged the words in his mind, knowing what he would say. *Please. Please be calm. This is what happens when jealousy and hatred are allowed to grow. This is the fruit we receive from the seed of prejudice and ignorance. This is the bitter feast we endure whenever we turn away from suffering.*

Words to salvage a presidency from ruin. Brave Hartmann, cool Hartmann, compassionate Hartmann. Hartmann before the eyes of a nation: a calming, competent leader in the midst of crisis.

Gregg stepped forward to the mikes. He looked out to the crowd and raised his hands.

Tachyon's left arm was locked about Braun's neck. His right lay across his chest. Blood stained the bandage over the amputated end. The pain from his broken ribs and his arm was so great that he couldn't lift his head from Jack's shoulder as the big ace cradled him in his arms.

Jack had returned to his place in the California delegation. The Omni smelled like a slaughterhouse, the air-conditioner unable to banish the sickly sweet odor of blood. The sharp scent of gunpowder still hung in the air, the smell of shit from the released bowels of the dead. Shock seemed to hold the entire convention.

James Spector was dead.

The hunchbacked assassin was dead.

But Hartmann remained.

Tachyon gnawed at his lower lip.

The candidate broke free of the clinging Secret Service agents. Head back, shoulders squared, hands outstretched in benediction, a gesture of calm, or reassurance.

He stepped to the microphone.

And in that moment Tachyon knew what to do.

Gregg began to speak, his gaze searching and pleading with the people in the seats. "Please," he began, his voice calm and deep and compelling.

And then . . .

. . . Tachyon was in his head. The alien's strong, insistent presence took Gregg's struggling ego and pushed it backward, stepping in front of him even as Gregg resisted desperately and uselessly.

"Please be calm . . . Hey, *shut the fuck up and listen to me!*" his voice shouted without any volition on his part, echoing throughout the Omni. He saw himself in one of the monitors above the floor, and he was *smiling*, smiling that oily, practiced campaign smile like nothing at all had happened.

"Oops, got a little too vehement there, didn't I?" He felt himself giggle, of all things, tittering like a child. Gregg tried to stop the laughter, but Tachyon was too strong. Like a helpless ventriloquist's dummy, he spouted someone else's words.

"But you have to admit you did shut up, didn't you? That's better. Hey, I'm calm. Let's all be calm. No panic in a crisis, not me. No way. Your next president doesn't panic. Uh-uh."

Down on the floor, the exodus had stopped. The delegates were staring at him. His casual, amused delivery was more chilling and horrible than any screaming fit could have been. Above the sobbing and moaning behind him, he heard Connie Chung in the VIP section shout into her mike, "Get the cameras on Hartmann! Now!"

Inside, he continued to fight uselessly against the bonds Tachyon had placed on his will. *So this is what it feels like to be a puppet*, he thought. *Let me go, damn you!* But there was no escape. Tachyon held the strings, and he was a practiced puppeteer himself.

Gregg chuckled, glanced back at the carnage, and then shook his head as he turned back to the crowd. He held his arm straight out from his body toward them, his palm down and fingers spread wide.

"Look at that," he said. "Not even a tremble. Cool as a damn cucumber. So much for the old '76 worries, huh? Maybe this is a good thing in the long run, if it puts all that business to rest."

John Werthen and Devaughn had come forward to pull him away from the mikes, and he watched himself flail his arms at them, pushing them away and grabbing at the mikes desperately. "Go away! Can't you see that I'm just fine? Back off! Let me handle this." John looked at Devaughn, who shrugged. Gregg tugged his hopelessly soiled suit coat back into position as they let go of him hesitantly. He gave that eerie smile for the cameras once more.

"Now, what was I saying? Oh, yes." He chuckled again and waggled a finger at the delegates. "This is *not* acceptable behavior and I won't have it," he scolded them as if talking to a class of schoolchildren. "We had a little problem up here but it's over. Let's forget it. In fact—"

He giggled and bent down to the stage. When he straightened again, his forefinger was dripping with a thick, bright red liquid. "I want you to write 'No More Violence' a hundred times as punishment," he said, and he reached out to the clear acrylic panel in front of the lectern and traced a large smeary "N" on it. The first loop of the "O" was barely legible.

"Oops, out of ink," Gregg declared gaily, and bent down to the stage again. This time he plopped something meaty and unidentifiable down on the lectern with a distinct wet *plop*. He dipped his finger into it like a quill pen into an inkwell. Someone was being noisily sick again behind him, and there were screams from down on the floor. He could hear Ellen sobbing and pleading with anyone who would listen: "Get him out of there. Please, stop him . . ." John and Devaughn came forward again, and this time they took hold of him firmly, one on each arm.

"Hey, you can't do this!" Gregg spluttered loudly. "I haven't finished yet. You can't—"

It was over. At least it was over. Tachyon's control dropped from him and he sagged in their arms, silent. Gregg tried not to see the horrified faces he passed as they escorted him backstage: Ellen, Jackson, Amy. He cursed Tachyon, knowing the alien was still there.

Damn you for this. You didn't have to do it this way. You didn't have to humiliate and destroy me like that. Couldn't you see that Puppetman was dead? Damn you forever.

11:00 P.M.

Tachyon lay in bed. They had wanted to put him back in the hospital, but he had fought that like a maddened creature, and Jack had kept him out of the hands of the doctors. He had allowed them to rebandage his stump, rewrap his ribs, but no more. He had even refused the pain pills. Because somewhere in this city was his grandchild, and Tach needed a clear head to find him. His brain seemed to be battering at the confines of his skull as he searched, but only darkness answered him.

Pain took him, and he hung over the side of the bed and retched. The memory of those final chaotic minutes at the convention reared up and added to his confusion. Hartmann's mind beating like a trapped and terrified animal at the iron confines of Tachyon's mind-control.

For an instant remorse gripped him, then slowly Tachyon raised the ugly ungainly stump, and studied it. Hate replaced the momentary flicker of regret. *I'll never do surgery again. Damn him to eternal wandering!*

His jaw set in a stubborn, bitter line, and he crawled from the bed. The Nagyvary lay in its case. City light filtered around the edge of the curtain and glimmered on the polished grain of the wood, danced on the strings. Gently he drew the fingers of his left hand across the strings releasing a sigh of sound.

Rage filled him. Snatching out the violin, Tachyon swung it hard against the wall. The wood splintered with a horrible brittle sound. Several strings broke with sharp jarring notes; a musical scream of pain.

His final swing pulled him off balance, and Tach instinctively threw out his right hand to catch himself. Screamed. Black spots danced before his eyes, and suddenly he felt hands on his shoulders. Someone lifting him.

"You damn fool! What now are you doing?" asked Polyakov, depositing him back in the bed.

"How . . . how did . . . you . . . get in?"

"I'm a spy, remember?"

The worst of the agony receded. Tach touched his upper lip with his tongue, tasting salt. "This isn't very good trade craft," said Tachyon.

"We needed to talk." George was rummaging about Tach's discarded clothes until he found the flask.

"You could have just left," the alien whimpered, and hated himself for his weakness. "Slipped away to Europe, the Far East . . . begun again. And left me to face the inharmonious music."

Polyakov gulped down brandy. "I owe you too much for that."

A tiny, bitter smile touched Tachyon's thin lips. "What? You don't believe in Gregg's tragic breakdown?"

"I believe that he had a little help."

A sigh. "It was damn close."

Polyakov grunted. "More exciting that way."

Tachyon accepted the flask, and took a sip. "You don't like exciting. You like subtle and efficient. George, what are we going to do? Share a cell at Leavenworth?"

"What do you want?"

"I'm not too proud to beg. Help me, please. My devil's stepchildren, my grandson, what will become of them if I am incarcerated? Please, please help me."

The mattress squeaked and shifted as the man seated himself. "Why should I?"

"Because you owe me, remember."

"We'll probably never see each other again."

"I've heard that before, too."

The Russian took another swallow of brandy. "How are you going to control Blaise?"

"Make him love me. Oh, George, where has he gone? Where can he be? What if he's hurt and he needs me and I'm not there!" His voice rose shrilly. Polyakov pushed him back against the pillows.

"Hysterics won't help."

Tach pleated the edge of the sheet, stared with strained eyes into the oblivion of the far wall.

"Let me ease your mind on one point. I've already called the FBI, and offered to roll over in exchange for your immunity."

"Oh, George, thank you." His head fell back wearily

against the pillows. "Goodbye, George. I would offer to shake hands, but . . ."

"We'll say goodbye the Russian way."

Polyakov bear-hugged him, and pressed hard kisses onto each thin cheek. Tachyon reciprocated in the Takisian fashion with a kiss to the forehead and lips.

The Russian paused at the bedroom door. "How do you know you can trust me?"

"Because I am a Takisian, and I still believe in honor."

"Not much of that around."

"I take it where I can find it."

"Goodbye, Dancer."

"Goodbye, George."

CHAPTER EIGHT

Monday
July 25, 1988

8:00 A.M.

"You're finished, politically," Devaughn said. His tone was almost jolly; Gregg wanted to smash his fucking face in. *With Puppetman it'd be easy.*

But Puppetman's gone. Dead.

"I'm not quitting, Charles," Gregg retorted. "Have you gone deaf? This is just a goddamn minor setback."

"Minor setback? Christ, Gregg, how can you say that?" Devaughn rattled the papers he'd brought. "The editorials are screaming. *USA* has a poll saying that eighty-two percent of the American public thinks you're nuts. ABC and NBC did overnight phone polls showing that you're now trailing Bush by sixty percent. CBS didn't even bother with that; by their poll, an even ninety percent of the public thinks you should flat out resign the nomination. As do I."

Devaughn did another turn of the deserted headquarters room.

"Jackson's really pissed, even if he's smoothing it over for you," he continued. "The committee wants your resignation in writing this morning. I told them I'd get it."

Gregg slumped in his chair. The television was replaying his—Tachyon's—breakdown again. Gregg got up and very calmly went to the set.

He kicked the picture tube in.

Devaughn raised his eyebrows but didn't say anything.

"Fuck the polls," Gregg said. He glowered at Devaughn as glass dribbled from his cuffs. "I don't believe in polls. Hell, let me debate Bush and I'll tear his nuts off. He's about as dynamic as dry toast. That'll turn the polls around."

"Bush won't debate you, Gregg. He won't come near a platform with you and he'll make you look like a fool when you insist. Resign, Gregg."

"Look, Charles, I'm the candidate. Don't you get it? It doesn't matter what you or anyone else thinks. This convention elected me and by god, I'm running. I've got Jackson—he's charismatic . . ."

"He'll also pull out of the ticket if you try to continue this charade," Devaughn sniffed like a prissy English lord. Like Tachyon. "You broke *down*, Gregg. America saw you on TV acting like a gibbering fool and they wonder how you'd react in a crisis in the White House. They don't want your finger on the button, Gregg. And frankly, neither do I."

"Damn it, that wasn't *me* that broke down, I tell you. It was Tachyon doing it. He took over my mind. I've told you that now a hundred times."

"So you say. You'll have a hell of a time proving it, though, won't you? Frankly, Gregg, that's going to sound like just another weak excuse. Or are you claiming Tachyon did it to you in '76, too?"

"Goddamn you!" Gregg roared. He pushed Devaughn with both hands, and the big man rocked backwards, a suddenly frightened look on his face. "I'm not resigning!"

"Take your hands off me, Gregg."

Gregg looked at Devaughn. *With Puppetman, I'd make the bastard crawl* . . . He took a deep breath and stepped back. He rubbed his hands on his pants as if they were dirty. "I've made up my mind on this," he said softly.

Devaughn stared at him scornfully. "Then they'll reconvene the convention whether you like it or not. If you fight, you come out with nothing. You'll be made to look like a total ass. Resign, and maybe you can salvage at least your dignity from this mess. That's my final piece of advice for you, Senator." He stressed the last word mockingly.

Gregg went over to the couch, picture-tube glass crunching under his wingtips. He flung himself down on it. He cursed monotonously to himself, Devaughn watching silently.

When he finally looked up, the words he spat out tasted like ash.

"I've been hanging on with my damn fingertips, and now you're getting your kicks jumping up and down on them until I let go, aren't you? Well, you get your wish. Tell Tony to write the damn resignation," Gregg said. "He can write whatever he wants; I don't care. You read it—you'll get the most fucking pleasure out of it. And tell Amy to make arrangements to get me and Ellen out of Atlanta. I don't want to see any reporters. You got it?"

Devaughn sniffed. His gaze was scornful and superior, and Gregg ached to tear it from his face, but he didn't have the power anymore.

"Tell them yourself. I don't work for you anymore." Devaughn shook his head. "I had it all for you and you blew it. I'm going to see if Dukakis can use my talents."

Devaughn left the room with prissy dignity. A Secret Service man stuck his head in, glanced at Gregg and the shattered glass on the rug, and shut the door again.

Gregg sat there alone for a very long time.

9:00 A.M.

Somehow over the years he had managed to spend a lot of time in morgues. And no matter how beautifully appointed, how perfectly cleaned, nothing could hide the essential fact— they were freezers for dead human meat.

"I appreciate your coming down here," the M.E. was saying as he led Tachyon into the operating room. His eyes slid to Tachyon's stump, and quickly away. "Especially after . . . but I've never seen anything like this, and you're the expert."

"No problem. It's sort of fitting somehow."

The M.E. helped him into gown and mask. They walked to the table. A wan-faced woman was clutching rib cutters to her chest, and eyeing the headless body with wary alarm.

The corpse had been slit from sternum to groin, the ribs cut and pulled aside. But pale yellow fat was growing across the glistening intestines. The ribs were putting out bony tendrils. Skin had grown across the severed neck, and pooching up from the center of the neck, like a finger thrust into a drum, was a tiny bud. Tachyon bent in for a closer look. Fascinated and horrified and unable to stop himself.

"It's almost as if it's . . . trying to . . . to . . . "

"To grow a new head, yes." Tach jerked back when he realized the embryonic head had *eyes*.

What if they suddenly opened? Would Demise's power remain? Would he make good his threat even from beyond the grave?

Stupid! He's always killed from beyond the grave.

Bending Tachyon slid his dagger from its boot sheath, and jabbed it sharply into a buttock. The body arched and jerked.

"*Shit!*" screamed the woman, and the M.E. didn't stop running until he reached the door.

Clinging to the swinging door, he stuttered, "Wha . . . what the fuck is that?"

"A mistake. A major miscalculation on my part. My nemesis and a reminder not to play God. May I suggest that we dispense with the autopsy, and move straight to cremation?"

"Great. You'll get no argument from me. What about the ashes? Are there any next of kin?"

A humorless smile touched Tachyon's lips. "I suppose I stand *in loco parentis*. I'll take them."

"Doc, you are one weird dude," sighed the woman, and she snipped off a rib that had grown beyond the edge of the chest cavity.

10:00 A.M.

ACES BATTLE IN CONVENTION BLOODBATH

Sara winced and let the newspaper fall into mud drenched by firehoses and churned by a thousand feet of various descriptions.

You're right, damn you, she thought, in case Tachyon happened to be listening in. He wouldn't, though; that Takisian honor of his. That damned expedient Takisian honor.

He'd laid it right on the line, as straightforwardly as he'd laid her Friday night, and even less gently: *You cannot unmask Hartmann. It would hand the election to Barnett on a platter. How many innocent joker lives are you willing to spend on your vengeance?*

"None," she said.

A couple of joker faces looked at her with shellshock blankness. None of them recognized her; she had a leopard mask on today. It had been lying in a gutter on Peachtree. The riot hadn't mashed it beyond usefulness.

Something crunched beneath her foot. She kicked at it until a sign emerged from the mud, hand-lettered at the JADL headquarters tent for last night's demonstration. The message almost made her smile.

> Judas Jack, 1950
> Traitor Tach, 1988
> Two of A Kind

With Mackie dead she'd been able to return to her own room. She was dressed today in blue jeans and a loose pale-blue blouse. She let her Reeboks carry her past a CBS remote van, where an earnest young black stringer was talking into a yellow-foam phallus.

"Piedmont Park remains virtually deserted after a night of rioting in which three hundred jokers were arrested. Several dozen jokers wander, as if dazed, among the trampled ruins of the tent city; Atlanta Mayor Andrew Young has rescinded his order that any jokers found on the street should be arrested on sight, following a personal plea in the early hours of this morning by Massachusetts Governor Michael Dukakis. Debate still rages over Governor Harris's refusal to declare martial law. . . ."

They were few enough, but they were in a sense her people. She walked among them for the last time. No joker would trust her again, and she had sworn on her soul never to reveal the secret that would vindicate her in their eyes. For their sake she had to let them hate her.

For my sake. Unless I never plan to pass another mirror with my eyes open.

Tom Brokaw spoke to her from a portable television resting on an upturned ice chest and being ignored by a listless black joker with glowing blue carbuncles covering his face and such of his body as his coveralls left bare.

". . . uneasy truce that prevails between a mixed force of police and aces and several hundred joker demonstrators outside the Blythe van Rensselaer Clinic. . . ."

The camera cut to a sign supported either edge by six green sucker-tipped fingers: "The Knave of Hearts Beats Every Joker in the Deck." Then it panned to a joker Sara knew named Canker, for obvious reasons, with the beleaguered J-Town Clinic for backdrop.

"Aces are helping the pigs oppress jokers on this street," he told the camera, gesturing at the cordon that kept the protesters at bay. "An ace did Chrysalis and a joker stands to burn for it. It's us against them!"

Tachyon, Tachyon, did you know what you were sacrificing? She knew. That was one reason she was willing to burn her own career and reputation at his behest.

The other was that she had her vengeance, and nothing else mattered.

Puppetman was dead—that was what Hartmann called his power, Tachyon said. Demise had killed it, sucked it right out through Hartmann's eyes before Mackie Messer decapitated him.

The evil wasn't dead; oh, no. No matter how much Gregg wept, how bitterly he protested his innocence. Puppetman had been the crystallization of Hartmann's lusts. Those lusts still lived.

But Gregg didn't have the ability to pull strings and make puppets dance to gratify his needs any more. *That* was what Demise had destroyed.

And Gregg would never have the balls to walk the night with a knife in his own hand.

Without his power, Gregg was trapped in hell. Sara no longer wished he'd die. Now she hoped he lived a long, long time.

She sat on an overturned trash can. *Andi*, she thought, *this is vengeance, isn't it? You wouldn't want me to ruin the life of every wild card in America just to buy you a little more?*

The spoiled little bitch probably would. But Andrea Whitman was dead now, too.

Sara shook out her winter-pale hair, smoothed it back from her face with her hands. A breeze blew across the park, almost cool. She lifted her head and looked out over the morning-after battlefield.

A black policeman rode around the outskirts of the park on a tall bay gelding. He watched her closely. *A pig hunting more victims? A frightened man trying to do his job?* It was a judgment call, and Sara Morgenstern was fresh out of judgments.

Victims . . .

Puppetman's strings were all cut. But Gregg Hartmann had one more victim left.

She stood up and left the park with a sense of purpose that tasted like an alien emotion to one who thought her purpose was all used up. She left the mask in a can that said Keep Atlanta Beautiful.

Tachyon closed the door to Gregg's suite behind him. Gregg looked up from the Samsonite suitcase he was packing. "Doctor," he said. "I'm surprised you came so quickly. Amy must have just called you a few minutes ago . . ."

"I suppose I felt I owed it to you." The alien was holding himself in stiffly, his chin cocked forward over a ruffled lace collar and a paisley, electric-blue silk shirt. Despite the pose, Tachyon was obviously on the edge of exhaustion. His skin was too pale, the eyes too sunken and hollow, and Gregg noticed that he held the stump of his hand behind him. "I feel no guilt about what I did to you. I would do it again, gladly."

Gregg nodded. He closed the suitcase, latched it, locked it. "I'm picking up Ellen at the hospital in a few hours," he said conversationally. Setting the luggage down on the floor, he gestured silently to a chair.

Tachyon seated himself. The lilac gaze was utterly expressionless. "Well, let us play it—the final scene in this little drama. But quickly. There are other people I need to see."

Gregg tried to stare him down. It was difficult to hold the alien's intense, unblinking gaze. "You can't say anything, you know. You still can't."

Tachyon grimaced and his eyes darkened as if in implicit threat.

"No, you won't," Gregg said softly. "You tell the press what you know about me and you prove that Barnett was right all along. There *was* a secret ace with his hands on the strings of the government. The wild card virus *is* something to be feared. The nats *do* need to do something to protect themselves from us. You talk, Doctor, and all the old laws will seem like freedom. I know you. I've had twenty years to watch you and learn how you think and how you respond. No, you won't talk. After all, that's why you did what you did last night."

"Yes, you are quite correct." Tachyon sighed and pressed his stump to his chest as if it pained him. "What I did went against all my principles—some old ones, and some newfound ones. It was not something I did lightly or at whim. You are a murderer and you should pay." He shook his head in weary frustration. "And ships should be stars, but they're not, and nothing can ever make them so."

"What the hell is that—the Takisian version of spilt milk?" Gregg paced across the room, then whirled to face the alien. "Look, you've got to know one thing. *I* didn't do it," Gregg told him. "Puppetman did it. The wild card power. *All* of it was the wild card. Not me. You don't understand what it was like to have him inside. I had to feed him or he'd destroy me. I'd have given anything to have rid myself of him, and now I have. I can make a fresh start, I can begin again—"

"*What!*" Tachyon's roar interrupted.

"Yes. Puppetman's dead. Last night on the podium, Demise took him. Look inside me, Doctor, and tell me what you see. You didn't have to ruin me; the evil was already gone. By the time you took my mind, I was free." Gregg studied his hands. A deep sorrow welled up in him, and he looked at Tachyon with eyes that shimmered with moisture. "I would have made a fine president, Doctor. Maybe even a great one."

Tachyon gazed back with unyielding steel in his gaze.

"Gregg, there *is* no Puppetman. There never *was* a Puppetman. There was only Gregg Hartmann and his weaknesses, a man who was touched by an alien virus and was provided with a power whereby he could feed the darkest corners of his soul. Your problem is not that you are a wild card, Gregg. Your problem is that you are a sadist. This feeble excuse of yours is almost classic guilt transference. You constructed a shadow personality so you could pretend that somehow Gregg was still clean and decent. That is a child's trick. That is a child's deception, and you are smarter than that."

Tachyon's harsh words were like a slap. Gregg flushed, angry that Tachyon would not understand. It was so obvious; it seemed impossible that Tachyon could not tell the difference. "But he's *dead*," Gregg cried in desperation. "I'll prove it to you. Go on," Gregg insisted. "I'm asking you to. Look inside me and tell me what you see."

Tachyon sighed. He closed his eyes, opened them. He turned away from Gregg, pacing the room silently for a long minute and then coming to a halt near the windows. When he looked at Gregg again, it was with a strange sympathy.

"You see, I told you," Gregg said, almost laughing with relief. "Puppetman died last night. And I'm glad. I'm so goddamn glad." Gregg felt the laughter becoming tinged with hysteria, and he took a deep breath. He looked at Tachyon, who stared at him sternly. Gregg raced to say the rest. "My god, the words are so fucking inadequate and stupid, but it's true. I'm sorry. I'm sorry for it all and I'd like to do what I can to start making up for it. Doctor, I've been made to do things that I hated. I lost a son because Gimli used Puppetman against me, I—"

"You are not listening to me. There was no Puppetman and Gimli died over a year ago. There was no Gimli either."

It took several long seconds before the impact of those words sunk into Gregg. "What?" he stuttered, then the denial came fierce and desperate and angry. "You don't know what the hell you're saying, Doctor. Gimli's *body* died, but not his *mind*. He found his way into my son. He was in my head; he nearly made me lose any control of Puppetman at all—that's how all this started. He threatened me, said he was going to make Puppetman destroy me and my career."

"Gimli died a year ago," Tachyon repeated, relentlessly. "All of him. You made up his ghost yourself, the same way you made up Puppetman."

"You *lie!*" The word was a shout. Gregg's face was distorted with rage.

Tachyon just stared at him coldly. "I was in your head, Senator. You have no secrets from me. You are a disassociative personality. You've denied the responsibility for your own actions by creating Puppetman, and when that threatened to get out of hand, you needed another excuse: Gimli."

"*No!*" Gregg shouted again.

"Yes," Tachyon insisted. "I will tell you once more. There was never a Gimli, never a Puppetman. Just Gregg. Everything you did, you did yourself."

Hartmann shook his head wildly. His gaze was pleading, hurt and vulnerable. "No," he said softly. "Gimli was there." His eyes went suddenly wide and frightened. "I . . . I wouldn't have killed my *child*, Doctor."

"You did," Tachyon said, and he saw in Gregg's eyes the deep wounds each word ripped into the man's soul, even though Gregg would not admit it. Already Hartmann was defiantly forcing himself into a semblance of calm and control. He smoothed his hair back with one hand.

"Doctor, I don't know what you want me to do. Even

assuming that I gave any credence at all to what you're saying—"

"Get help."

Intent on his own words, Hartmann almost missed Tachyon's. "Hmm?"

"Get help, Gregg. Find a therapist. *I'll* find you a therapist—" Suddenly Tachyon realized how impossible that was. A therapist would have to be told too much, and it would all come out. Somehow, it could all unravel. Tachyon's face twisted in frustration. He did not like the only answer he could see. "We're going to spend a lot of time together, Gregg."

"What do you mean?"

"As of now, I am your physician. You are under my care."

Gregg spat laughter, turning his back on the doctor. "No," he said. "Uh-uh. I don't need a damn shrink because Puppetman's gone. You're not even human, Doctor. I doubt you're particularly well-qualified to act as a psychologist."

"Consider it a compromise position. It will guarantee my silence."

"I tell you the power's gone, and the power was at fault."

"And we go around again? Admit the truth of what I'm telling you, Gregg. You won't even look at me. I saw your guilt, Gregg. You can deny—even to yourself—but I know the truth. It's time for you to start facing the reality."

Long silence stretched between them. Finally Gregg said, "All right, Doctor. I'll grant you a compromise—politicians are used to them. Your silence for my business, huh? I suppose you'll need some paying customers when the funds are cut off."

Tachyon did not dignify the insult with a comment. "I will contact you as soon as I return to New York."

"Fine." Hartmann sighed. He tried to give that professional smile of his and failed. Walking over to the suitcase, he swung it off the bed.

"Well, this is it, then. I'm going to pick up Ellen. She's understandably confused and hurt by all of this." The self-conscious smile flashed again. "I'm going to tell her I'm sorry, too. Goodbye for now. I guess I'll be seeing you soon . . ."

Hartmann thrust out his hand to Tachyon.

Tachyon stared in bitter disbelief at the proferred hand. He wondered if this was not some final, cruel joke of Gregg's. *Hey, all's forgiven. Let's shake and make up. Buddies again.*

But I can't shake, you bastard. You saw to that.

Hartmann suddenly realized what he'd done and yanked back his hand. He didn't say anything. He went to the door and opened it. They left the room together.

"Walk with me to the elevators?" asked Hartmann.

"No."

"I'll be calling for that appointment, then."

Tachyon watched him walk away—a soft, overweight man with pale white scalp like wings where the hair had receded. He had always thought of Gregg as a dynamic, handsome man. Now he realized that that too had been a function of his power.

Was I wrong to speak the truth about his power? Perhaps it would have been better to simply let him believe in his possession by Puppetman and Gimli.

NO! He escaped punishment. I'm not going to let him escape the guilt.

But for all intents and purposes Puppetman *was* dead. Now it was up to Tachyon to keep it that way. Which meant he had to remain close to Gregg Hartmann. The thought was nauseating.

The alien walked to the stairwell. Sat down on the concrete step and leaned his head against the cold metal handrail. His arm was throbbing again, claws of pain that seemed to rip up his arm and into his shoulder. This might very well be the place where Jack had died, he thought wearily. And, right down there, Gregg killed his own child.

I'm dead too. But nobody's realized it yet because I'm still walking around.

Eight days in July. Eight days in which to lose so much: his oldest friendship on Earth; his belief and respect in Gregg Hartmann; the love and respect of his jokers.

His hand.

His innocence.

But Jack hadn't died. And he wasn't dead yet either.

"Stop feeling sorry for yourself, Tis, and get on with the business of living."

But I have to deal with Hartmann! his mind wailed.

"Tough. Someday after he's dead and buried you can present a paper on him at the AMA."

He began to climb the stairs.

11:00 A.M.

"I don't need it!"

"Stop being such a royal asshole, your Takisian excellency." Jack unfolded the chair and placed it by Tachyon's hotel bed.

"I've managed all morning without you or that damned wheelchair."

"Yeah, and look at you, you look like something the cat threw up."

"You should be out looking for Blaise," Tachyon said. He was propped up on pillows suffering whitely.

Jack sighed. "The police are looking for him. The FBI has been alerted. Even that fatuous jerk Straight Arrow is poking around. What can I do that they can't?"

Tachyon's face was haunted. His one hand clutched the bed covers. "I *must* find my grandson. I must. He's all I have left."

Jack sat on the room chair, and reached for a cigarette. "The police say he was with that Popinjay guy, that Jay Ackroyd, at the hospital Saturday night after your operation. They were watching the TV in the waiting room. One of the nurses remembers that something on the TV caught their attention, and that Popinjay turned to Blaise and said 'You wanna go play detective?' Or words to that effect."

"Ideal." Tachyon bit his lip. "If Popinjay has involved my grandchild in one of his intrigues . . ."

"The police are trying to find out what channel they were tuned to." Jack shook his head. "I wasn't any help there either. I was partying Saturday night." Depression invaded him. "I thought the right candidate had got the nomination."

"I have been trying to phone Hiram," Tachyon said. "I thought he might have seen Blaise, but he's vanished too."

"He left yesterday morning."

"No he didn't. I inquired, and he hasn't checked out of the hotel."

"I saw him in the lobby. He was carrying a trunk."

Tachyon frowned. "Jay and Hiram are the closest of friends. If Ackroyd were in trouble, Hiram would be the person to whom he would turn." Tach dropped into a thoughtful silence.

"Since they're all missing they aren't going to be very much help to us. What you need is some rest."

Tachyon leaned back against the pillows. "You are right." He closed his eyes. "Perhaps I should try again to detect Blaise's mind signature. Would you please turn out the lights? It might help my concentration." Almost inaudibly he added. "I am weary. So very weary."

"Will it disturb you if I have a belt of bourbon?"

"Not at all."

Jack turned out the light, leaving only the trickle of sunlight coming in under the drapes, and then he carried his cigarette in the direction of the bottles on Tachyon's table. He put some ice in a glass, then reached in the near darkness for one of the bottles. It turned out to be James Spector's ashes. He put the urn down and picked up another bottle. It seemed to have liquid of the right color. He poured.

Scotch. Damn.

It was sure one of those days.

It all felt very strange.

Gregg didn't know the Secret Service guards who rode with him in the rented limo on the way to Ellen's hospital. Their faces were unfamiliar and they didn't speak to him. They were strangers, hidden and masked by dark glasses, dark blue suits, and dark frowns.

They would *always* be strangers. Their minds were locked away and Gregg no longer had the key to open them.

It felt very strange to be so silent in his own head, to be unable to sense the tidal flow of feelings around him, to find it impossible to swim in the bright salt ocean of emotion, to be powerless to change its swift currents.

This must be what it's like to go suddenly blind or deaf or mute. Then: *Puppetman?* he mind-called again, and again there was only the echo of his own thoughts.

Dead. Gone. Gregg sighed, feeling lost and sad and hopeful all at once, looking at the people around him, touching him, and yet isolated. Apart.

He didn't know if he'd ever get used to that.

All he wanted to do was get away from the furnace of Atlanta, to go back home and be alone and think. To see if he could heal some of the wounds and begin again.

It wasn't my fault. Not really. It was Puppetman and he's dead. That should be punishment enough.

Gregg didn't know exactly what he was going to say to Ellen. She, at least, had tried to comfort him yesterday. She at least had said that it was okay, that it didn't matter, that it would all be all right again. But behind the words, he knew she wanted to know why, and he didn't know how to explain it. Part of him ached to simply let the horrible, awful truth spill out and beg forgiveness. Ellen cared for him. He knew that from Puppetman; he had seen her love given to him even without the power's help.

Yes, he'd give her a part of the truth at least. He'd tell her that yes, he was an ace, that he'd abused his abilities to enhance his own power, that he'd manipulated people. Yes, even her.

But not all of it. Some of it couldn't be said. Not the death and the pain and the violence. Not what he'd done to her and their own child.

Not that, because then there'd be no hope at all. Ellen was the one thing Gregg could salvage from this wreckage. Ellen was the only person who would help him find a path.

Gregg needed her. He knew just how desperate that need was from the churning in his stomach and the cold fear in his gut.

"Senator? We're here."

They were at the side entrance of the hospital. The Secret Service riding in back with him pushed open the doors. Heat and sunshine hit Gregg like a fist as he got out, blinking behind his sunglasses. He leaned back into the cool, leather-scented interior to speak to the chauffeur. "We'll be back in a few minutes," he told him. "We're just going to get Ellen and her things—"

"Senator," one of the bodyguards outside said. "Isn't that her?"

Gregg straightened to see Ellen being wheeled out of the hospital behind a clot of reporters, her own Secret Service personnel keeping back the flurry of videocams and cameras. Gregg frowned, puzzled.

The heat rippling up from the blacktop went cold: behind Ellen, he could see Sara. She was standing inside, her face pressed against the glass doors.

"No," Gregg whispered. He half ran to Ellen, the Secret

Service men pushing a path through the reporters around her. He saw her bag, sitting alongside the wheelchair.

She stood as he approached. Gregg smiled for the cameras and tried to ignore the specter of Sara just a few feet away.

"Darling," he said to her. "Did Amy call—?"

Ellen looked into his face and his voice trailed off. Her examination of him was long and intense. Then she looked away. Her mouth was a straight, tight line, her dark eyes were stern and solemn, and a bitter loathing lurked behind them.

"I don't know if it's all true, what Sara said," Ellen husked out. "I don't know, but I can see *something* in you, Gregg. I only wish I'd seen it years ago." She was crying now, oblivious or uncaring of the reporters circled around them. "*Damn* you, Gregg. Damn you forever for what you did."

Her hand lashed out unexpectedly. The slap jerked Gregg's head around and brought tears of pain to his own eyes. He fingered the crimson flush on his cheek, stunned.

He could hear the cameras and the excited buzz of the reporters. "Ellen, please . . ." he began, but she wasn't listening.

"I need time, Gregg. I need to be away from you." She took her bag and strode past him toward a waiting car. Behind the glass doors, Sara snagged Gregg's eyes as his hand dropped from his burning face.

Bastard, she mouthed silently, and turned away.

"Ellen!" Gregg wheeled around, the image of Sara's accusation staying with him. "Ellen!"

She wouldn't look back. The driver placed her bag in the trunk. Her guards held the door open for her.

With Puppetman, Gregg could have made her stop. He could have had her run back into his arms in a glorious, happy reconciliation.

With Puppetman, he could have written a happy ending.

Ellen got into the car and slumped back against the seat. They drove away.

12:00 NOON

The maître d' was waiting in vain for his C-note. The hotel had emptied out, and the Bello Mondo was no longer crowded.

Jack had brought Tachyon to lunch, but he couldn't make

him eat. Half a sole filet was abandoned on the plate. Jack finished off his New York cut.

"Eat, eat, my child. As my mom used to say in German."

"I'm not hungry."

"Build up your strength."

Tach glared at him. "Of the two of us," he said, "Which one is the doctor?"

"Which one of us is the patient?"

Tachyon's answer was stony silence. Jack took a drink— bourbon at last. Tachyon's violet eyes softened. "I'm sorry, Jack. My anxiety has rubbed away my manners."

"That's okay."

"I owe you my thanks. For this. For trying to find Blaise."

"I only wish I *could* find him." Jack put his elbows on the table and sighed. "I'd like something good to come out of everything we've been through."

"There might be something."

"A George Bush presidency, that's for sure." Jack stared at his plate. "That's the last political activity you're going to see from me. Every time I try to change the world, everything goes into the crapper."

Tachyon shook his head. "I have no thoughts to comfort you, Jack."

"All I did was screw up. I even *died* for god's sake. And the one thing I did right, I did for the wrong man." He took another drink. "I guess I'm about as confused as I've ever been. Hell." Another drink. "At least I'm rich. In this world, you can always fall back on money."

Jack leaned back against the cushion. "Maybe I'll write my memoirs. Get it all down. Then I'll maybe know what it means, if anything."

Memoirs, he thought. God, was he already that old?

When Jetboy died, he'd been twenty-two and looking younger. He hadn't aged since then.

At least he'd seen a few things. Been a movie star. Changed the world, back before the roof fell in. Saved a lot of lives in Korea, and that was *after* he'd become a world-class fuckup. He'd even seen *The Jolson Story.*

As good a place as any, he reflected, to start his memoirs. *When Jetboy died, I was watching* The Jolson Story.

No one said anything for a long while. Jack realized that Tachyon had drowsed off. He paid the tab, then pushed the wheelchair out of the restaurant and headed for the elevators.

On the way Jack saw the man who'd been selling gliders in the mall, table folded and his merchandise in a pair of paper sacks, talking to a friend. Jack parked the chair, then bought the entire line. When he came back, carrying his gliders, he saw that Tachyon was awake. He held up the gliders. "For Blaise," he said. "When we find him."

"Bless you, Jack."

For the first time in a week, Jack got an elevator right away. He pressed Tachyon's floor and the surge of vertigo as the glass elevator took off almost took him off his feet. To keep his mind off heights, he began assembling a glider.

A foam Earl Sanderson looked sternly at him from behind his flying goggles. Jack wondered dimly if, even after all these years, he had anything at all to say to Earl.

Besides an apology, of course. Better start with the basics.

The elevator lurched, and Jack's stomach lurched with it. The doors opened, and with a shock Jack saw David Harstein step into the elevator.

Tachyon was rolling a guilty white-rimmed eye at him. Jack had a feeling his own face held the same expression of stupid, overdone innocence.

"You *know*," Tachyon said.

"*You* know?" Jack replied.

"Hey, we *all* know," corrected David with hearty bonhomie.

The glass box lurched for the sky. Jack's stomach lurched with it. He could feel the sweat popping out on his forehead. He searched for something to say.

The elevator slammed to a stop again. The door opened and Fleur van Renssaeler stepped aboard, looking over her shoulder and waving goodbye to a friend. The door closed, and Fleur turned.

Everyone stopped breathing for a long moment. The elevator staggered upward. Suddenly Tachyon lashed out with his right arm, striking the STOP button with his bandaged stump.

The alien let out an animal-like howl of pain. David knelt quickly by the wheelchair as the elevator jerked to a halt. "Hush, it doesn't hurt."

And of course it didn't. Or at least it didn't matter.

Tachyon blinked hard to clear the moisture from his eyes.

"David Harstein," said Fleur, her voice expressionless.

* * *

Tach felt a chill go through him.

"Just now I remembered from when I was little." Fleur gave a thin smile. "The man who lost China to the Reds. And all these years you've just been hiding under that beard."

Smiling again, she turned to Jack. "An old friend of the family," she said scornfully.

The big ace yanked out a handkerchief and mopped his brow. "It seemed like a good idea at the time," he said weakly.

The glider of Earl Sanderson held limp, forgotten in Jack's hand. Tachyon reached out, and took it. He laid it gently in his lap.

"I count myself in nothing else so happy," David said, "as in a soul remembering my good friends."

Tach looked up at him. "Yes, all the ghosts have gathered."

Fleur stared hollow eyed at Tachyon. "I am *not* my mother!"

"You have your father's eyes," David said, his voice gentle.

It was a simple statement. No accusation. No hidden meaning. It left her confused, uncertain, the belligerence draining out of her. "You don't know me," Fleur whispered.

"No," David said. "Sadly."

For a moment Fleur looked like she wanted to hug him. In fact, Tachyon wanted to hug him. Silence spun like cobwebs between the four of them. Fleur stared into David's compassionate dark eyes. Tears welled up, and spilled slowly down her cheeks. But the fear came back. She pressed her hands against her cheeks, and backed away. "No, don't do this to me."

Tachyon sighed. "We must speak, Fleur."

"I'm going to scream." Her voice was a frightened thread.

"Please don't," David said. "You have nothing to be afraid of."

Fleur quieted, but still managed to say, "No, I do have something to be afraid of. I'm alone with all of you."

"Are we so fearsome?" David asked. "An old actor, a one-handed man . . ." He glanced back at Jack. ". . . and a weenie."

"Hey," Jack began, but then he paused and rubbed his

jaw thoughtfully as he considered and then acknowledged the truth of Harstein's words.

Fleur hugged her elbows. "You don't understand. You honestly don't understand, do you?" The three men stared at her. "You stand there with these powers that can hurt us and twist us, and you wonder why we're afraid."

Jack looked with some confusion at the glider in Tach's hands. He spoke slowly, reaching hard for each word. "I think Earl would say you can't be afraid of people just because they're different, because you can never draw a clear line. Do you fear them because they've got the wild card, or because they have different beliefs, or because they have the wrong color skin . . .?"

"I fear them because they can *hurt* me," Fleur insisted.

"There are a lot of people who can hurt you," Jack said, "and very few of them have the wild card."

"Easy to say, when you're one of those who do," Fleur replied. "You know what you call the rest of us. The nats. Naturals, that's what it's supposed to be short for, but there's another meaning. Gnats. Little insects. Little bothersome insects waiting to be swatted by you. We're supposed to obey the laws, and treat you nicely. But those same laws don't apply to you. You don't have to be nice to gnats. Not with all your power."

"Fleur," said David. "You have all the power here. You hold my life in your hands."

Fleur hesitated a long time, looking at him. The wailing of the alarm was like an ice pick in the brain. "You don't have to worry," she said at last. "You're safe from me."

David nodded, as if he'd known that all along. "Start the elevator," he said quietly.

Tachyon slewed around awkwardly, and hit the button. The elevator shuddered and shot upward.

"Not to throw cold water on this love feast," Jack said to David, "but you do remember Mao? Mao Tse Tung, Chinese guy? Sooner or later we've got to let her off this elevator, and then she's going to blow the whistle."

"That is her right."

That shook Tachyon out of the dream state which seemed to hold him. "No."

David turned those dark eyes on him. "Yes." Gently. "I

knew the risks. I've paid the price before. I'm prepared to pay again."

They reached her floor. The doors opened. She stepped out.

"Fleur," Jack Braun said. "Think twice before you start naming names. I didn't. I'm still paying for it."

Fleur looked at them all for a long time. Tach wondered what she was thinking. Easy enough to find out. Better that he didn't. She walked off without saying a word.

The doors shut. Tachyon stared at the flashing numbers.

"We must be crazy to let her walk off like that," Jack said.

"You have to take a gamble on someone sometime," David replied.

"She's her father's daughter!" Jack said.

Tachyon stirred in his wheelchair, and handed the Earl Sanderson glider back to Jack. "And her mother's too."

The elevator, with its cargo of ghosts and survivors, continued its lunge for the sky.

CLOSING CREDITS

STARRING	CREATED & WRITTEN BY
Jack (Golden Boy) Braun	Walter Jon Williams
Senator Gregg Hartmann	Stephen Leigh
Mackie Messer	Victor Milán
Sara Morgenstern	Victor Milán
James (Demise) Spector	Walton Simons
Dr. Tachyon	Melinda M. Snodgrass

co-starring	created by
Jay (Popinjay) Ackroyd	George R.R. Martin
Blaise Andrieux	Melinda M. Snodgrass
Rev. Leo Barnett	Arthur Byron Cover
Billy (Carnifex) Ray	John J. Miller
Hiram Worchester	George R.R. Martin

featuring	created by
Joshua Davidson	George R.R. Martin
Tom (Gimli) Miller	Stephen Leigh
Georgy Vladimirovich Polyakov	Michael Cassutt
Fleur van Renssaeler	Melinda M. Snodgrass

with	created by
Nephi (Straight Arrow) Callendar	Walter Jon Williams
The Gatekeeper	Victor Milán
Amy Sorenson	Stephen Leigh
Charles Devaughn	Victor Milán
Tony Calderone	Walton Simons
Doughboy	Victor Milán
The Great and Powerful Turtle	George R.R. Martin

THE STRANGE HISTORY OF
THE WILD CARDS

It all began in 1946 . . .

When a bizarre gene-altering virus was unleashed in the skies over New York City. It came from an alien planet, brought by scientists who regarded humanity as nothing more than useful guinea pigs. One of their number found the plan ignoble, unworthy of Takisians. In orbit above Earth, he battled against his fellows . . . but lost.

His spacecraft was crippled. The other—the ship carrying the virus—crashed, and its Takisian passengers were killed. Before any authorities could reach it, the deadly virus was released. . . .

The street was full of stopped cars now, for as far as Croyd could see in either direction. There were people on the tops of buildings and people at every window, most of them looking upward.

He rushed to the sidewalk and turned right. His home was six blocks to the south, in an anomalous group of row houses in the eighties. Joe's route took him half that way, then off to the east.

Before they reached the corner they were halted as a stream of people flowed from the side street to the right, cutting into their line of pedestrian traffic, some turning north and trying to push through, others heading south. The boys heard cursing and the sound of a fistfight from up ahead.

A man lay upon the pavement. He was having convulsions. His head and hands had swollen enormously, and they were dark red, almost purple in color. Just as they caught sight of him, blood began to rush from his nose and mouth; it trickled from his ears, it oozed from his eyes and about his fingernails.

"Holy Mary!" Joe said, crossing himself as he drew back. "What's he got?"

"I don't know," Croyd answered. "Let's not get too close."

Croyd saw a reptilian face through a windshield then, and scaly hands clutching at a steering wheel that had been torn loose from its column as the driver slowly slumped to the side. Looking away, he saw a rising tower of smoke from beyond buildings to the northeast.

When they reached the corner there was no place to descend. People stood packed and swaying. There were occasional screams. He wanted to cry, but he knew it would do no good. He clenched his teeth and shuddered.

"What're we going to do?" he called to Joe.

"If we're stuck here overnight we can bust the window on an empty car and sleep in it, I guess."

"I want to go home!"

"Me, too. Let's try and keep going as far as we can."

Croyd saw a man perform a series of dancelike movements, tearing at his clothing. Then he began to change shape. Someone back up the road started howling. There came sounds of breaking glass.

During the next half-hour the sidewalk traffic thinned to what might, under other circumstances, be called normal. The people seemed either to have achieved their destinations or to have advanced their congestion to some other part of town. Those who passed now picked their way among corpses. Faces had vanished from behind windows. No one was in sight atop the buildings. The sounds of auto horns had diminished to sporadic outbursts. The boys stood on a corner. They had covered three blocks and crossed the street since they had left school.

"I turn here," Joe said. "You want to come with me or you going ahead?"

Croyd looked down the street.

"It looks better now. I think I can make it okay," he said.

"I'll see you."

"Okay."

Joe hurried off to the left. Croyd watched him for a moment, then moved ahead. Far up the street, a man raced from a doorway screaming. He seemed to grow larger and his movements more erratic as he moved to the center of the street. Then he exploded. Croyd pressed his back against the brick wall to his left and stared, heart pounding, but there was no new disturbance. He heard a bullhorn from somewhere to the west. ". . . The bridges are closed to both auto and foot traffic. Do not attempt to use the bridges. Return to your homes. The bridges are closed. . . ."

An army truck rolled from the side street at the corner ahead of him. He ran to it. A helmeted face turned toward him from the passenger side.

"Why are you out, son?" the man asked.

"I'm going home," he answered.

"Where's that?"

He pointed ahead.

"Two blocks," he said.

"Go straight home," the man told him.

"What's happening?"

"We're under martial law. Everybody's got to get indoors. Good idea to keep your windows closed, too."

"Why?"

"It seems that was some kind of germ bomb that went off. Nobody knows for sure."

"Was it Jetboy that . . . ?"

"Jetboy's dead. He tried to stop them."

Croyd's eyes were suddenly brimming.

"Go straight home."

The truck crossed the street and continued on to the west. Croyd ran across and slowed when he reached the sidewalk. He began to shake. He was suddenly aware of the pain in his knees, where he had scraped them in crawling over vehicles. He wiped his eyes. He felt terribly cold. He halted near the middle of the block and yawned several times. Tired. He was incredibly tired. He began moving. His feet felt heavier than he ever remembered. He halted again beneath a tree. There came a moaning from overhead.

When he looked up he realized that it was not a tree. It was tall and brown, rooted and spindly, but there was an enormously elongated human face near its top and it was from there that the moaning came. As he moved away one of the limbs plucked at his shoulder, but it was a weak thing and a few more steps bore him out of its reach. He whimpered. The corner seemed miles away, and then there was another block. . . .

Now DR. TACHYON, the sole surviving Takisian, dedicates his life to the study of the Wild Card Virus and how it might be cured. Unfortunately, it's too late for thousands of people. Many of the survivors of Wild Card Day would be forever changed. Some were called Aces, gifted with extraordinary abilities; others were called Jokers, cursed with bizarre disfigurements.

Their progress through the decades of an ever-altered Earth would not be easy. Aces and Jokers alike had to face disdain, jealousy, and fear as America struggled with the anticommunist hysteria of the 1950s, the summer-of-love '60s, and the '70s of Vietnam and Watergate.

Young Croyd, altered forever in the chaos of Wild Card Day, became known as THE SLEEPER. Trapped in an ever-changing form, he tries desperately to resist sleep . . . because every time he wakes he is something new, something strange, something frightening. . . .

Others you will meet in Volume I of the WILD CARDS series include:

GOLDEN BOY—a football hero and actor whose superhuman strength and power brought a meteoric rise and an equally rapid fall.

THE BLACK EAGLE—the powerful, thunder-throwing champion destroyed by the forces of fear in the hate-ridden '50s.

PUPPETMAN—who used his gifts to enslave.

THE GREAT AND POWERFUL TURTLE—a mild-mannered Ace who fought to become a true hero.

WILD CARDS II—ACES HIGH

The year—1979. The place—New York City, home of Aces High, glamorous lounge atop the

Empire State Building, and Jokertown, squalid residence of the city's underclass. The victims of the Wild Card Virus are no longer new and strange, but neither are they accepted by a world that still fears them.

But as the '80s dawn, all eyes are drawn to the skies and the Wild Cards may be the planet's only hope, as an abomination called the Swarm arrives to threaten Earth. . . .

A pillar of darkness rose over Princeton. The android saw it on radar and first thought it smoke, but then realized the cloud did not drift with the wind, but was composed of thousands of living creatures circling over the landscape like a flock of scavenger birds. The pillar was alive.

There was a touch of uncertainty in the android's macroatomic heart. His programming hadn't prepared him for this.

Emergency broadcasts crackled in his mind, questioning, begging for assistance, crying in despair. Modular Man slowed, his perceptions searching the dark land below. Large infrared signatures—more Swarm buds—crawled among tree-lined streets. The signatures were scattered but their movement was purposeful, heading toward the town. It seemed as if Princeton was their rallying point. The android dropped, heard tearing noises, screams, shots. The guns on his shoulders tracked as he dipped and increased speed.

The Swarm bud was legless, moving like a snail with undulating thrusts of its slick thirty-foot body. The head was armored, with dripping sideways jaws. A pair of giant boneless arms terminated in claws. The creature was butting its head into a two-story suburban colonial, punching holes, the arms questing through windows, looking for things that lived inside. Shots were coming from the second floor. Christmas lights blinked from the edges of the roof, the ornamental shrubs.

Modular Man hovered overhead, fired a precise burst from his laser. The pulsed microwave was invisible, silent. The creature quivered, rolled on its side, began to thrash. The house shuddered to mindless blows. The android shot again. The creature trembled, lay still. The android slipped feet first into the window where the shots had been coming from, saw a stark-naked fat man clutching a deer rifle, a teenage boy with a target pistol, a woman clutching two young girls. The woman was screaming. The two girls were too stunned even to tremble. "Jesus Christ," the fat man said.

"I killed it," the android said. "Can you get to your car?"

"I think so," the fat man said. He stuffed rounds into his rifle. His wife was still screaming.

"Head east, toward New York," Modular Man said. "They seem to be thickest around here. Maybe you can convoy with some neighbors."

"What's happening?" the man asked, slamming the bolt back and then forward. "Another Wild Card outbreak?"

"Monsters from space, apparently." There was a crashing sound from behind the house. The android spun, saw what looked like a serpent sixty feet long, moving in curving sidewinder pattern as it bowled down bushes, trees, power poles. The underside of the serpent's body writhed with ten-foot cilia. Modular Man sped out the window, fired another burst of microwave at the thing's head. No effect. Another burst, no success. Behind him, the deer rifle barked.

♥ ◆ ♠ ♣

Other heroes and villains you'll meet in *Aces High* include:

JAMES SPECTOR—possessor of one of the deadliest Ace powers, he can kill with a mere look.

KID DINOSAUR—a starry-eyed teenaged boy whose strange powers earned him a place in the action.

CHRYSALIS—though her skin is transparent, no one can see through to the mysteries she hides within.

JUBE—the walrus who peddles newspapers and, on the side, masterminds an attempt to save the human race.

WILD CARDS III—JOKERS WILD

Every year on September 15, in remembrance of the original Wild Card Day, the streets of New York erupt in celebration. The anniversary is a time for excitement, for grief and joy, for remembering the dead and cherishing the living. It is a day for fireworks and street fairs and parades, for political rallies and memorial banquets, for drinking and fighting in the alleys. With each passing year, the festivities become larger and more fevered.

This year—1986, the fortieth anniversary—promises to be the biggest and best Wild Card Day ever. The media and the tourists have discovered the celebration, and taverns and restaurants expect record-setting business. But lurking in the background is a twisted mind which cares nothing for fun and festivity. The Astronomer has only one concern. Destruction. . . .

The Crystal Palace smelled like any other bar in the morning—like stale smoke and spilled beer and disinfectant. Fortunato found Chrysalis in a dark corner of the club, where her transparent skin made her nearly invisible. He and Brennan sat down across from her.

"You got the message, then," she said in her phony English-public-school accent.

"I got it," Fortunato said. "But the trail's cold. The Astronomer could be anywhere by now. I was hoping you might have something else for me."

"Perhaps. You know a yo-yo calls himself 'Demise'?"

"Yes," Fortunato said. His fingernails dug use-lessly at the urethane finish on the table.

"He was in about an hour ago. Sascha got a reading off him, loud and clear. 'He's going to fucking kill me. That twisted old fuck.'"

"Meaning the Astronomer."

"Right you are. This Demise seemed completely round the bend. Had quite a lot on his mind, Sascha said."

"You mean there's more," Fortunato said.

"Yes, but the next bit's going to cost you."

"Cash or favors?"

"Blunt this morning, aren't we? Well, I'm in-clined to say favors. And in honor of the holiday, I'll even extend you a line of credit."

"You know I'm good for it," Fortunato said. "Sooner or later."

"I don't like charging for bad news, in any event.

The other line Sascha heard was, 'Maybe he'll be too busy with the others.'"

"Christ," Fortunato said.

Brennan looked at him. "You think he's going on some kind of killing spree."

"The only thing that surprises me is that it took him this long. He must have been waiting for Wild Card Day."

Aces High introduces these Aces and Jokers:

BAGABOND—she commands armies of animals and can send them against predators, human and superhuman.

SEWER JACK—hidden deep in his mind is a monstrous reptile driven by a desperate hunger.

ROULETTE—she kills men with love.

FATMAN—he can command gravity itself.

WILD CARDS IV—ACES ABROAD

Though the Wild Cards Virus burst into existence over New York City, the plague that followed was not confined to the United States. It spawned Aces and Jokers in every country on Earth. Now a fact-finding mission seeks the truth about how Wild Cards are treated in other nations. From the jungles of Haiti to the Great Wall of China and behind the Iron Curtain, the Wild Cards team investigates the fate of their fellows everywhere.

My name is Xavier Desmond, and I am a joker. Jokers are always strangers, even on the street where they were born, and this one is about to visit a number of strange lands. In the next five months I will see veldts and mountains, Rio and Cairo, the Khyber Pass and the Straits of Gibraltar, the Outback and the Champs-Élysées—all very far from home for a man who has often been called the mayor of Jokertown. Jokertown, of course, has no mayor. It is a neighborhood, a ghetto neighborhood at that, and not a city. Jokertown is more than a place though. It is a condition, a state of mind. Perhaps in that sense my title is not undeserved.

I have been a joker since the beginning. Forty years ago, when Jetboy died in the skies over Manhattan and loosed the wild card upon the world, I was twenty-nine years of age, an investment banker with a lovely wife, a two-year-old daughter, and a bright future ahead of me. A month later, when I was finally released from the hospital, I was a monstrosity with a pink elephantine trunk growing from the center of my face where my nose had been. There are seven perfectly functional fingers at the end of my trunk, and over the years I have become quite adept with this "third hand." Were I suddenly restored to so-called normal humanity, I believe it would be as traumatic as if one of my limbs were amputated. With my trunk I am ironically somewhat more than human . . . and infinitely less.

My lovely wife left me within two weeks of my release from the hospital, at approximately the same time that Chase Manhattan informed me that my services would no longer be required. I moved to Jokertown nine months later, following my eviction from my Riverside Drive apartment for "health reasons." I last saw my daughter in 1948.

I am the founder and president emeritus of the

Jokers' Anti-Defamation League, or JADL, the oldest and largest organization dedicated to the preservation of civil rights for the victims of the wild card virus. The JADL has had its failures, but overall it has accomplished great good. I am also a moderately successful businessman. I own one of New York's most storied and elegant nightclubs, the Funhouse, where jokers and nats and aces have enjoyed all the top joker cabaret acts for more than two decades. The Funhouse has been losing money steadily for the last five years, but no one knows that except me and my accountant. I keep it open because it is, after all, the Funhouse, and were it to close, Jokertown would seem a poorer place.

Next month I will be seventy years of age.

Mary and I often talked of a trip around the world, in those days before the wild card when we were young and in love. I could never have dreamt that I would finally take that trip without her, in the twilight of my life, and at government expense, as a delegate on a fact-finding mission organized and funded by the Senate Committee on Ace Resources and Endeavors, under the official sponsorship of the United Nations and the World Health Organization. We will visit every continent but Antarctica and call upon thirty-nine different countries (some only for a few hours), and our official charge is to investigate the treatment of wild card victims in cultures around the world.

There are twenty-one delegates, only five of whom are jokers. I suppose my selection is a great honor, recognition of my achievements and my status as a community leader. I believe I have my good friend Dr. Tachyon to thank for it.

But then, I have my good friend Dr. Tachyon to thank for a great many things.

The heroes and villains of ACES ABROAD include:

PEREGRINE—the winged beauty whose talent is to drive men sexually mad—before she flies away.

FATHER SQUID—the kindly pastor of the Church of Jesus Christ, Joker. He delivers his moving sermons through the tentacles that hang over his mouth like a constantly twitching mustache.

FORTUNATO—the handsome half black/half Japanese ex-pimp whose special powers depend on his sexuality.

WILD CARDS V—DOWN AND DIRTY

When rival gangs stage a bitter war for control of the streets of Jokertown, District Attorney Rosemary Muldoon asks for Ace volunteers. But then Muldoon is exposed as Rosa Maria Gambione—a Mafia don—and all the Aces are under suspicion for connections with organized crime. In the meantime, the killings continue, and other events stir the lives of Aces and Jokers alike. . . .

"Captain Ellis doesn't approve of this protection racket," Digger Downs bulled ahead. "She says somebody's going to get hurt and it ain't gonna be the bad guys."

"I would submit to the good captain that the protection rackets have all been coming from one direction. And she's being unduly pessimistic. I think we can look out for ourselves. Ideal knows we've had enough practice," Tachyon added dryly, recalling all the years when the police were curiously uninterested whenever a joker was beaten or killed, but Johnny-on-the-spot whenever a tourist howled. Things were better now, but it was still an uneasy relationship between New York's jokers and New York's finest.

Digger licked the tip of his ballpoint pen, a silly, affected gesture. "I know my readers will want to know why these patrols consist only of jokers. With you heading up this effort why not pull in some of the big guns? The Hammer for example, or Mistral or J.J. Flash or Starshine."

"This is a joker neighborhood. We can take care of ourselves."

"Meaning there's hostility between jokers and aces?"

"Digger, don't be an ass. Is it *so* surprising that these people choose to handle this themselves? They are viewed as freaks, treated like retarded children, and ignored in favor of their more fortunate and flamboyant brethren. May I point out that your magazine is titled *Aces*, and no one is panting to found a concomitant magazine entitled *Jokers*? Look around you. This is an activity born out of love and pride. How could I say to these people you're not tough enough or smart enough or strong enough to defend yourselves? Let me call in the aces."

Which was of course precisely what he had been going to do until Des had opened his eyes. But Digger didn't need to know that. Still, Tach had the grace to blush as he shamelessly appropriated Des's lecture and passed it on to the journalist.

"Comment on Leo Barnett?"

"He is a hate-mongering lunatic."

"Can I quote you on that?"

"Go ahead."

"So who's going to be the white knight? Hartmann?"

"Maybe. I don't know."

"I thought you two were real tight."

"We're friends, but hardly intimates."

"Why do you think Hartmann's been such a friend to the jokers? Personal interest? His wife a carrier, or maybe an illegitimate joker baby hidden away somewhere?"

"I think he is a friend to the wild cards because he is a good man," replied Tachyon a little frigidly.

"Hey, speaking of monstrous joker babies, what's the latest poop on Peregrine's pregnancy?"

Tachyon went rigid with fury, then carefully uncoiled his fists, and relaxed. "No, Digger, you're not going to get me again. I will never stop regretting that I let slip that the father of Peregrine's child was an ace."

WILD CARDS VI—ACE IN THE HOLE

It's 1988, an election year. For the first time the victims of the Wild Card Virus have a candidate who isn't afraid to stand up for jokers' rights. And Greg Hartmann stands a good chance of winning the Democratic nomination, even against competition like Jesse Jackson, Michael Dukakis, and Leo Barnett, the fiery anti-Wild Cards preacher.

But there's more than speeches going on at Atlanta's Convention Center. Behind the scenes a killer ace is on the prowl, and several important lives are at stake. . . . *On sale now!*

Editors Gregory Benford and Martin H. Greenberg
ask the provocative question

What Might Have Been?

* if the Egyptian dynasties—and their Hebrew slaves—had survived until modern times?

* if Mahatma Gandhi used passive resistance when the Nazis invaded India during World War II?

* If Lawrence of Arabia faced Rommel in North Africa?

These star-studded anthologies include stories by some of the most imaginative authors writing speculative fiction today, including Poul Anderson, Gregory Benford, George Alec Effinger, Harry Harrison, and Tom Shippey, Barry Malzberg, James Morrow, Larry Niven, Frederik Pohl, Robert Silverberg, and Judith Tarr to name a few. Here are stories that will engage the mind and challenge the imagination!

☐ Volume One: **Alternate Empires** (27845-2 • $4.50/ $5.50 in Canada)

☐ Volume Two: **Alternate Heroes** (28279-4 • $4.50/ $5.50 in Canada)

Buy **What Might Have Been?** on sale now wherever Bantam Spectra Books are sold, or use this handy page to order: